IR

D0380266

RIVETED

DISCARD
Westminster Public Library
3705 W 112th Ave
Westminster, CO 80031
www.westminsterlibrary.org

ALSO BY JAY CROWNOVER

The Saints of Denver Series

Riveted

Charged

Built

Leveled (novella)

The Breaking Point Series

Honor

The Welcome to the Point Series

Better When He's Brave

Better When He's Bold

Better When He's Bad

The Marked Men Series

Asa

Rowdy

Nash

Rome

Jet

Rule

RIVETED

A Saints of Denver Novel

JAY CROWNOVER

wm

WILLIAM MORROW

An Imprint of Harper Collins*Publishers*

This is a work of fiction. Names, characters, places, and incidents are products of the author's imagination or are used fictitiously and are not to be construed as real. Any resemblance to actual events, locales, organizations, or persons, living or dead, is entirely coincidental.

HarperCollins books may be purchased for educational, business, or sales promotional use. For information please e-mail the Special Markets Department at SPsales@harpercollins.com.

FIRST EDITION

Designed by Diahann Sturge

Library of Congress Cataloging-in-Publication Data has been applied for.

ISBN 978-0-06-238600-7

17 18 19 20 21 LSC 10 9 8 7 6 5 4 3 2 1

Dedicated to Elma Mae Bruce.

I am a changed person because your story and my story intersected, no matter how brief that chapter may have been. Your support as a reader meant the world to me as an author, but the impact you had on me as a person . . . well, that is unforgettable, and I will be forever grateful that I was able to share both your triumphs and disappointments as you fought the good fight. It is true what they say . . . not all heroes wear capes.

We are all going to leave a legacy behind us when we go. Be it big or small, I hope that all of us take a moment, a minute, a split second to invest in making sure the one that we are building is one that we can be proud of, one that makes others smile and think fondly of us, because it's so easy to forget the good when the bad seems to always be out front and center. Leave the lives you touch better off for having had you in them.

Also FUCK YOU, cancer . . . you are literally the worst and we're all pretty sick of your shit.

If you're going through hell, keep going.

—Winston Churchill

INTRODUCTION

So I'm sure it's no surprise that I consider myself kind of a badass (on occasion at least). Not much fazes me. I'm pretty willing and able to roll with the punches and I've always been a "take the bull by the horns and make him your bitch" kind of gal. That being said there are things that are bigger and badder than me, things that scare the ever-living stuffing out of me and I really didn't stop to think about how I handled the fear, or rather didn't handle it, until I started working on this book.

If you follow me on social media at all I'm sure you know I have three dogs that I'm obsessed with. They are my best furry friends and my family. I love them unconditionally and fiercely. The boy Italian greyhound, Duce, (I know, I know, it isn't spelled right, but even before writing books I was doing weird stuff with names) is getting older and last year he got sick . . . and I mean really sick. It was terrifying. It was heartbreaking and I handled it like shit. I broke down and turned into a tantrum-throwing idiot, which helped my dog and the situation zero percent. Quite frankly I didn't know what to do or how to help him and that lack of control, no matter how much money I threw at the problem, turned me into a lunatic. I was terrified that I was going to lose him even though logically I knew he couldn't stick around forever.

Eventually I got him to an amazing veterinarian . . . shout-out to Northwest Animal Hospital here in Colorado Springs and Doctor Sudduth, who took great care of him, got him diagnosed, and promised that it wasn't his time to go yet. Duce is still old, still sickly, but he's on meds and kicking right along. The last year was a struggle but we spent it together at home for the most part, which means I owe my readers and everyone that supports my books even more than you will ever know.

None of it changes the fact that I'm eventually going to have to say good-bye.

It still scares me. It makes me tear up even thinking about it. It's going to be one of the hardest things I'm ever going to have to do . . . but writing this book . . . focusing on how Church handles love and loss, how we have this stoic, tough-as-nails soldier that has been through hell and back, but has things bigger and badder than he is that he can't get out from underneath, was eye-opening. No matter what kind of armor we wear, all of it has a chink, a dent that speaks to a battle we fought and lost.

I know now that when the time comes I want to focus on the good, on the years we spent together, and all the wonderful memories my furry little guy gave to me. I don't want any of that goodness and enduring love to be overshadowed by the pain of letting go. I need to be strong when the little guy can't be . . . seriously, he's only like seventeen pounds . . . so small to be poked, prodded, and medicated the way he is. He handles it like a boss though. ☺

I can't lie and say I'm not still scared, terrified even. Every time I leave home for an event I spend most of my free time checking in on the old man. But I like to think that I now have the wherewithal to be there for my four-legged bestie the way he has always been there for me.

So yeah . . . this entire book was kind of inspired by my sick dog . . . the good and the bad . . . Church and Dixie represent both sides of that . . . lol . . . I promise it will make sense when you read it.

Welcome to my love and loss . . .

Xoxo
Jay

Prologue

My mom met her Prince Charming when she was a freshman in college and my dad leaned over and asked to borrow a pen so he could take notes. Rumpled, obviously hungover but flashing a smile that promised a good time and with a twinkle in his eyes, he was impossible to resist. She always told me and my sister that it happened that fast. In a split second she knew he was the one for her.

It was a sweet story. One that my parents shared with us often, both still sharing private smiles and eyes still twinkling, but neither one of us gave it much thought until my younger sister met her very own prince before she was old enough to drive. It was during a hard time for my family, hard for all of us, but especially for her. She'd always been the baby, been spoiled and treated like a princess. When the attention was yanked off of her in a really ugly way, she was lost and let the family tragedy consume her. Lost in grief and confusion she somehow managed to sign herself up for auto shop instead of an extracurricular that actually made sense for my very girlie, very feminine younger sibling. She spent five minutes in that noisy, greasy garage, but she spent years and years leaning on and loving the quiet, enigmatic auburn-haired boy she met in those five minutes. He saved her and even though she was way too young to know anything about anything, she had the same story that my mother did . . . she just knew he was the one for her.

It happened fast in my family. We fell hard and we didn't get up once we fell. We stayed down and we loved hard and deep. I also learned as I watched all my friends, the men I worked with, the women that I considered sisters of the heart, that when it was right for anyone it happened fast and that they did indeed *just know.* They knew when it was right. They knew when it was going to last. They knew when it was worth fighting for. They knew when they had found the person that might not necessarily be perfect, but that was without a doubt perfect for them. *They just knew.*

So I waited, admittedly impatiently and anxiously, for my shot, for my turn to fall. I waited through my family healing, for them to come back with a love that was even stronger. I waited through my sister screwing up and desperately trying to repair her perfect. I waited and watched so many weddings and babies that weren't mine. I waited through danger and drama. I waited through one bad date and one failed relationship after another. I waited through nights alone and nights spent with the occasional someone I knew wasn't *the* one for me. I waited and waited as good men fell for even better women, all the while wondering when it would be my turn. I waited and watched love that was easy and love that was hard, telling myself I was far more prepared for my fall than anyone else around me was. I wanted it so bad I could taste it . . . but the more I waited the more certain I became that I was never going to fall.

I would be lying if I said that I didn't think Dash Churchill was something special the second he walked into the bar where

I worked—all coiled tension, sexy swagger, and with a swirling, threatening cloud of attitude hanging over him that would dim even the brightest summer days. I had eyes and I had a vagina, so all the things that I thought were special were the things those parts of my anatomy couldn't miss. Long limbed, with a body that looked like it was ripped from the cover of *Men's Health* magazine, bronze skin, unforgettable eyes, and a mouth that even though it was constantly frowning brought to mind every single dirty, sexy thing a pair of lips like that was capable of doing. I liked the way he looked . . . a lot . . . but I couldn't say I much liked him. He was sullen, distant, uncommunicative and there was an air about him that marked in no uncertain terms that he was dangerous and volatile. He came across as a very unhappy individual, and no amount of rest, relaxation, and good friends seemed to shake that dark shroud of discontentment that hung over him. His amazing eyes flashed warnings that I was smart enough to heed. I liked my days spent basking in the sun, not dancing in the rain.

I was friendly to Church because I was friendly to everyone. The first month or so we had an uneasy working relationship that involved me dancing around him while every other single and not-so-single woman that came into the bar where we worked did their best to catch his eye. It worked out well for me and seemingly for him, so I went back to waiting for my perfect, my fairy tale, my heroic knight, my unmatched hero. He had to be out there somewhere and I was starting to think if he wasn't looking for me I needed to start looking for him. My patience was wearing thin and my typically affable attitude was starting to get just as gloomy and gray as the one that hung over Church.

But then it happened and *I just knew*. I knew like I had never known anything as clearly and as unquestionably in my whole life. I knew with a rightness that shot through my soul and made my heart flip over in my chest.

I was trying to cash out a group of overly intoxicated and obnoxiously difficult young men. It wasn't anything new. I'd been a cocktail waitress for a long time and knew how to handle myself and the customers. This drunken group was no better or worse than any other one I'd had to deal with in all my years slinging drinks and working the floor, but they were loud and the things they were saying were easily heard throughout the bar. Some of it wasn't so bad. They liked my hair (curly and strawberry blond—who didn't like my damn hair?) and they liked the way my shirt fit tight and snug across my chest. I was a solid D cup, so again who didn't like my tits? But they also had a lot to say about my ass. Apparently it was too big for my small frame, and they didn't love my freckles. That red hair was authentic and as real as it could be, so there wasn't much I could do about the colored specks that dotted the bridge of my nose and brushed the curve of my cheeks.

I had pretty thick skin, you had to when you worked in a bar and liquor loosened tongues, so I was ready to brush the entire conversation off and snatch the credit card off the table when I felt a hand on my lower back and a storm not just brewing off in the distance but collecting and gathering, ready to unleash hell at my back.

"You good, Dixie?" The question made me freeze and it wasn't because it was asked into my ear with an unmistakable slow and very southern drawl. It wasn't because he was so close I could feel every line of muscle in his massive body and both the heat of his skin and the chill of his icy anger pressing into my back.

No, I froze, riveted to the spot and stunned stupid, because in twenty-six years no one had ever bothered to ask me if I was good. They always assumed I was.

I was the girl that could handle myself and everyone else around me.

I was the girl that never asked for help.

I was the girl that always smiled even when that smile hurt my face.

I was the girl that always had an ear to bend or a shoulder to lean on for a friend even when I really didn't have time.

I was the girl that everyone ran to with a problem because I would drop everything to help fix it even if it was unfixable.

I was the girl that never let anything or anyone drag her down and fought to keep everyone else up with her.

I was the girl that everyone always assumed was good . . . so they never asked . . . but he had and the world stopped.

I gripped my pen and struggled to clear my throat. "I'm good, Church." My voice was barely a breath of sound and I felt his touch press even deeper into my lower back.

"You sure?" No, I wasn't sure. I was as far from good as I had ever been and I had no clue what to do about it.

I gave a jerky nod and blew out a breath, which had him taking a step away from me. I looked at him over my shoulder and he returned the look. There was no warmth in his fantastic eyes. There was no change in the harsh expression on his face. There was no knowledge that he had fundamentally changed my life in the span of a few terse words.

He was simply doing his job, making sure everything in the bar was okay and that the staff was safe. Meanwhile I was shoved unwillingly into the kind of love that had my arms flailing, my legs kicking, while a-scream-ripped-from-my-lungs in love with him. Of course I did that all silently and in my head as he walked away from me, because I might have now *known* he was it for me, but it was evident Church didn't have a clue.

No one had ever given me any idea how to handle it when the right one came along, but you weren't the right one for him.

There is no such thing as darkness; only a failure to see.

—Malcolm Muggeridge

Chapter 1

Dixie

"Um . . . I had a lovely evening." No, I hadn't. It was awful. It would go down as the worst first date in the history of first dates, which was something considering my recent run as the awful-first-date queen. But it wasn't in my nature to say so. All I wanted to do was say good-night and go hide in my bedroom with a glass of wine and my dog for the rest of the evening.

"Aren't you going to invite us in for a drink?"

I fought to hold back a cringe and looked over the shoulder of the very cute but painfully shy young man I had accepted the date with after several weeks of online chatting. I'd met him through one of the dating apps I had signed up for when I decided I was done waiting for my perfect to realize that I was perfect for him.

My terrible luck in love had held true and this date, with this cute boy . . . and his mother, the person who had asked about coming in for a drink since my actual date seemed incapable of speech. Yep, it solidified the fact that I was bound to end up alone. That beautiful blinding thing that everyone important in my life that I loved seemed to find with such ease was clearly not in the cards for me. I wanted a fantasy but every day was faced with the fact that all I was getting was cold, hard and very lonely reality.

I sighed and reached up to push some of my wayward, strawberry-colored curls out of my face. I was annoyed that not only had I clearly been cat-fished—there was no way the son was the one running his dating profile, not if he couldn't string two words together, and not if he couldn't look at me without blushing and trembling nervously—but by the fact that I had wasted a perfectly cute outfit, killer hair, and a face full of flawless makeup on this sham of a date. I was typically a very low-maintenance kind of girl, so pulling myself together like this took time and effort that I would never have expended if I had known it was all for a woman with crazy eyes and a psychotic interest in finding her grown child a suitable mate. Honestly, I was surprised the woman hadn't asked for blood and urine samples before the appetizers arrived. She'd grilled me like I was a POW for the entire date and when my answers didn't meet her expectations I could feel her disappointment wafting from across the table.

Anyone else would have gotten up the instant their date showed up with parental supervision. They would have chalked it up as a loss and deleted the guy off the app. I, unfortunately, wasn't wired that way. Nope, I was predisposed to believe every situation, no matter how bad, had a silver lining. I thought maybe my date would loosen up and tried to reason that it was actually kind of sweet he was so close to his mom. I figured after dinner and the interrogation I would be vetted enough that maybe he would want to do something without our eagle-eyed chaperone.

I thought his shy demeanor made him seem vulnerable and that he was even more adorable in person than he was in his profile picture.

It didn't get better.

It got worse, and I quickly realized the lining was never going to be silver because it was made out of lead, and I was sinking with it to the bottom of the bad-date ocean. I tried to think of a polite way to get out of the rest of the evening but the woman wouldn't give me a minute to breathe. She even went as far as to follow me to the bathroom so I couldn't send out an SOS call to one of my friends for a convenient escape. It was brutal, but I powered through, thinking once they followed me home and saw me to the door in an old-fashioned but still over-the-top gesture that it would be over. I had a boatload of nosy neighbors and a big dog in my apartment, so I didn't fret too much about him knowing where I lived (the mom was a different story).

I was wrong.

I shifted my weight on my feet and bit back a sigh. I should have known she was going to be persistent, but I was done playing nice for her when it was clear her son was so beaten down that he was too scared to make a move or even speak for himself. She was a tyrant and I wasn't going to subject myself to her vile company anymore. As soon as I slipped inside my apartment I was going to delete all the dating apps I had on my phone.

"I have a dog and she's leery around strangers." That was partly true. I did have a dog, a massive blue pit bull that I rescued from a shelter just days before she was supposed to be put down. Dolly looked like a brute, but she was a sweetheart and had never met a human she didn't want tummy scratches and love from. We were kind of kindred spirits in that way. I mean I didn't need my ears scratched or my belly rubbed, but I was afflicted with the same pressing need to be liked and accepted by pretty much everyone I came in contact with. It was ingrained in me to at least try to make everyone a friend, and if they didn't reciprocate my kindness it only forced me to try harder. Sometimes I hated that about myself, and sometimes it was my favorite personality trait because the men and women in my life weren't the easiest nuts to crack. They all loved me and let me in because I'd refused to let them shut me out.

Well, all except for one man.

I couldn't hold back my flinch when he crossed my mind because he had warned me about online dating from the get-go, and I hated that he was right about it. I also hated that he was the reason I was desperate to find a man . . . a man who wasn't him . . . in the first place.

Mommie Dearest shook her head and clicked her tongue at me. "Joseph is allergic to dogs. Your pet will have to go as things progress between the two of you."

I felt my eyes pop wide and the forced smile I had plastered on my face for the entire evening finally slipped away. I already knew she had a few screws loose, but she was taking her crazy to another level if she thought she could tell me to get rid of my dog or what to do with anything in my life.

I straightened my shoulders and tilted my chin up. It was a look that worked on the drunks and unruly college kids that I hustled out of the bar where I worked every night.

"That's not going to be a problem because things are not progressing beyond my front door. Thank you both for dinner, but if you'll excuse me I'm going to go inside and cuddle my dog and erase every online dating app there is."

The woman narrowed her eyes and stepped around her son. The young man made a noise low in his throat and his eyes widened. I thought he was scared of his mom, but the closer I looked at him the more obvious it became that he was scared for me as the woman advanced. He reached out a hand to grab his mother's elbow, but it fell away before making contact like he knew the repercussions for intervening would be severe and drastic.

"Listen here, you little . . ." I lifted my hand before she could throw at me whatever insulting word she was going to label me with. I don't think the woman was used to anyone standing their ground with her because she gasped and fell back a step.

"Stop. I thought I was talking to Joseph. I thought he was a nice guy, maybe a little sheltered and awkward . . . but a nice guy. Obviously it wasn't him running his dating profile and there was some other agenda here from the start. I'm well past the age where I need a mother's approval or permission to date her son, so I'm going to go into my apartment and end this date before either side gets nasty." I looked at the shell-shocked young man hovering behind his mother and mouthed *good luck* before turning my back on both of them and inserting my key into the door. Dolly barked loud and deep from the other side, which was both comforting and reassuring.

I turned the knob on the door and pushed into the apartment without looking back. Once the door was shut and my dog was happily rubbing against my legs, I tossed my head back and let out a sigh that felt like it was tied to my soul. I was tired, so tired.

I loved my life. I had a job that I enjoyed going to every day, and I worked with people I adored and admired. I was never going to be a millionaire doing what I did, but I was good at it and most of the time it felt more like spending time with friends than actual work. I loved and was deeply loved back by my family, even if my younger sister was an idiot. I had a cute apartment, an active social life, and great freaking hair. There wasn't a lot I could complain about on a day-to-day basis and things that did get under my skin were things I had a hard time explaining to anyone that didn't grow up knowing love at first sight was real and that when you found the other half of your heart life was infinitely better.

I was only twenty-six, still plenty of time to live life and settle down, but I felt ancient and overlooked when I compared myself to my younger sister. She'd found the fairy tale our parents had laid out for us when she was still in high school and I got nothing but lonely nights and a string of dates so bad no one believed me when I tried to tell them how awful they really were.

I jolted when there was a knock at the door behind me, making my ears ring since my head was still resting against the wood. Dolly growled low in her throat when she felt me tense up, so I put my hand on the top of her broad head and used the peephole to see who was interrupting my pity party.

My new neighbor, the girl who moved like a ghost and spoke so softly I often had to struggle to hear what she was saying, stood on the other side. Poppy Cruz, quiet, withdrawn, but so sweet and smitten with my dog. I'd totally leveraged that love she had for my pet into a budding friendship that Poppy was obviously reluctant to have.

I knew some of her history through stories from her friends and family who were all regulars at my bar, so I was careful not to push too hard even though all I wanted to do was cuddle her and tell her the clouds have to part on even the darkest of days. She was comfortable enough with me now to knock on my door well past the acceptable visiting hours, so there was no way I was going to leave her standing in the hall, even if that meant my wine and sob-fest were further delayed.

I pulled the door open and Dolly immediately lunged for the visitor on the other side. Poppy was willowy but she had no trouble bracing for the impact from the dog and she seemed just as excited to receive the slobbery kisses as Dolly was to give them.

"I heard you talking out in the hallway and I just wanted to see how your date went. It didn't sound like it ended on the best note." Her quiet voice drifted to me as I shook my head and snorted.

"It didn't start on a great note either. He showed up with his mom, can you believe that? I need a glass of wine, do you want one?"

She wrinkled her delicate nose and wrestled the big dog into the apartment so she could shut the door behind her. "I don't drink, but thank you."

She didn't do much of anything. The product of a very strict and religious upbringing, Poppy was as straight and narrow as one could get. She'd suffered severely at the hands of a man her father had handpicked for her and it was clear that every single day was one more step in the process of healing from that.

"I forgot. I'm in the bar so often I forget that there are humans in this world that can cope without alcohol." I lifted an eyebrow at her and made my way into the kitchen. "I'm not one of them."

She laughed lightly like I meant her to and followed me into the tiny galley-style kitchen.

"So his mom?" Her eyes were the color of hot cider and they gleamed with gentle humor. She was impossible not to like and as much as I wanted a different life for myself I also wanted one for her. I hated that her history was so ugly, but I loved that she'd survived it and was pushing herself to live beyond her experiences. That was beautiful and hinted at an inner strength her delicate appearance kept hidden.

I snorted again and rolled my eyes. "I thought the guy that took off halfway through the date with my wallet was as bad as it could get. I was wrong. Really wrong."

"I can't believe it gets worse, Dixie." She shook her hair at me and I wanted to reach out and touch the bronze strands. They glimmered like they were lit from within. Everything about her was meant to shimmer and shine through the shadows that surrounded her. Eventually that inner glow was going to break free and I hoped I was around to see it. "I didn't think it could get worse than the guy who wanted you to be third person in a ménage à trois with his wife."

I sucked back a mouthful of wine at that and shuddered. "Yeah, when he told me it was fine because their kids were with his parents for the weekend I almost threw my water at him. That was bad, but this mother was still the worst. It was a shame because her son was actually really cute and I think if he wasn't so browbeaten he might actually be a good guy." I lifted a shoulder and let it fall. "Oh well, you live and you learn."

Something crossed her beautiful face, something tragic and painful that hurt to look at, but it was only there for a second and then her typical serene and unaffected expression was firmly back in place. "If you're lucky you get to live. So no more online dating?"

I nodded and finished off the rest of my wine. "No more.

There seems to be an infinite amount of crazy out there in the world and I'm a magnet for it."

They can be whoever they want to be on the internet, Dixie. You'll never know who you're dealing with, and that's dangerous. Church's warning drifted through my mind and it made me want to hit something. He was right. He also always seemed to be looking out for me, which would be thrilling, exciting, and exactly what I wanted if he had been doing it out of something other than some misguided need to watch out for me because we worked together. If he cared about what happened to me because he cared about *me* in some way, shape, or form, I would be over the moon. But really it all boiled down to the fact that I was important to the people that were important to him, so he didn't want to see anything bad happen to me.

I was turning to pour another glass of wine when Poppy and I both started as someone started pounding on the apartment door. I gasped a little as Poppy jumped to her feet in a panic with a startled yelp pealing out of her throat. Alarmed by the human's distress Dolly started to growl and stalked to the door like the born protector that she was. She let out a sharp bark that had me practically sprinting across the room to see who was causing the commotion so that her gruff growling and sharp yapping didn't wake up the neighbors.

I glanced at Poppy and frowned when I saw that she was as white as my countertop and looked like she was going to pass out. Her hand was to her throat and her fingers were shaking so badly I could see the tremors all the way across the room. She was terrified. I wanted to fix that for her but I didn't know how.

"Dixie, open the door. I left Kallie and I need a place to crash for a few days." The voice on the other side of the door was as familiar as my own. His words made me swear out loud as I pulled the door open without another thought given to the fact that Poppy might end up facedown on the carpet.

"You left Kallie?" I barely got the words out before my little sister's obviously furious and clearly frustrated fiancé barreled into the tiny living space. I shut the door behind him. Dolly went about her typically happy greeting once she realized she knew the tall, lanky, auburn-haired man that was now frantically pacing through my living room, raking his heavily tattooed hands through his messy hair.

"She's been cheating on me . . . again. I was such an idiot to believe her when she told me it would never happen again after the last time. How could she do this to me after all we've been through together?" His heated blue eyes locked on me and I could see he was struggling to keep both his emotions and the moisture trapped in his eyes in check. "We're supposed to be getting married in a few months." His voice cracked and I couldn't stop myself from walking over and wrapping my arms around his trim waist.

"Oh, Wheeler. I'm so sorry." My sister was an idiot, but in all honesty so was he. My sister didn't know how to be an adult without him and he didn't know how to be a family without her. They were scarily dependent on each other and had been since they were kids. Now Kallie was barely twenty-two and had everything I wanted in the palm of her hand—the brand-new house Wheeler bought for them to start their lives together, an engagement ring that made my heart squeeze with envy. I would treasure the love and promises she had been given and part of me died every single time I watched my sister be careless and reckless with what Wheeler had handed her. "You can stay here for as long as you need to. Do you want me to call her?" If I did I was going to rip her a new one. I loved my sister dearly, but at the moment I would gladly strangle her with my bare hands.

I felt his broad chest rise and fall where I was squeezing him. He heaved another deep sigh and pulled back so that he could shake his head in the negative. "Not tonight." He growled from low in his chest and roughly dragged his hands over his face. "I need a minute . . . or ten."

There was a delicate clearing of a throat and we both shifted our gazes to where Poppy was pressed against the front door like Wheeler could grow razor-sharp claws and mile-long fangs to eviscerate her at any moment. Her eyes were twice their normal size and her teeth were buried so deeply into her bottom lip I was surprised she wasn't drawing blood.

"I'm going to go." Her voice quivered and her hands were still shaking.

I felt Wheeler tense where I was still holding on to him, and I watched his eyes narrow as they locked on Poppy. His gaze was normally a mellow light blue that looked amazing with his reddish hair and the dimples that dug into his cheeks. Tonight it flared like the blue at the base of a flame and those adorable indents in his cheeks were nowhere to be found.

"Sorry. I didn't mean to interrupt anything. It's been a shitty night on top of an even shittier week and I'm not thinking too clearly at the moment. I didn't mean to barge in and make an ass out of myself." And that was why I loved Hudson Wheeler with every single bit of my heart and soul. His world was crashing down around him. He was drowning in an ocean of his own bad choices (and I would call Kallie a bad choice to her face for this bullshit) and misery, but he still had the wherewithal to gentle his tone and rein in his temper so that he didn't further terrify the young woman plastered against the only exit. He was a good guy . . . no, a great guy . . . and Kallie was a world-class moron for screwing around on him . . . again.

"It's fine. You're . . . um, fine. Dixie, I'll see you later." She leaned down to pet Dolly one last time and then slipped out the door shutting it silently behind her. She moved like smoke and vanished just as fast.

I pulled away from the man that was set to be my brother-in-law and tunneled my fingers through my wild hair and squeezed my head. "That's my new neighbor."

He grunted and threw himself down on my well-worn couch. The springs protested under his weight and then groaned again when Dolly climbed up next to him and put her head on his denim-clad thigh.

"I know her. She's Salem's sister and Rowdy grew up with her back in Texas. He brought her by when she needed a new car. I tried to sell her a '64 Bonneville that needed a little work. She would've made that car look gorgeous. She ended up with a Toyota Camry. It was a goddamn travesty. A girl that looks like that should have a car that stands out, not something safe and predictable." I forgot that Wheeler knew a bunch of the boys that frequented my bar because they were family, some by blood and some by something more, with my boss, Rome Archer. Rowdy St. James also worked at the tattoo shop that was responsible for the majority of the ink that covered Wheeler from head to toe. I should have realized he would have run across Poppy at least once or twice since she'd come to Denver, even if Kallie tended to keep him on a tight leash.

I lowered myself onto the only available seating left in my small living room and kicked my feet up so that they were resting on my coffee table. "Poppy isn't really the standing-out type and she can do with a little safe."

His gaze shifted to mine and his mouth pulled into a frown. "That's a damn shame, too."

I agreed with him, so I didn't say anything else.

After a solid hour of sulking I finally got up and took Dolly out for her nightly ritual. I dug up some sheets and blankets to make a temporary bed for Wheeler on the couch, a temporary bed that was going to be as uncomfortable as hell considering his long legs, and eventually found my way to my own bed.

I wanted to cry for all of it. For Wheeler's broken heart, for my sister's stupidity and blindness to what she had thrown away, for Poppy's obvious emotional scarring and her fear of other people, for Joseph and his creepy relationship with his insane mother, and for me. Unrequited love sucked. I hated it.

No tears fell as I climbed under the covers. Like I always did, I told myself there was bound to be a light at the end of the tunnel . . . there had to be because I refused to live my life in the dark.

Keep your face always toward the sunshine and shadows will fall behind you.

—Walt Whitman

Chapter 2

Church

"You've been awfully quiet tonight."

The southern drawl was lighter than mine, more lyrical and smooth. The Blue Hills of Kentucky rolled thick and unmistakable in Asa Cross's twang as he looked at me steadily from behind the massive oak bar he was currently in the middle of wiping down.

"I talk when I have something to say." No one would ever accuse me of being the chatty type. When I did choose to speak the Mississippi Delta was deep and locked thickly around all my words. My drawl was much slower than the blond bartender's and far less practiced. Asa used his inflection and his southern charm to work whoever was sitting on the other side of the bar like they were one of his marks in a long con. He turned up the south in his voice to make hearts flutter and to fool drunks into thinking he was far less sharp than he was. His Kentucky-flavored tone was nothing more than a tool he used to his advantage whenever he needed it, while my unhurried inflection reminded me of a home I hadn't seen in far too long. That was one of the reasons I never had much to say. Every time I opened my mouth the sound of my voice, like molasses over gravel and deep as the Mississippi River, took me back to a place I had been actively avoiding for over a decade.

I'd spent a little over ten years serving my country in various capacities while enlisted in the army. I'd been around different types of men from a million different walks of life. In all that time I'd never met anyone as hard to unravel as the man standing across from me. He had eyes the exact same color as the aged whiskey on the shelf behind him, and they were picking me apart with a perceptiveness that made me uneasy. I wasn't used to being so transparent. Whatever shield I had up, whatever ironclad curtains I had pulled around me, Asa Cross saw right through them.

"You are usually quiet, but tonight you didn't say a single word. You look like you have something on your mind." His eyebrows lifted and that smirk on his face turned into a grin that I wanted to put my fist in. He wouldn't be half as pretty as he was with missing teeth and a bloody nose. "Dixie had a date tonight. I figure you were worried about her since she's been spending time with those internet guys over the last few months, and the bar is never the same on her nights off."

My back teeth clicked together in aggravation and a low growl escaped my throat. My hands curled into fists at my sides without me being aware they were doing it and I could feel a furious heat climb up the back of my neck.

The idea of Dixie, sweet, sunny Dixie, out there with God only knew what kind of troll she was going to find on the internet made me want to destroy everything. I wanted to break the bar top in half. I wanted to throw chairs through windows. I wanted to smash all the meticulously placed bottles displayed behind Asa into smithereens. I wanted to dropkick the remaining few stragglers nursing their last-call drinks out the door and I wanted to get my hands on whoever had taken Dixie out tonight and throttle him within an inch of his life.

Logically, I knew there were decent, normal individuals using the internet to find love and sex . . . the sex being more likely. There were millions of people online dating and while I thought that was okay for them I refused to think it was an option Dixie should be utilizing. I hated the idea of her dating at all, but there was something about her meeting strangers, meeting men that hadn't had the opportunity to see her in person before taking her out, that really rubbed me the wrong way.

Dixie Carmichael was the nicest girl I had ever met. She didn't have a mean bone in her perfectly curvy and petite body. She was always smiling, always laughing, and there wasn't a moment spent in her company where it didn't feel like the sun was shining directly on you. She embodied warmth and care. Someone behind a computer monitor would never understand that. They would never feel the way her innate ability to make everything seem like it would be okay made the world seem like it was worth saving. There was a lot of bad shoved at us all on a day-to-day basis but somehow Dixie was a filter for it, and when you were around her it seemed like the only thing you could focus on was the good she let through.

She needed someone that could appreciate that. She needed a man that shined as bright as she did and that would hold her above the shit that was always trying to drag everyone else down. I doubted that guy was on Tinder or Bumble. In fact, I doubted that guy existed at all.

"I don't keep track of her comings and goings." I rubbed a hand over my mouth and watched as Asa's eyebrows shot up and his lips twitched. I was a damn good liar. I lied to myself for years and years about the kind of man I was in order to convince myself that the choices I made were the right ones. But I was currently trying to lie to a man that was a professional liar, so it was no surprise that he saw right through the bullshit I was laying down.

"Ahh . . . I see. You have no interest in the fact she might be out there with a serial killer that wants to turn her pretty hair into a coat for his pet hamster?"

I glowered at him and crossed my arms over my chest. I was a big guy. Years of doing PT and boredom in the desert had led to a strenuous fitness routine I still maintained, partly out of habit and partly because when my muscles burned and I made myself sweat I could shut off all the other stuff that was crowding my head. Some of it nagging, niggling regret from the past, a whole lot of it new nightmares and realizations from my present. I had a couple inches in height on the Kentucky charmer and a whole lot more brute strength. Yet none of that or the glower that I was sure was stamped across my face kept Asa from keeping his stupid, sound advice to himself.

"Dixie is a good girl, she deserves someone who can give her that kind of good back." I could see the surprise on Asa's face as I finally gave him something that was wholeheartedly true.

He pushed off the bar and hollered that it was time for the last few customers to finish up. There were some grumbles but everyone left was a regular and as soon as the clock hit one thirty they would move towards the door without any hassle. I liked nights like this, where there were no fights to break up, no crying girls to console, no puke to clean off the floor, no amorous couples to shoo out of the bathrooms. Typically on a night like this I would watch Dixie scamper around shutting the bar down while pretending I wasn't looking at her. I couldn't help myself. My eyes were pulled to her and when she laughed or smiled I felt it in my gut like a punch. She did things to me that no woman had ever done to me before.

She made me want to smile and that alone was enough to have my feet itching to hit the road before I did something stupid, like fall in love or take her up on her blatant invitation into her bed. I wanted to fuck her, but I knew if I did it would fuck us both. She was nothing but good and when I got good in my life it always went bad, so I didn't allow myself, or her, to go there. She shone as bright as the sun every single day but I was a man that knew all too well that too much time in the sun could lead to some serious burns.

I'd spent the last few months biting my tongue until it bled while she dated men that weren't me and I went to bed alone each night wondering why I didn't just pick up one of the barflies that hung around making it known they were ripe for the picking.

I'd never been the kind of guy that burned through women. My mother, and subsequently the women that stepped in to raise me after my mom was gone, Elma Mae and Caroline, taught me to understand that women's hearts were fragile and you had to be careful with them. They tried to teach me how to take care of the good when you had it, how to respect it and earn it. I kept the lessons close because they were some of the only things I had left of the women that shared them with me. I never played with a woman's body if I didn't know for sure her heart was kept in a separate box somewhere. I liked my hands on soft tits and full hips, and silky legs wrapped around my back as much as any other guy. What I didn't like was wiping away tears, explaining myself, and dramatic good-byes when I didn't stick around after a good time. I was picky about who I went to bed with and I made sure they understood all my hard and fast rules about not committing or sticking around before I ever put my hands on them.

"Denver was just a pit stop." I rubbed my hand over the top of my buzzed head and looked down at the wooden floor under my boots. "With everything that happened with Brite and Avett a few weeks ago I think it's about time I put some space between me and the Mile High." A friend and his daughter had recently run afoul of some really nasty people. My old commanding officer and current boss and I had moved in to help in any way we could, which ended with bullets and blood and some seriously pissed-off drug dealers. Holding a weapon in my hand and kicking in doors was second nature to me. I missed the fire of combat in my blood and the adrenaline coursing through my veins. I was made to fight, not to rest on my laurels. "Well past time I made my way home and tried to mend some fences."

This was why Asa was such a good bartender. He pulled your story out of you whether you were planning on telling it or not, and he listened like he cared even if my story was told in fewer words than he was used to.

He nodded at me and pushed a rocks glass filled with amber liquor towards me. He typically drank Scotch at the end of the night, but I was a bourbon guy through and through. "I know all about mending fences, brother. Not a day goes by that I don't have to dig a hole for a new post and string up some new wire." He took a swig of his own drink and plastered that arrogant smirk back on his face. "Plus you might as well run before that girl you've been watching when she isn't watching you fall in love with someone who ain't you."

I was going to hit him. My intent must have been clear because he put his glass down on the bar and lifted his hands up in a gesture of surrender. "My girlfriend is armed and she likes my pretty face the way it is. Keep that in mind, soldier."

I slammed back the rest of the bourbon and let it burn its way down my throat. "Fuck you, Opie."

He chuckled at me and turned to cash out the register behind him. "That's why they say the truth hurts, Church."

Before I had been Church I'd been Dash. And before I had been Dash I'd been Dashel. It was already hard enough being a kid with less than white skin and with parents in an interracial relationship, but having a name that was as uncommon as mine down in the Deep South was fuel on an already burning fire. I'd hated it growing up and even with shortening it to Dash I'd still struggled with it. But now I'd been Church for a long time, and he was a man that didn't give any kind of shit what anyone else thought of his name. I'd earned that nickname through service and blood. It wasn't a name that was given to me. It was one I had taken and made my own. Elma Mae was going to hate it and she was still going to call me Dashel even when I begged her not to but there was a part of me that couldn't wait to hear the stubborn old woman tell me, *I'll call you by the name your mother picked out for you, son. That's the name she wanted for you and you should respect it.* I should, but there were a lot of things I should have done to make my mom proud that I didn't do.

The truth Asa was laying down did hurt, because there was no hiding from him that part of the reason I was ready to bolt was because I really couldn't stomach the idea of watching someone else take Dixie's heart.

"Didn't ask you for the truth." I stuck my head out the front door and watched as the last two bar patrons climbed into their Uber. I locked the front door and shut off most of the lights and made my way back to the bar.

I liked the operation Rome had set up here. I liked the people, both the ones who worked for him and the ones he served, and I liked that the atmosphere was usually festive but pretty mellow. On the nights that heads needed to be cracked and tempers needed to be tamed I enjoyed the exertion and physicality of that as well, but I wasn't meant to be a bouncer. I had too much training, too much experience, and frankly too many demons that needed an outlet, to babysit drunks and party girls for the long haul. It was time for me to stop drifting.

Asa finished up with the money and shot a glance at his phone. I could tell by the genuine smile that crossed his face and the way his gaze sparked that his gorgeous redheaded girlfriend was the one behind the message. Royal Hastings, the pretty Denver policewoman had recently moved in with the annoying southerner and it wouldn't surprise me if she ended up with a ring on her finger before the year was out. The cop and the con had something special going on even if I firmly believed it was doomed to fail.

"Most folks don't ask for the truth but that doesn't stop me from giving it to them." He gave me a look that told me if I was any kind of man I would take that truth he was so fond of and do something smart with it. I didn't bother to tell him good and

I didn't really see eye to eye. We made our way to the back door after a quick stop at the office to lock the money up in the safe. Asa scribbled a note to Rome and then quickly checked the security cameras. He typed out a message on his phone and by the time we hit the parking lot at the back of the bar a brand-new Toyota 4Runner was pulling in with a smiling redhead behind the wheel.

Asa clapped a hand on my shoulder and gave me a look that burned with understanding and seriousness. I felt like he was speaking directly into my soul when he told me quietly, "The real truth is, I let something good go, so I know how that feels. Got it back and would move heaven and earth to keep it by my side, so I know exactly what you're walking away from, soldier. Be smarter than I was and don't let all that goodness slip through your fingers." He turned around and walked backwards for a second while flashing me that shit-eating grin of his. "It's always better to be warm than it is to suffer the cold, Church."

He moved towards the SUV and I had to look away when he leaned into the driver's side window to kiss his girl. There was so much intimacy there, so much passion that it made everything I swore I knew about love and togetherness pull against the reins that held it tight.

I gave a halfhearted wave as Royal honked the horn at me and pulled out of the parking lot, then made my way over to my Harley. It was still nice enough weather to ride, another reason I needed to get my ass in gear and head south. In a few weeks it was going to be too cold to have the bike on the road and I wasn't interested in putting the beauty on a trailer and driving her like some expensive piece of luggage back to Mississippi.

I was swinging my leg over the chrome-and-leather beast

when my phone vibrated in my back pocket. It was after two in the morning so I knew anything buzzing through at this time of night couldn't be good. Considering I'd recently shot Denver's top drug supplier's right-hand man and put down another one of his henchmen for good, I was dreading seeing what was waiting for me on the display.

It was almost as bad as I expected it to be. The number was one I'd been ignoring since I landed in Denver months ago. It was a number that belonged to a man that I owed more than some simple conversation or a handful of words. It was a call I would have continued to ignore if it hadn't come in the middle of the night and on the heels of three other calls throughout the day that I had turned a blind eye to.

It was time to stop running from my past.

It was time to man up.

It was time to be a better man, the man the person calling had tried his best to raise me to be.

"Hey, Julian." I rested the Harley back on the kickstand and ran a hand over my face. I could practically feel the shock wafting across the phone line. He hadn't expected me to answer and that made me a special kind of asshole.

"Dash." His voice was even deeper and coarser than mine. People often told me I sounded like Johnny Cash but Julian Churchill really had the Man in Black's rough growl embedded throughout his tone. "I didn't think you were going to answer."

I sighed and felt like the wild five-year-old he had tried to wrangle all over again. "Been busy. Took a while to settle in and get used to sleeping without bombs going off overhead."

He didn't say anything for a long minute and when he spoke I could tell he was trying really hard to keep the hurt and censure out of his deep voice. "You have a perfectly good bed here and last I heard there weren't any bombs in Lowry." Lowry was the small town where I had been born and raised, just outside of Tupelo, Mississippi. There weren't bombs there but there was a bucket load of memories that blasted me with emotional shrapnel that hurt worse than the kind I'd had surgically removed from my skin.

"I needed time, Jules."

"Had more than enough time, son. You need to come home." I bristled just like I always did when he tried to tell me what to do. I thought I'd squashed that urge after we stood side by side and lowered my mom into the ground but there was something about him talking to me like I should know better that always made me feel like an unruly kid.

"Planning on it. Have to tie up a few loose ends around here, and I have to make sure I don't leave my friend that helped me out in a lurch." Rome would send me on my way with a pat on the back and a foot in my ass if he knew the real reason I was hiding in Colorado instead of hightailing it home. He was understanding, but the man was all about family first and he wouldn't abide the way I'd been avoiding mine for the last decade or so. I was a coward and I didn't want a man I'd been in the trenches with, a man I would die for and knew would die for me, to know just how deeply that weakness ran.

"Dash." There was a sigh and then Julian cleared his throat, so I knew he was struggling to keep his emotions in check. "Elma Mae had an accident."

I almost dropped the phone as I bolted up from my lounging position on the bike. "What do you mean she had an accident?" My fingers tightened around the phone to the point that my knuckles hurt and the blood rushing furiously between my ears made hearing his response difficult.

"She was carrying her laundry in off the line and tripped going up the stairs. She fell backwards and busted her hip. A neighbor heard the commotion and ran to help. They had to airlift her to the hospital in Tupelo. She's also got a dislocated shoulder and a sprained wrist. She's back in the Lowry hospital now recovering and she should be going home at the end of the week."

"Jesus." Elma Mae was chasing down eighty if she was a day. None of us knew her exact age and she refused to tell. She would just smile at us and tell us we kept her young. Those kinds of injuries were serious for someone in their prime. In a woman Elma's age they were life threatening. "She gonna be all right?"

"Elma is a tough old bird. It'll take more than a tumble to keep her down. She's been asking about you."

Well, if that wasn't just a fucking red-hot poker right through the guts. It was also a slap across the face with the reality of everything I'd purposely been avoiding and denying for way too long.

"I bought a Harley. Gonna have to ride it home, so I'll be there in a couple days." My homecoming was happening sooner than I'd planned, but there was no way I couldn't be there for the woman that had always been my true north. When nothing else in my life made sense there was Elma Mae. She was the only safe place I had ever known and if she needed me I was going to be there to return the favor. I owed the woman everything and the fact I'd waited so long to see her after years of deployment was a startlingly clear reminder of why I was correct and considerate in staying the hell away from Dixie.

She lived in the light and I was far more comfortable hiding in the dark.

"I'll let her know. That will make her day." He paused for a second, which made me brace for whatever was coming next. "She mentioned a girl. Elma told me the reason you weren't in any hurry to come home from Denver was because of a girl. That true?"

Son of a bitch. The truth might hurt but the lies I told, and they were more gray than white, were going to outright kill me. "There's a girl." And there was, but she wasn't entirely the reason I wasn't ready to face Julian or anyone else back in Lowry. She had been one of my reasons for sticking around Denver longer than I'd planned. She was an excuse that would buy me time and one that wasn't entirely untrue.

"Do me a favor and see if you can bring her with you. Elma would love nothing more than to see you happy, to know you're finally settling down and moving past the things that happened with your mom and with Caroline. You bring your girl home with you and give all of us some peace of mind. Make an old woman happy, Dash. You owe Elma a few years where she doesn't have to worry about you catching bullets or ending up alone."

Shit. I rubbed my temples and kicked at the loose gravel under the soles of my boots. "I'll see what I can do." That was bullshit. Dixie would drop everything and come with me if I explained the situation. She was too nice and too sweet to tell me no. Elma Mae was going to goddamn love her after she gave her a ration of hell in order to make sure she was the right girl for her boy.

"If the girl cares about you then she'll figure out a way to be here. If she can't figure it out, she isn't worth your time. Come home, son, we miss you."

I missed home, too, but I could do without the memories and

reminders that had kept me away since the day I signed my life away to my country.

It was my turn to sigh. "I'll see you soon, Jules." He hung up and I wanted to kick myself because after all these years and all the time and effort he put into raising me I still couldn't call the man Dad. He deserved the title, after all it was his last name I carried around with me, not that of the man who had knocked my mom up and run. He had earned it much like I had earned my name, but whenever I tried to say it the word got stuck and I fell back on something that seemed less important. It felt like I was fooling God and everyone under the sun about just how important Julian was to me if I refused to call him the only thing he had ever been to me. I was trying to trick fate so Jules didn't end up the way so many others I loved had.

I was also going home, and I was going to put some sunshine in my pocket and take it with me.

Chapter 3

Dixie

I'd been working bar hours long enough that it took some major commotion and ruckus to pull me out of bed before lunchtime. Even Dolly had adapted to middle-of-the-night walks and breakfast at noon since I was a worthless and cranky blob of indignation if I was forced to abandon my comfy bed while the morning sun was still in the sky. It was the one and only time I let myself be grouchy and hate everything, which meant anyone that knew me well gave me a wide berth in the mornings. My days and nights had been flipped for as long as I could remember, so when loud voices pulled me from a sound sleep the next morning well before noon, and well before the time that most people got up to start their day, I was livid. I hadn't slept very good the night before, so it felt like I had just shut my eyes even though several hours had passed, but that didn't mean I was in any kind of mood to be startled awake or to play referee.

I heard Wheeler's sharp tone as I crawled out of bed almost pushing Dolly to the floor in the process. I was stunned when it was another deep, obviously angry male voice that replied and not my sister's. I figured Kallie would show up with her tail between her legs any minute now begging Wheeler to take her back. That's what she'd done the last time he caught her stepping out on him with another guy. She wasted no time in trying to force him to forgive and forget.

She knew exactly where her bread was buttered and there was no way she was going to let the guy that had taken care of her, coddled her, given her everything she'd ever asked for get away from her. There was also no way in hell my vain, spoiled little sister had the backbone and fortitude to weather the embarrassment of canceling her long-anticipated wedding this close to the date. If word got out exactly why Wheeler had pulled the plug on their dysfunctional relationship, Kallie would wither away from embarrassment. She might want to have her cake and eat it too, but if someone pointed out how gluttonous it made her seem she would fall apart. The girl couldn't take criticism to save her life, which was why she had kept hold of Wheeler for so long. He loved her and everything about her . . . at least he had until she'd drop-kicked his heart.

I recognized the rough, growly voice with its southern drawl right away. I couldn't figure out why Church was at my apartment this early, and I couldn't figure out why he and Wheeler were barking at one another like two dogs staking their claim over territory in my living room. I thought that maybe I was still dreaming until I stubbed my toe on the back of the couch as I rushed into the front of my apartment to see what in the hell was going on.

I swore loudly and hopped around on one foot, which drew both of the snarling men's attention to me. Dolly, curious about the early morning visitor, gave me a sympathetic look then happily trotted over to Church, who was standing with his arms crossed over his massive chest while he glared at me out of those amazing eyes of his. People would call them hazel for lack of a better term but hazel didn't cut it. Hazel was too ordinary a word for a color that was so brilliantly extraordinary. Those eyes of his were something else, pretty much all of him was designed to make vaginas surrender without putting up any kind of fight. There were men that were pretty like Asa, and there were men that stole breath with their masculine beauty like Rome Archer. Then there were men who had the best of both those worlds like Dash Churchill.

"What are you doing here before Starbucks is even open, Church?" I rubbed at my sleepy eyes and stiffened when his gaze drifted down from my messy hair, which I was sure looked like I stuck my finger in a light socket, to the oversized T-shirt I was wearing that had a giant cartoon taco on the front wearing a scowl with the words "I don't wanna taco about it" scrawled underneath. Obviously it wasn't something I would have ever worn to bed if I'd known he was going to be my six-foot-four, testosterone-fueled alarm clock, but there wasn't anything that could be done about my ridiculous sleepwear or my out-of-control hair now. There was also nothing that could be done about the fact I wasn't wearing pants and even though my taco shirt was big it was still just a T-shirt and barely, and I do mean barely, covered up all the things it needed to in order for me to keep my modesty.

I cleared my throat as that mesmerizing gaze drifted down the length of my legs and back up to my heated face. I took a careful step behind the couch and crossed my arms over my chest to mimic his badass pose. Mine was more to hide the fact I didn't have a bra on and to cover up that even though he was pissed and clearly annoyed his mere presence still had all my lady parts shaking off sleep and waking up bright and early.

"I need to talk to you. I wasn't expecting you to have company." The way he said it wasn't very nice.

I stiffened and shifted my gaze to Wheeler, who was standing at the doorway not letting Church and his palpable anger all the way into my apartment. Dolly was sitting between the two men watching them like they were opponents in a tennis match. She was probably waiting to see who would give her attention first but the visual still made my lips twitch as the dog's head swiveled back and forth.

"Wheeler, go ahead and let him in. If I'm going to be up this early I need coffee and I don't want either of you or your male posturing to scare Poppy." I shuffled from behind the couch and into my tiny kitchen as my no-longer-future-brother-in-law stepped to the side. It was only when Wheeler was fully clear from the door that I realized all he had on was a pair of low-slung jeans. His heavily tattooed torso was on full display and his mahogany hair was mussed and messy from a night of aggravated hands pulling at it. If I was on the other side of the door and couldn't see the tangled mess of Wheeler's haphazard bed still on the couch, I would probably be jumping to the same conclusion that Church obviously was.

I wanted to rush to reassure him that it wasn't what he was thinking, that Wheeler was family, but the big, broody man stomping through my living room had me eyeing him warily as Wheeler snorted and muttered, "Come on in, *Church*."

Church's head swiveled around and his jaw went tight. I thought I was going to have to take the sprayer from the sink and hose them both down. "Appreciate the hospitality, *Wheeler.*"

I rolled my eyes as Dolly whined when the tension ratcheted up a notch and it was no longer fun to be caught between the two men.

"All right, enough. You both have badass names and I'm sure you're both remarkably well endowed." I felt like I should offer them rulers to measure just to break through the hostility. "Can we chill out with the pissing contest until after I'm properly caffeinated? Please?" I looked at Wheeler because out of the two of them I knew he would be easier to sway with tired eyes and a weak smile. He looked properly annoyed by my comment about what he was or wasn't working with behind the fly of those low-slung jeans.

He gave me a narrow-eyed look and walked over to the couch so that he could pull his shirt on. "I'll take Dolly out for a little bit so you guys can talk." He gave Church a pointed look as he walked towards the door with my dog happily trotting along behind him. "I'll only be gone a few minutes." The implication was clear, Church better state his business and go. Wheeler wasn't a fan of the early morning wake-up call or the judgment that came with it either. His eyes flicked to me and his lips quirked. "You're still in fine form in the morning I see."

I rolled my eyes at his back as the door closed behind him. I popped a pod into my Keurig and looked at Church over the counter that separated us as he paced back and forth in the minuscule space that was supposed to be the dining room. I saw him pause and his step faltered when his gaze hit the tangle of sheets on the couch. He turned to look at me and I watched as a muscle in his cheek twitched as he considered me silently for a long moment.

"He wasn't your date from last night, was he?" He walked towards the counter and curled his fingers around the edge. If I didn't know any better, I would think he was looking for something to hold on to.

"Nope. Wheeler is supposed to be marrying my little sister in a few months. He broke up with her last night after he caught her cheating again." I tapped my fingers on the lower counter and tilted my head to the side. "Even if he was my date from last night that doesn't give you the right to show up here at the crack of dawn and growl at him." I expected a flinch or a look of contrition. I didn't get either.

Then he lifted a hand to his face and dragged it down. I noticed he looked as tired as I felt. "You're right. I'm sorry." He didn't look or sound very sorry, but I decided I was still too groggy to fight with him about it.

"So why are you here?" Maybe he would answer me now that he knew I didn't kick Wheeler out of my bed to answer his knock on my door.

He sighed and his eyebrows dipped low over his fantastically-colored eyes. "Because I need a favor."

I couldn't control myself from taking a step back. I'd been subtly throwing myself at the man for months and had resigned myself to the fact that all we would ever have was an uneasy friendship because he didn't return my interest. I couldn't fathom what kind of favor would have him calling on me first thing in the morning.

I blew out a breath and watched as it sent a loose curl dancing across my forehead. "We're friends, Church. I care a lot about you, of course I'll do you a favor." I felt like I would do anything for him and not just because I would do anything for anyone I cared about. He was someone special and whatever I could do to chase some of that thundercloud he lived under away I would do it.

He barked out a laugh but there was no humor in the sound. His deep voice dropped even lower as his gaze shifted away from mine. "You probably want to hear what I'm about to ask you to do before you blindly agree."

I felt my eyebrows shoot up at his somber tone. "That sounds ominous. Just spit it out." It was too early in the morning for my brain to be firing on all cylinders.

He pushed off the counter and resumed his pacing. He put a hand to the back of his neck and I watched as his fingers flexed as he squeezed. "I haven't been home since I enlisted in the army. That's a decade, Dixie. That's a long time to be gone." He shook his head a little and let out another one of those laughs that hurt to hear. "I knew Rome was still in Colorado, so I asked him to hook me up with something until I could get my feet back underneath me. I knew he would understand." He cleared his throat. "It's time for me to go home."

I nodded absently and snatched up my cup of coffee. I felt like I might need to Irish the dark brew up a little bit to get through the entirety of this conversation. I asked Church if he wanted a cup and was waved off. He was struggling to get to the point and obviously didn't want any distractions.

"Denver has always been temporary." He stopped and turned to look at me. I was trying desperately not to freak out that this was essentially him telling me good-bye. I'd never had him, but I was far from ready to let him go.

"When are you leaving?" My voice cracked and I didn't bother to hide how deeply his words were affecting me. When you fell you eventually had to land but nobody warned me that part hurt like a bitch.

He stopped moving and put his hands on his hips. It was his turn to incline his head at me while he watched me unwaveringly. "I'm leaving this afternoon."

I lost my grip on the coffee mug. The heavy ceramic fell out of my suddenly numb hands and hit the kitchen floor with a shattering impact. I didn't even hear Church call my name as hot liquid splashed up on my bare legs. I was frozen, stuck in place as every fantasy I'd built around the man that was rushing towards me, demanding to know if I was okay, imploded inwards. Dying dreams ripped at my heart as blood rushed through my ears in a waterfall of what could be. If only he knew the way I knew.

I gasped so hard that it made my lungs hurt when hard hands landed on my shoulders and gave me a little shake. Before I could tell him that I was fine I found myself swept up in a single fluid motion. I was clasped to a rock-hard chest as arms that felt like boulders held me aloft. His boots crunched across the broken pieces of mug on the floor as he demanded directions to the bathroom so he could make sure my naked lower half was okay.

I'd wanted his hands on me for what felt like an eternity and when I finally got them there he was getting ready to take them away forever. This wasn't enough of his touch. This wasn't even close to being the way I wanted to be held and handled by him but if he was going then I would soak it up like a sponge and savor every fleeting second of it.

He didn't put me down until he found the bathroom, on his own since I was mute and immobile. He set me down on the edge of the vanity and crouched down in front of me. I'd had a lot of really X-rated fantasies about him being in that exact position. In them I wasn't wearing a shirt with a taco on it, sporting morning breath and rocking hair that looked like a strawberry blond rat's nest. I also had on underwear that was far sexier than the plain, cotton boy shorts I was pretty sure Church currently had a clear view of, but none of that mattered because he was using the edge of a towel he'd torn from the rod behind him to gently rub the spots on my shins that were turning an angry shade of red.

"You might blister." The Delta was thick in his voice as he looked up at me. His accent never seemed to change, it was always languid and syrupy thick with the south in it, but while he knelt in front of me, eyes hooded and concern for my well-being stamped all over his beautiful face, it was stronger, more pronounced. Always there making sure I was okay, for all the wrong reasons. I never asked to be his duty. My heart twisted painfully as I struggled to pull it together.

"It'll be fine. I'm pale, so it always looks worse than it is. I need to go clean up the mess before Wheeler brings Dolly back. Her food and water is in the kitchen and I don't want her in there until it's safe." We'd never been this close before. Normally my want for him prickled under my skin, annoying but manageable. This close, his hands brushing across my tender skin made longing burn along every nerve and my blood come alive with hunger that was throbbing heavy and hard in every single part of me that was female.

He grunted at me and rose to his feet, which immediately made the bathroom infinitely too small for both of us. He shifted to reach the shower and cranked it on. After dousing the towel in cold water and dropping it back on my legs, he leaned back against the wall and resumed his favorite pose with his arms across his chest. I tried not to ogle the way the fabric of his plain black T-shirt strained around the circumference of his biceps and failed. He was effortlessly a whole lot of eye candy and there was no denying I had one hell of a sweet tooth.

"I'll clean the mess up but, Dixie, I gotta ask you . . . Will you come to Mississippi with me for a few days?"

He asked it so casually that I swore I misheard him. "What?" I lifted my fingers to my ears and gave each one a poke and a tug. "I must've heard you wrong. It sounded like you just asked me to go to Mississippi with you."

One of his eyebrows lifted and the corners of his mouth twitched. It wasn't a smile, but it was the closest thing to one I had ever seen on his handsome face.

"I did ask you to go to Mississippi with me. It's a long story, and if you agree I promise to tell you all the important parts of it." I stared at him in stunned silence for a long moment feeling like I'd been dropped in an alternate universe. There wasn't much between us aside from that friendship I forced on him, so this favor seemed way out of the boundaries he had established and way out of character for the man that made it known he rode that Harley of his solo.

"I need more than that, Church. You can't really expect to ask me something like that and want an answer with no explanation." Everything inside of me was surging and rushing, trying to catch up with this new, unexpected turn of events.

He heaved a sigh that lifted and dropped his thickly muscled chest. "When my family asked me to come home, instead of telling them I needed time, that I wasn't ready to face them and the real world yet, I told them I was hanging out in Denver because I met a girl. I thought it would get them off my back, and it did . . . sort of."

I sucked in a breath and shifted my legs under the now clammy and cool towel. "You lied to your family?" I didn't like that one bit.

"I've been lying to them for years. When they wanted to know where I was, what I was doing . . . I lied. Every time they asked if I was safe and I told them things were fine, it was a lie. This was just one more lie that I told so they didn't have to worry about me. I wasn't ready to go back, now I am, but I need you to go with me. There's an eighty-year-old woman that's counting on me to come through for her and I need you to make that happen." He said it all so point-blank and matter-of-factly that I was convinced maybe I was dreaming the whole thing. Maybe I was still wrapped up in bed with Dolly snoring next to me. Maybe my last date had been bad enough that I'd officially gone off the deep end.

I reached out and grabbed the taut skin above the top of his jeans. There wasn't any fat there to trap between my fingers but I still managed to get a solid pinch in. Church swatted my hand away and took a step towards the door. "What in the hell was that for?" He rubbed the spot through his T-shirt and glared at me.

"Well, clearly I've stumbled into a terrible romantic comedy and Hugh Grant is going to burst through the door any second, either that or you've been reading too many romance novels and are using the plot that's in pretty much all of them to fuck with me. You can't possibly be asking me to pretend to be your fake girlfriend in real life. That shit doesn't happen." I kicked the soggy towel off my legs and climbed to my feet. I pointed a shaky finger at him. "You better not be asking me to lie to your family for you, Church, because that is something I won't do and I won't forgive you for asking me to do."

He swore again and held up his hands in a gesture of surrender. "I'm not asking you to lie, Dixie. You keep telling me we're friends, well, I need you to be exactly that. I just need you to be my friend in front of my family."

I scoffed at him. "That's ridiculous."

When he was within touching distance he reached out and put one of his hands on my shoulder and used the knuckles of the other to tilt my chin up so that I had no choice but to gaze up at him. "I'm asking you because you are the only person that can help me. I'm asking you because I know you mean it when you say you care about me." The pad of his thumb moved along the edge of my jaw and again I forgot how to breathe.

"That's not fair, Church." I didn't like that it felt like he was using my inherent desire to see the people I cared about happy and whole against me.

"Never claimed to be the kind of guy that plays fair, pretty girl."

Pretty girl.

It was like a knife in my already bleeding heart.

"I don't know if this is something I can do." I wanted to because I wanted him to find the peace he was obviously lacking, but I also wanted to be able to look at myself in the mirror every day and not hate the woman I saw staring back at me. I wanted the fairy tale my mom talked about, the dream guy my sister managed to land, but I never wanted to be desperate or pathetic in order to get it. Love was supposed to make you better, not make you hate the person you became in order to obtain it.

His gruff voice rumbled from somewhere over my head since I couldn't force myself to look up at him as my mind whirled and my heart thudded heavy and painful in my chest. "I know it's asking a lot, but I'm asking anyways because I don't have a choice." That was probably true. He was a man that very much handled things on his own terms and in his own way. He was a creative problem solver, proven by the fact he was standing in front of me regardless of the hell he had seen and the terror he had witnessed firsthand.

"You should've been honest with your family from the get-go. Neither one of us would be in this spot if you had been." I didn't mean to snap at him but I felt a little cornered and he was still stroking my jaw, which was making my head fuzzy and my resolve weak.

"That ship sailed a long time ago." He sounded mad about the fact, but all the anger was directed inwards, into that void of darkness that lived in the center of him.

"I don't want you to be a liar, Church." That wasn't the kind of man that had made me fall so far and so fast.

"I promise on my mother that I won't ever lie to you, Dixie." He sounded so sincere, so earnest that my heart finally overthrew my brain's tyranny over my common sense. He needed me, and I think we both knew from the outset that there was no way I could deny him help when he asked for it. It wasn't in my nature to deny someone I cared about my help and there was no way I could tell the person that I was stupidly sprung on "no."

I blew out a breath that made the floppy hair in front of my face dance. I lifted my hands so I could wrap them around his wrists. It made me shiver when I couldn't even get my fingers to touch as I tried to close the circles around them. His pulse kicked hard under my fingertips.

"I need to make sure it's okay with Rome that I go, and I need to get someone to watch Dolly for a few days. If I can get all that squared away then I'll come with you." I was convinced any kind of happy-ever-after for me involved him but I was starting to wonder if his was a different kind of happy-ever-after that had nothing to do with realizing I was the one for him. It sounded like his happy-ever-after involved closing rifts and knitting breaches that stretched far and wide. He needed me in an entirely different way than I needed him. The knowledge stung but I still couldn't deny that I wanted to be the one that he turned to for help. I also wanted to be the one to help him even if it hurt my heart.

He stared at me without speaking for a long, drawn-out moment and then slowly nodded. He let go of my face and stepped back.

"I already cleared your time off with Rome. We had a long talk this morning when I told him I had to leave. He called Avett in to cover for you the next week or so. I told him I wasn't sure when I was putting you on a plane back home."

I scowled a little bit and started to follow him out of the bathroom. "You were so sure I was going to agree to this nonsense?" That was annoying.

He looked at me over his shoulder and his lips quirked again like he was trying to smile and he simply forgot how. "I was. You always come through for your friends, and even though I never gave you reason to, you've considered me a friend from the get-go. I'm gonna go clean up that mess in your kitchen. Maybe you want to put some pants on before your guest gets back with the dog."

I looked down at my still-splotchy legs and then back up towards his retreating back with a huff. At the sound he turned around and looked at me over his shoulder with a lifted brow. "I think it's pretty cute you're all grumbly and scowly when you first wake up. You're like a furious kitten looking for something or someone to put your claws in."

I sat there with my mouth hanging open and staring at the space he was no longer in. No one thought I was cute in the morning. No one except Church apparently. I groaned and dropped my head into my hands.

I should have stayed in bed. Nothing good ever happened before noon.

Chapter 4

Church

I should have been elated that she'd agreed to go with me, it saved me the hassle of trying to explain why I lied to my family, but all I could feel was all-encompassing relief that the good-looking redheaded man that had answered the door was family and not someone who had had the pleasure of spending the evening in her bed.

I'd wanted to rip his heavily tattooed arms off and beat him within an inch of his life with them when he pulled open the door looking understandably irritated at my early morning visit. He'd seemed far too comfortable in Dixie's home and there was no stopping the flood of jealously and the flickering flames of rage that raced through my blood when he looked at me like I was the interloper. I'd held myself back because I didn't want to hurt her and I didn't want to hurt myself, but seeing someone else in the place that I knew was rightfully mine made all my good intentions burn like acid deep inside my gut. Whenever I tried to do the right thing it somehow managed to go horribly wrong.

Dixie had good timing. She'd put the fires of jealousy out and started a different kind of burn under my skin by doing nothing more than standing there looking rumpled and endlessly cute. Her hair was always kind of wild and unkempt, but straight from bed it looked like it had taken on a life of its own and was looking towards world domination. Her soft brown eyes were even darker than normal when filled with leftover sleepiness and her dusting of freckles stood out even more since she wasn't wearing any makeup. If she looked that rumpled and messy after a night alone in bed I couldn't keep my mind off of wondering what she would look like after hours of hungry hands and an eager mouth having their fill of her soft skin and sweet smile. It was a struggle to keep my eyes off the bare expanse of leg peeking out from the bottom of her ridiculous T-shirt because I could tell the other guy had his eyes on me and he didn't like the way my eyes were on her at all. He was protective . . . and he should be. None of the thoughts I had while trying not to blatantly check her out would make him very happy.

The relief that she wasn't hooking up with a guy who wasn't me was short-lived as I scrambled to get everything needed for the two of us to hit the road together. I wasn't sure what the weather was going to be like, so that meant I needed to stock up on a little bit of everything to make the long ride down south. It was almost twenty hours, most of it through the plains of Kansas and tips of Missouri and Arkansas. That meant the conditions were going to be varied across the board weather-wise and it was up to me to make sure my passenger had everything she needed to make the ride as comfortable as possible. Now that she'd agreed to ride with me I wanted to make sure there was no reason for her to back out. I'd never been on the Harley for that long of a ride either, but I figured after years of riding around in tanks and other armored vehicles and flying in and out of hot spots in cargo planes that my ass was well beyond up for the job.

Rome actually gave me a helmet he had sitting in his office that was small enough to fit Dixie. He told me it was his soon-to-be wife's, but she hardly ever used it now that they had two kids under the age of five. The free hours they had to ride together were few and far between and with winter on the horizon he was looking at parking his bike for the next several months anyway. I took the helmet gladly but the conversation that had come before it about why I needed to borrow the headgear in the first place had come begrudgingly.

Rome knew a little about my history. It was impossible to keep from him considering he was my CO for most of my military days. When news came from home, good or bad, it was always filtered through him first. As expected he listened to me lay out my laundry list of sins without saying a word and when I was done all he did was nod, tell me I would be missed around the bar, let me know I would always have a place in Denver and a sympathetic ear if I needed to talk, and agreed with me that it was well past time I got my ass back to Mississippi. Just like I knew he would, he told me that family was everything and if I was the kind of man he knew me to be I would go do right by mine.

It wasn't until I told him that I was asking Dixie to go with me that his demeanor changed. His dark brows snapped down, the scar that bisected his eyebrow pulled tight, and made him look like a man very capable of making me regret any bad decision I may make where the bubbly redhead was concerned. I'd been to war with Rome Archer, so I knew exactly what he was capable of and I knew things wouldn't end well for me if I misstepped with someone he considered part of his family.

"You send that girl back here with a broken heart and we're going to have issues, Church." Those issues would very likely end up with me in the hospital waiting on broken bones to heal.

"I don't plan on hearts being involved in any way, shape, or form, boss man. I need a favor and she's the only one that can do it for me. We're friends." We weren't really but we were something close to that and I knew there was no way Dixie's affable and eager-to-please personality would let her tell me no. I needed her and she had this way about her that made it known if you were someone she cared about, someone that mattered to her, there was no way she could abide letting you down. She was also a chronic fixer and had an openly bleeding heart, so I was also aware of the fact that when I explained there was a rift that needed mending back home her desire to meddle and tinker with the lives of those she loved would automatically kick in. It worked for me, though I had serious doubts that any of this would work for her.

Rome shook his head at me and a knowing grin played around his mouth. I hated it when he looked at me like he knew something that was bound to knock me on my ass when I figured out whatever it was for myself.

"It's cute that you think you can actually have a battle plan with it comes to your heart, soldier. You go ahead and let me know how well that works out for you." He pointed a finger at me and lowered his voice. "You take care of my girl like she's one of your men out there in the firefight. You watch her six and I guarantee that she'll watch yours. You mark my word that this is going to be the biggest battle you've ever fought and you'll never have been so happy to lose when you finally surrender."

I rolled my eyes at him. He had no idea what he was talking about. It would only be a fight if I had something to give up and since I didn't believe in love, or soul mates, or the kind of forever that shined so brightly out of Dixie's dark eyes, I wasn't at risk of losing anything.

After the lecture from Rome and securing the agreement to ride south from Dixie, as well as earning a few deadly glares from her couch surfer, I swung by the closest shop that would have women's riding gear and picked up everything that Dixie could possibly need for the upcoming ride. The zip-up chaps that the sales guy brought out immediately had my mind diving into the gutter with all kinds of inappropriate thoughts. They were meant to be worn over jeans and zipped all the way up the sides for easy removal but all I could imagine was what they would look like on her tiny frame with nothing else. She had the prettiest pale skin, flawless and cream colored with just a few adorable little freckles across her nose and the tops of her shoulders. The idea of all black leather against all her sweetness was enough to make the fit of my pants a little tighter. The image of Dixie covered in nothing but leather and me wasn't something that should be playing through my mind if I was going to make the effort to keep things in the friend zone but I couldn't stop it. I never wanted her friendship, but now that I had it and needed it for my own end I knew I needed to not mess it up by letting my dick make decisions for me.

She wasn't the type of woman that I was normally attracted to. She was too soft, both in spirit and in life experience. I tended to drift towards the women that were just as jaded and just as world-weary as I was. I'd seen a lot in my lifetime, both at home and in the far-flung places my previous career had sent me, so it was hard to look at life through anything but cynical eyes. When I first met Dixie I was convinced her "I never met a stranger because everyone is a friend" act had to be forced and fake. I couldn't get my head around the fact that there was someone in the world that hadn't had their spirit crushed by how truly terrible things could be. I figured she had to be working an angle, that her entire bubbly, sunny disposition was nothing more than a front to work the customers for bigger tips, but as time went on, as days turned into weeks and weeks bled into months without the slightest falter or crack in that brilliantly bright façade I realized Dixie really was that upbeat, unflappable, and positive all the time.

Being the cynic that I was I told myself that the only way she could be that happy, that cheerful day in and day out was because she had lived a life where she didn't have to witness what a ruthless bitch fate could be. I figured she'd never had to live through loss or fight through all the things that came after. I convinced myself she'd never seen a struggle or had to battle hardships, but one night after closing the bar down I'd had a few too many cocktails and let my theory slip to Asa. The other southerner had shut me down before I finished spewing all those bitter accusations.

He'd pointed out that it was much easier to let life beat you down, to put up a shield and hide behind walls when life kicked you around, than it was to keep on smiling. More truth that seriously hurt just like he'd intended it to.

I tended to think that all I had endured during my time serving my country and all the tragedy that had come before it made me invincible, and unbreakable. I'd taken the worst that fucking fate had to throw at me and I was still ticking. I told myself I was stoic and knew that the only things in life I could actually control were myself and my reaction to the things happening around me, but after Asa's harsh, behind-the-bar truth I wondered if I'd taken my emotional lockdown a step too far and had simply stopped allowing myself to react to or feel anything altogether. Being numb served its purpose when you were in the middle of hostile territory but I was home now and that numbness and coldness weren't getting me anything other than a lonely bed and an estranged family that I still needed to beg forgiveness from. I wasn't stoic, I was scared and that made me feel pathetic and weak.

I wasn't the only member of my family that had been kicked in the heart and stabbed in the guts by tragedy, but I was the only one who'd decided a war zone was an easier place to be than home. I tucked tail and ran. I purposely chased after danger and disaster because I was positive that if I made it a point to put myself in the heart of conflict and peril whoever was in charge up in the great beyond would finally leave the people that I loved alone. It made no logical sense but to an eighteen-year-old kid without many options and with way too much loss in his life, it seemed like a brilliant plan. I was surrounded by death, I might as well go to a place where all of it made sense, where there seemed to be some kind of rhyme and reason to the loss and letdown. As asinine as my thinking might have been it worked . . . at least it had until Elma Mae took her tumble down the stairs.

As I guided the big chromed-out bike to the curb in front of the brick apartment building I had to admit that it felt a little like I was poking fate with a stick by heading down south. Things weren't exactly sunshine and roses after I left but no one else had been taken from this Earth too soon while I was overseas. Jules didn't have to put another woman he loved in the ground and my younger brother didn't have to weep over the loss of another mother while I was away. Things were good for them, and then they weren't. It logically couldn't be tied to my return from the desert but man, it sure felt like someone out there really had it in for me and those that cared the most about me. Six months after my boots hit American soil the woman who was our de facto matriarch, who was our guiding light, and who took care of all the Churchill men when we were unwilling and unable to care for ourselves, had gone down when nothing else in this life had been able to level her. I wouldn't say I was a superstitious man, but I had to wonder if that was some kind of cosmic reminder of how drastically I managed to fuck things up. I got a little bit of good and I destroyed it effortlessly. It kind of felt like the universe was warning my family of how destructive love could be when I was around. That also didn't bode well for the perky redhead that was standing on the edge of the curb tapping her booted toe as she talked to another young woman I vaguely recognized from my nights watching over the bar.

The young Hispanic woman was probably the most objectively beautiful woman I had ever laid eyes on. Everything about her seemed like it had been handpicked by the keepers of beauty and grace. The long waves of her caramel hair belonged in a frilly shampoo commercial and her skin was perfectly golden and so flawless that she almost looked like she couldn't be real. She was too skinny and way too fragile for my particular taste. She looked like she was ready to bolt back into the building the second I turned the engine off and leaned the bike to the side on its stand. She had to know there was no way I would hurt her, I'd spent the last several months making sure any female that crossed the threshold of the Bar knew they were coming into a safe space, but her eyes still got big and her hands still fluttered like nervous birds. Some of that gold went white in her face and I could see it was an actual struggle for her to stay where she was next to Dixie's side as I approached.

Dixie gave me a lopsided smile and handed the leash she was holding over to the other woman. She crouched down in front of the big pit and gave the animal a kiss right in the center of its furry forehead. The dog looked up at her with sad eyes, like it knew she was getting ready to leave it behind, and I felt the beast's pain. When Dixie got on a plane back to Denver I knew it was going to be the last time I saw her face always smiling, always laughing, always looking at me like I was something more than I was. It hurt. The good things in my life always seemed to.

"So Wheeler is going to be in my apartment for a few days until he figures out what to do with my sister. For now, he's letting her stay at his house because he doesn't want to fight. If your boss doesn't want you to bring Dolly with you during your shift you can just leave her with him. If you need anything just hop next door and Wheeler can help you out." Dixie rose to her feet and reached out a hand and put it on the younger woman's shoulder. I watched as she flinched at the touch. It made my back teeth grind together. No one as soft and as dainty as she was should have that reaction from a simple touch. It made me want to injure whoever had made her afraid.

The pretty brunette slipped away from Dixie and laid a hand on the top of the big dog's head. "Other vet techs bring their pets in all the time. As long as Dolly doesn't get aggressive with the other animals or the staff it will be fine." She shifted her feet nervously and darted her tongue out to lick across her bottom lip. She was so pretty it was impossible not to stare at her but I could tell the attention made her even more anxious than she already was so I reached for the bag at Dixie's feet and turned back towards the bike without a word. "I shouldn't have to bother . . . Wheeler." Her already quiet tone went even softer when she mentioned Dixie's couch surfer.

Dixie let out a soft sigh and shrugged. "Well, if you do need him he won't bite. He's actually one of the best men I've ever met in my entire life and my sister is a complete jackass for royally screwing things up with him. Speaking of which, don't be surprised if a tall blonde shows up creating a racket. I know you hate other people's drama but Wheeler pulling out of the wedding is going to make Kallie lose her damn mind. Call me if she won't take the hint or better yet call the cops. Maybe a night in jail will finally force her to grow the hell up." Dixie sighed and bent to pet the dog one last time. "Thanks again for offering to take Dolly. I'll shoot you a text when I'm on my way home."

The soft-spoken woman tucked a piece of that honeyed hair behind her ear and forced a smile. It was obvious she wanted to mean it, she just wasn't in a place where she could yet. I really wanted to do some physical damage to the person responsible for stomping all over such gorgeous terrain.

Dixie made a move like she was going to try to hug the other woman but thought better of it when the brunette tugged the leash so that Dolly was placed firmly between them. With a strained good-bye and one last reminder to call if she needed anything, my traveling companion finally turned to me with cocoa-colored eyes filled with obvious sadness for her friend.

I tilted my chin in the direction the woman and the dog had taken down the block. "The person responsible for making her so twitchy still in the picture?" Dixie sighed again and took her bag from me.

"No, he's dead. Took his own life right in front of her after kidnapping her and torturing her for two days." She stiffened as the words rushed out. "The worst part is I don't think he was the first person to knock her around, he was simply the one that made her determined to keep everyone at an arm's length. If you can't get close enough to touch her then there is no way you're close enough to hurt her. That's a lonely way to live."

It was. I knew that intimately because I was living pretty much exactly the same way. I cleared my throat and gave my head a little shake to get my thoughts out of that particular gutter and back into the one that involved Dixie dressed in leather and wrapped around me pretty much nonstop for the next few days.

"You ever been on a bike before?" She was dressed like she was ready to ride. She had on jeans that were tucked into the tops of black boots that had heavy soles and laced up to right below her knees. She was also wearing a fitted plaid shirt with a white tank peeking out the top under a lightweight denim jacket that had shearling at the collar. Her mass of bright curls was tamed in a poofy ponytail at the back of her head and it made my fingers itch to set them free. I liked her wild and uncontrollable hair. It made her look like a pussycat with a lion's mane as she gave me attitude and promised me everything I didn't deserve with nothing more than a look. Keeping her tresses tied as we screamed down the asphalt made sense but I knew without a doubt before the day was over I was releasing them from their little rubber captor. That was absolutely not a friendly thought to have but I had it anyways.

Dixie rolled her dark eyes at me and reached for the helmet that I held out to her. "Of course I've been on a bike. Do you think Brite would have hired me back in the day if I couldn't talk shop with his clientele? The bar used to be one of the biggest baddest biker hangouts in all of Denver. I think that was the first question he asked in the interview. Darcy made him clean the place up when Avett started getting old enough to come hang out in the kitchen with her." She smirked at me and slapped the borrowed helmet onto the top of her head. I knew the history of the place that Rome now called his but I guess I never really stopped to think about the integral part this little spitfire had played in all of it before now. "Plus, before the accident my dad used to ride. Not a Harley, but still. I was on the back of a motorcycle a lot when I was younger."

She strapped the chin strap in place and hefted the backpack that was loaded down with whatever she had packed for the week over her shoulders. She was so goddamn cute it made everything inside my chest feel too tight and had all those naughty thoughts about what could happen once it was just me and her and the road roaring back to the forefront. It also made my blood heat up and dick twitch in a way she was bound to notice if she bothered to look in that direction.

I cleared my throat and reached for my own helmet as we moved to the bike. "Your dad was in an accident?" That was the thing about separating yourself from the people around you, they didn't get to know me, but I also missed out on really knowing anything about them. Typically, I thought that distance and indifference were for the best but as I swung a leg over the bike and settled in, waiting for Dixie to climb on behind me, I really started to resent the fact I didn't know anything beyond the superficial where she was concerned.

The leather creaked as she wiggled into place with her legs clamped around the outside of mine and the soft press of her breasts into my back. Her hands slipped around my waist like she had held on to me a thousand times before when in reality today was the most we had ever touched. I knew why I was compelled to keep my distance. Once her palms flattened onto my abs under the material of my open leather jacket and the soft whoosh of her exhaled breath hit the back of my neck I knew I would never be able to sit on this bike again and not feel her there behind me. She was going to be a memory I couldn't shake.

"Yeah." She breathed deep and low, her chest rising and falling where it pressed into me. I had to bite back a groan as her fingers curled into my tense stomach muscles. "The summer right before I started high school he got into an accident on his motorcycle. A truck changed lanes and didn't see him. He was thrown over a hundred yards and had to be airlifted to Denver General. He was fortunate he had his helmet on or else he wouldn't have made it."

I could feel a tremor move throughout her tiny frame as she recounted the story. I turned to look at her over my shoulder and noticed the corners of her mouth pulled into a frown. "He's lucky, then."

She lifted a shoulder and let if fall. "He survived, but he's been in a wheelchair ever since. So yes, he's lucky, we all were because he's a great dad, he was before and he continued to be after the accident, but our family was changed forever."

We stared at each other for a long, silent moment. Sometimes it felt like it was easier to communicate with her through a look than it was through words. It wasn't lost on me that she had survived something horrifying and life changing at the hands of the very machine she was currently propped up on. The amount of trust and faith she had to have in me in order for her to agree to ride for days on the back of something that had almost taken a parent from her was humbling and terrifying. I hadn't done anything to earn that kind of conviction from her but now that I knew I had it I was going to do everything in my power to live up to it.

"I'm not going to let anything happen to you on this trip, Dixie. I promise that you will be safe with me." I meant it. I would keep her safe from everything, including me and the way it was impossible to ignore the heat of her pressed against the plane of my back.

"I wouldn't have agreed to go with you if I didn't believe that you would take care of both of us, Church." Her voice was quiet but I heard the truth in her words loud and clear.

I cranked the key in the ignition and let the growl of the V-twin motor drown out the sound of the taunting voice in the back of my head chanting the word "friend" over and over again. I might have to tattoo the damn reminder on my forehead before we crossed the state line.

She was cute. She was curvy. She was sweet and sunny . . . What she wasn't was a chick I could take to bed and walk away from no harm no foul, and I needed to keep that in mind even as she flipped me a nervous grin in one of the mirrors that jutted off the handlebars. Everything about Dixie Carmichael screamed forever, and I knew probably better than anyone on this planet that forever wasn't something that was real, no matter how good you had it. Forever was an illusion that soft hearts and warm brown eyes built dreams around. It wasn't something a man that knew how quickly everything could be ripped away and shredded to pieces put much stock in.

It also surprised me that Dixie had been through something that very easily could have crippled someone else and she was still nothing but sunshine and roses. I on the other hand took life's unexpected misfortunes and let them mold me into a man I could hardly stand to face most days.

I wanted her because she was Dixie and there was something about her that shed light on all the dark places I'd been living in for so long, but I knew with every fiber of my being I didn't deserve her and that if I wanted what was best for her I wouldn't let either of us believe for a single second that I could keep her.

Chapter 5

Dixie

It was late afternoon by the time we got on the road. The fall sky went dark early as we headed out of the city and into the endlessly flat landscape that was everything east of the Rockies. When the sun went all the way down Church stopped at a truck stop a few hundred miles from the Kansas border and ordered me to put on a pair of leather riding chaps that zipped up the outside of my legs and buckled around my waist. It wasn't that cold, but there was definitely a nip in the air as the wind rushed past us on the highway. I didn't think I needed the leathers but there was something about the look in his eyes as he ordered me to go put the stiff garment on that made me swallow any argument I was going to give him. The blue in his eyes burned and there was heat in his eyes that wasn't from the air slapping across his stern face. I never considered myself a leather kind of girl but apparently Church had different ideas about that.

I took the leathers from him as he turned to top off the tank. The truck stop was busy enough that it took me a few minutes to maneuver my way across the parking lot and around to the side of the building where the sign indicated that the restrooms were. I found myself quickening my pace as a couple of truckers leaning against the side of the building tracked me under the bills of their stained hats. I didn't like the way they looked at me and I really didn't like the way they looked over at Church.

I could have pulled the chaps on while standing in the parking lot but all that vibration and rumble underneath my backside meant Church was going to have to get used to stopping every few hours so I could use the restroom, just like I was going to have to get used to the questioning and not altogether friendly looks that were being fired his way. If he was one of those guys that was determined to make the best time from point A to point B with as few stops in between as possible, he was in for a rude awakening. And I may have stretched the truth a little bit about how recently I had had my rear end planted on the back of a motorcycle.

In high school I'd dated a wannabe rebel without a cause that rode a busted up Victory that he swore would be worth a fortune when he fixed it up. It hardly ever ran and when it did it crawled rather than roared, but other than that I tended to avoid anything that drove on two wheels instead of four. I'd let Brite take me home after work a few times when my car was in the shop and I'd ridden with Rome a time or two when he wanted me to go with him for stuff related to the bar. My dad's accident hadn't exactly put me off of motorcycles, but I was very cautious and careful about getting on one, and my willingness to do so was directly related to who was driving the machine. I had never done a long road trip on the back of a bike before and so far I was a fan, but that might have been directly related to the fact that

I got to spend hours upon hours clutching Church like my life depended on it, because it kind of did.

I'd wanted to have my hands on the man in a totally inappropriate way since the first time I laid eyes on him, so there was no way in hell I was going to squander the opportunity to touch all the places that I was supposed to be touching as I curled into him and held on for dear life. He felt just as hard, just as hot, just as heavenly as I always figured he would, and I was really starting to resent the soft cotton of the long-sleeved T-shirt he had on for keeping all that golden skin from my fingertips. I wanted to scratch my initials into his abs and rub my palms all over the carved ridges that flexed and bunched under my hands every time he changed lanes or looked over his shoulder to check on me. I already knew Church was built like a mythical deity, but having the fact confirmed for hours upon hours as muscle moved against me was making me twitchy and damp in places that weren't exactly comfortable against rough denim.

The truck stop bathroom wasn't the worst I'd ever seen but it was far from the best. It was obvious women's comfort was low on the priority list as I took in the cracked mirror and hanging door on one of the two stalls. I gingerly picked my way across the stained laminate floor, careful not to step in any of the unidentified puddles of liquid marring my path, and slipped into the stall with the working door.

I handled my business while reading the endless amount of graffiti carved on the wall—apparently there were a lot of women available for a good time if called—and used my foot to flush because there was no way I was touching anything more in this bathroom than I had to. I found a relatively clean spot in front of the mirror to wiggle into the leathers and wasn't surprised at all when I went to wash my hands that there was no soap and barely a trickle of water leaking out of the faucet. Thankful I never went anywhere without a stash of hand sanitizer, I gave myself one last once-over, decided that I might be able to pull off a little bit of badass biker babe after all, and made my way to the door.

I gave it a tug and groaned when my fingers touched something sticky. I shook my head when nothing happened thinking that I needed to push instead of pull to escape the nastiness. I frowned when changing tactics didn't release me from Satan's bathroom either. I pulled harder and then resorted to using my shoulder and shoving with my entire body weight in the opposite direction but still the door remained shut. I gave a shudder and wiped my hands on my leg.

"I wonder if it's stuck." There wasn't a response because I was the only soul brave enough to enter this hellhole and my voice echoed off the broken tiles that surrounded me. I heaved a sigh and tried again to pry the door open, this time putting a foot on the wall and pulling back with my entire weight. There wasn't even a creak or a groan to indicate I was making any kind of headway.

Swearing, I patted my pockets futilely looking for a cell phone I knew good and well was in the front pocket of the backpack I had left sitting next to the bike. I didn't want to risk it falling out of my pockets and shattering on the highway but now, trapped and getting more and more panicked every second, I wished I had thrown caution to the wind and kept the thing on me.

After a few more minutes of pushing and pulling to no avail

I started looking for another way out of the bathroom. I figured that was my only option for escape unless someone else was in desperate need of the toilet and managed to Hulk the door open from the other side. I assumed Church would wonder where I had disappeared to and eventually come looking for me, but just in case he didn't get curious fast enough to suit my now racing heart and sweaty palms I wanted to make sure there was another way out. There was a small window in the stall with the broken door that I wasn't sure I was going to fit through. I was fairly petite, but my ass was not. I was round in all the places a woman was supposed to be round so even if I managed to get my head and shoulders through the opening I doubted the girls and my back end could squeeze through. It didn't matter though, if someone didn't come and set me free in the next minute I was going to try to force my way through the too-narrow opening even if I got stuck. Someone was bound to see my head sticking out of the side of the building.

"Hey! The door is stuck!" I cupped my hands around my mouth and shouted in my best "last call" voice. "Someone come and let me out of here!" I used the side of my fist to pound on the door and winced as my shout bounced off the walls around me.

I kicked the door with my boot and swore again. This was actually the perfect way to end a day that had started off too early and kind of crazy.

I pulled the hairband out of my hair so I could tug on my curls. It was a nervous habit I'd always had. There was something soothing about watching the ringlets go straight and then immediately bounce back into their spiral as soon as I let them go. I started to pace anxiously back and forth in front of the door, eyeballing the window like a junkie eyed a fix. I told myself one more minute then I was climbing through regardless if I fit.

I called for help one more time and let my shoulders fall in defeat when there was no response. I was starting to really freak out and I was honestly annoyed that Church didn't seem to find it at all odd that I had been gone for well over fifteen minutes at this point. I wanted to believe that there was a part of him that cared about me, at least a little bit, but now with his obvious lack of interest in my whereabouts it was pretty clear I was searching for affection and feelings that simply weren't there. He kept an eye on me when it was his job and when my safety was in his hands, but when I was out of sight apparently I was also out of mind.

"Fuck this." Throwing my hands up in the air I marched to the broken bathroom, far less careful about the goo on the floor than I was before. I was going to need an hour-long shower to even feel remotely clean after my time stuck in this craphole. I had one foot on the toilet seat and a hand on the back of the tank when I heard my name being called from the other side of the door.

There was no mistaking Church's southern twang or the annoyance that was clear in his impatient tone.

I wilted with relief that I wasn't going to have to climb out the window and rushed back over to the door. "It's stuck. I've been in here forever!" My tone was just as irritated and annoyed as his. He should have come looking for me long before now. I crossed my arms over my chest and frowned when the door didn't immediately swing open.

"It's not stuck. There's a piece of pipe shoved through the handle." I heard the sound of metal scraping across metal and then there was a whoosh as he pulled the door open. There was a scowl on his face and a rusted metal pipe in his hand as I rushed past him and towards freedom. "Why would someone jam the bathroom door?" He tapped the pipe against his leg and looked at me like I had the answer to that very strange question.

I put my hands on my hips and narrowed my eyes at him. "Why did it take you so long to come looking for me?"

His eyebrows snapped down over his eyes and his mouth tugged down into a frown. He looked like he was going to give me attitude right back, but then his eyes traveled over me, taking in the curls that were now everywhere from my nervous fingers and my legs encased in all that black leather. Whatever he was going to say died and the gold in his better than hazel eyes sparkled and shined with something that made me want to blush and shift my weight on my feet. I knew I was all right to look at, hell, on the days I put effort into it I could be better than all right, but I'd never had anyone look at me like I was the best thing ever before, especially not someone who really was the *best* thing ever. It made my heart flutter and all those dreams he'd willfully crushed pulsed with new life.

Church gave his head a hard shake and cleared his throat. He tossed the pipe towards the side of the building and motioned that we should head back towards the Harley. "I was headed over here to check on you when some guy stopped me and asked me if I could help him with his car. There was smoke billowing out the front of it, so I couldn't exactly ignore him." He lifted his hand and rubbed his knuckles along his jaw. "I told him it was a busted radiator hose and then I came to find you."

I huffed and moved to follow him, some of my anger dissipating since he had a reasonable excuse for not rushing to my rescue and he actually did sound sorry. "Probably just kids that thought it would be funny. It wouldn't have been so bad if someone bothered to clean the restroom at least once this millennium." I didn't want to think about the truckers with their narrowed eyes and tight mouths as they watched me walk away from Church. Suddenly getting locked inside the devil's restroom alone didn't seem as bad as it might have been.

He grunted and turned to look at me over his shoulder. "I should have been paying closer attention. I told Rome I would watch your six, and so far I've done a piss-poor job of it. You shouldn't be walking around a truck stop after dark without my eyes on you. Anything could happen, and getting locked in a dirty bathroom is the least of it." His words mirrored my nervous train of thought to a T.

I wrinkled my nose at him as I wrestled my hair back into a band so I could fit the helmet back on my head. Some of my panic was fading and it was replaced with a healthy dose of self-recrimination. "I work in a bar, Church. I don't get off shift until three in the morning. I know how to watch my surroundings, and I know how to take care of myself. I should have paid closer attention or waited for you to walk with me." I swore I could feel him whenever he was close by. The air felt different, heavier, and thicker. My skin tingled while my heart raced. I would know if he was missing without even having to look for him. I would elementally know it, that's how attuned to him I was.

He stopped at the side of the bike and turned to face me. There was a muscle ticking furiously in his jaw and his hands flexed like he couldn't control them at his sides. "I told you I would take care of you, that I wouldn't let anything happen to you on this trip. I know you can take care of yourself, pretty girl, but for the next few days it's my job to take care of you. Not happy that I dropped the ball right out of the gate."

He was mad.

I could see it in the set of his wide shoulders and in the way his mouth tightened. His gaze swirled angry and furious with a riot of clashing colors as he took a step towards me, looming and glowering as we stared at one another.

I couldn't function. All I could do was blink up at him slowly because it was exactly like the time he asked me if I was good. I was so used to being on my own and handling whatever I was handed all by myself that it made me forget how to breathe and made my knees weak when I thought about being able to lean on his strong shoulders and to have someone else there to carry the burdens I was often loaded down with.

"Oh." The word squeaked out, too high and too thin. I didn't want him to give me hope that there could be more when he snatched that option away every chance he got, but his words, those beautiful words, they made all those fantasies that centered on him and I together forever pulse and pound hard in my blood.

He reached out a hand and used the tip of one of his fingers to tuck a loose curl back behind my ear. "I will do a better job of keeping an eye on you while you're in my hands."

I wanted to turn my face into his palm and let him caress my cheek but it was all too much for my tender heart to take. The only thing I'd wanted since I fell for him was to be in his hands and for him to find a place for me inside of his heart. I'd wanted all the things he was saying to me from him when I thought there was the possibility of a future for us. He was going home to a life that didn't include me and I was going back to Denver and a life that wasn't going to be nearly as satisfying without him. Him giving all of this to me now felt wasted and trivial. He could throw pretty words and sentiment at me because he knew we were going to head our separate ways soon and he wouldn't have to live up to them for very long.

I took a step away from him and tugged on the end of my coat so that I didn't reach for him. "It was just a prank gone wrong. I'm sure it will be smooth sailing from here on out. We'd better get going if you want to make it into Kansas tonight. You said you wanted to ride at least a few more hours as long as the weather cooperated."

He looked like he wanted to say something more to me but instead he gave a jerky nod and moved to strap his own headgear on. He swung a long leg over the bike and waited for me to situate myself behind him before starting the motor back up. I didn't hold him as tightly as I had the first part of the ride and I didn't lean as close to him as I could. My body wanted the contact but the rest of me couldn't take it. He had my emotions on overload and my hormones battling against common sense. This favor felt like it might be the death of me and we hadn't even crossed any state lines yet.

I had my hands low on Church's ribs, but kept a pretty tight grip on him with my legs. It didn't feel as intimate as curling myself into his back and even though the distance was minimal it felt like we were miles apart. His big body was just as stiff as mine was as he muscled the motorcycle through some heavy traffic the closer we got to the border of Kansas. It was semi-truck after semi-truck whizzing by making air rush around us and provoking me to be even more alert and tenser than I normally was when riding. Being on a motorcycle was already dangerous, being on a motorcycle surrounded by twenty-ton trucks seemed even more hazardous. If Church lost focus or got distracted at all, things weren't going to go well for either of us. Luckily he drove the bike like he did everything else, with single-minded determination and unwavering intensity. There was nothing casual or relaxed about him as he zipped around the big rigs. I wasn't sure that was how he normally handled the bike or if he was simply being extra cautious because of my history but either way I was grateful for his palpable concentration and consideration.

It took us another hour to hit the very flat and, even in the dark, very boring landscape of Kansas. We had the entire state to drive through tomorrow and I knew from a previous road trip that I had taken with my family when I was younger that we were in for a lot of corn and cows. I was ready to call it a day. My backside was starting to get numb and my spine hurt from sitting so straight so that I could keep some breathing room between me and Church's leather-clad back. I was also hungry and still needed that hour-long shower to wash away the grime and gunk from the truck stop bathroom. Not to mention I'd been pulled from bed way earlier than I was used to, so I was struggling to keep my eyes open and to stay alert to what was happening around us.

I was leaning forward in order to holler into Church's ear that he should stop when we got to the next town that looked like it might have a decent hotel or motel for us to crash at for the evening. I was jolted from my position when all of a sudden an engine revved, tires squealed, and headlights cut across the black asphalt far too close to us for any kind of comfort.

I couldn't stop the shrill shriek of terror that ripped out of my throat as the massive machine I was perched so precariously on rapidly veered to the right. I felt a wobble and heard the motor protest underneath me.

Pride be damned. I threw myself into Church's back and wrapped my arms so tightly around his middle that I wouldn't be surprised if he had to struggle to breathe. I squeezed my eyes shut and sent a silent prayer up to the sky just in case some divine being wanted to cut me a break today. I didn't see my life flash before my eyes but everything that could be did.

The family of my own I would never have.

The perfect wedding that I'd dreamed of ever since I was little looking at the pictures that hung in my house from that magical day my mom and dad shared.

The guy . . . who wasn't perfect . . . but still made my heart flutter and my knees weak. The one that I wanted more than anything I had ever wanted before . . . the one who felt cold yet refused to let me warm him up.

And the sex . . . good God the sex. The mind-melting, soul-stopping, heart-healing, and body-bending sex. The sex that would make all other sex meaningless and forgettable. The sex that would make everything old feel new again. The sex that would be unforgettable and extraordinary. The sex I was never going to have because the man I wanted to have it with didn't know what I knew.

It made me want to cry for what could be and for what should be. It made me hurt for both of us because even though my heart was invested and his wasn't I knew Church deserved more than a life spent alone staggering through the dark.

By some miracle the bike stayed upright and neither one of us went flying off the seat and into a field of corn. Church pulled the motorcycle over onto the shoulder of the highway and propped the heavy machine up on the kickstand so that we both could climb off and catch our breath. Big trucks continued to zoom by oblivious to the near-death experience that left us both shaken and rattled.

Church ripped his helmet off and glared down the highway like his fury alone was enough to stop the reckless driver in his tracks so that vengeance and quite possibly an ass kicking could be doled out. He shifted his furious gaze to me and put the helmet on the seat of the bike so that he could catch me when I started to wilt to the ground. My legs wouldn't hold me up anymore and my spine felt like Jell-O as I folded towards the asphalt.

I was shaking so hard that he had to struggle to find a good grip on my arms to keep me upright. "It's okay, Dixie. I told you I wouldn't let anything happen to you."

I couldn't do it anymore. The space was too much. I needed his strength and his quiet confidence to keep me from falling apart on the side of the road.

I wrapped my arms around his waist and pressed my face into the center of his chest. I could hear his heart beating just as fast as mine was but while I quaked and quivered, struggling not to cry, he stood sturdy and strong, unruffled and as cool and calm as always. He was like a tree standing tall and unmoved after a terrible storm. There was so much comfort in that steady self-assurance that my legs quit trembling and my lungs remembered how to work.

I breathed him in and exhaled the terror and panic out. I thought he was going to stand there immobile and immovable but his hold shifted from my upper arms so that one arm wrapped around my shoulders clutching me to him almost as tightly as I was clinging to his waist, while the other moved so that one of his hands was cradling the back of my head, helmet and all. He held me to him letting me know that if pieces started to break off if I did indeed shatter, he was there to catch them and put them back in place. It was singularly the most important and most impactful hug of my entire life.

After a few minutes of headlights hitting us and exhaust fumes choking us I gave him one last hug for good measure and pulled back enough that I could look up and barely make out his features in the shadows.

"I totally believe that it's in your best interest to keep me alive, Church. I'm having serious doubts other motorists feel the same way. That was way too close for comfort." My voice was slightly shaky and the humor I attempted was forced at best.

He gave a little nod of agreement. "Way too close. If I hadn't been paying attention that would have been bad . . . really bad." I appreciated the fact he didn't sugarcoat things for me. I hated the fact that he seemed to be taking some sort of responsibility for the poor driving habits of someone else when he told me, "I shouldn't have asked you to take this trip with me. I should have just bought you a plane ticket and met you at the airport. I'm used to the risk and I was being selfish and shortsighted as usual."

I lifted a hand from his waist to the side of his face. His cheek was warm despite the chill from the night air around us. He also had the start of a golden scruff that made him look even more attractive . . . if that was possible. His jaw felt like steel under the tips of my fingers but the curve of his bottom lip was soft as I ran the pad of my thumb over it. The touch must have startled him because his lips opened on a soundless sigh and his breath whispered out to touch my fingers.

"I told you I am well aware of the hazards that are associated with riding motorcycles. I am intimately acquainted with all the things that can and do go wrong. My dad was a very skilled rider and he still got hurt. Sometimes bad things happen and all we can do is learn to adapt and work with what comes next. I knew the risks involved and I said yes anyway." I was talking about more than the risks involved with spending endless hours on a two-wheeled death machine and he knew it.

We stared at each other in silence for a long time until he gave a jerky nod against the fingers that were still tracing the lush outline of his very kissable mouth. "I think we should call it good for the day. We can pull off at the next exit and find a hotel to crash in."

I nodded in agreement. "Okay." But there was something I had to know before we tempted fate by getting back on the bike. "Hey, Church." My voice was husky and rough in the darkness that surrounded us.

"Hey, Dixie." His always gruff voice rasped like sandpaper across my overly sensitized skin.

I shifted my hand to his cheek and lifted the other one up to his thickly muscled shoulder so I could get the leverage I needed to lift myself up onto the tips of my toes to reach those delectable lips that had been calling to me since day one. He grunted a little as I leaned fully into him so that we were chest to chest and almost lip to lip.

If I was going to risk my neck on the back of his bike with all the crazies out here on the road, not knowing what could happen to either of us from one moment to the next, I was going to do it knowing what it was like to kiss him. I was going to know what his mouth felt like on mine and how he tasted on my tongue. I was going to memorize every single nuance and every little sound because when I went back to Denver this kiss and the memory of what it felt like was going to have to last me a lifetime.

Chapter 6

Church

She kissed me.

Her lips touched mine and she destroyed me. This tiny ray of light that seemed determined to chase the darkness inside of me away unraveled me with nothing more than the brush of her very soft lips against mine.

I should've pulled away, either that or gone all in. The attraction between us was only going to end one way, with me inside of her as we scorched through one another, so a real kiss with tongues and teeth and grabbing hands was inevitable, especially if she was holding the door wide open in invitation. I was already struggling with the friend thing and this wasn't helping at all. I stood there, holding her, feeling her as she rubbed her mouth over mine, the barest hint of pressure as she took a taste, as she feathered her lips against mine like she was trying to memorize the shape, the feel, the flavor of them. It was the singularly softest touch I'd ever experienced and yet it had the power to make my knees weak and my blood pop with a desire so sharp it felt like it could pierce right through my skin.

Her hand cradled my jaw, her fingers shaking with some of the same things I was feeling. This thing that lived between us was hungry and tired of being ignored. It buzzed around us, electric and hot, refusing to be cooled by the chill in the night air that surrounded us. If we weren't careful the passion that was starving and needy between us would consume us, devour us, and leave us nothing more than hollow husks filled with fading satisfaction and jagged disenchantment because no matter how good we were together it couldn't and wouldn't last. I didn't want any part of me to be responsible for burning her out. I liked that her light chased my shadows away and that meant I wasn't going to have any kind of hand in dimming the way she glowed.

Her breasts pressed into the center of my chest as she leaned more fully into me and I could feel the pointed peaks of her nipples stab into my skin. The sensation made my dick twitch behind my zipper and had all the available blood that was still above my belt rushing south. I'd always liked the way Dixie was built. She was on the shorter side, but every single part of her small frame was curved and lush. She looked like a woman that you could grab ahold of without having to watch yourself. She was delicate but in no way did she come across as fragile or breakable. She looked like she could take everything I had to give her, all the pent-up longing, all the nights of frustration I spent hard and alone, all the denied hunger that made me want to eat her up and then go back for seconds and thirds because I knew there was no way I was going to have my fill of her honeyed lips and velvety skin in one go.

There was so much of her to experience, and I wanted to

know what all of it felt like, tasted like, sounded like. I wanted to watch her come from every possible position I could get her in, and then I wanted to find some new ones, ones no man had ever had her in before, and watch her come in those, too. Because I knew once I got her she would let me have her in ways she hadn't let anyone else. Her eyes, so pretty and dark, made me all kinds of promises, and I wanted to take her up on every single one of them. But there wasn't anything I could promise in return, and that always kept me from crossing the invisible line.

She ran the tip of her nose along the edge of my jaw and that little nuzzle made my entire body shudder. She had the ability to bring down all the walls I'd so carefully built up around us in order to keep both of us safe. She didn't have any clue the kind of damage I could do if I ignored all the warning bells ringing loudly in the back of my mind. I knew the ways in which I could wreck the women in my life that I cared about and there was no way on God's green and often unforgiving Earth that I would subject her to that. I barely survived the loss of the last woman I loved, I knew if I let Dixie sneak her way inside my heart and something happened to her there would be nothing left of me. There wouldn't be anyplace left for me to run.

I hated that she still had her helmet on. I wanted my hands in that wild mane of hair. I wanted to hold her close and let myself absorb how good it felt to have her in my arms after wondering how we would fit together in the dark for so long. We fit just right. She was small, but mighty. She had no trouble getting herself where she wanted to be and the side benefit of all her stretching and grabbing on to me meant that every soft and sweet part of her was pressed fully and tightly against every hard and hot part of me. Her body yielded to mine and I swore I would never survive if it did the same thing while she was stretched out naked and wanting underneath me. It felt better than anything ever had even though we were standing up, fully clothed on the side of a highway. There was no way my starved senses and achingly lonely soul were going to be able to withstand the sensation overload that would follow getting Dixie naked and my hands and mouth on every part of her creamy, freckled skin.

The very tip of her tongue darted out and gave the center of my bottom lip a little lick. It was the best kiss I'd ever had and it was barely a kiss at all. She fell back on her heels and gave my shoulders a little push so that I would let her go. I took a step back and used the tip of my own tongue to chase the way she tasted off my lips. Sweet. Everything about her was always so damn sweet. Her taste was going to be branded on every part of my memory long after she was gone, just like I could feel the touch of warmth against my skin and know she had been in the room recently. She thought I wasn't aware of her. The truth was she was the only thing I'd been aware of since getting back home and turning in my fatigues.

She gave her head a little shake and blinked her eyes up at me like she was struggling to see me. A truck flew past us and blasted the horn, which made her jump and had me scowling after it as it disappeared down the road. "We should probably get moving. Being parked on the side of the highway in the dark isn't much safer than riding down it."

She nodded absently and waited for me to get back on the bike. When she crawled on behind me I expected her to sit stiffly the way she had been for most of the evening. I was a little surprised when she curled into my back and even more surprised when I felt the press of her cheek between my shoulder blades.

It was nice to have a pretty girl that I had a hard-on for wind her way around me and hold on like she would never let me go.

The next exit was about twenty miles up the road and luckily there was a motel that didn't look like it was a frequent sight for crime scenes or used as a meth lab, so I pulled over and stopped. I wasn't sure if there was going to be an awkward talk while we discussed if we were sharing a room or not, honestly I was fine either way. I was used to sleeping in barracks and under the desert sky, so anything that even remotely resembled a bed was fine with me, but I never had the opportunity to ask because she shoved her credit card at me and told me to put her room on it as she hefted her backpack over her shoulders and told me she would be at the diner across the street when I was done.

I couldn't tell if she was really that hungry or if she was cutting me some slack and taking the choice and the conversation out of my hands. I went into the office, pleased that the clerk didn't look like an extra from *The Texas Chainsaw Massacre* and secured us two adjoining rooms. Of course I paid for both. This long-overdue and overly dramatic homecoming was all of my making, so I had no intention of letting her pay for anything along the way. I already owed her more than I could ever repay.

I moved the bike so that it was in front of our rooms, dropped my stuff off inside the room I decided would be mine, and then made my way over to the diner. Dixie was already at a booth, a chocolate milkshake in front of her as she chatted with a waitress who looked tired but was still smiling because it was impossible not to smile at the redhead when she turned that infectious grin and those big doe eyes on you. I slid in across from her and got a raised eyebrow from the waitress. Her keen gaze skimmed over me and she turned to give Dixie a wink that made me frown. I ordered a cheeseburger without looking at the menu and narrowed my eyes at Dixie as she stuck the straw sticking out of the frothy drink into her mouth and sucked.

The way her mouth puckered and her cheeks hollowed out immediately made me think of her sucking on something else like that, which had me shifting uncomfortably on the seat and trying to discreetly adjust my jeans. "Why did she wink at you before she walked away?"

Her tongue darted out to catch a stray dollop of whipped cream that dotted her lip and I had to bite back a groan. "I told her I was waiting on the best-looking guy she was going to have in her section all week. She's working a double because the girl that was supposed to relieve her called in sick and that means she had to leave her kids with their dad who has a live in girlfriend that is barely over eighteen. You walked in and proved me right. She needed something to make her smile."

The waitress walked over and poured me a cup of coffee without asking if that's what I wanted. I wasn't really the smiling type but I did manage a stiff lip twitch for her when she let her gaze roll over me. There was a twinkle in her tired eyes that I knew Dixie was entirely responsible for. She simply had that effect on everyone that crossed her path.

"Did I ever tell you that you remind me of someone I used to know? Someone that also thought it was her job to make everyone she came into contact with smile." I picked up the coffee and gave it a sip. It was surprisingly good.

She stuck a finger in the whipped cream on the top of her drink and stuck it in her mouth. I didn't bother to hide my reaction to her innocent seduction. I could feel the heat in my gaze as I stared at her and I watched as it made her cheeks turn pink.

She was cute but when she blushed she was so fucking adorable that it felt unfair.

"You've never told me much of anything, Church." Her words cut because they were true. She lifted a shoulder and let it fall. "When my dad got hurt he couldn't work anymore and my mom was juggling a lot. She was trying to take care of him and of me and my little sister. She had to find a job but she had been home with us for so long that she wasn't really qualified to do much besides service industry jobs. We had to downsize and move. We had to change schools. Things were really rough at home and everyone was in a pretty bad place. I figured the least I could do was try to be the one that stayed positive about things. I've always believed that you get what you put out there in the world and my family was putting out enough bad vibes that someone had to counteract that before karma kicked all of our asses. Sometimes it's so much easier to focus on what went wrong rather than what went right." She shrugged again. "It must have worked. Dad settled into his new normal and actually ended up being way better at staying home with us than my mom ever was, Mom got promoted at the hotel she was working at from banquet server to a conference planner, so she ended up making more than my dad did when he was working full-time, and a few years later my sister met Wheeler and he managed to curb some of her worst spoiled-brat tendencies. Having a positive attitude and an optimistic outlook on life didn't cost me anything, and it was what my family needed from me. I guess I never stopped being everyone's cheerleader." Her chocolate gaze narrowed fractionally. "Who do I remind you of?"

I considered her thoughtfully for a minute as her attention was stolen by the arrival of our food. She looked like a cheerleader. She looked like the kind of person that would never let you believe that you would fail. Everything about her inspired the belief that things would indeed work out the way they were supposed to. Just like the woman that had stepped up to take care of me, Jules, and my brother after we were forced to say good-bye to my mom. Caroline was never my stepmother. She was my second mother and her bright, positive personality was very similar to Dixie's, which was crazy considering she had also been handed some really shitty circumstances she had to work her way through while maintaining that smile.

I smothered my burger in ketchup and smashed the top bun back down with my palm. Dixie did the same with hers and made a sound that I knew she would make if I ever got inside of her as she took her first bite. It made the fit of my jeans even more uncomfortable than it already was after watching her with that milkshake.

"My dad remarried when I was a teenager. The woman he married was a lot like you. She saw the best in everyone and in every situation. She was quick to smile and quick to forgive." She was also the reason I knew that having something good and pure in my life wasn't in the cards for me.

I leaned back in the vinyl seat knowing I'd opened the door to a line of questioning I couldn't avoid forever. Talking about Caroline meant talking about my mom and how things had ended so tragically with both of them.

She arched her eyebrows a little bit and went back to her melting drink. "Who exactly are we going to see besides the woman that fell and hurt herself? You said you swore on your mother and now we have your second mother, so I assume we'll be crossing paths with at least some of your parents at some point in the next week." Anyone else might be a little intimidated by that but Dixie was likeable and she liked everyone, so I knew she would fit right in with the remaining members of my family. "What are they like?"

It was an easy question but one that I tended to dance my way around when it was asked. Typically, strangers asked it because they were wondering how I came by my unusual coloring and they wanted me to lay out my family tree and walk them through my genetic makeup. I knew Dixie could care less what color skin and eyes the people who had made me had, and since I knew that I had no problem trying to help her climb my complicated family tree.

"My mom was a beauty queen. A pretty blonde with blue eyes that wanted to be the next Miss America. She got knocked up with me her freshman year in college and was effectively disowned by her parents." The corners of my lips turned down, and I couldn't stop the flare of outrage I always felt on my mother's behalf that my grandparents were so close-minded and cold. "She never told me if the reason they were so pissed was because she pretty much tanked her education and her pageant future by getting pregnant, or because she got knocked up by a guy who was biracial. It was like she was doubly defying their antiquated and racist views. He was African American but he also had a solid chunk of Middle Eastern in him, too. He played soccer at the same school but didn't stick around long when Mom told him she was keeping me." I'd never met the guy, but she often told me I looked a lot like him. "Things were pretty rough for her when I was young."

Dixie sucked in an audible breath and I could see how deeply my words were affecting her. She was hurting for me and I hadn't even gotten to the parts that actually wounded and left scars yet. My frown dug deeper into my face and my hands curled tightly around the mug in front of me. "My grandparents never bothered to contact either of us. Not once. Not even when she died when I was thirteen."

I knew it was a bomb to drop and that I should have given her that information more tactfully but the words rushed out. I'd held them inside, never sharing them with anyone, so they took their chance to escape and fell heavily between us.

"Oh, Church." She sounded like she wanted to cry for me.

I lifted a hand to hold off the rest of her sympathy. "When I was five my mom met a guy named Julian Churchill. He's now the sheriff in Lowry, but back then he was a patrol cop and he pulled her over for speeding. He told her he would let her go if she agreed to a date." It was totally unethical and completely illegal, but luckily my mom liked the look of Jules, remembered him from high school, and agreed to go. It was a story they always told with smiles and shared laughs. It made me want to grin but I knew how it all ended and that in turn made me want to break something. I also never talked about the fact that initially I hated Jules. I hated that I had to share my mom with him. Hated that he showed up and took care of her when that was my job. I also resented the fact she picked another man with dark skin to fall in love with. I wanted her life, and mine by association, to be easier and without judgment and speculation and to my immature and untried mind it seemed like she was going out of her way to keep it hard by falling in love with someone who didn't look a whole lot like either one of us. I was too little to understand why all of that thinking was wrong and that who my mother loved was completely out of my control but there were a lot of years where

I was nothing short of terrible to Jules. As an adult I would like to take those actions and a lot of those words I hurled at him back.

"Jules is a good guy. He took me as part of the package without blinking an eye. They got married a year later and he asked if it was cool if he could adopt me before the ink was dry on their marriage license." I remember trying not to cry when he asked me if it was all right. My mom was good. My mom and Jules together was better. No one other than my mom had ever wanted me, in fact I spent most of my childhood feeling distinctly unwanted, but there was Jules, big, badass Jules, telling me he was choosing me to be his son despite the attitude and anger I so carelessly tossed his way. It would go down forever as one of the most significant moments of my life. "They had a perfect marriage and I thought we were a perfect family but Mom wanted more kids and struggled to get pregnant for a long time. Jules just wanted to make her happy, so he consoled her through several miscarriages and a round of failed in vitro treatments. Right about when she resigned herself to the fact that it wasn't meant to be, she got pregnant. She called it a miracle." Really it was a curse.

I rubbed a hand over my face at the memories of how happy she was, how excited she was for the little blessing to join our family. "She spent most of the pregnancy on bed rest but it was touch and go the entire time." I remembered being scared because she seemed so weak, but the truth was I hadn't been scared enough.

Dixie's eyes were twice their normal size and she had a shaking hand covering her mouth. She could see where my story was going and even though I wanted it to have a different kind of ending, it didn't.

"She went into labor early. It was obvious something was wrong as soon as it started. There was way too much blood and even though she didn't want me to worry I could see how much pain she was in. I called an ambulance and Jules met us at the hospital but it was too late." So much blood. I remembered the way it covered everything. I remembered the way I could literally see the light blink out of my mom's eyes as she told me she loved me. She told me to be a good boy for Jules and to help him take care of my little brother. She would be so disappointed to know I hadn't done either of those things. "The placenta detached and she bled out. They barely managed to save my little brother's life. He was in the NICU for almost two months and when he got out Jules found himself stuck as a single dad with two kids that he never necessarily wanted and definitely wasn't prepared for."

Dixie gasped and didn't bother to wipe away the single tear that escaped her eye. She looked as injured as I felt on the inside. Even after all these years the memories sliced to the bone and left jagged tears across my soul. "You have a little brother?" Her voice was rough and I could tell she was holding even more emotion back since we were in public.

I nodded jerkily and rubbed my face again. "Dalen. He's in high school, plays football, gets good grades, and Jules couldn't be prouder of him if he tried." The kid had worshipped every move I made when I was around when we were younger but I hadn't heard from him in over two years. I couldn't say I blamed him.

"You haven't seen him since he was five?" The way she asked it made me feel about as low as I could, but I deserved it. I had a little brother that was well on his way to becoming a man and I hadn't been around for any of it.

"I haven't seen either of them since they dropped me off at Camp Shelby for basic training." And that was something I would have to live with for the rest of my life. I was waiting for the questions about why I left and why I stayed gone but they never came. That was Dixie, always giving the benefit of the doubt.

She pushed her half-eaten burger away and folded her hands on the top of the table in front of her. "So your dad and your brother are there, but who is the other woman you mentioned? Caroline?"

I grunted and felt memories and pain slide icily down my spine. Talking about my mom was hard, talking about Caroline was harder because I was older and totally knew the way I acted while she was still alive wasn't okay. I missed my mom but cherished every minute I'd had with her. I missed Caroline as well but all I could think about when it came to her was regret. "Caroline was one of Dalen's NICU nurses. She took care of him while he was in the hospital. She watched out for him while Jules and I buried my mom."

I heard her gasp but I couldn't look up at her.

"Jules spent a lot of time with Caroline while Dalen was getting healthy enough to come home. Like I said, neither one of us really knew what to do with a newborn, and Caroline stepped in to teach us the basics." I kept my gaze on my plate. "It took a year or so. Dalen had just started to walk when Jules realized that he was feeling more than gratitude towards her. He asked her out on a date and I think she'd been in love with him from the first minute she saw him hold that baby, so of course she said yes. They got married a couple of years later when Dalen was a toddler. She was a good woman and she loved us hard. She was sick when she was younger, so she couldn't have kids of her own, but she always said it didn't matter because she had us. She was a good mom to Dalen, and I loved her because she never tried to replace my mom while she loved me. I was super lucky to have been raised by two special women." I loved her but by the time I realized it, it was too late. I spent more time resenting her and keeping her at an arm's length because I was scared to care about someone so deeply after losing my mom. I'd also been bitter that Jules had moved on even though he had every right to find happiness. It felt like betrayal until Caroline left me no choice but to love her. Again there were too many wasted minutes and moments I wanted back.

Dixie's tiny hand covered mine where they were clutched together on the tabletop, my knuckles white as I squeezed them together. "You don't have to tell me the rest if you don't want to, Church." She wanted a happy ending and I couldn't be the guy to give that to her because I'd never experienced one myself.

"I had just turned sixteen when she was diagnosed with breast cancer. It was the second time I saw Jules cry. She'd been in remission for years and years but as soon as she became a part of my family, as soon as I let myself love her she got sick again." I bit out a tortured laugh and threw my head back so I was looking at the ceiling. "She fought. She fought harder than I've ever seen anyone fight for anything, and I've seen war up close and personal. She didn't want to leave us, but it was no use. I watched her lose her hair when she started chemo. I watched her get skinnier and skinner as she tried to keep taking care of us and the house. She was determined to make it to my high school graduation. She wanted to see me in my cap and gown."

Dixie's hand tightened over mine and I wasn't sure if she was trying to comfort me or herself.

"Did she make it?" Her voice was so quiet I could barely hear her.

I shook my head and cleared my throat as emotion threatened to choke me. She hadn't made it because when good came into my life it left before I could fully appreciate it.

"No, she didn't. Neither did I. I enlisted and was at boot camp the day after we put her in the ground. I didn't stick around for graduation." I didn't stick around for Jules or Dalen either because they still had a shot at something good and I didn't want to be around to taint it.

She let go of my hands and leaned back in the booth. Eyes wide and her chest rising and falling in shallow breaths. "Wow. Is that all?" She sounded bewildered and a little baffled, not that I could blame her. It was a lot and none of it was particularly pleasant.

"Not quite. There's Elma Mae." If there was one thing in the world that actually made me smile it was Elma Mae. I couldn't stop my lips from twitching when I thought of the feisty older woman who had lived across the street from me for as long as I could remember.

"She lived down the street from me and Mom when I was growing up and when my grandparents didn't want anything to do with us she made sure to fill in for them. She took care of me after school when Mom worked. She helped Mom and Jules out with whatever they needed and she was there when Dalen was a newborn and Jules was in way over his head. She always had homemade cookies and cold sweet tea ready and waiting. She is the epitome of what a proper southern lady should be and she taught me more about family and forgiveness than anything or anyone else has."

Her head cocked to the side and she considered me thoughtfully. "Why couldn't you tell them the truth, Church? Why couldn't you just say you weren't ready to come home yet? Surely they would understand." It was a reasonable question but my reasons for not doing exactly that were anything but.

"I never told them when I was promoted into Spec Ops. I always let them think that I was still in infantry or that I was doing guard duty. When I went in I was an MP for the first few years, so I let everyone back home keep right on thinking that I was still doing nothing more than watching the gates at the base and regulating unruly soldiers. I didn't want them to worry. Everyone had suffered enough loss and I didn't want anyone to lose any sleep wondering where I was and what I was doing. So no one back home knows how desperately I really needed the downtime. They have no clue that I came back a different man than they remember." I carried a lot of heavy shit around inside of me and there was no way the people that loved me were going to miss the way I was weighed down. I blinked at Dixie realizing in the twenty minutes or so we had been talking that I had given her more, shared more with her than I had with anyone since I left home. Not even Rome knew the reason I kept communication to a minimum back home was for them and not for me.

She made a face at me. "You should be honest with them. They'll understand."

They would, but the way I left, the way I shut myself off from them and the grieving and healing we should be doing together, that was going to be harder for them to forgive and understand. "Are you ready to go? I want to get on the road pretty early in the morning and I know you aren't exactly the type that likes to rise and shine." There was also only so much of my heart and soul that I was willing to show her at one time. Turned out I had a lot to say when I was talking to someone that looked at me the way she did.

I hated feeling this exposed and raw. I knew the sun could burn when you let it shine on your unprotected skin for too long. That's what it felt like after giving Dixie so much and having her still look at me like I was something special.

She nodded and made like she was going to reach for her wallet but I waved her off and tossed a couple of bills on the table, sure to leave a tip that would make the waitress having to stay late sting a little less. I slid out of the booth but almost fell back into it when Dixie suddenly launched herself at me.

I wasn't used to being hugged. It wasn't something that happened when you kept everyone at an arm's length and made sure that a scowl was your default expression. Her arms circled my waist and her cheek rested right over my heart as she squeezed me tight. I curled an arm around her shoulders and let the fingers of my free hand twist and twine in the endless curls that cascaded down her back. They felt like silk as they wrapped around my knuckles and tickled my palm.

"What's this for?" I wasn't surprised that she was a hugger but I was surprised that she was hugging me for no apparent reason. That wasn't the type of relationship we had, at least it hadn't been before she gave me that kiss that I could still taste and feel.

"It's for the little boy that lost both his moms and for the man that hasn't seen his family in a decade. No one should go through the things you've been through without a hug, Church. Everyone needs one every now and then, even big, badass former soldiers."

I couldn't remember the last time someone had hugged me. It might have been Jules and Elma Mae when they dropped me off for basic, because I sure as hell wasn't into hugging the women I took to bed or the men I'd been deep in the trenches with.

I hugged her back but it was awkward and stiff. I wanted my arms around her for something other than comfort.

We broke apart and headed for the doorway. The waitress gave a wave from where she was standing behind the counter.

"You were right, darlin', he is pretty but he does need to smile more. You two have a good night."

Dixie laughed and pushed the door open and since her back was to me she didn't see it but I almost very nearly did smile. It was impossible not to around her.

Chapter 7

Dixie

The knock on my door came way too early the next morning. I tried to go to bed almost immediately after getting into the room and taking my long-awaited shower, but my body was far too used to being awake late into the night and sleeping when the sun was in the sky. Not to mention I couldn't stop my mind from spinning pretty fairy tales around that taste of Church I had snuck on the side of the road. I was stupid to think a single kiss was enough to satisfy the way I had been craving him since the beginning. I wanted more. I wanted it all and the way his big body tightened and shivered against mine was a pretty big indication that he was willing to give me what I desired, but the look in his eyes warned that it was only physical on his end. He would give me every single thing I asked for except for a way into that heart he guarded with iron bars and bulletproof armor.

I also couldn't stop thinking about what was waiting for us when we got to Mississippi. His story hurt to hear. I hated the idea of him feeling unwanted and I couldn't believe anyone could ever look into those beautiful eyes and consider his mother's choice to keep him and raise him a mistake. I knew there was more to why he hadn't been home in so long than him needing a break once he got out of the service.

I watched Church with Rome and Asa. I watched him with the other guys that filtered in and out of the bar that made up the tightly knit family that had surrounded and supported Rome when he was going through his own adjustment period after coming home from the desert. Church might think he was a lone wolf but it was obvious to me that what he actually was, was an alpha in search of his own pack to lead. He missed the camaraderie of having a band of brothers, he missed being a part of a group of like-minded individuals that would watch out for each other come hell or high water. He still had that bond with Rome, but for reasons that I didn't understand and was more determined than ever to figure out, he held himself aloof and apart from anyone else willing to welcome him into their fold, his family included.

I tossed the covers off the bed and made my way to the door blurry eyed and rumpled. When I pulled it open Church was on the other side looking like he had been awake for hours. He even had a white to-go cup of coffee in his hand and something in a paper bag that smelled heavenly.

"I sent you a text when I got up but obviously you didn't get it." He sounded amused and I realized his gaze wasn't on my sleep-tangled hair or my practically naked lower half. No. He was focused on the words "Tequila Made Me Do It" where they stretched across my chest on the long tank top I'd worn to bed the night before.

I shoved my hands through my hair, not thinking that the

motion would pull the hem of my shirt up well past my waist, giving Church an unobstructed view of my underwear. I blushed, but took solace in the fact that this time they were at least cute and lacy. I tugged the end of the shirt back down so that I was barely covered and took a step back into the room. "I need to get dressed and do something with my hair. Give me half an hour and I'll be ready to go. My sister called me no less than twenty times last night, so I had to turn my phone to silent. That's why I didn't get your text."

I fisted my hair in a hand and lifted the snarled mess up off my neck. I shouldn't have gone to bed with it wet. There was little to no chance that I was going to be able to wrangle the curls into any kind of order. I thought he would take the hint and head back to his own room, instead he walked farther into mine and placed the coffee and paper bag on the dresser where the TV sat. He made himself comfortable on the edge of my unmade bed and crossed his long legs at the ankle while he watched me with amused eyes.

"Everything okay back home?" The genuine concern in his honeyed voice had more heat working its way through my body. I spun on my heel, snatched up my jeans from the day before, grabbed my bra from where it was dangling on the bathroom door handle, and slid inside the little room so I could put some layers on between me and the walking, talking seduction that was Dash Churchill.

"Wheeler told her the wedding is off. He also told her she has until I get back home to find somewhere else to live. Kallie hasn't ever kept a full-time job and has never had to support herself, so she's freaking out. Also my parents invested a lot of time and money into their wedding, and she's panicking that Wheeler is going to tell them the reason he's walking away is because she cheated on him. She's always been the baby, the one they coddled, but they love Wheeler like a son, so it's going to be bad." I wiggled into the rest of my clothes and finger combed my hair. It was useless. The curls had taken over my head and they wouldn't be stopped.

I stuck my toothbrush in my mouth and looked at him in the mirror. He was watching me with hooded eyes and there was tension in his shoulders and arms that wasn't there when he walked in. He looked like he had been cast in bronze by a great artist that wanted to capture what true masculine beauty was all about. He was so strong and hard, but there was no denying that he was also all kinds of gorgeous and flat-out dazzling.

"Why do you think your sister stepped out on him?" I ran my tongue over my now clean teeth and wasn't surprised one bit that instead of minty freshness I still tasted him. I was certain I was going to taste him forever and that it was going to slowly drive me insane.

I trapped my hair in pigtails on either side of my head, which made me look like I was twelve years old. Well, a twelve-year-old with some serious cleavage. I made a face in the mirror as I slathered on some tinted moisturizer and some ChapStick. I figured it would be wind in my face and more truck stops today, so there was no need for me to doll myself up. Besides, today was the second morning in a row Church had seen me the way I was when I woke up, so there was no putting lipstick on a pig after that. I figured he couldn't be too repulsed by my au naturel state if he hadn't run out the door yet and I tingled when I remembered that he'd told me he thought I was cute when I was all grumbly and growly in the morning.

"Who cares why she did it? Wheeler is a good guy and this is the second time she's had no regard for how her actions will hurt him. There is no excuse that can justify what she's done." And I'd told her the same thing in no uncertain terms last night. I was pissed at her, and her tears and woe-is-me attitude over a situation of her own making only served to make me angrier as I talked to her. Eventually I'd had to hang up on her, which hadn't stopped her from calling or texting me well into the wee hours of the morning.

Church lifted an eyebrow at me as I made my way to where he had stashed the breakfast goodies. I wasn't fully awake yet but my stomach sure was. I didn't hold back a delighted squeal when I found frosted doughnuts in the paper bag. I was going to need to figure out a way to fit a treadmill in my apartment after all of this road trip food but I wanted to eat now and worry about my ass later.

"Seems to me if she isn't typically a bad person then there is more to why she did what she did than her getting tired of the same cock. There's usually a reason why good folks do bad things." He was watching me carefully and I felt like his somber words were some kind of warning I was supposed to heed.

I popped a sugary sweet bite of dough into my mouth and chewed while we stared at each other. It tasted like heaven and the jolt of sugar was enough to kick my sluggish system awake.

"I don't care what her reason is. I care that she hurt someone I care about and I'm pissed that she was only thinking of herself, not how her actions could affect the rest of the people in her life that love both her and Wheeler." I sounded sharp and slightly petulant but I didn't care. I couldn't imagine Kallie saying anything to me that would make the circumstances she had set in motion okay. I didn't care where her head was at while she was carrying on behind Wheeler's back, all I cared about was that her thoughts hadn't been on the man that had given her everything or the family that had claimed him as one of their own.

Church lumbered to his feet and ran a hand over his closely cropped hair. His eyes were serious and intent as he told me, "Her reasons might not matter to you, but they could be everything to her. Sometimes people make choices that hurt other people because they feel like it would hurt the people they care about even more if they didn't make that choice."

I cocked my head to the side as the chocolate frosting from my doughnut started to melt all over my fingers. "Are we still talking about my sister, Church?" I wondered if he was trying to explain why he had felt compelled to stay away from home for so long in a roundabout way.

"We're just talking, Dixie. That's what friends do." He looked at me, intensity and things I couldn't decipher burning bright in his brilliant eyes as he made his way to the door. "Finish your breakfast. I want to see if we can get to at least the Arkansas border today."

I licked along the side of my thumb and heard him suck in a sharp breath. I grinned at him and nodded. "Thanks for breakfast. Chocolate is my favorite."

He gave me another look, this one followed by a smirk, and then disappeared out the door with a snort. He didn't smile but there was definitely a lip twitch involved. I would take what I could get and consider the almost grin a win for the morning.

He was already on the bike with the motor running when I made my way to the parking lot. I had the leathers on so I wouldn't have to take any unnecessary trips to scary bathrooms and he tilted his chin in approval. He had on mirrored sunglasses, so I couldn't see his eyes anymore, but something instinctive told me that he more than liked the way the leather covered my legs and framed the part of me that fluttered and went damp as soon as I put a hand on his rock-hard shoulder so I could get the leverage I needed to climb on behind him. By the end of this trip I was going to be nothing more than one giant orgasm waiting to happen. He was going to accidentally brush up against me and I was going to make a fool of myself as all that desire finally burst out unable to be contained. I was bound to look like Meg Ryan in *When Harry Met Sally*, only my public climax was going to be very real because there was no faking that he turned me on and inside out.

I chuckled at the image, which had Church whipping his head around to look at me questioningly. I shook my head and smiled at him. There was no way I was going to pass along the information that all it would take for him to turn me into a sexual time bomb was the touch of his hands. Something told me he would use that intel to his advantage. His eyebrows winged up so that I could see them over the rims of his sunglasses but he turned back around and guided us back onto the highway. We had a long way to go, both in miles and in what it was going to take for Church to actually find his way back home, and there wasn't any time to waste.

Kansas was a straight shot, and I made it almost all the way through the entire state before we had to stop. This time Church wouldn't let me out of his sight, so I had to go to the bathroom while he waited outside the door. I wanted to tell him it was overboard, but honestly I felt better knowing I could do my thing without worrying about what was happening beyond the closed door. The truck stop had a diner attached to it, so we stopped for lunch and he ordered a steak that was the size of my head. When I questioned him he said he was used to a high protein diet and that typically he worked out enough that he needed the fuel. I was already burned-out on all the greasy food we'd been eating, so I tried to order a salad. Unfortunately, the only salad they offered was driven towards trucker taste, so it came in a fried tortilla bowl with taco meat, cheese, and sour cream on it. It was really good but I could feel the waistband of my jeans getting tighter with each bite.

I was rumbling about calories and the lack of healthy options on the menu when Church cut me off with a raised hand and a furious scowl. "Do you like the way you look?"

His sharply spoken question surprised me into silence. I nodded slowly and mumbled, "I do. I mean my hair can be a pain in the ass and when I was younger I hated having freckles everywhere but for the most part I know I'm pretty cute."

He nodded at me and his scowl turned into a leer. "You are very fucking cute. There is something to love about all women, no matter what form they take, so eat your salad and enjoy your chocolate doughnuts. If a man can't appreciate what's right in front of him then he isn't a man that was raised right and he doesn't deserve a taste of that sweet skin, no matter how much or how little of it there may be."

I was so stunned by his words that I let my fork fall back into my very unhealthy salad with a click. "Wow. I don't think you've ever said so many words in a row before." Minus last night when he was filling me in on his tragic family dynamics. "Leave it up to you to pick some of the best words I've ever heard to be the ones you go with when you decide to finally venture into small talk."

He made a noise that might have been a laugh low in his throat. "I grew up not being white enough for the white kids and not black enough for the black kids. I had grandparents that wouldn't acknowledge me and a mother that looked like a supermodel but dressed and lived like she was an orphan, because she pretty much was after she had me. She had a baby with one guy of color and then married another one even after she knew firsthand how difficult interracial relationships could be in the south. As far as we've progressed as a nation when it comes to acceptance there is still a long, long way to go. You gotta like the way you look because how you look tells your story and fuck anyone that doesn't want to appreciate that."

I was stunned into silence, so all I could do was gape at him with my mouth hanging open. I looked ridiculous, but I couldn't get my head around someone as gorgeous and as perfectly built as he was ever being anything other than admired and sought after. Even now in this nowhere truck stop, every pair of female eyes was on him . . . and some of the men couldn't look away either. Not all of the male attention was admiring. Truck stops in the middle of nowhere the farther south we went meant more and more narrow-eyed looks and tight-lipped scowls were sent his way. They seemed even worse when we walked side by side and when he put his hand on my lower back to usher me into the booth across from him.

"I . . . well, I can't believe anyone could ever look at you and not want the story behind those eyes. You're beautiful." He was, but it was the hardness in his face and the scars that dotted his arms and that peeked out of the collar of his shirt that begged to tell their tale.

"Sometimes all people can see is what's different, but those differences are what make us who we are. For instance you might fight with your hair but I've never met anyone else whose hair I want my hands in all the time. It's soft and I like the way it feels when your curls don't want to let me go. I like that you look a little bit like a lion when you get up in the morning even though I know you're a pussycat. And don't even get me started on the freckles." He gave me a look that clearly indicated he would like to find out exactly how many I had and where they stopped. The answer was a lot and they didn't. I had them all over, so if he wanted to find them all he was going to be a very, very busy man.

"Can you just keep talking? I've always liked your voice but it's even better when you're saying such amazing things." It really was. I fell for him in an instant when he went out of his way to make sure I was okay. I knew then that he was it for me, but now that he was letting me actually *know* him it stung even more to realize that my heart had chosen wisely even though his still couldn't see what was standing right in front of him. He was a good guy, smart and resilient. I didn't want anyone to ever look past how amazing and important he was again.

We finished lunch in relative silence after and I wasn't surprised when he appeared to be done talking for the day. He had used up his daily allotment of words to make sure I knew that he liked the way I looked and that I should like the way I looked just as much. In his own subtle way he also addressed the fact that he wasn't oblivious to the stares and side-eyed looks coming from the people in the truck stop that weren't interested in his story. He knew they were there, he just didn't care.

I wanted to kiss him again, instead I climbed back on the bike behind him and settled in as we pushed our way through Kansas City and all the way through Missouri until we both agreed it was time to stop right before we hit the Arkansas border. We would roll into Lowry late tomorrow afternoon at the pace we were going, which worked well since Elma Mae was due to go home from the hospital the following afternoon.

The ride today had gone much smoother than the hours spent on the asphalt last night. There weren't any almost accidents, and we were lucky that the weather had stayed temperate and dry. I needed to stretch my legs and work out some of the numbness in my backside when we stopped. Church found a tiny little place that looked like it was a bunch of individual cabins for us to spend the night. Unfortunately, there was a celebration happening in town called the Ozark Festival, so there was only a single room available for the night. The entire town was packed with tourists in for the event and it was one of the only vacancies. The festival brought in people from all over the Ozarks and was a pretty big deal. The guy that handed us the room key mentioned we should plan on waiting if we headed out for dinner anywhere. I did a quick search on my phone to see if there were any other options and came up with nothing unless we wanted to ride another fifty miles down the highway.

I wasn't sure how I was going to manage sharing a bed with him and keeping my hands to myself, but I was a grown-up and told myself I could make it through one night unscathed . . . maybe.

"I need a beer, and maybe a shot . . . or three." Definitely more than one if I was going to lie next to that big, hard body all night and not touch. I could drink until I blacked out ensuring I would keep my hands to myself and not whisper into the dark all the ways my heart longed for him. "We drove past a couple bars when we pulled into town that are within walking distance. Wanna grab a drink?"

"I'm not sure that's the best idea." He sounded gruff and leery of my plan.

"Come on. It'll be fun. I promise your virtue, and the rest of you, is safe with me." I smiled at him and reached out so I could grab his hand. I started walking towards the road, thinking he would oblige me, but was pulled up short when his massive frame didn't budge an inch.

"It's not my virtue I'm worried about. It's all those Confederate flags hanging out of the back of the pickup trucks parked out front." I paused and frowned at him over my shoulder. "I'm used to not being safe, it's you I would worry about."

That wasn't something I even noticed, but I wasn't surprised he had and his words had my tummy twisting into knots. Every single time he mentioned keeping me safe or taking care of me it made that thing I *knew*, that knowledge I had that he was it for me, settle deeper into my bones. It made me want to kick myself for wasting a second on those stupid dating apps. I couldn't trick my stubborn heart into thinking there was a substitute for the man that didn't want it. When the heart *knew*, it just *knew*. "Okay. Well, I guess we can find a liquor store and have happy hour in our room." I didn't want to put him in a situation where he was uncomfortable or unappreciated. He was a lot bigger than me but I really wanted to shield him and protect him from some of that ugliness that he'd experienced throughout his life.

He grunted and gave his head a shake. "No, let's just go to the bar. I'll be fine and I'll make sure you're fine." Something in his tone told me that it probably wouldn't be fine and he was lying through his teeth.

"Really, I just want a drink. I don't care where it comes from." I yelped as his fingers curled around mine where I was holding him and he started to march up the side of the road practically hauling me along behind him. There was no way I could keep up with his long-legged gait, so I ended up almost having to jog to keep pace with him.

"I haven't been around the good ole boys in a long time. It's probably good to have a refresher course before we hit Lowry and it can't hurt anything for you to see what you very well might be up against when we cross into the city limits. Jules used to have to come and get me from school for fighting all the time. Now he'd have to come get me out of jail if someone rubbed me the wrong way."

I tried to pull him to a stop so I could urge him to go back to the cute little cabin with me but now he was a man on a mission. I wasn't sure if he was trying to teach me a lesson or prove something to himself, but either way it wasn't exactly a pleasant experience. All I wanted was a drink, not to be caught in the middle of one of his memories or a bad memory in the making.

I felt him stiffen the minute we pushed through the doors. I saw his back go board straight and the way his shoulders braced like the ceiling was going to fall down around us. I couldn't see his face, but I knew that if I could the expression on it would be fierce enough to keep anyone from venturing too close to us. However, as we walked farther inside the honky-tonk it was clear the loud country music wasn't going to stop playing. None of the patrons stopped the conversations they were having, and the bouncer sitting at the door much like Church did at my bar didn't flick an eyelash or even shift his weight. The only person that seemed to care about us at all was the blonde cocktail server in shorts that were way too short who swung by and told us there was a table in the back if we wanted to sit down. She apologized for the crowd, mentioned the festival, and told me she liked my tank top after mentioning they had a two-for-one special on Patrón.

I ordered a round before we sat down and gave Church a look from under my eyebrows as he sat sulkily and silently across from me, eyes darting around the room like he was waiting for a confrontation that didn't seem like it was in any hurry to find him. The waitress smiled at him exactly the same way I would if I was the one dropping off his bourbon, lots of teeth, lots of eye contact, and enough of an invitation that I was now also scowling. She hurried about to take care of the rest of her tables as Church's gaze found its way back to mine.

I let the silence drag on through the first two shots but by the time the blonde brought the third I had settled enough that I was brave enough to ask. "So I take it this isn't your usual experience in a place like this?"

I tossed the third shot back and chased it with a swig of beer. My head was starting to get a little fuzzy and my limbs a little loose.

He picked up his glass and gave the amber liquid a little taste, his multicolored eyes seeming to swirl together like an abstract painting. "Been in a lot of places around the world. I learned you never know what to expect when you walk into any place not looking much like the locals."

I frowned a little bit and licked at the salt I had poured on the back of my hand I'd used to chase my tequila shot with. I made a face as I sucked on a slice of lime. "That sounds exhausting. Being on alert all the time, always waiting for the other shoe to drop. That doesn't sound like much fun."

He grunted at me. "Fun doesn't have anything to do with it." He didn't sound bitter about the fact, just matter-of-fact and resigned. It was the way it had always been for him and he didn't expect it to be any different no matter where he was. "If you don't plan for the worst and you're caught with your ass hanging out in a bad situation there is no one to blame but yourself. Especially if you know firsthand how bad it can get."

I lifted an eyebrow at him and licked my lips. "What about plan for the worst but expect the best? Why can't you have a plan for if it goes bad but go into a situation ready to experience all the good things it may have to offer?"

He made a noise low in his throat and picked up his drink so that it covered his lickable lips. "I know my way around bad like the back of my hand, good not so much."

I ordered another round of shots and glared at him as he lifted his eyebrows questioningly at me. "Are you having a liquid dinner tonight?"

He smoothly changed the subject and I noticed that his attention was now squarely on me and not on searching out hidden danger. I pointed a finger at him and realized it was less than steady. "We're sharing a bed and that means I'm drinking enough that I'll be too hammered to do anything inappropriate in my sleep and if I do get clingy I'll be too drunk to remember it in the morning."

There it went again, that little lip twitch that was trying so hard to be a smile. "You don't have to share the bed if you don't want to. I can sleep on the floor. Believe me, I've laid my head down in worse places."

I groaned and put my face in my hands. "I do want . . . that's the problem."

He chuckled at me and pulled the shot I still hadn't taken out of my hand. "How about we play a game and if you win then I'll give you back your shot."

I pouted at him and crossed my arms over my chest. "What kind of game?" I worked in a bar and had for a long time. If he thought he could beat me at pool, darts, quarters, or any of the other common barfly games I was constantly surrounded by he had another thing coming, even if I was well on my way to a pleasant buzz.

"Let's play two truths and a lie. You tell me three things, two that are true and one that's a lie and I have to pick the lie out. If you win you get your drink and if I pick the lie, then we get to go." He sure did seem like he was in a big hurry to get back to the room we had to share but my brain was a little bit too fuzzy to pick up on the heat in his eyes and the sexy twist of his lips.

"Fine, I'll play." I was a terrible liar, so there wasn't a chance in hell he wasn't going to win. I tapped my fingers on the table in front of me and narrowed my eyes on his in concentration. Two truths were easy, it was the lie I was struggling with. I held up a finger and smirked at him. "Number one, is the first boy that I ever kissed ended up being gay. He was beautiful and it broke my heart when I found out. Number two, I am not a real redhead, all of this—" I picked up one of my poofy pigtails and let it fall "—is fake." His eyebrows danced up and I saw his gaze sharpen on me in the dim light offered up by the neon glow surrounding us. I could tell he was trying to see if I had roots showing or not but I just smiled at him and held up a third finger. "Third, I've been calling my vibrator Church for the last six months. It never had a name before but since I've practically burned the thing out since you came to town it only seemed fitting I named it after you."

He almost dropped his glass.

His eyes flared to life in a way I had never seen before and those lips that were made to kiss and to whisper dirty, sexy things in the dark parted as a breath wheezed out of him.

"Jesus, Dixie." My name sounded like the direst word he could think of and at the same time like something decadent and sweet he wanted to indulge in.

It was my turn to lift eyebrows and smirk. I pointed at the shot he was still holding captive. "You were the one that wanted to play."

His eyes burned with colors that there weren't words to describe. "I don't want to play anymore." His words were nothing more than a guttural growl. "Are you ready to go?"

Was I? A day ago I would never have considered bed-breaking sex with him because I knew it would lead to nothing but heartache considering I was way more into him than he was into me. I wanted the whole fantasy, the entirety of my own version of perfect, but after a few drinks and long minutes lost in that multicolored gaze, having something instead of nothing didn't seem quite so bad. Maybe I wasn't the girl meant for happy-ever-after. Maybe I was the girl that was going to have to take happy for now because that's what was on the table. It wasn't what my parents had, it wasn't what Kallie had thrown away with Wheeler, but I wasn't them and Church didn't know what I knew.

This wasn't the dream. This was reality.

I leaned across the table so I could get my fingers around the glass. I pulled it back to me and let the tequila burn its way down my throat.

Liquid courage.

Tequila really did make me do it, but it wasn't like I'd stood a chance against him and the way I wanted him from the start. My body was all for making decisions my heart was going to pay for later on down the road. I wondered if he realized the danger sitting right across from him. I had a feeling that if he knew how into him I really was, beyond the physical, beyond the fact that I knew he would rock my world, that he would back off because he was compelled to protect me and he had the power to hurt me. I knew without a doubt hurting me would hurt him far worse than facing the silent judgment of strangers did. Even with that I still whispered, "Let's go." Because I always expected the best and refused to think about the worst.

Chapter 8

Church

She was a little bit drunk and a whole lot turned on, which in turn had me battling my desire to take care of her and the burning need to fuck her. I wasn't sure yet which instinct was going to win out.

I could feel it in the way she stumbled and used it as an excuse to hold on to me as I hauled her sweet ass out of the rollicking honky-tonk. Her hands held me a little tighter than they needed to and her lips landed right below my jaw on the side of my neck. Instead of one of her bubbly little laughs brushing across my overheated skin I felt the wet flick of her tongue as it lashed its way up along the throbbing vein that lived there. I couldn't hold back the groan when her teeth nipped into the lobe of my ear. I slid a hand around the curve of her waist and walked her backwards until her back hit the bricks that lined the outside of the bar. Her pale skin was bathed in the blue and red lights from the sign advertising PBR tall boys and her eyes were at half-mast and darker than they had ever been with warm desire. I wanted her so bad it made my balls hurt and my insides feel like fire.

"Told you I didn't want to play, Dixie." Her hands were crawling across my abs and up the wall of my chest under the fabric of my shirt. She touched me like she was making it a point to leave her fingerprints on every inch of my skin. I wanted to take what she was offering, it's what I'd wanted from the start, but I knew if I took it without giving anything back it would be one more sin that I had to atone for and frankly I had enough to repent for without adding this sweet, considerate, and effortlessly tempting girl to the list. Everything inside of me demanded that I take her back to the room, spread her across the bed we were going to share, and get inside of her as fast and as deeply as I could but there was that lingering wistfulness shadowing the heat in her gaze as she continued to stroke me and kiss along my jaw.

I put my hands on either side of her face and bent down so I could press my lips to hers. It was the same kind of soft kiss she had given me. The kind of kiss you gave to someone that mattered. The kind of kiss you shared with someone you didn't want to hurt. She tasted like the promise of dirty, hot sex and smoky tequila. She tasted like all the best things men stuck at war dreamed about and told themselves they were fighting for. She tasted like potential heartbreak and the good things I knew I was never meant to have. I bit into her lower lip and rubbed my tongue along the supple flesh I trapped between my teeth. I felt her entire body shudder against mine and her palm flattened over my heart where it thundered and roared into her touch.

I put a hand next to the side of her head and braced myself over her. We were around the side of the building, the side that wasn't visible from the road, but there was a door a few feet away that anyone could come out at any time and burst the sensual little bubble the two of us seemed to be trapped in.

Her hand that wasn't tapping along to my furious heartbeats made its way around my waist, her fingertips taking the time to track across every raised mark, to memorize every scar and imperfection that marred my body. She was reading my history, my story that was written on my skin, and I could see that it wasn't one that she was particularly enjoying.

"But I didn't get my turn, Church." Her voice was quiet. "I want those two truths." It grated that she felt like she had to taunt and pull them out of me. I gave her more truth than I had given anyone else in a long time. I'd kind of hoped it was enough but apparently not. She wanted more.

I lowered my forehead, and then dropped it down some more until it rested against hers. "Fine then, I'll tell you three things that are absolutely true because I promised I would never lie to you." She made a little noise in her throat and the fingers of her hand that was resting on my chest curled into a fist.

I shifted my head so I could kiss her on the ridge of one of her freckled cheeks. "Number one; I miss the army. I miss knowing that every single day I'll have something that feels important to do. I miss the regimen and at the same time the unpredictability. I was a damn good soldier and that mattered to me because I wasn't a very good son or brother."

Her eyebrows twitched and the fingers of the hand she had curled around my side dug into my skin. I felt the bite of her nails and could feel the way she sucked in a breath as I leaned to the side and let my lips land on her other cheek. "Number two; I hated the fucking army. I hated watching my friends die. I hated being in a place where it was so easy for kids and women to get killed. I hated the way it felt like no matter how much effort any of us put in, the impact we had on the people we were there to help was minimal. I hate the way it's so hard to leave the battles in the places they were actually fought. You bring all of that shit home with you and it's up to you to figure out where you're going to store it. There is no handbook, no instruction guide, and too many people end up letting that baggage overrun their entire lives. Every day I try and make sure my shit is sorted and stored in a safe place. Sometimes I do a better job at keeping it on a shelf and out of sight than others."

Her softly whispered "Oh, Church" brushed across my lips as I planted my third truth directly on her parted lips. "Third; if I could promise you all the things your eyes promise me, I would. I'm not that guy, I don't have it in me to pretend that I am even if it means you want to turn around and walk back into that bar so we don't tear each other up wanting the same thing but with different outcomes. I can take you to bed and guarantee it'll be worth your while, but nothing else I have to offer is, mostly because I don't have anything else to offer . . . anyone." I knew what it looked like to love and to lose and I wasn't strong enough or brave enough to ever put myself back in that position even if this sunny, sexy woman tempted me to throw caution to the wind.

She lifted herself up on her toes and sealed her mouth to mine.

This kiss was different.

This kiss wasn't soft or kind. This kiss had bite and desperation in it. This kiss was a kiss that you gave to someone that you knew you shouldn't be kissing because kissing them was going to lead to nothing but disappointment. This was a kiss that was flavored with anger and had the tang of frustration laced all throughout it. Her teeth clicked against mine as tongues invaded and dueled for control. Lips took hungrily as breaths bled together and chests heaved rapidly up and down. She made my head spin and I made her hands shake. I could feel them as they danced erratically across my skin, frantic and furious as they scrambled to free themselves from under the fabric of my shirt.

I slanted my lips across hers at a different angle, tasting her deeply and thoroughly. Her mouth was velvety and sweeter than I ever imagined that it could be. She kissed me like it was the only thing that mattered. She kissed me like it was important, like I was important. She kissed me like she loved me even though she knew there wasn't any way possible for me to love her back. I tasted more than tequila on her tongue, everything she wanted from me was there as well and I knew the burn and singe of it would linger with me for an eternity.

It took my brain a few seconds to catch up considering it was clouded and fuzzy with her taste and the feel of her caught between me and the wall. I liked her not having any other option than to lean into me. I also really liked the way her fingers were steady and sure as they dipped behind the button and the zipper at the top of my jeans. She sucked in an audible breath when her touch landed on aching and hard flesh. There was no hiding the erection that had the metal of my zipper digging into my skin. The one that kicked and jerked so that it brushed along the backs of her fingers, begging for attention and acknowledgment.

"Dixie." Her name was a guttural warning. I'd used up all my restraint and good intentions and somehow my mind slipped from how exposed we were and the possible ramification of being out in the open with her like this to the fact that we *were like this*. Everything else faded away and my world narrowed to the woman in front of me and the places she was touching me.

She was playing with fire and was going to find herself over my shoulder and hauled back to the hotel room in a second if she didn't stop what she was doing, no matter how badly that was going to end.

She licked her bottom lip, and I swore when it was obvious that she was savoring the little bit of myself I'd left there. Her strawberry eyebrows arched and her freckled nose wrinkled in a way that shouldn't make me harder but did. My pants felt way too tight and my dick pulsed hot and hard where she twisted her hand around so that she was lightly tracing the throbbing lines and turgid flesh that was hurting all because of her. I put a hand on her wrist as the hand that wasn't occupied playing with my cock started to work on the opening of my pants. We were outside a bar, which I typically wouldn't complain about, but if she was going to pull my dick out for any reason I didn't want to be interrupted. Dixie with her hands on my cock was not something I wanted to share with anyone.

She popped the button on my jeans and I sucked in a breath as cool air and her warm hand covered the tip of my exposed cock. She was making it hard to think. She was making everything hard, period. I was supposed to be looking out for her but somehow she always seemed to end up looking out for me. My zipper sounded unnaturally loud as she slid it down and leaned in closer to me. If anyone walked out the door there was no way they could miss the torrid situation I should be putting a stop to, but I couldn't, or wouldn't use the words that might make her stop.

My dick pointed towards my stomach. Aching and already damp at the swollen tip. Her thumb rubbed an erotic circle around the head, tracing the flare and rushing along the super sensitive underside. My blood went thick and my breaths whooshed in and out of my lungs like I had run a marathon.

"Is this really what you want?" My words felt like they were being dragged out of me. I was having trouble keeping my thoughts in line. All of my attention was focused on the way my cock felt cradled in the palm of her tiny hand. She handled me like she had done it a thousand times. She seemed to know right where to touch, exactly the kind of pressure I liked. I hadn't had a girl work me over like this since high school and it sure as shit didn't feel this good back then. My ab muscles pulled tight and my biceps bunched and locked as I threaded my fingers through the soft hair at her temples. The curls wrapped around my fingers like a silken shroud.

Her eyes gleamed up at me, dark and getting darker as tension pulsed thick and tangible between us. None of this was a good idea but common sense and reason fled the minute she put her hands on me. There was no planning for the worst, there was simply giving in to the promise of one of the best things that might ever happen to me. "It's what I want right now." That answer was cryptic and didn't make much sense but before I could pull more out of her she kissed my chin, right in the center, and then she started to slide down the wall I had her pinned against. I tightened my hands in her hair to keep her standing upright but she gave her head a little shake to let me know my hold on her was hurting rather than helping. "We don't have to do this." I shouldn't let her do this, not here and not now. I owed her and felt like it was my duty to put a stop to this before some guy in a trucker hat and Carhartts came stumbling out the door and caught us in the middle of something that shouldn't be happening in the first place.

Her big brown eyes were glassy with boozy desire and there was an attractive pink hue coloring her cheeks and making her freckles stand out even more than normal. "Let me go, Church."

I let her go and a second later she was on her knees in front of me and my cock was engulfed in the damp, warm cavern of her mouth. I'd watched her suck on that straw yesterday and wondered what it would be like to have those pretty, pouty lips wrapped around my dick. My imagination didn't have shit on reality. She blew my mind while she proceeded to blow me outside of a bar in the middle of nowhere Arkansas after too many shots of tequila and too much honesty. It hurt my heart but the rest of me really fucking enjoyed it.

I leaned forward when she made a satisfied noise as precum hit her tongue. I braced an arm on the brick wall and rested my forehead on my arm. I put a hand on the top of her head as she bobbed up and down, tongue swirling, cheeks hollowing out as my hips kicked forward involuntarily towards her. It was glorious and it was torture. I'd spent many a night with my hand wrapped around the same rigid flesh she was sucking, licking, taunting with licks and vibration as she gave repeated hums of satisfaction. My own fist would never do now that I knew what the reality of Dixie's warm, welcoming mouth felt like. She had ruined jacking off for me and I hated and loved her for it at the same time.

I pressed farther into her as she sucked my length back into her mouth as far as it would go. She wrapped a hand around the base because there was more of me than she could fully take and twisted her wrist as her tongue did an erotic little dance along the heavy vein that ran along the underside of my erection. The girl was beyond good with her mouth. She had me weak-kneed and blurry eyed as she sucked and swallowed as I bucked against her far more violently than I meant to. I should be reverent and respectful. This was far more for me than it was for her but my baser instincts were taking over and all I seemed able to do was grunt and demand more from her as she worked me deeper inside her mouth and farther down the back of her throat.

It was the dirtiest and at the same time most worshipful experience of my life. I never wanted it to end but I also wanted to rush through it because it still felt like the wrong place and the wrong time and I was absolutely the wrong guy . . . but she was right. Everything about her and the way she made me feel as pleasure coiled low at the base of my spine, while it had my thighs locking and my hands clutching at her head like it was my only anchor to this moment, felt so much like it should be, was meant to be, like it was the only right that had happened in my life in a very, very long time.

"You're about to get more than you asked for, pretty girl." My voice sounded like it had been dragged over gravel and dipped in acid. The drawl was thicker than it had ever been and I couldn't keep my eyes open as pleasure pressed down hard on me and had my balls drawing up and my cock kicking hard where it was trapped between her lips.

She hummed again, twisted her hand the other way, dug the fingernails of her free hand into the curve at the top of my ass where she was holding on for balance, and then she licked across the steadily weeping slit that was touching her tongue. She pulled back just a little bit and I couldn't take it anymore. I swore and then growled her name as I pressed the back of her head closer to my waist. It wasn't delicate or kind. It was greedy and gluttonous. I wanted her to take all of me as I flooded her mouth and filled her up with pleasure that would no longer be contained. She swallowed just as voraciously, taking it all while she stared up at me with those unendingly dark eyes. I didn't deserve any of this, but it was a moment, a memory that I would treasure until I took my last breath. She made me feel like a hero when I was the furthest thing from that.

She fell back on her haunches after placing a kiss right below my belly button. She leaned her head back against the brick wall and stared up at me as I figured my situation out and got myself adjusted back in my jeans. I couldn't stop looking down at her. She made me take risks I would never take, not just because I knew better than to get distracted, but because when I was distracted I couldn't keep her safe. She might have done a spectacular job going down on me but my mind was blown just as much as my cock had been. She made me forget to be on the lookout for the bad things that always seemed to chase the good ones out of my life.

Her mouth was puffy and swollen. Her cheeks were hot pink and there was no missing that her typically wild hair was even more unkempt from my hands pulling at it. I opened my mouth to say something, to say anything, but I was saved from tripping over useless words when the side door to the bar swung open and the cute cocktail server that had been taking care of us inside stepped out, cigarette in hand.

Her gaze slipped over us, me looming over a very flushed and very wide-eyed Dixie, and a knowing grin tugged at her mouth.

"That's a popular pit stop, but you guys might want to relocate before last call if you don't want to give the whole town and all the tourists a show." She winked at me as I reached out a hand to pull Dixie to her feet. She wobbled a little and I pulled her to my chest, where she buried her flaming face.

"She needed a minute." My voice sounded like it was traveling over sandpaper when I gave the waitress the weak excuse for our compromising position. Dixie let out a snort that the cocktail server echoed.

"I bet she did. By the looks of you I bet she needed more than one." Dixie let out a strangled laugh and pulled back. She shook her tangled pigtails out of her face and waved a hand in my general direction.

"I mean look at him. Can you blame me?" The blonde let her gaze roll over me and she gave Dixie a nod.

"Nope. Not at all." They shared a look that must have required a vagina to understand as I hooked a hand under Dixie's elbow and gave her a tug towards the road.

"We need to hit the road early if we're gonna make it to Lowry with enough time for me to swing by the hospital and see Elma Mae before they release her." What I needed to do was get her somewhere alone and private so I could get my head around all the ways the dynamic between us had just shifted. I was starting to settle into the idea of having her as a friend, a friend I wanted to fuck but still a friend. None of what happened inside or outside of that honky-tonk felt very friendly. It felt like the start of something that was going to kill me when I had to finish it.

Dixie gave a sloppy nod and waved at the still-smiling cocktail server. She let me wrap an arm around her shoulders and hold her to my side as we made our way back towards the cabin-like motel.

"She's used to it. Before Rome put up cameras in the bar I can't tell you how many times I would walk out the back door and stumble onto something that should be on cable late at night." She gave a little giggle that made me think the tequila was still thick in her blood. "Rome can't ever fire me because I can't tell you how many times I've walked in on him and Cora doing stuff that leads to all those babies they have."

I grunted and hauled her even closer to my side. "You deserve more than a quick fuck in a back office or up against the side of the bar." She deserved a guy that would be careful with her and give her back all the goodness she handed out so freely.

She dug an elbow into my side and pushed until I let her go. She stumbled closer to the edge of the street than I was comfortable with, so I pulled her back but she immediately shook my hand off her arm.

"Sometimes it isn't about who deserves what. Sometimes it's simply about what makes you happy. Sometimes it's okay to take what you can get and be satisfied with that because you know more will eventually come along." She cut me a look out of the corner of her eye and then let out a deep sigh. "Let's just call it too much temptation and too much tequila."

What had just happened between the two of us was the most selfless I'd ever had any woman be with me. Sure, I'd had other mouths attached to pretty girls wrapped around my cock, but it had never felt as personal and as important as it felt with Dixie. And none of them had looked at me like I was doing them some kind of courtesy by allowing them to suck me off. I sighed, louder and much more exasperatedly than she had. "You make me feel like you getting me off with the best blow job I've ever had was me doing you some kind of favor. Believe me, the pleasure was all mine."

She gave her head a little shake, which sent her captured curls bouncing, and I wanted to punch myself in the nuts for the way her eyes filled with shadows of sadness. "Fair warning before we fall into that bed together, if you put your hands and your mouth on me, Church, I'm going to want more. My stupid heart is going to spin big dreams that lock you and me together forever even though my head knows better. You gave me the little bit you just did and I can already feel every single piece of me is wanting to gobble it up and demand more. I'm happy right now, but if you take me to bed and make me feel special I won't be happy when I realize that isn't true. I'd rather stay happy and if I had to guess I would bet you want to stay happy, too." Her lips twitched and she leaned into me. "Well, as happy as a big, broody former soldier and prodigal son can get."

Her words stabbed at me with the unvarnished and unsheathed truth. "Everything inside of me is screaming that I need to give you what you gave me, pretty girl."

She gave me a smile that nearly broke my heart in half. "I'm not looking for you to balance the scales by giving me as many orgasms as I give you. I put your cock in my mouth because I wanted it there. I've been thinking about how you would taste on my tongue and getting myself off imagining everything that is you for fucking forever. I didn't go down on you because I wanted you to owe me anything, I went down on you because I saw my shot to live out a fantasy and I took it."

I let her pull away from me and when we got into the cabin she silently disappeared into the bathroom. When she came out much later she was freshly showered and smelled like orange and honey. Her curls hung down to the middle of her back with the weight of the water still stuck in them and all she had on was her tank top and a pair of black boy-short panties that covered more than a bikini bottom would but made my cock jolt nonetheless.

"You want me to crash on the floor?" It was the least I could do since she wanted me to keep my hands to myself. Chivalry sucked and I really wanted to be less than gentlemanly at the moment. But she told me she wanted to stay happy and I couldn't bring myself to do anything to mess with that even if she looked delectable and sweet enough to eat.

She shook her head in the negative. "Nope, but don't take it personally when I build a pillow fortress around myself. I'm a middle-of-the-night cuddler."

I wanted her to cuddle me . . . naked. She crawled under the covers and surrounded herself with all the extra pillows on the bed. There wasn't a chance that we would accidentally roll into one another in the night and that fact made me grind my back teeth together and curse my inability to be the kind of guy that truly appreciated having a woman like her in the same bed.

It was a restless night for both of us. She tossed and turned while I laid as still as possible, eyes locked on the ceiling. She let out a tragic-sounding sigh every hour or so and when the sun filtered through the curtains on the window we were both ready to keep pretending we were asleep and silently agreed that being on the road was better than being in the bed, so close yet so far apart.

We rode hard and fast. We pushed on through the rest of Arkansas with the minimum of stops and ate an awkward and mostly silent lunch when we crossed into Mississippi. Every mile we rode closer to Lowry made me nostalgic and nervous at the same time. A man never forgot where he came from, even if he had tried his hardest. I didn't exactly feel very welcome when we stopped and I had to endure several obvious sneers and dirty looks as I escorted Dixie to and from the ladies' room. Some things didn't change no matter how much time had gone by and it reminded me why, even though this place was home, I had decided to leave it behind and not look back. I was used to tuning out that kind of reaction and judgment, but there was no way to stop the way it made me tense up and get overly territorial where Dixie was concerned. I didn't want her to get the same kind of flack I remembered my mother getting. Neither one of them deserved that kind of reaction just because of the company they chose to keep.

We blew through Tupelo, Dixie oohing and awing over the old plantations with their stately columns in the front and the giant weeping trees. She kept telling me to slow down as the main roads turned into barely paved country roads so she could snap pictures with her cell phone. I was anxious to hit the county line but I couldn't deny her simple request, so we were cruising along, slow and steady when suddenly red and blue lights lit up behind us.

The siren whirred and Dixie went ramrod straight behind me. "We're barely moving. Why would they stop us?"

I didn't want to tell her it was a common occurrence in Lowry. If you didn't look like everyone else the cops had no problem pulling you over just so they could let you know they were watching you. That had happened less when I became a cop's kid but there was only so much Jules's position could shield both me and Mom from.

"No big deal. Probably just wondering what we're doing in town." That was partly true because I didn't want to lie to her.

I didn't want to share with her the other reasons they could be pulling us over, so I kept my mouth shut and my eyes on the vehicle behind us.

I watched in the side mirror as the cop grabbed his hat and climbed out of the car after we both stopped on the side of the road. The tall figure was achingly familiar and recognizable as he ambled his way up to the side of the bike. A face that I hadn't seen in a decade stared down at me from behind mirrored shades. He looked like he hadn't aged a bit except now there were threads of gray in the ever-present goatee that surrounded his mouth.

I took my sunglasses off and tilted my chin up at the tall man. "Jules."

The cop's mouth twitched and his head turned to take in my pretty passenger. "Glad to have you back, son."

"Glad to be back." And I was. That surprisingly wasn't a lie.

"We got a situation, Dash." Jules's deep voice sounded like home but his tone was serious and it made my very honed instincts stand up and take notice.

"What kind of situation?" I felt my eyes narrow as his head turned so he could look at Dixie where she was silently taking in our exchange.

"Got a call into the station about an hour ago about a kidnapped woman. The call hit dispatch in Tupelo a couple hours ago and they passed it on to us to keep an eye out. Got a description of a redheaded woman, small in stature, last seen in Arkansas. Caller said she was abducted by a man on a brand-new sportster with temp plates out of Colorado. The description that dispatch operator sent along sounded awfully familiar."

Dixie stiffened behind me. "Wait . . . you're saying someone reported me kidnapped?" She sounded incredulous and alarmed.

Jules lifted a hand and rubbed it over his mouth, a gesture I must have picked up from him along the way somewhere. It took time and distance but I could now see a lot of the man that had picked me to be his in myself. I wondered if that gave him a sense of pride or disgusted him seeing as how I'd left him and the good life he'd tried so hard to give me through thick and thin.

"That's what it sounds like."

"No way. That's crazy. Church asked me to come a couple of days ago and I agreed. I'm with him by choice."

She was with me by choice and through a little bit of coercion, but I was starting to wonder if her being unable to tell me no when it came to something I really, actually needed her for was the worst mistake she had ever made. After all, she was nothing but good and I had a really bad track record when it came to being able to keep a good thing going.

Chapter 9

Dixie

The cop looked almost exactly like Shemar Moore. The afternoon sun glinted off his shaved head and cast his confident swagger in shadow as he approached us. He even had the neatly trimmed goatee surrounding his mouth and the kind of smile that made me forget my own name. I was having a really hard time listening to what he was saying and not gawking with my tongue hanging out. He was tall, built, and gorgeous, just like the man sitting stiffly in front of me. They might not be related by blood, but there was no mistaking that Church was every inch his father's son and there was also no missing that his dad felt it was long past time his eldest returned home.

"I am very obviously not kidnapped." I couldn't believe that someone had reported me missing. For a second I wondered if it could be Kallie going above and beyond to get my attention since I wasn't around to keep her world from crumbling around her like I normally was. I wouldn't put it past her, but I quickly dismissed the idea when the hot cop took his sunglasses off and pinned me with a hard, chocolate-colored stare several shades darker than my own.

"You give anyone a reason to report you missing before you left Denver?" His voice rumbled like distant thunder and his drawl was so thick and low that I really had to listen to understand him.

I shook my head vehemently no as Church swore. "I pissed off a drug dealer before I blew out of town. Could be payback for that. Got some looks outside Kansas City and some more once we hit the Mississippi state line. Could be that." He tensed up and practically growled at the man standing stoically next to us. "You know how it goes." He sounded pissed and his words made the man he didn't refer to as Dad look angry.

"I do know how it goes, son." It sounded like it didn't go well for either of them in the past.

"Someone locked Dixie in the bathroom at a truck stop the first night. They jammed a pipe in the door and she was stuck there while I helped some guy out with his radiator. Someone also tried to run us off the road the first night. I'm thinking none of that was coincidental now."

"You got a description of the guy?"

Church shook his head. "No, sir. I can't tell you what kind of car he drove or what he looked like. I can tell you all of Acosta's guys are Hispanic."

"Acosta, the drug dealer?" It was so formal, so regimented. I couldn't believe neither man was an emotional mess after spending so many years apart. There were no hugs exchanged, not even a friendly handshake. It was all facts and information exchanged in clipped sentences. It was almost painful to watch.

"Yep. He's tangled up in federal court right now, but he's got a dirty lawyer that I wouldn't be surprised to learn is helping him run things from behind bars."

The cop switched his attention to me and his lips lifted in a half grin. Dear Lord, if Church ever let go of all that history and horror that made it impossible for him to smile he would be devastating. He was already the prettiest man I had ever seen, and if he ever got to the point where he could comfortably flash his pearly whites my heart wouldn't be able to take it . . . and I was pretty sure my vagina would spontaneously combust.

"You see the car that tried to run you off the road, Curly Sue?" I couldn't hold back the giggle at the nickname. When Church called me "pretty girl" it made me feel all kinds of hot and bothered. The "Curly Sue" from his dad made me feel welcomed and enfolded in the warmth of a family that was missing a piece. I didn't have anything to do with bringing the prodigal son home, but the cute nickname and the lazy smile that showed all of his strong white teeth made me feel like I was the key to putting all the fragments back together.

"No, I didn't see anything, but I wasn't paying attention because I was too busy watching my life flash before my eyes."

He nodded and put his sunglasses back on. "It's been my experience that most drug dealers tend to be more in-your-face with their retaliation, but this guy might be more subtle if he's looking at federal charges. Not sure what's going on and it's going to be a paperwork nightmare to get the alert pulled on you two, so I would keep an eye out for anything else that seems out of sorts. Pretty easy to spot the things that don't belong in a small town."

Church snorted. "One of these things is not like the other."

The cop frowned and shook his head. "You've been gone a long time, son. Things change. The boy you were may have struggled here, that doesn't mean the man you are now can't find his place."

"Not sure my place is here, Jules." I saw the admission hit the older man like it was a bullet fired from a gun. Julian Churchill had been waiting for his son to settle for a long time, and the fact Church couldn't see that made me want to smack him upside his helmeted head.

"As long as you find a bit of peace when you find that place I don't care where it's at. I've got to get back to the station and try and untangle this missing-persons mess. You headed to the house?" He said it like it was a given that Church and I would be staying at his childhood home. I saw Church start to shake his head no, and I decided it was enough.

"We're going to the hospital to see Elma Mae first, but when visiting hours are over we'll be there. Church mentioned that you live close to her, so we can stay there and help her out once she gets back home. It'll be great." I purposely ignored the daggers that I was sure Church was throwing at me with his eyes behind the lenses of his sunglasses. I could see his big body lock with tension and refusal. His dad must have picked up on it, too, because before Church could offer up a suggestion that didn't have us under his father's roof the cop mentioned that he would call his other boy and make sure that he had the place tidied up. He excused himself in a rush and turned and walked back to his cruiser.

Church's jaw clenched and a muscle in his cheek twitched. "I was planning on getting us a couple of rooms in town."

"You haven't seen your family in ten years. It's obvious that your dad wants time with you, and I think we both know you need the time with him and your brother. It won't kill you to stay with him until you figure out where you want to be." I sounded like I was scolding a child, but frankly he was kind of acting like a toddler that had skipped nap time. I could understand him wanting to take it slow while he salvaged the remnants of the bridges he had burned, but the pace he seemed to be moving at rivaled a snail for speed.

"Jules's place isn't very big. There isn't an extra room for guests. That means you and I are going to be in close quarters until you go home." The way his twang made the word "close" sound had heat rising into my face and made me tug at the collar of my shirt.

"We'll survive it." I sounded more confident than I felt. Last night had been torturous. There was nothing worse than that necessary distance that I had to keep between the two of us. All I longed to do was reach out and touch him. Every inch of my skin prickled and ached for me to let him touch me. I wanted his arms around me and his hard, heavy body pressing into mine. I wanted it with every part of my being, but I knew once I got it there was no way I was going to survive letting it go. He refused to entertain the idea that we could have more, that he could be more to me than a hard and ready cock and every time he reminded me of the fact it was like having a bucket of icy water poured over my head.

I'd lost my mind a little last night outside the bar. He just smelled so good, and when he looked at me like I could be the thing he built his dreams on there was no stopping me from taking a little taste. I was like a starving person that was offered a cupcake. I wanted to lick all the frosting off and shove the rest of all the deliciousness in my mouth with both hands. It shouldn't have gone as far as it did. I knew he wasn't going to understand that it had been more about me than it had about him, and I couldn't blame him for that. It was hard to explain that making him happy and giving him what he wanted since I knew that there was no way I was getting what I wanted from him fulfilled me in a complex and emotional way. His satisfaction gave me a little bit of my own. It was a pretty powerful thing to be the girl that made a man that had brooding and suspicion down to an art form drop that ever-present shield he held up to keep the world at bay. That glimpse of Church unprotected and vulnerable would stay with me forever. He might not love me, but he trusted me and he lowered his defenses for me. That might be enough to keep me going when it was time to walk away.

I made his eyes glow. That better than hazel color had lit up the night and nothing had ever made me feel so accomplished or satisfied. The darkness that seemed to follow him everywhere lifted for a split second and I would never forget that I was able to chase his shadows away for that moment, no matter how brief it may have been.

"How long you think a pillow fortress is gonna keep my hands off of you?" I jolted as he rocked the bike up off its stand and turned the motor over. Clearly he didn't want my response and I was secretly glad I didn't have to give him one because the only thing I didn't really want him to keep me safe from was *him*.

The drive to the small hospital took almost no time at all once we hit the actual city limits, though "city" was a bit of a stretch. The town of Lowry looked like it could be the set of a family drama set deep in the heart of the south. It was adorable, quaint, and looked like every single person living there had taken an oath to keep the streets clean and the main street just kitschy enough to be ironically cool. The entire place could have fallen off the front of a postcard, it was that picturesque and pristine. It almost felt like stepping back in time and I sort of loved it. I was a Colorado girl to my core but part of the reason I loved the Mile High so much was because it was a big city with a small-town mentality. People were kind to their neighbors. There was a sense of community, and it really felt like I couldn't go anywhere without running into someone I knew. I was tickled pink by this actual small town, and I waved back at everyone who lifted their hand in greeting and smiled at everyone who offered up a grin as Church barreled down the narrow two-way street. I wasn't sure if they recognized him and that's why everyone seemed so friendly or if this was just the kind of place where strangers were friends until proven different. If that was the case this place was my kind of town.

The hospital wasn't a massive, sprawling structure. In fact, the entire building looked like it would fit inside of the bar where I worked back home. However, the inside was a bustle of activity and there was no shortage of medical equipment or hospital staff scurrying around in colorful scrubs. The outside might not have been very impressive but the inside sure was.

Church stopped at the information desk and asked where we could find Elma Mae. The woman seated behind it gave him a smile and proceeded to tell him that she remembered him from when he was little, that his brother was growing up to look just like him, and that she knew his dad and was so happy when Julian decided to run for sheriff. For all the forgetting Church had been trying to do it appeared that the people he had left behind had long memories. The woman thanked him for his service, to which he blushed and stumbled over a "Much obliged, ma'am." We hadn't been back for very long and already his accent was twice as pronounced as it normally was. He might have thought he cut himself loose when he enlisted and ended up on the other side of the world, but his roots ran deep no matter how tangled and snarled they might be.

On the way to the room he was stopped twice more. Once by a nurse that told him they went to high school together and that she was glad to see that he'd made it back home in one piece, and the second time by a doctor that mentioned he had been the one taking care of Elma Mae and knew that his visit was going to mean the world to her. Apparently the older woman talked about the Churchill men like they were family. Church didn't bother to tell the man that they *were* family, he simply replied that he would be around for as long as Elma needed him. That got him a pat on the back and a toothy smile.

When we got to the room I grabbed Church's elbow and pulled him to a stop before he could push the door open. "I'm going to give you a few minutes alone with her. I'm sure she missed you and I don't want to intrude. Come and get me when you're ready, I'll hang out here in the hallway." I really needed to find a cup of coffee. My sleepless night and the stress of wondering who would have possibly reported me missing had me strung out and feeling spread a little too thin.

He put his fingers over mine and met my look with one of his own. "I'd rather you come in with me. She's been through enough and doesn't need to get all worked up about where I've been and what I've been doing. She's southern through and through, so there is no way she'll throw a fit in front of a stranger." His explanation for wanting me by his side sounded reasonable, but I could see there was more to it than that. He was scared . . . more than scared . . . he was terrified to step inside that room on his own.

His mouth was pinched. His eyebrows were pulled into a V over the top of his nose and he was pale under the natural golden hue of his skin. The fingers that covered mine had a slight tremor to them, and I really got the sense that he wasn't going to cross that threshold until I pushed him or agreed to walk in beside him.

I huffed out a breath and tugged my hand until he released it. "Fine. I'll come in with you, but if anyone starts crying then I'm gone." I said it jokingly because I was pretty sure that if anyone was going to succumb to waterworks it would be me. I was a sucker for a happy reunion and no one needed someone to throw their arms around them and welcome them home more than Church.

The slender figure in the center of the hospital bed looked like she could be Helen Mirren's twin sister. She was elegant and stately even in a pink pajama top covered in what appeared to be kittens wearing sunglasses. She had the covers pulled up to her waist but the bulk of the leg immobilizer was impossible to miss, so were the sling around her shoulder and the black eye marring her flawless complexion. Church mentioned she was in her eighties or close to it on several occasions, but I wouldn't have put her a day over sixty-five if I hadn't known better. She was in the hospital with a broken hip and her hair and makeup looked better than mine did on any given day of the week. I was impressed, but as her keen gaze went from elation at seeing Church to accusation as it landed on me, I could tell the feeling wasn't mutual.

"Well, aren't you a sight for sore eyes. Look at you, all grown and handsome. Get over here and give Elma a hug. I missed you something terrible, Dashel." I had been shocked to hear his dad call him Dash. I almost fell over when this woman called him Dashel. It was a stark reminder that I didn't know the man that had been my obsession and my downfall nearly as well as I wanted to.

Church worked his way around the edge of the bed and bent to carefully wrap his arms around the woman. Her hands fluttered along his corded shoulders, but her cutting gaze never left me as I watched the reunion with wide eyes, holding my breath for so long it made my lungs burn. I was afraid if I moved, if I so much as twitched the wrong way I would somehow ruin this moment for him. I was trying to be as unobtrusive as possible even with the old lady glaring at me like I was the sole reason he had been gone for so long.

She shifted her attention to Church as he straightened. She lifted her hands to each side of his face and turned it from side to side like she was searching for the teenager that had left a decade ago.

"You're taller now. You look so much like your momma and wait until you see Dalen. He's such a handsome boy. He looks a lot like you now that he's growing into his feet. It's good to have you back, Dashel. You were missed. Talking to you over Skynet isn't the same as having my boy home where I know he's safe."

I couldn't hold back the laugh that forced its way out. "Skynet? Isn't that the computer system that takes over the world in the Terminator movies?"

He chuckled and wrapped his hands around Elma's wrists as she narrowed her eyes at me once again. "She means Skype. I tried to check in on everyone once a month while I was overseas. Jules set up Skype for Elma on her computer so she could see for herself I was all in one piece. I told you I was taking care of myself." He gave her hands a little squeeze and stepped back.

"You need someone to take care of you for a change, my boy. Isn't that why you stayed in Colorado with your girl instead of coming back home?" Her words were pointed, and I was starting to doubt Church's assurance that she wouldn't want a scene in front of a stranger. She seemed more than willing to call me out for any hand I may have had in keeping her boy from home when his tour of duty was done.

Church exhaled a breath and shot me an apologetic look. "Elma Mae, Dixie is a good girl. Believe me when I tell you the last thing she needs is another person to take care of, especially when I am perfectly capable of taking care of myself. I told you there was a girl and that things were complicated, you didn't believe me. Well, she's the girl and things are no less complicated now that we're here instead of there."

Those overly observant eyes practically pinned me to the spot. She was looking at me like she could see all the things I had been covering up with smiles and humor for longer than I cared to remember. Church told me I was the sun shining on even the cloudiest of days, but the truth was there were times when I couldn't get through the fog. There were days when all I wanted was a hug and for someone to tell me that it would all be worth it in the end. Every grin, every pat on the back, every thumbs-up and unwavering positive reinforcement I handed off to others, there were days when I longed to know that the universe would turn that back around on me and I would finally be rewarded with the simple dreams that I had nurtured for so long. It kind of felt like time had run out on that karmic windfall considering I was never dating again, and the only person I wanted to love unconditionally didn't even know it. Not to mention the more time I spent with him on his journey home, the more I was wondering if I had ever really known the man my heart was so stuck on.

The broken soldier looking for some peace. The brooding bouncer. The beautiful and aloof hero that didn't have the time or patience for wasted words and actions. The loyal friend. The southern gentleman. The consummate loner with miles and miles of walls erected around him. Those were all the parts of Church that I knew and still managed to fall for, but there were the new parts that I wasn't so fond of. The battle-weary warrior carrying years and years of war around inside of him, so heavy and weighted down he couldn't move forward. The man who had lost too much. The standoffish son. The reluctant to return small-town boy. The jaded child scarred from years of being told he was different and not enough of one thing to be a whole anything. The man that needed me to help him out but didn't want me enough to step out of his comfort zone. There were a lot of sides to Church that should knock the rose-colored glasses right off of my nose, but my foolishly determined heart was having a hard time letting go of all the things it decided it loved about him.

"You've had a situation that needed figuring out here since you left." She turned her sharp gaze to him and Church ducked his head. "I don't care why you stayed away, alls I care about is the fact you're back. One of these days me and you are gonna sit down and you're gonna tell me why you couldn't come home. You're gonna tell this old woman why you went chasing after bad guys and nearly broke your daddy's heart, but for now you're gonna give me another hug and promise me that you aren't going anywhere until I got two good legs so I can chase you if you decide to run again."

He bent down and wrapped his arms around her and gave her

a squeeze that made her laugh. He put a soft kiss on her cheek before he stood to his full height once again.

"I'm home for the foreseeable future. Dixie is hanging around with me for a little bit so we can get you settled. I told her all about your cookies and your sweet tea."

"You aren't stayin'?" The woman was sharp as a tack and didn't miss a beat.

"Well . . . I . . . ugh . . . I'm here for as long as Church needs me to stay." I winced when she narrowed her eyes at me when I used the only name I knew him by and it obviously irritated her.

"I don't know anyone named Church. I know an adorable boy that wouldn't want to disrespect his momma by throwing away the name she picked out for him." I shifted my gaze to Church and watched as he moved his weight nervously from foot to foot. Well, wasn't that adorable. Add chagrined and scolded Church to the list of parts of him that were impossible not to care for.

"Haven't been Dashel in a long time, Elma. Went to war and earned the name Church. I got it from a man I respect and admire, a man that I still call a friend. I think Mom would understand." His voice was quiet and the sentiment was clear. He liked his name and he was proud of how he came by it. He wasn't a kid that needed her to look after him anymore, he was a man that had seen things and done things that fundamentally changed a person. He couldn't be Dashel anymore. That innocence and naïveté had been stripped away.

The older woman made a noise low in her throat and threw up her hands in exasperation. "Fine, you be Church for your woman and for everyone else, but for me you'll always be little Dashel with the wild eyes and the too tender heart. I'm so mad I fell, but God was looking out for me and He had a plan. If that tumble was what brought you home to me and your family, then I would gladly take a hundred more."

Church rumbled out a laugh from low in his chest and walked over to where I was still hovering by the doorway. His shoulder brushed mine and he reached down to grab my hand. His fingers were no longer shaking but there was a coiled tension running all throughout his body, making him so rigid and stiff that it felt like I was standing next to a stone statue.

"No more falling. I'll borrow Jules's truck tomorrow, assuming he still has it, and come and pick you up when it's time to go home. I missed the shit out of you, Elma."

"Language!" She shook a finger at him and gave me one last knowing look. "This old woman missed you more than you will ever know. Looking forward to seeing what's so special about your girl, Dashel."

Church muttered another good-bye and hustled me out of the room before he had to further defend my honor. We were in the elevator when I told him flatly, "You brought me all this way, and she hates me."

He gave me a hooded look as he crossed his arms over his chest. "She doesn't hate you. She's just protective of me, and it's been a long time. I don't think she was ready for the actuality of me being grown and having lived an entire life she had no part of."

"One of these days do you plan on sharing why she had no part of that life?" I tilted my chin back so that I could look him in the eye. "I think that's a story I would like to hear. Also I'm not at all surprised you were scared to go see her on your own. She's something else."

His eyebrows shot upwards so fast I was amazed they didn't

go flying off his forehead. His gorgeous eyes widened and colored with disbelief. "I wasn't scared to go into her room alone."

I made a face at him and pushed past him so I could get out of the elevator. "Oh right. You're a big, badass soldier, you aren't scared of anything. That's why you were pale and shaking at the door. I get it, she talks to you like you're five and you clearly adore her and don't want to let her down. I would be nervous about my reception, too."

Once we pushed out the front doors and back into the idyllic scenery that made up his hometown he grabbed my arm and hauled me around so that we were nose to nose. He was breathing hard and there was an unhinged panic in his eyes that I had never seen before. This was Church close to the edge. The edge of what, I had no clue, but I was smart enough to recognize that I needed to shut my mouth or else there was a real risk I would end up pushing him over.

"Elma Mae loves me and nothing I could do or have done would ever make her stop. I wasn't nervous or scared about how she would handle seeing me after all this time." His eyes flashed a million different emotions at me and his lungs pushed out breaths as rapidly as he could pull them in. "I didn't want her to be dead."

He dropped the bomb at the same time he let me go. I rocked back on my heels and put a hand over my chest where my heart was racing, trying to keep up with his erratic behavior.

"Why would you think that? You knew she was doing fine other than her injuries. Why would you think that she would be dead just because you finally made it to see her?" He wasn't making any sense but I could see he was as serious as could be.

His eyes drilled into me and his voice was icy cold and devoid of all emotion when he flatly responded, "Because the women I care about don't make it. I get a good thing in my life and it goes away before I realize just how good it is. Bad can always get worse and there isn't a damn thing I can do to stop it." He pulled his eyes away from mine and turned his back on me as he started walking towards the motorcycle. "Why do you think I refuse to let myself think about there being a me and you, pretty girl? You're all good and I don't want to bring you into the kind of bad I can't seem to shake."

His words floored me. They left me frozen on the spot and unable to think straight. He started the bike and refused to look at me while I stood stuck and immobile a few feet away.

We needed to talk. I needed to understand. He needed to make what had just happened here make some kind of sense, because I knew for a fact Church was a lot of things, some I liked more than others, but none of those things was bad.

I was starting to see what all those dark clouds and shadows that hovered over him were made of.

Memories and regrets and a whole lot of loss that he couldn't stop. He was still feeling old wounds like they were freshly sliced into his soul. I didn't know if there was a sunny day bright enough to shine through all of that but I'd be damned if I didn't try to find one for him.

Chapter 10

Church

I'd spent the last ten years of my life putting myself in dangerous situation after dangerous situation. I'd lost friends and come close to losing myself on more than one occasion. I'd been injured and broken down. I'd been exhausted and pushed to the limit, but in all of that time I'd refused to let fear be a factor in how I did my job. It was there, always hovering on the periphery of my consciousness, but I tuned it out and ignored it. I focused on the task at hand, on the mission, and I never froze. I believed I was bigger, badder, and my mission was more important than the things that scared me and I brazened my way through every situation I found myself in, even the ones that *should* have terrified me. I went into the army with a purpose.

Today all of that long-practiced bravado fled.

Today I couldn't wrestle back the fear and camouflage it with bluster and balls.

Today my hands shook so badly I couldn't even hide my fear

that another person I cared so deeply about had left this world for whatever was beyond.

There was no hiding the stark terror that had made it almost impossible for me to open the door keeping Elma Mae from me and there was no stopping the truth from rocketing loose from the jagged place in my soul when Dixie questioned my obvious hesitation. It ripped free from the place inside where I kept it perched high and visible to constantly remind me why I refused to let myself care about anyone in a deep and meaningful way. I couldn't withstand the loss of another vital, beautiful, loving, and generous woman. I already carried around the weight of the loss of both the women Jules had loved, and if there was any more added to the load I would buckle and never be able to get back on my feet. Senseless and wasteful. There was no rhyme or reason to why we couldn't keep the women we loved safe and that shredded me, especially when I thought about the way I squandered time with one of them and wasted days being mad at the other because they both chose to love a good man. I should have done better, been better.

I knew Dixie wanted an explanation. I could feel her tiny frame practically vibrating behind me and it had nothing to do with the rumble of the motorcycle and everything to do with the conversation she was waiting to have. A conversation I wanted to have about as much as I wanted to spend another year eating nothing but MREs. Telling her about my mother passing far too soon had been hard and had forced me to be far more honest than I wanted to be with anyone. If she pinned me down and made me tell her about how I knew things could go from bad to worse especially when it came to Caroline there would be no more softening of her eyes when I asked her if she was okay and no more little grins when I told her I wanted to keep her safe. She looked at me like I was a hero and I selfishly wanted to keep it that way. The truth was anything but heroic.

Taking her from the hospital to the house I grew up in was a literal trip down memory lane. I absently catalogued all the things that were the same in the sleepy suburb where Jules's sprawling brick ranch home was located, but it was all the things that were different that really stuck out. I forced myself to believe that home was better off without me, and me without it, but I hadn't really prepared myself for home to go on and grow and prosper without me. The streets were lined with new homes and happy families playing in the perfectly landscaped yards. There was a park on the corner that hadn't been there years ago, and instead of a single stoplight in the center of town there were now three—and a slew of convenience stores and a new chain superstore that felt woefully out of place in the memories I had of my hometown.

Luckily when I pulled into the driveway of my childhood home, Jules was just pulling in as well. That meant I could put the conversation Dixie was chomping at the bit to have on the back burner for a little while longer. She liked me too much to strip me bare and drag me over the coals in front of a man I obviously respected and admired. My relationship with Jules was complicated at best, and I knew the spunky redhead well enough to know that there was no way she would want any part of driving the wedge any further between me and the man in the sheriff's uniform that greeted us with an easy smile and a warm, fatherly glint in his dark eyes.

"How was Elma?" Jules offered Dixie a hand as she clamored

off the back of the bike. When she grinned up at the man her smile was so easy, so bright I was surprised Jules wasn't temporarily blinded by it. I knew that when she looked at me like that I felt like I couldn't see anything but the sunshine that glowed out of her too-big heart.

Dixie took her helmet off and shook out her hair. I wanted to comb my fingers through her rowdy curls and bury my face in them. They always smelled like fresh air and sunbeams. They felt like warm silk and luxurious satin. She was like the perfect day if the perfect day was a human being.

"She looked good to me, but she did not hide the fact that she thinks it's my fault Church didn't come home as soon as his discharge papers were signed. She was not a fan of this particular Yankee."

Jules threw his head back and let out a laugh that made his entire body shake. "The old bird did not call you a Yankee."

Dixie laughed. "She didn't, but I was waiting for her to."

Jules laughed again and reached out for the backpack that she had been hauling around with her for the last few days. I growled a little under my breath. It was such a simple gesture, a basic act of chivalry, and I hadn't thought to do that for her the entire time we had been together. I'd been home for less than a day and already I was being reminded of the ways I wasn't ever going to live up to the example Julian had set for me.

"Did you tell her your name is Dixie? That might have softened her up a little bit. You can't be a Yankee when you're named after the south."

Dixie smiled up at him and shook her head, which sent her curls bouncing. "We didn't get that far. She gave Church the what for and told him that she would throw herself down the stairs a hundred more times if that's what it took to finally get him home. She was equal parts impressive and terrifying."

Jules nodded in agreement and paused at the front door. It was like stepping back in time. I remembered the first time we walked across that doorstep as a family. I also remembered the first time Jules and I walked over it grieving my mother, both of us at a loss as to what we should do with a newborn. I remembered him bringing Caroline over for the first time and refusing to come out of my room to say hello to her. I remembered her tripping and stumbling, sick from chemo and still trying to reassure me that she would be all right. All the memories raced around, the good colliding with the bad. The happy getting shredded by the sorrow that was so much sharper.

"She's protective of both my boys. She never wanted Dash to leave, none of us did. She's going to be greedy and possessive now that he's back. She'll warm up. Just give it some time." Jules talked like Dixie was going to be around forever. She cast a look over her shoulder at me and I silently wished that was the case. Forever and her right in the center of it weren't the worst things that could happen to me even if I was pretty sure *I* was the worst thing that could happen to her.

"Dixie has a life and a job back in Denver she has to get back to, Jules. She agreed to ride down with me so we could extend our good-bye, but she isn't staying." I was surprised that the thought of letting her go of my own free will hurt almost as much as letting go of a loved one when I had no choice in the matter.

Jules gave me a hard look as he unlocked the door and pushed it open. He shifted his attention back to Dixie and his expression softened because it was impossible to be anything but soft with her, well, impossible for everyone but me, but luckily she seemed to like it when I was hard. "Well, if that's the case I suggest you make the most of the time you do have while you're here together. Let Elma fawn all over Dash. Help her out, but don't make her feel like she's an invalid, and make sure she gets her tea in the afternoon. Take a minute to make sure her garden is watered and her flowers are tended and you'll have a fast friend. She knows how to Skype now so don't be surprised if she wants to keep in touch after you head back to the mountains."

"I'll keep all of that in mind. Thanks for the tips."

Jules said something else but it was drowned out by the rush of blood into my head and the whoosh of it in my ears as I was engulfed in memories and history when I finally stepped into the house.

The neighborhood and the surrounding city might have changed but the home where I had grown up hadn't. Sure, there was a new couch and a massive flat screen in the living area but the pictures on the walls that showed a happy family and then another happy family were all the same. There were no signs of either of those families being ripped apart and tattered. There were smiling faces and joy. No signs of everything that had been lost and buried. Jules was focused on what he'd had, not on what he'd lost.

There were new additions as well. Pictures of me in my football uniform and pictures of Dalen in his. Even with me being gone and communication between the two of us sparse and stilted it was obvious Jules wanted reminders of both his children front and center in his home. That knowledge hit me like a punch right in the center of my chest. It hit me so hard that I had to put a hand on the wall to brace myself as I stumbled over my feet. All this time I thought he would be disappointed in the way I left, in the way I abandoned him and Dalen to deal with the same grief we shared on their own. Those pictures made it seem like he was as proud of me now as he was when I stood by his side both times he married the women he loved.

"You all right, son?" I was going to nod in response when a teenager that was almost as tall as me came around the corner. Tall and lanky, Dalen in person bore a striking resemblance to me when I was the same age. He had the same darker than gold skin tone and the same not quite brown or blond hair color as I did. His features took strongly from his father, but his eyes were like mine, a hazel that borrowed heavily from the ocean blue that his mother had been blessed with. He wasn't a baby or a little boy anymore. He was a young man, a teenager with an obvious chip on his shoulder if the way he narrowed his eyes at me and tilted his head in blatant challenge was any indication. I'd missed watching my little brother grow up, missed watching him become someone that I knew I would be proud of, and while the desert was an easy place to forget about that, here in this house where I had grown up it was impossible to ignore.

I felt my mouth open, but no words came out. My brother and I stared at each other, me stunned and in shock as the real ramifications of my disappearance slammed into me hard enough to knock me over. Dalen didn't look happy or relieved to see me, and I couldn't blame him. I was a stranger . . . made one through my own bad choices.

"Hi. I'm Dalen." He took a step towards Dixie and extended a hand. She gave the massive paw a shake and smiled at him. His voice was deep like Jules's and echoed the same strong southern tones that colored all of our speech. The boy was good-looking and polite. I had a pang of worry that this town couldn't appreciate everything he had going for him the way they had squandered my distinctive contributions. I never felt like I belonged anywhere until I joined the army and I didn't want that for him.

"It's nice to meet you. I'm Dixie. I'm a friend of your brother's."

Dalen shot me a look from the corner of his eye as he let Dixie's hand fall. "I would say I've heard a lot about you but that would be a lie. We haven't heard much about anything where Dash is concerned in a long time. I had Calvin's mom stop so I could pick up some barbecue for dinner when she picked us up after practice." He turned so that his back was to me and asked Jules with scorn clearly threaded into his tone, "I already ate. Is it cool if I go do homework in my room?"

He didn't want to be around me. I sucked in a sharp breath and gave Jules a little chin lift when he looked at me over his other son's head. I wasn't about to force the boy to endure my company or any kind of brotherly bonding.

"That's fine but you aren't going to make a habit of hiding out while your brother is home. I haven't had both my boys under the same roof in way too long. You're going to indulge your old man and let me enjoy having my family all together." He clapped the teen on the shoulder and gave him a little shake. "We've got to get Dash out to one of your games while he's here."

Dalen snorted in a very teenaged way and stepped away from Jules. He shot me a scathing look and turned on his heel. "Like he suddenly cares what's going on in our lives. He's more worried about what's happening to strangers in a different country than he is about what's happening here. He wouldn't have bothered to come home if Elma Mae hadn't hurt herself." The words were sharp and cutting. They were also far too cynical to come from someone so young.

"Dalen." Jules didn't even bother to sound like he was going to lay into the boy for putting the truth out there but he did sound exasperated, which let me know this wasn't the first time my little brother had mentioned how he truly felt about my absence in his life.

I held up a hand before Jules could launch into dad mode. "It's cool. Dalen doesn't have to hang around if he doesn't want to. He's old enough to decide who he invests his time and energy in. I made some hard choices when I was close to his age and I can't stand here and say I don't regret most of them. I'm not going to force my company on you, Dalen, and I'm not going to ask you to pretend like you're happy to see me if you aren't."

The kid gave me a look over his shoulder that spoke volumes. I had secret fears and insecurities that I struggled to keep at bay, so did my little brother, and me being home had more than mine rearing up and fighting to break free. He left us standing in the entryway locked in an awkward silence.

Jules sighed and lifted a hand so that he could rub it over the top of his head. "Sorry about that. I guess I shoulda warned you that he's been a little out of sorts since I told him you were on your way home. He was so young when you shipped out . . . I don't think he remembers that he used to look at you like you hung the moon and the stars."

I grunted and reached for Dixie's bag that he was still holding on to. "Can't say I blame him. I did a shit job trying to be a part of his life these last ten years. I'd be pissed if I was in his shoes. You want this stuff in my old room?"

He dipped his chin in a nod. "Yeah. Haven't changed it much since you left. Guess I wanted it to be familiar when you came back." A wry grin tugged at his mouth and made his goatee twitch. "Reminds me of the good ole days when I stick my head in there."

I cringed. "We had good ole days? I don't recall those." They were obscured by too much tragedy and misfortune. The bad memories tended to engulf the good ones. They fed on them like hungry vultures and left nothing but bones picked clean.

"Then you need to try harder, son. You two go and get settled. I'll leave dinner in the kitchen. Don't feel like you have to rush on my account. It sounds like you had a long trip to get here."

I grabbed Dixie's hand and tugged her down the hallway to where my childhood bedroom was located. There were more pictures on the walls that made my knees weak and that had my heart trying to turn itself inside out. Those were the good ole days that Jules wanted me to remember, and the days I had tried my damnedest to forget. There was no outrunning the past. Somehow and someway it always managed to catch up to you, and when it did you were so tired from all the running that when it wrapped its arms around you there was no possible chance of evading it again. It held on too tightly.

"Jules and Dalen have the rooms on the other side of the house. The bathroom is across the hall here." I pointed to a closed door that was a few feet down from the door that was cracked open to reveal the time capsule that was my old bedroom.

"Oh my." Dixie's voice broke on a laugh as she followed me into the blue-painted room that really hadn't been touched since I was a teenager.

Luckily I'd always been a big guy, so the bed that was covered in a dark blue and white striped comforter was queen-sized, but that was the only sight for sore eyes in the space. There were still trophies from when I played high school sports on the dresser, along with an outdated video game system that some hipster would probably pay an arm and a leg for now. There were posters of hip-hop artists and sexy pop singers on the walls that hadn't had hits in a decade. Tucked into the side of the mirror that hung over a small desk with a computer on it that probably ran the first version of Windows were snapshots of a much younger me and the few friends I did have back in the day.

"He really didn't touch anything in here did he?" I tossed her backpack on the bed as she wandered over to the mirror and started looking at the pictures pinned there. "You're actually smiling." She ran her finger over the image of me and the girl whose name I couldn't remember that I took to senior prom. I only went because Caroline forced me to and I was only smiling because even when she was sick it was impossible not to around her. She told me I needed to get out of the house and that no son of hers was going to spend his last year of high school on death watch. Always looking out for me, just like the woman shooting me a look over her shoulder and muttering sarcastically, "I wasn't sure you knew how to do that."

Right after that prom picture was when I'd run to the closest recruitment office and signed my life away. It was the day that I knew for certain that it wasn't better to love and lose than to never love at all. You could survive without love. It was a hollow, empty existence, but it hurt less than living each and every day knowing what you were missing, knowing how awful it was to love someone and lose them.

"It's so weird to see this and know you were a normal teenager at some point in your life. I can't get my head around you being anything but broody and badass."

I ran a hand over my face and took my jacket off and tossed

it on the bed next to where her stuff had landed. "Well, I'm sure you weren't this much of a ray of sunshine before your dad got hurt. Our experience shapes who we are, good and bad."

She shrugged a little and tapped a finger on a picture of me as a teen with Jules and a pretty blonde woman who wasn't my mother holding on to a baby Dalen. "I always tried to focus on the positive instead of the negative, even before my dad got hurt. I let it out a little more after the accident. I stayed buoyant and refused to sink like everyone else that seemed all too willing to drown in their own sorrows. My experience maybe should have changed that but I'm glad it didn't." She changed the subject so quickly it took me a minute to catch up with her. "Who is this woman? You're older in these pictures, so it can't be your mom."

I walked over so that I was standing directly behind her. That picture had the air locking in my lungs and my hands curling into fists at my sides. "That's Caroline."

She sucked in an audible breath. "Oh." She cocked her head to the side and a soft smile toyed at the corners of her mouth. "She looks really happy with you, Church."

I sighed and moved away from her to sit on the edge of the bed. "She was, when I finally let her in."

I heard her soft gasp but I couldn't look up at her. Her experience should have dampened her spirits. It should have knocked some of that constant cheer out of her but she refused to be defined by the hand fate dealt her. She was a thousand times stronger than I was. I took what fate handed me and let it not only define the way I would live my life but also dictate the man I would become. "When Jules first started dating her he didn't tell me. Can't say I blamed him, I was a little shit when my mom first brought him around. I guess I didn't like to share." I rubbed a hand over my face and looked at the floor between my feet. "Wasted a lot of time being angry that the people that I loved and that loved me were happy when I wasn't. I treated Jules like an interloper and he didn't want that for the woman that did her best to keep him together when my mom passed. He taught me better but I still acted like an idiot. I didn't want him to replace my mom and I didn't want another woman in my life that might eventually matter. I had Elma and that was good enough."

The bed dipped as she sat down next to me on the mattress. Her tiny hand covered both of mine where they were clutched together between my legs, my knuckles white as I squeezed them together. I looked at our hands until our skin blurred. "Couldn't not love Caroline. She was sweet, sunny, and soft. She never tried to force her way in but one day she was . . . all the way in. I was looking for her in the mornings, I was rushing home from school to have her help me with homework. She put a Band-Aid on my broken heart and I didn't even realize that's what she was doing. She pulled this family back together and she did it with nothing more than a smile. I had to love her and when I knew I was going to lose her it killed something inside of me. I hated myself for making her earn my love at first and I hated myself for letting that love take root. I already knew how it felt to lose a mom and I never wanted to go through it again."

She rested her head on my shoulder and a soft sigh whooshed out and tickled my neck. "You had to do that twice. That's two times too many, Church."

I agreed. "I was a little bastard to my mom when she picked Jules. I was a little asshole to Caroline when Jules picked her. I wasted time with both of them for nothing. I've had good handed to me, hell I've had the best, two great women that loved me and raised me right, but I've also lost that goodness and I'm not willing to go through it ever again. I keep anything that might be good, that might make me happy at bay and I do it knowing I'm not a man that's strong enough to survive another blow. Pushed my own little brother away because that was easier than thinking about having him ripped away." I tilted my head so that my cheek rested on her curls and told her the truth about the man I was. I was a coward, not a hero. "Left the only person in the world that ever picked me, the man that chose me, in the dust because I woke up in the middle of the night choking on fear thinking about the things that could happen to him while he was on the job. I was almost a full-grown man when I made the choice to run away from home because it hurt too bad to be here and I abandoned everyone that needed me so I could fight monsters that made sense. If I was going to be surrounded by death I figured it might as well be in a place where it wasn't a shock to lose someone." I ran a hand over my face. "You didn't let your circumstances ruin you when your world got turned upside down. I let mine destroy me. I wasn't a son anymore. I wasn't a brother or friend. I refused to be a boyfriend or a partner. I became a soldier, a man that forgot the past and refused to focus on the future. All that mattered was the moment and staying alive. I refused to be all those things that I had been before the army because I was bad at being them. I was a good soldier. Even on the worst days I was still good at war."

She was crying. Silent tears rolled off the ends of lashes that were spiked together with moisture. I didn't want her to cry for me. I didn't deserve her sympathy but I knew her heart was too soft for the kind of brutal kick to the teeth my past carried with it. I leaned towards her and touched my lips to the crest of her damp cheek. I heard her breath shudder out as she sighed and leaned into the touch of my lips.

"You weren't bad at being all the things you were before you became a soldier, Church. Life just made being them more challenging for you than they typically are for everyone else." One of her hands reached up to curl around the side of my neck and I felt her fingers trace the line of my pulse that pounded there.

"You don't need to make excuses for me, Dixie. I know what I did was wrong. I know I took the coward's way out. Sometimes I think I'm going to choke on self-loathing. It tastes bad and it lingers for a long time. I buried my head in the sand and pretended that all the bad things happening here didn't affect me. One look from Dalen, the distance between Jules and I, there is no getting around the fact that I fucked up. They needed me here and I needed to be anywhere else."

Her hand slid around the back of my neck and her fingers scraped over the short hair at the back of my head. It was soothing. She was trying to tame the vicious sorrow that howled and pawed at my insides like a wild, living thing.

"You were a scared kid, Church, and yeah, maybe you were kind of a bratty one but you were still just a kid. A lot of kids act out when their parents introduce a new dynamic into the fold. I can't say that I blame you for wanting to run or for wanting to find a place where loss and devastation make sense. Especially after having suffered so much. It takes a big man to recognize the mistakes he's made and try to repair the damage he has done. You are moving in the right direction now."

I kissed her on the tip of her nose and lifted a hand so that I could wrap it around her slender wrist. "You will always see the best in people even when they give you every reason imaginable not to."

She exhaled softly and moved her head so that her lips were touching mine. "All I see is what you're showing me, Church." The kiss was swift and not nearly enough. "Now let's go eat and spend some time with your dad. You have fences to mend."

She slid off the bed and held out a hand so that she could tug me to my feet. I could still feel the sting of those memories all across my insides but when I rose to my feet and towered over her I also felt lighter. This time when her arms wrapped around my waist in a hug I managed not to screw it up and embraced her back.

It felt as natural as breathing. I thought distance was the answer to keeping myself safe from all that bad that was lurking, I was starting to wonder if I was very, very wrong.

Chapter 11

Dixie

Dinner was tense and a little bit painful. It was clear both father and son were trying but the damage had been done and the road back to uniting this family was rocky and being navigated in the dark. They found common ground talking about how the town had grown and discussing the fact that it had taken the rest of Jules's shift to get the missing-persons report on me revoked. Jules joked that we were lucky we hadn't been pulled over on the way here from the hospital. Church didn't think it was funny. It was weird and a lot concerning. Disgruntled and disgusted looks from strangers were one thing, going out of the way to cause trouble and strife for a stranger based solely on the color of their skin was another. I didn't like anything about it and I hated that both Church and Jules acted like it was nothing new.

Dalen stuck his head in the dining room and asked his dad for help with his homework. It was an obvious ploy to tear Julian's attention away from Church but neither man called him out on it. Church was going to have his work cut out for him with his younger brother and I wondered if either sibling could see how unmistakably similar they were. Church clearly looked up to and idolized his father and had pushed him away for complicated reasons I still didn't fully have my head wrapped around. Dalen noticeably looked up to his big brother but was viewing his tentative homecoming with understandable skepticism. They were two apples that had not fallen far from the very handsome tree that had raised them.

I offered to do the dishes and told Church to take the bathroom first. The Harley meant I'd had to pack creatively for the trip south and I was out of wardrobe reinforcements, so I asked Jules if it was okay if I borrowed his laundry room. He nodded absently as he headed towards the opposite side of the house from where Church and I were staying. Church told me he would find something for me to sleep in for the night and took the chore of laundry out of my hands by mixing a load of his stuff and my stuff together before disappearing into the bathroom. I waited until I heard the shower shut off before starting the dishwasher and wasn't surprised at all when my phone rang and Kallie's number was the one that flashed on the screen.

I made my way to the front steps of the sprawling house and blinked in surprise as bugs with glowing backsides swirled around me the minute I sat down.

"I already told you I'm not getting into the middle of this with you and Wheeler." I didn't even give her a chance to launch into her defense. I didn't want to hear it.

"I went to try and talk to him today. He was with another girl." She was crying and sniffling. If I hadn't known that she was the chef behind this particular shit stew, I would have felt really sorry for her.

"He does not have some girl in my apartment, Kallie. I've known Wheeler for years and I don't believe he's the type to jump into a revenge fuck. You broke his heart . . . again."

"He was with another girl and she was gorgeous. She answered the door and then bolted when I demanded to know who she was. Apparently she's your neighbor."

I sighed and put my forehead in my hand. I didn't even want to think about how terrified Poppy probably had been when she was faced with my sister's misguided wrath. "Poppy. She's watching Dolly for me while I'm gone. She was probably just over to get more dog food or some of Dolly's toys. She wasn't there with Wheeler. Not that you get a say in who he spends time with after what you did."

There was a soft sob on the other end of the phone. "I have eyes, Dixie. It didn't look innocent."

I heaved a sigh. There was no way I was going to waste the breath it would take to explain why it wasn't possible that there was anything going on between Wheeler and my stunning neighbor. Kallie was too caught up in her own drama to have the empathy Poppy's situation called for.

"You need to leave Wheeler alone, sis. It's time to go your separate ways. You can't care more about him after you threw him away than you did while you had him in your grasp. He deserves better than that."

She hiccupped a little and I heard her blow her nose. I moved the phone away from my ear and made a face. "What about me, Dixie? What about what I deserve? I've been with Wheeler since I was fourteen. I've loved him since before I understood what love was."

I swore under my breath and pushed my hair off my forehead.

"You screwed up more than once, Kallie. He forgave you the first time. I don't think it's fair to expect him, or the rest of us for that matter, to keep forgiving you for the same mistake. You should only have to touch a hot stove once to know that it's going to burn."

"I don't know what I'm going to do without him." She sounded genuinely terrified and I couldn't blame her. He'd made her life pretty easy up until this point and now she was going to have to figure out that her actions had some really harsh consequences.

"You should have thought about that when you went to bed with a guy that wasn't him then." I didn't mean to scold her but I couldn't stop the censure from creeping into my voice. I was really disappointed in her and in her choices. Even I was having a hard time finding the silver lining this go-around.

The line went silent and I almost hung up because I thought she had disconnected. I barely heard her when she whispered, "It was a girl."

I dropped the phone. It hit the cement and bounced. I was sure the screen was going to be shattered when I picked it up and breathed a sigh of relief when it was still intact. "Did you just say what I think you said?"

It was Kallie's turn to sigh. "I didn't cheat on him with another guy, it was a girl. The first time I was unfaithful it was because I thought something was missing in the relationship. Our sex life has always been fine. Wheeler is sexy and very intent on making sure things are good, but I wasn't into it and he could tell. I thought it was me. I thought we'd outgrown one another." She sniffed again and I mumbled her name softly. "I hated it. I hated the sex with the other guy so much. I hated that it hurt Wheeler. I hated myself. It was awful. When Wheeler agreed to take me back and we got engaged I told myself I was going to make it work no matter what. I thought something was wrong with me and that if I ignored it, it would go away."

"Why didn't you say something to someone, Kallie?" She was around when I was in high school and crushing hard on Remy Archer. I had had a thing for Rule and Rome's brother for the longest time. I'd taken my shot at a party one weekend and cornered the handsome and preppy half of the Archer twins and stolen my first kiss. It had been exactly like Kallie described. Fine. There were no fireworks, the world didn't move, and it was clear I was way more into it than Remy was. Years later after Remy had passed away and Rule had married his best friend the news that Remy had been gay had made the rounds. It was far from shocking and all of us that knew Remy when he was younger wished he hadn't had to spend so much of his life pretending to be something he wasn't. My tummy flipped itself into knots thinking that my sister had put herself in the same boat.

"Because I didn't know what was going on, Dixie. I love Wheeler, I really do. I love the life I have with him, but I met Roni and . . . sparks. Seriously, sis, I felt like I'd been living in black and white and she flipped the switch and everything was suddenly in color. I didn't want to hurt Wheeler but I couldn't say no to something that felt so right either."

Good people usually have a reason for doing bad things. Church's words hammered into my head as I gave another sigh.

"You have to tell Wheeler, and you need to be honest with Mom and Dad." That would go a long way towards making this situation more understandable.

"I didn't mean for any of this to happen. I went to talk to Wheeler today and I saw him with that girl and I realized everything I was going to lose and panicked. I don't know how to live a different kind of life than the one I've always lived."

She was wrong. "That's not true. We all learned how to live different lives when Dad was hurt. It takes some time and it isn't easy but eventually you figure it out. We'll all figure it out as family just like we did before. Obviously the experience you had with this Roni was worth everything you might lose. Don't diminish that because you're scared of the fallout that comes from such a major change."

"It's scary, Dixie. I don't want to lose anyone's love." She sounded like a scared little girl.

"You won't lose it, Kallie. Love doesn't go away because the person it's attached to has changed. It simply changes with them. I'm sorry I'm not there to give you a hug. It sounds like you could really use one."

She gave a dry laugh, and I could clearly picture her pulling herself up. "I could use a hug, but I guess it's time I put on my big-girl panties and try and fix the mess I made. Telling you the truth was a huge step, and it didn't hurt half as bad as I thought it was going to. You're right, you know." She blew out a breath. "The experience with Roni was worth losing everything. I had to have it in order to know that what I had with Wheeler was never going to work out in the long run. I did it the wrong way, but it was the right choice to make. I miss you. I hope you're coming home soon."

"Soon enough. I'm just a phone call away if you need me." We chatted for a few more minutes and when I hung up I was exhausted and felt like I had been emotionally drained. I made my way back into the house, and sent a silent thank-you towards the ceiling when the bathroom was empty and waiting for me.

There was a folded-up T-shirt on the edge of the sink that Church had left for me and it felt so good to strip out of my tank top and jeans that I had to take a minute to stretch out all my tired limbs. The sexual tension and stiffness from being on the back of the bike was rigid in my muscles and tendons. I couldn't wait to stand under the hot water and loosen up.

I scrubbed my hair with shampoo that smelled like mint and rubbed my body down with something that smelled like it was designed to cover up teenaged-boy stink. It made me laugh and when I got out and dried off I laughed even harder when I noticed that the shirt Church left for me appeared to be a jersey from when he was younger. It was an unflattering mustard yellow with maroon writing on the back that spelled out his last name and had the number twenty-one. Clearly he had always been giant-sized because the hem fell almost to my knees and made the fact that I was sans underwear more tolerable as I bolted across the hallway and into his room.

I figured Church would be in the living room watching TV or even better talking to his dad but he was standing in front of the mirror that had the pictures tucked into it. His expression was wistful and far away but the second his eyes locked on me they flared to life with an internal heat that was hot enough to scald my damp skin.

"Go team." I meant for it to be funny and lighthearted but the words came out breathless and laced with an invitation I wasn't a hundred percent sure I was ready to extend.

His eyes took a leisurely perusal over my wet hair and down to my bare toes. When he was done his lips twitched so hard that the smile trapped there almost broke free. "I played for a few years. Nothing serious like Dalen is involved in. I liked the cheerleaders, and it was easier to talk them out of their skirts if I had a jersey on." His lips twitched again and this time his teeth flashed as well. It was a sorry excuse for a grin but it was a grin just the same. "I guess I've always had a thing for girls that have spirit and pep." He reached out a finger and hooked it in the neck of the jersey. He gave the fabric a tug. I took a step towards him knowing that he was getting a pretty nice view down the shirt. It made my skin pebble up and had my breath catching in my lungs. "I used to try and sneak girls in here all the time. When your old man is a cop that doesn't work so well. Gotta say the one I finally got in here puts all the others to shame. You look good wrapped up in my memories, Dixie."

He made it so hard to resist him. He made the space that I knew I needed feel useless and painful. He made the way I wanted him and the way he admitted to needing me seem like the beginning and ending of everything that existed between us. We were nothing more than two entities that craved one another, that lived to satisfy and to surrender to the other. Desire made the fact that he was the wrong Mr. Right seem inconsequential and insignificant.

"You look good when you let your memories make you happy, Church." I gasped a little as his fingers skated over my collarbone and over the top curve of my breast. His jersey was giving him easy access to all the things I should be keeping out of his reach. My nipples pulled tight and beaded into hard points as he reached past my head and shut the door with a definitive click.

"You're a memory that will always make me think about good things, pretty girl. I'm not so sure you will be able to say the same thing about me." His hand lifted and curled around the side of my throat. His thumb pressed against the line of my jaw so that I had to tilt my head back and look up at him. His eyes swirled with too many feelings to put names to but the lighter colors at the center lit up and I felt the warmth from that like a touch on every single part of my exposed skin. "Your Mr. Right will come along and you'll forget about me but I will always, and I do mean always, remember every single second we spent together."

I was going to give in to him because I was tired of trying to fight against something I wanted so desperately anyways. I had to have him, whatever part of himself he was willing to give me because I couldn't not have it when he was the one offering it. Happy for now was all we were going to get and that was going to have to be enough. I was going to have to accept my own version of the fairy tale, including the ending that didn't have me getting everything I wanted. There would be no cute story or shared smiles to hand down to my own kids because whatever and whoever came after Church wasn't going to be the one my heart recognized as its own. There would never be any forgetting him, there would simply be loving him differently after he broke my heart. The poor, fractured thing would never work the same once he was done with it.

I lifted my hand up and circled his wrist. I smiled up at him and took a step closer. I felt my thighs clench and the center of my body throb the closer I got to him. His chest rose and fell, rubbing against the silky finish of the jersey and dragging the slick fabric across my puckered nipples.

He dipped his head and his extraordinarily long lashes dropped to shade his vibrant eyes. "I tried really hard to do the friend thing, Dixie. The second you put my dick in your mouth you made that impossible. I never wanted to let anyone else in, but every time I give you another piece of the past I feel you there . . . all the way in."

His words send a fiery trail of delight zapping down my spine. I wanted to be in because he was all the way in with me. In under my skin. In, buried between each erratic beat of my heart. In deep within all the places that throbbed and ached at nothing more than the sound of his honeyed drawl. It hurt that he didn't look thrilled about the fact I was getting to him the way he got to me, but I was all about taking what I could get when it came to him. "I want to make you smile. Focus on the good instead of the bad and remember how to smile, Church."

I wanted that almost as much as I wanted him to love me back.

I let out a strangled yelp as one of his hands snaked around my back and slipped under the bottom of the jersey. His palm landed on a lot of naked ass as he jerked me to him, the front of his jeans digging into my stomach and letting me know he was ready, willing, able to make good on his promise to give me better than I ever had before.

"Give me something good to smile about and I'll see what I can do for you, pretty girl."

Challenge accepted.

I lifted up on my toes and planted my lips over his as his hand worked its way over my backside and up along my spine, taking his jersey with it. In a matter of seconds, I was naked in front of him and being devoured by his hungry gaze. He took a step towards me, which forced me to take a step back. He leered at me the entire time he advanced and I got the distinct feeling that I was being herded and hunted towards the exact spot where he wanted me. There was something infinitely arousing about being pursued by a man that you knew very rarely had to work for his prey. I liked the idea of being a challenge, especially considering how much work it had been for me to get even the smallest peek into those shadows that obscured who he really was.

The back of my knees hit the bed and down I went. Before I could catch my breath he was on his knees between my spread legs, using his wide shoulders as leverage to keep me open and exposed. He used his hands to pull me to the very edge of the bed and bent his head so that he could rub the scruff on his chin along the super sensitive skin of my inner thigh. It made me tingle. It made my core clench and my tummy muscles tighten. He was staring at me like he wanted to eat me up and couldn't decide which part of me he wanted to put his mouth on first.

"You are without a doubt the prettiest thing I've ever seen, Dixie." He trailed a rough fingertip around the side of my knee and up the inside of my thigh until he reached the damp folds that were slick and glistening with anticipation. My entire body jolted at the light touch and I practically came up off the bed as that dangerous digit took a sudden detour and slipped inside my aching center. "And you feel like a fucking dream. So hot. So tight. So goddamn wet and ready for me. If I'd known you felt this good there's no way I would have wasted my first shot at having you by fucking that smart mouth of yours. You're good with your mouth but this pussy is as close to heaven as I've ever been."

I blinked because I wasn't used to hearing him say so much and I definitely wasn't used to having him say such delightfully dirty things to me. The way his drawl dragged the words out and made them roll across my already overly stimulated skin had my hands curling in the covers and hips canting upwards chasing each syllable and breath.

"I liked having you in my mouth." I was panting and breathing in a choppy rhythm that made talking hard. He added another finger to my now drenched opening and used the pad of his thumb to circle that little hidden nub of pleasure that was swollen and reaching for his attention.

"Good. Because I plan on being there as much as possible in the next few days, that is when I'm not buried in all this sweetness you have waiting for me right here." His fingers pumped in and out, trailing moisture in their wake and making me squirm. It was a simple caress but coming from him it felt like the first time I had ever been touched. "Been a lot of places over the last few years. Never found one where I wanted to stay." His thumb pressed down on my throbbing clit and it made me want to scream. Acutely aware that his brother and father were somewhere not too far away I balled up a fist and shoved it in my mouth. My teeth sank into the skin hard enough to leave impressions, which made him chuckle. "I could stay right here, right where you are so pretty and pink forever. You can't control the way you want me and that makes me feel like king of everything. I could convince myself that I belong between your legs, Dixie."

My whole body was quaking as he felt me up and used his fingers to fuck me. He was watching everything, every little tick and movement. I'd never been under such intimate and intense scrutiny before. It made my blood feel too thick for my veins and it had all of my muscles quivering as my nerve endings popped and fizzled with awareness. He was driving me towards the edge relentlessly and he wanted to watch as he shoved me over. He was ushering me towards an orgasm that we both knew was going to be unforgettable and he had no plans to stop before I reached the breaking point.

With a fist still in my mouth and my legs shifting restlessly where they were propped up on his shoulders I couldn't control my other hand from finding the tender tip of one of my breasts. My nipples were beaded little points that were starving for some kind of attention. I caught the turgid peak between my fingers and gave it a little tug. I felt the response all the way down to my toes and I heard Church growl low in his throat when the slippery channel he was torturing with his skilled touch spasmed and pulsed around his moving fingers. Clearly he liked that and wanted to see for himself what my pleasure tasted like.

Those thick, questing fingers disappeared only to be replaced by a probing and swirling tongue. I gasped into my hand as my fingers lost their ability to play under the onslaught of sensation that followed his first lick. My back arched up and my thighs clamped down around the sides of his head. His teeth grazed my clit with the softest bite I had ever felt and everything inside my body became nothing more than points of light that sparked and flickered where he touched and tasted. I was going to do exactly the same thing he claimed he regretted and waste my first shot at having him by coming in his very talented mouth. He seemed determined to even the playing field but I wanted him inside me, I wanted my body surrounding every inch of that impressive erection that was straining the front of his pants the first time he dropped me over the edge and into oblivion.

He was using the tip of his tongue to rapidly flick the distended flesh of my clit, so I had a hard time making words work when I told him to stop. Immediately his head lifted and he pulled back so that my legs fell off of his shoulders. I knew I had to move quickly before he got the wrong idea, so I gathered strength I didn't have and stumbled from missing coordination as I slid off the edge of the bed and onto his lap. We stared at each other with chests heaving and I grabbed at his shirt and tried to get it off over his head. I sighed in delight when he did that thing that only guys seemed able to do by grabbing it in one hand at the back of his collar and yanking it off. My hands tingled in excitement as all that golden, perfectly imperfect flesh was bared to my greedy touch.

I lowered my head and grazed my lips over a particularly nasty scar that ran along the line of his collarbone.

"I want my first shot at having you to be me and you together. I want you inside of me. I want to know how we feel when we're together."

He made a noise that might have been a laugh, but then he put a hand on the side of my face and leaned in so that he could kiss me. All the desire I had for him was there on his lips. The way he made me want and the way he made me need slid across my mouth as he kissed me deep. My back was against the bed and the mattress moved with our weight as he pressed closer into me and reached for his leather jacket. I kissed him back as he fumbled around in the pockets and took my fill of tracing across all his bunching and flexing muscles as he held me on his lap and frantically looked for something in the dark.

The metallic wrapper of a condom glinted dimly but the flash of teeth as Church grinned at me shone like a thousand-watt bulb. It wasn't a full smile, but it was something. There was no mistaking that this moment between us had him forgetting that he wasn't the type of guy that grinned.

"I knew these would come in handy. Always pays off to be battle ready." I wasn't sure that I appreciated having sex with me compared to combat but I was too busy getting his pants undone and pulling out his rigid cock to engage in a war of words.

His erection pulsed heavy and hard in my hand. The head already slick with precum and pointing at me like it knew I had the perfect place for it to go. I circled the rounded flesh with my thumb and bit my bottom lip as it kicked eagerly in my hands. Church handed me the condom and I could see the golden part of his eyes gleaming at me. There was no going back to pretending that I was nothing more than his friend after this, not that I had done such a great job at pretending before I had his dick in my hands.

I ripped the foil packet open with my teeth and took the time to cover his considerable length. I was glad he was prepared because safe sex hadn't even crossed my mind when I decided to jump into the oncoming disaster feetfirst. I'd like to think I had enough common sense that when it came to sealing the deal I would have held off until both of us were safe but he went to my head faster than a shot of tequila, so who's to say I wouldn't have made this already terrible decision even worse by not being able to say no even when I really, really needed to.

The denim of his jeans was rough against my thighs when he lifted me up a little and dragged me closer to his proudly erect cock. There was something a little sensual about being totally naked and uncovered while he still had the majority of his clothes on. It was kind of reflective of how we both approached our relationship. I'd been transparent and uncovered with the way I felt about him from the beginning and while he was starting to reveal parts of himself to me, there were still big portions that he kept covered up.

The tip of his cock dragged enticingly through my wet folds.

The thick head nudged playfully against my still-sensitive clit and it made my eyes roll back in my head. He repeated the motion a couple of times as I wrapped an arm around his shoulders and rocked my hips into the teasing caress. My body was begging for him and he seemed to like torturing it. I mewed in desperation and dug my fingers into the back of his neck. I kissed him hard and let my teeth drag across his plush bottom lip.

Finally, he used his thumb to angle his rigid length towards my now soaked and very eager opening. He slid inside and I panted and shook as he spread me open and split me wide. I'd never been with someone that was as well endowed as Church was. I could feel him . . . everywhere. I could feel him touch every nerve. I could feel every part of my pussy move and stretch to accommodate him. I felt my muscles clench and relax as they worked to pull him deeper and deeper. I could feel every quiver and quake as pleasure coiled along my spine and ripped through my veins. This was more than having sex. This was being claimed. This was being invaded and taken over. This was being conquered by the king of everything and made the queen of all that was important to him.

"I lied." His voice was ragged against the side of my neck. "If there is something better than heaven that's what being inside of you feels like."

He used his hold on my hip to urge me to move. I started sliding up and down, his cock pulling along swollen, sensitive flesh with each downward glide. It made my eyes roll back in my head again and had my toes curling. His free hand skated up the ladder of my ribs and worked its way under the heavy weight of my bouncing breast. His thumb circled my nipple on one side as his head shifted so that he could catch the other one in the heat of his mouth. The dual sensation caused me to throw my head back and moan up at the ceiling. I was well past the point of worrying that someone was going to hear me.

I rode him hard.

I rode him fast.

I rode him wild.

I rode him rough.

I felt his fingers digging into my hip and I knew I was going to have a bruise but I didn't care. His teeth were scratching roughly across my nipple as I panted into his ear with each collision of our bodies. I could feel my orgasm chasing me down. It was pushing, shoving me towards the edge that I was scared to drop over. Once I did I knew the only person that would know where to look for me after I landed was the one driving me towards the verge of a pleasure so intense it was going to change who I was and what I was willing to accept for the rest of my life.

"Church." I whispered his name into the darkness and let my lips skim along the curve of his shoulder. He was salty with sweat and his skin was warm on my lips.

"Goddamn, Dixie, you make it really hard for me to remember why I thought it was a good idea to stay the hell away from you." I squealed in surprise as he suddenly lurched to his feet and maneuvered us onto the bed. He urged me to curl my legs up around his pumping ass as he held on to my hips. I locked my ankles at the small of his back and groaned when he ordered me to put my fingers between my legs. I did as requested, sliding fingers through my own wetness and almost purring in delight when his hardness brushed across the back of my knuckles as he pounded into me.

I used a much lighter touch than he had when I circled my clit.

My fingers barely made contact as I brushed the engorged little nub. I whispered his name again, not really sure if I was asking for more or asking for mercy, either way my little caress was the last step I needed to go over.

My body bucked against his thrusts and clamped down tightly on his pistoning cock. I gushed pleasure and leaked desire in a flood that wouldn't be stopped. He rumbled something animalistic and raw from deep within his chest. He told me that I was better than anything that had been before me. He told me I was beautiful, that I felt beautiful. He promised me that I would feel him in the morning and every time I moved for the next day. He told me that he'd never had anything perfect but if he had to guess what it felt like it would be the two of us together. He was constantly telling me that he was a liar . . . but with him over me, with him inside of me . . . I believed every word he said. The truth was in his hands, in his mouth, in the way his cock moved in and out of me like he couldn't get enough of me . . . or of us together.

When he came his eyes were like a kaleidoscope of passion and pleasure colliding. I got lost in the sheer beauty of everything that was Dash Churchill. It was hard to keep my eyes open but there was nothing that could pull my gaze away.

He was breathing hard and uneven as he braced his big body over mine. He was comfortable in the dark, so I knew he could see me clearly while I struggled to take in everything that was hidden in the dimness.

We watched each other, both changed in unspeakable ways as our heart rates returned to normal. I put my hands on either side of his cheeks and lifted my head so I could give him a kiss. There, against my lips, I felt his lips twitch and move. Slowly at first. Rusty and out of practice. He smiled as I kissed him and I felt it all throughout my soul.

I had given him something good to replace the bad and he had given me something that was going to be cherished and unforgettable when this moment with him was nothing more than my favorite memory.

Chapter 12

Church

I couldn't remember a night that I slept throughout without waking up. My body was trained to doze lightly and to wake when even the slightest thing seemed off. I never rested easy when I was in a new place and I very rarely managed to out-sleep the sun going up even after working the extreme bar hours I'd been keeping as of late. It was an instinct honed over years of catnapping under a sky set on fire by missiles and gunfire. It was a reaction that had saved my ass more than once.

My childhood home wasn't exactly hostile territory and bedding down with Dixie sprawled heavy limbed and orgasm drunk all over the top of me definitely wasn't sleeping with the enemy, but there were enough differences in my usual routine that it should have been a restless night without much shut-eye. The opposite was true. I slept better than I had in ten years. I wrapped my arms around the warm, pliant woman that had blown my mind . . . and other parts of me . . . closed my eyes, and drifted off like I didn't have the kind of history behind me that usually led to nightmares instead of sweet dreams. Granted I was more than worn-out. The reunion with my family, getting an earful from Elma, the puzzle of who was trying to make this trip home more difficult than it already was, all of that weighed heavily on my mind, and then Dixie had her way with the rest of me and every muscle I had, every tendon and bone felt like it had turned to mush. I'd never considered myself a man that had the ability to go soft for a woman, but dammit all if she didn't make me malleable and pliable with nothing more than her sexy moans and wicked demands whispered in my ear. I told her I would give her the best of what I had. I didn't anticipate the need, the overwhelming desire to give her better than my best because that's what she gave me.

I woke up when Jules and Dalen were rambling around the house getting ready for work and school respectively. I heard them down the hallway in the kitchen and contemplated getting up and bringing breakfast back for the woman who was still breathing slowly and evenly into the center of my chest. Her uncontrollable tangle of hair was brushing my chin and sticking to the scruff that I had yet to find the time to shave off. One of her hands was folded under her cheek, lying across my heart, and that little traitor leaped at the knowledge that if I dared to let her hold it there was no way she would handle it with anything but gentle care and delicate reverence. Her other arm was tucked along my side where my arm was curved across the sexy dip of her hip. I had no idea when my palm took up residence on the luscious swell of her ass but I wasn't going to complain about it and I was in no rush to move it.

I liked her goofy T-shirts with their silly sayings that she seemed to prefer sleeping in, but if I had a say she wouldn't be in this bed with me with anything covering her up for the rest of our time together. I was still finding cute little freckles that I hadn't yet put my tongue on and there was no way I would be able to find them all if she was keeping those lush curves of hers hidden.

She had one of her legs cocked at an angle between mine and while my morning erection was always alert and ready to go before I was, this morning it was particularly insistent that I get my shit together and take advantage of the fact that what felt like an endless amount of silken smooth female flesh was pressed against it, warm with sleep and soft from lingering satisfaction. She felt good draped across me. She felt like she belonged there.

My fingers stroked across the supple skin like they had a mind of their own. Dixie mumbled something drowsily and rubbed her nose on the hard line that divided my pecs. The heavy muscle flexed involuntarily, and I sucked in a careful breath as her knee grazed the very sensitive part of my anatomy it was resting against. My dick twitched and lifted, pressing pointedly into her thigh. I couldn't tell if she was on board with this particular wake-up call but the hand along my side moved so that it was resting under my ribs and her freckled cheek brushed against my chest like a kitten searching for affection. I took the hand that was resting behind my head and tunneled my fingers into her fiery mane of hair. I loved the way it coiled and snaked around my fingers. It was the only trap I would walk willingly into time and time again.

"You awake?" My voice was raspier than normal and I could hear the throb of desperation in it. I really, really wanted her to be awake or I wanted to wake her up in a way she wasn't going to be able to forget anytime soon. We'd gone at each other hard last night, several times over. I could feel it in my thighs and in my back, so I had no doubt she was probably sore and tender in all the places I wanted to leave even more marks and memories on. "I know it's before noon, but if you rise and shine I can guarantee you won't regret it." It wasn't lost on me that my asking her to let me in had more than one meaning. I wanted inside all the sweetness that would go wet and ready for me in an instant, but I was also starting to feel like I needed inside, past all the warmth and kindness she had for everyone, to the real heart of her.

The tip of her nose rubbed back and forth over my collarbone as she shook her head and mumbled something else I couldn't make out but her leg shifted between mine again, this time more deliberately. This time it was a caress. This time it was her leg sliding along the underside of my very erect cock, rubbing it up and down, causing it to pulse against her and making me shift my hips under her so I could chase the sensation. She made me desperate and entranced me with very little effort. I'd wanted to take her to bed from the minute I saw her, but now that I had her there it felt so much more significant than getting off and getting a piece of her. It felt like something I had been fighting for, something I had been working towards without even knowing I was taking those steps.

I buried my face in the side of her neck and licked along the creamy column. It was easy to maneuver her so that we were lying face-to-face and I growled in satisfaction against her skin, now damp from my mouth, when her leg moved so that it was on the outside of mine, giving me unfettered access to her pretty, pink center. I was kissing my way up to her ear and rubbing my hands all over her back while retaining my hold on her ass when I vaguely heard the trill of some song I didn't recognize coming from somewhere on the floor.

I was wrapped all around Dixie, I had the tip of my dick nestled perfectly between folds that were warming up and getting slick and ready when she suddenly made a noise that indicated she was no longer half asleep. Her eyes popped open and she stared at me for a minute before her teeth sank into her bottom lip, and she put her hands on my shoulders and pushed back a little bit until I loosened my hold on her enough that she could roll away from me towards the side of the bed. She didn't have her typical morning scowl and blurry-eyed annoyance stamped on her pretty face. It was nice to know if I woke her up with foreplay her claws stayed retracted, not that it bothered me when she sunk them in.

"That's Wheeler. I need to answer it. Some crazy stuff went on with my sister yesterday, and he might need to talk."

I heard her hands patting the floor where everything had landed after our acrobatics on the bed last night. I shook my head to get my thoughts together and frowned at her back even though she couldn't see my sour expression.

"Can't you call him back when it's a better time for you?" I knew she went above and beyond for the people she cared about but there was no missing the way her body responded to mine. She wanted what I was about to give her, half asleep or not.

She looked at me over her shoulder with her strawberry brows pulled into a scowl. I couldn't tell if it was directed at me or at the interruption. "It'll just take a second. I have to be there if he wants to talk."

I scowled right back at her but mine lacked the heat hers had because in her haste to answer the call she forgot to pull the sheet back up and her plump, rosy nipples were poking out at me looking like the most delectable little berries. That was the kind of breakfast in bed I was talking about. My frown quickly morphed into a smirk as I asked her, "What about what *you* want? When do you get to put your own needs first?"

Her scowl deepened as she issued a breathy greeting into the phone. Maybe she didn't like me pointing out that she was always putting others first, but at some point the girl deserved to have hers and damn everyone else. I felt my lips pull upwards as I continued to watch her. Her cheeks heated, and she put a hand out to ineffectively ward me off as I leaned towards her. She wanted me to smile. I wasn't quite there yet but I could grin, and I could do it wickedly and mischievously because I didn't care that she was on the phone trying to fix someone else's life. I cared that she wanted me and there was no reason to deny herself, or me. She deserved to come first every now and again . . . in fact I was going to make it my mission to make sure she came first whenever we were together for the foreseeable future and not just when we were in bed.

"No. Don't chase after Poppy, Wheeler. That's the worst thing you can do. If you go pounding on her door she won't open it." Her eyes widened as I reached for her and started to pull her back across the bed towards me. She held up a hand and shook her head frantically while I continued to grin at her. I ignored her swatting hand as I rolled her much smaller frame under mine and trapped her with my bulk.

She continued to glare at me as I caught the hand that wasn't busy with the phone in one of mine and pinned it to the bed next to her. Her wiggling only served to make a space for me between her legs that I immediately took advantage of. I captured one of the plump, pert tips between my lips and used the tip of my tongue to circle around and around. Her whole body went still and I heard her suck in a breath and then assure the tatted-up caller on the other end of the phone that she was fine.

"I just have something caught in my throat. Why are you worried about how Poppy feels? I know Kallie can be intense, but shouldn't you be concerned with what she came over to tell you and not how the confrontation affected a total stranger?"

I heard a masculine voice rise on the other end of the call and took advantage of the fact that Dixie moved the phone away from her ear to get my mouth on her other breast. I wanted them glistening and wet. I wanted them slippery enough that I could slide my cock between them until the tip touched her lips. That image had me growling around the stiff tip locked between my teeth. The vibration had her legs shifting against mine where I had them immobilized in a different, more restless and less combative, way.

"Uh . . . what? No, no, I'm listening to you and I'm not taking Kallie's side. I just think you need to listen to her. What she has to say isn't going to make the fact she cheated on you hurt any less, but it will go a long way towards both of you finding some kind of closure. I think my neighbor should be the least of your concerns at the moment." Her words were coming out faster and faster. Instead of trying to wiggle away from me she was pressing her chest up into my mouth as I licked across her collarbone and stopped to suck on the hollow at the base of her neck hard enough to leave a mark. She made a pained little sound and moved her legs more aggressively against mine.

Because I wasn't done showing her that she should put her wants and her needs before others' occasionally and because I was enjoying the slow and sweet torture of touching her without having the luxury of having her hands undoing me in turn I wrapped an arm across her chest and rolled us so that her back was plastered all along my front. My throbbing dick found a very happy home nestled along the sexy crevasse of her backside. The rounded flesh pressing into my erection had me sucking in a breath that was loud enough to be heard by the person Dixie was struggling to have a conversation with.

"Jesus, Wheeler. Do you really want me to get into all the ways in which it isn't your business who that was? You have enough on your plate without worrying about me." She swore softly and turned her head to glare at me over her shoulder as I grabbed her knee and propped it up on the outside of mine. She could play at being mad all she wanted, that pussy that was what dreams were made of didn't lie. It was shiny and all kinds of perky and eager. Her desire was evident and I wasn't about to deny either of us the otherworldly gratification we could give to each other. "Listen, I have to go." She sure did. I curled my hand around her knee and lifted it up so that I could prod her swollen entrance with my cock. Her body pulled at me, tugged at my rigid flesh until I couldn't resist the lure and pushed all the way into her. She made a strangled sound that I figured Wheeler had to recognize because a split second later Dixie was muttering, "Talk to Kallie. I'll check on Poppy later. Bye." The phone fell to the bed as I started to thrust slowly in and out of her.

She was still looking at me over her shoulder but the heat that was angry was quickly switching to arousal. "I'm super mad at you right now." The words had no force behind them and I couldn't stop another grin from escaping as the hand that had been using the phone lifted up and bent behind her so that she could hold on to the back of my head as I latched my teeth on to the delicate dip at the base of her neck.

"I don't believe you. You don't feel mad. You feel like you want to come. You feel like you need to come." From this position behind her I couldn't get as deep. My thrusts were shallow, slow and deliberate. I could feel the way my cock dragged across tender flesh and sensitive nerves. It was delicious torture for both of us but there was no way either of us were going to get off with this teasing, taunting pace. "You feel like you want something just for you, Dixie. Take it. You're allowed to come first, pretty girl."

She tossed her head back so hard that I had to jerk my chin out of the way to avoid getting knocked silly. I rubbed my fingers across the gentle swell of her belly, stopped to circle her tiny belly button with my pinky, and then found my way to the spot where we were joined. I slid my fingers through her wetness, spread her slick folds open so I could get my questing fingers on her sweet spot. Her clit leaped at the first press of my fingertips and her entire body arched forward and away from mine as I circled the tender little nub relentlessly. I kissed the back of her neck under the fall of her hair and let out my own strangled sound when one of her clever hands disappeared between us so that every time I moved forward into her heat the base of my cock also slipped along the flat of her palm. She used her fingertip to tickle the ultra-sensitive globes that hung heavy between my legs and I knew I was about at the end of my rope when it came to gentle, playful fucking. I wanted to have an easy touch with this woman who shined so bright but she made me feel savage. She made me want to take, and take, and then take some more. Everything she offered up I wanted more of because I was driven and determined to give it all back to her. I felt like I had something to prove, but I had no clue what that something was.

I played with her clit until I felt her body start to hum and quake around me. I couldn't finish like this but I had no problem holding her and watching her come apart in my arms while she did. Her head turned and her eyes sought mine out, dark with desire and desperation.

"You want me to come first?" Her voice was just a breath of sound as she panted and moved with me.

"I want you to get what you want, period." My words had her body clamping down on mine like a velvet vise. Everything about her was a satin trap I never wanted to escape from. I would happily be her prisoner forever.

"Then I want you to fuck me for real, and I want you to come with me." Well, shit. Just when I thought there wasn't any possible way she could be any more perfect. I might actually be able to make a relationship work if we never had to leave this bed.

I kissed her cheek and chuckled into her soft skin. "I can fuck you if you aren't too sore, but I can't come with you, pretty girl. No more condoms." We'd blown threw my limited supply last night. It was risky being inside her the way I already was but it was a perilous chance I couldn't seem to stop from taking.

"Oh." Her eyes widened and her teeth dug into her bottom lip.

I lifted an eyebrow at her as I pulled out of her welcoming heat leaving a trail of moisture on the inside of her leg. It was a sexy glimmer I didn't seem able to look away from. Before I could tell her that it was fine, that I fully planned on getting her off regardless of any obstacles in our way she turned away from me, braced her hands on the mattress, lifted her gloriously round and perfectly curved ass in the air, and looked at me saucily over her shoulder. She always looked good, cute and charming, but bent over, that slit between her legs shining and wet and her backside ready and arranged for the taking she had never looked better. Her wild hair slid across her pale shoulders and I couldn't stop myself from running my fingers along each dip and divot in her spine.

"I trust you, Church." Her eyes pleaded with me to do the right thing. To tell her this was a bad idea even if she claimed to want it but I kept telling her I wasn't that guy. I wasn't her Mr. Right or even her Mr. Right Now. I was the guy that was going to take her every single way there was to take her until either of those preferred options showed up.

"You shouldn't, but I'm lucky as hell that you do." I fisted a handful of her hair and pulled her head back at the same time I curled my other palm around her hip. I loved that she had a little something there to hold on to. It made her seem less breakable, able to withstand all the things I wanted to put on her.

I leaned into her, curving myself over the tantalizing bow of her back, and pulled her hips back towards mine. She was already wet and ready from my earlier ministrations, so I slid in easily. We both gasped loud and long as I bottomed out, touching places inside of her that made my head spin and had my heart beating erratically. I kept her head pulled back as she rocked into me. I let my lips trail over the side of her neck as I braced myself on the mattress with a locked arm.

I surged into her. Powered myself in and out of her soaking channel as my vision blurred and my lungs burned for air. She bucked back into me, moving against me as violently as I was moving into her. Our bodies slapped together filling the room with the sounds of sex and satisfaction. Thank God I actually knew what to do with her once I finally managed to get a girl naked and under me in this room. I was glad I didn't have any other experience here to compare to this one. Anything before Dixie would be pale and unremarkable in comparison.

She was already primed and close from the way I'd handled her body earlier. She was moaning low and loud. I took a minute to hope that my dad and brother had already left but if they hadn't I didn't care. The noises she made urged me on, begged me to go at her harder, so there was no way I was going to remind her that we possibly weren't alone.

The arch of her neck was so delectable. I wanted my teeth on it. I wanted my hands wrapped around it. I wanted to lick it and suck on it as her blood pumped furiously through her veins. I could see her pulse throbbing under the alabaster color of her skin and it had my balls tightening and pleasure kicking hard at the base of my spine. I was close and she still hadn't come first. I needed to get her there and get her there fast.

I let go of my hold on her hair and put a hand between her shoulder blades so that she had to lower her top half to the mattress. She rested her cheek on the wrinkled comforter as I clutched both her hips in my hands and really started to pound into her. I didn't stop to think that she was still tender from the night before, my only intent was to drive her to the brink so that she was as out of control as I was.

She screamed my name and I saw her hands convulse where they were wrapped in the fabric of the bedding. Her pussy locked down on my cock and engulfed it in waves of liquid pleasure. She scalded me with satisfaction and blinded me with bliss. This was perfection. This was more than I deserved. She was everything and I had no doubt I was bound to ruin her.

That thought was sobering enough that I managed to get it

together enough to pull out of her engulfing heat before my own completion hit. I wrapped my cock in my fist, gave it an obligatory stroke that almost wasn't needed, and watched with a primal sense of accomplishment as I marked her in the rawest and most basic way a man could. She was covered in sweat and sex. She had the sticky remnants of my orgasm glistening on the curve of her still-lifted backside as she collapsed on the bed underneath me. It was an image that was going to be burned into my brain for an eternity. It was the picture I was going to pull up every time I was alone and missing her. I was going to remember that for this second, this moment she was undeniably mine. The proof of it was clinging to her gorgeously speckled skin.

It was my turn to lean over the side of the bed and rummage on the floor for something I could use to clean us both up with. I retrieved my shirt from the night before and scowled when it was my phone that rang and interrupted the quiet moment after the hurricane-like sex that had just consumed us. I swiped the cotton across Dixie's skin, feeling a little like a teenager scrambling to hide the evidence of what had just taken place.

I felt my eyebrows lift when I noticed it was Dalen's number on my phone. I sent him a few text messages on holidays and his birthdays when I was deployed after Jules told me he got the boy his own phone. I typically didn't get a response back, so I couldn't imagine why he was calling me now that I was under the same roof in the same city as him.

"Did you pocket dial me, kid?" Dixie shifted in the bed next to me and turned her head so that she was looking up at me, chocolate-colored eyes alight with curiosity.

"I need you to come and pick me up." He sounded funny, not that I knew how he normally sounded but his voice was shaky and missing some of the resentment it'd had last night.

"I gotta go get Elma Mae from the hospital and bring her home. Aren't you at school?" I swung my legs over the edge of the bed and reached for the pants I'd carelessly dropped last night.

"Forget about it. I should have called Dad. I don't know why I thought you would show up when I needed you. You never have before." Sucker punch. I sucked in a breath through my teeth and rubbed a hand over my face as the kid hit me with a shot that took more out of me than any of the bullets and shrapnel that had ripped through my skin.

"I'll come get you, Dalen, but you need to tell me what's going on so I can tell Jules. I'm not going to get between you and your dad my first day home."

"He's your dad, too, asshole." My little brother wasn't pulling any punches. "I'm at the Stop N' Save on route 12. I skipped my first class with a couple of other guys on the team. There was an assembly on something stupid, so we slipped out and decided to grab something to eat at the gas station." He swore and I heard his voice shake when he went on. "I was waiting for my buddy Drake to come out of the store. He's old enough to drive, so I was chilling by his truck when these guys in another truck pulled in and blocked us in." He cleared his throat and I felt my blood start to boil and fury flare to life blazing and explosive inside my veins. "They started saying some really ugly stuff, Dash, really ugly. I thought they were giving us a hard time because we were kids. I figured they maybe supported a rival school and were pissed we had Lowry colors on." He sounded like he was crying and I wanted to level the entire fucking town in order to make him stop.

"I'm on the way. Are you okay, Dalen?"

"They messed me up, Dash. I mean I'm a big dude and I take hits day in and day out on the field, but there were three of them."

"Son of a bitch. Do you need to go to the hospital?" Dixie gasped and bolted up next to me. She put a hand on my arm and patted the muscle that was locked in a battle-ready position. I would rip anyone that hurt the kid apart limb from limb. I would make them suffer in ways they couldn't imagine. I would hunt them down and run them to ground if it was the last thing I did.

"No. My face is busted up. Split lip, couple black eyes, and my knuckles are busted open, which is going to piss coach off. I tried to call Dad but he got a call out to the Holler and won't be back in city limits for another hour. I told my buddies I would find my own way home. I don't want them in trouble for skipping school. Coach will bench all of us for the next game if he finds out."

The Holler was a trailer park way out in the boonies. It wasn't easy to get to and the people that called it home weren't easy to deal with. Jules was going to be pissed when he found out what had happened.

"Hate to break it to you, kid, but once the old man catches sight of the damage done he's gonna want to talk to your friends. They're witnesses to an assault. I'm headed out the door right now, so sit tight."

He mumbled a sullen agreement as I turned to look at Dixie, who was also climbing out of the bed, her curls clasped in a hand to hold them away from her face.

"I gotta go get Dalen. The kid is in bad shape, and I need to call Jules so I can fill him in. Can you go get Elma Mae and get her settled at her place? I know that's asking a lot." She nodded without hesitation and grabbed some clothes from the pile I'd brought in from the laundry room last night.

"Of course I'll go get her. I hope your brother is okay."

I clasped the back of my neck and squeezed the thick coils of tension that were suddenly there.

"He'll be all right. The redneck assholes that fucked with him won't be able to say the same thing. I'm glad he called me. Surprised but glad."

She paused and gave me a serious look as she covered her nakedness with her bundle of clothes. "Of course he called. He's giving you the opportunity to show up because he wants you to prove that you still care about him the way he still cares about you. You were his idol and he's giving you a shot to reclaim your position as his hero. He could have called the police, in fact he probably should have. He could have called a friend's parent or another adult he trusts, but he called you. Don't screw this up, soldier. This is a mission you cannot afford to fail."

She was right about most of it. She was wrong about me being any kind of hero.

A hero wouldn't have bolted when things got tough at home. A hero wouldn't have let the man he idolized and adored grieve alone for the second woman he'd loved. A hero wouldn't have abandoned his little brother with no explanation and no justification. A hero wouldn't make love to the woman of his dreams over and over again knowing he was going to end up doing irreparable damage to her heart. A hero wasn't terrified to let himself fall in love, because all real heroes knew that pain was unavoidable and it was the suffering that was optional. Hell, half the guys I served with had those very words inked on their skin somewhere. It was a reminder that I didn't just choose to suffer, I embraced the suffering until it was the only thing I could feel aside from duty and obligation.

I had been many, many things in my fairly short and most definitely exciting lifetime but a hero wasn't one of them.

Chapter 13

Dixie

Julian's massive 4x4 dwarfed me. The shiny red truck had wheels that came up to almost my hip and gleaming chrome runners that ran along either side under the doors that I most definitely needed to use when I pulled myself up into the motorized beast. I was sure I had to look ridiculous behind the wheel but the interior of the truck was nicer than anything I had inside my apartment and I couldn't deny that I felt almost as badass sitting up so high and on top of so much horsepower as I did in the leather chaps Church was so fond of. I couldn't resist snapping a selfie, complete with duck face to send to Wheeler, because even though the truck was newer and not one of the classics that he preferred, I knew that he would appreciate the hilarity of me being the one behind the wheel of the beast.

I got a text back filled with question marks and a whole bunch of confused-face emojis followed by one that simply said *sweet ride*. I owed him an explanation as to why I'd been so distracted and dismissive on the phone earlier, not that I could figure out one that wasn't a lie. We were close and shared a lot, but I doubted we were "talk about the amazing sex I was having with the guy you almost threw down with in my living room" close. Hell, apparently there had been issues behind closed doors with him and my sister for a while now and neither one of them had bothered to fill me in. How was I supposed to help if I didn't have all the information?

Maybe Church was right. Maybe it wasn't my problem to try to fix. Maybe it wasn't my place to wade in and play peacemaker even though that's what I had always done. Kallie had to find her way to the truth and I couldn't walk Wheeler by the hand to forgiveness if he didn't want to go. Even if all the mediator tendencies I harbored and hoarded were screaming at me to do something to smooth everything over so that my family could stay the way it was. I wanted everyone to be happy, but spending these last few days with Church and being dropped into the center of his fractured family had shown me that sometimes wanting happiness wasn't enough. You had to work for it, and once you had it, you had to cultivate it and care for it. I liked to pretend that everything was always coming up sunshine and roses, but being on Church's home turf reminded me that every day had a night. That the sun had to go down and that as pretty as flowers were they all eventually died, no matter how carefully maintained they were. There was no good without the bad, no joy without sorrow, no peace without war, and there definitely couldn't be love without the sour taste of hate. You had to know what one felt like to fully experience and appreciate the other. All of the things I wanted and strived to bring into my life and the lives of others couldn't be experienced without the furious backlash of the opposite emotion.

I took up two parking spaces. I felt bad about it for a second and then rationalized we would be leaving soon, so it really didn't matter. I was going to have to pull the mammoth machine around to the front when they wheeled Elma out in the wheelchair she was going to be confined to for the next few weeks anyways. I didn't envy the physical therapist or the home care nurse that were going to be spending the next six weeks getting Elma Mae back on her feet. The feisty white-haired terror was going to put everyone through their paces during her recovery.

I maneuvered my way through the small hospital, acutely aware that I was drawing a lot of curious looks that I hadn't been on the receiving end of yesterday. It could have been the very obvious sex hair I was rocking. It could have been the fact that without Church by my side I was an unfamiliar face in a place where everyone seemed to know everyone else. Or more than likely it could have been my tightly fitted T-shirt that had a cow on the front with the words "I'm Not in the Mooooooood" printed below it. I thought it was cute and kind of funny but the side eyes and the lifted eyebrows from everyone I passed indicated they didn't share my quirky sense of humor.

I actually owned a closet full of normal, non-hilarious clothes but they weren't things I wanted to roll into a ball and shove into a backpack that may or may not have ended up sliding across asphalt. In fact, my ridiculous T-shirts were a big hit at the bar when I wore them. They were a conversation starter and it gave the guys that were going to stare at my boobs anyways an actual reason to have their gazes locked on my chest. So as silly as they were I had no plan on ditching them, no matter how many turned-up noses and divisive snorts were fired my way. Plus, Church didn't seem to mind them, not that I would retire them even if they were suddenly a deal breaker. I would miss his dick, but I would miss that little piece of me even more.

I knocked on the door to the room where Elma Mae had been the day before and braced myself as a sweetly southern "Y'all come on in" came my way. I knew she wasn't going to like the fact she was stuck with me instead of her boy but I was determined to put on a happy face and force the old battle-ax to like me.

"Hi, Elma Mae. Church ran into an emergency with Dalen, so he asked me to come and get you. Sorry you're stuck with the Yankee." She was sitting up in the bed much like she had been yesterday only today instead of kittens, her top had owls on it. Not just owls, but owls wearing headphones. Owls that were apparently waiting for the bass to drop. I couldn't stop the little laugh that escaped, but it died almost immediately as Elma narrowed her eyes at me as she took in my messy hair and casual attire.

"Well, bless your heart, dear. You didn't have to rush over and get me without taking the time to get ready. I'm not going anywhere with this busted stump." She sounded sweet but I'd been around Asa and his sister, Ayden, enough to know that when anyone from the south blessed anything they weren't actually sanctifying you or praying for your well-being. The opposite of that was actually true. "Bless" pretty much meant "eff you and the horse you rode in on." I wasn't gaining any brownie points with Elma Mae.

"Church didn't want you waiting around when you finally got your walking papers, so I hurried over. Do you need to see the doc before we spring you?" I refused to let any kind of annoyance at her rudeness show. My smile stayed firmly in place and I used the same placating tone I often employed when I had to talk a drunk into giving up their last drink when it was time to shut the bar down. It rarely failed me, but Elma gave me a sharp smile that let me know she knew exactly what I was doing. There would be no killing her with kindness, at least not today.

"No need to bother the doctor. He's a busy man. Let me just call the nurse so they can bring the chair and help me into it. I need to be home before noon. That's when the home nurse and the physical therapist are showing up to get my house invalid ready. What happened to Dalen? Did he get hurt at practice? I keep telling Julian that football is too violent. That boy is too smart and too handsome to be rolling around in the mud with the rest of the boys his age." I opened my mouth to deflect, to give a vague explanation as to what constituted an emergency serious enough that Church couldn't be here when it was what he had come home to do, but before I could she pointed a finger at me and told me, "Don't you piss on my leg and tell me it's raining, girl. You tell me where my boys are, and if they're okay or not."

I cringed at the visual her words conjured and cleared my throat. "Umm, well, I wouldn't ever piss on anyone's leg, so you're safe."

She gave an exasperated sigh and tossed her thin arms up in the air. "It means don't lie to me, child. I can see the wheels turning under that mane on the top of your head."

I subconsciously lifted a hand to my curls and tugged on one until it straightened and sprung back. This lady was tough as nails. I'd never had anyone be so overtly nasty to me before, well, aside from the third-wheel mother that tagged along on that date from hell. I sighed and gave her as much of the story as I could.

"Dalen skipped a class this morning and ran into some

trouble. It sounded like some other guys surrounded him and started a fight. He was roughed up and worried about getting his friends in trouble if he called the cops or went back to school. Jules was out at something called the Holler, so Church had to go get him. He's angry, really angry. The guys that messed with Dalen picked the wrong little brother to mess with, because his big brother is back home and not going to tolerate that kind of hate or ugliness."

"Lowry is a quiet town. We have our problems, just like anywhere else, but Dalen has lived here for fifteen years and never had anyone so much as say boo to him. Most folks round these parts know his daddy's the sheriff and those that don't know the kid is a future hall of famer. No reason for him to run into trouble other than the fact his big brother is home and brought you with him." She reached for the control on the side of her bed and pushed a button. "Something's not right."

I sighed again and struggled to get my toothy armor back in place. She was making it feel impossible, and I hated that my usually cheery façade was so easily navigated around. "I'm sure Church and Jules will figure it out."

She narrowed her eyes at me and crossed her arms over her narrow chest. "Chipper little thing, aren't you? Never would have pegged you as Dashel's type. When he was younger he liked sweet southern girls. Ones that knew how to dress and speak properly. Do you even have a job? Or are you planning on mooching off a military pension for the rest of your life?" She sniffed at me and turned up her nose. The archaic and clearly old-fashioned snub was the last straw. I was done playing nice when she was throwing cheap shot after cheap shot at me and not getting called for a foul.

I put my hands on my hips and cocked my head to the side. "I have a job. I'm a waitress at a bar." I held up a hand before she could drag my beloved profession through the mud. "Don't even start with how that isn't a real job because let me tell you, I make more on a busy weekend than most of the people I know that have degrees. I like working with people. I love my boss, and I never would have met Church if it wasn't for the bar. I'm never going to own a yacht or be able to afford a vacation in Saint-Tropez with Harry Styles and the Kardashians, but I live a good life and more days than not I'm really happy." It was my turn to point at her and turn my nose up in her direction. "I understand that you think I somehow kept Church in Denver when you would have preferred him home, but you do realize he is a grown-ass man, a man that served his country, a man that made the choice, be it the right one or the wrong one, to leave all those years ago. He's also the one that made the choice to not come home during that entire time when I didn't even know him. You can blame me all day long for delaying his homecoming because I care about him, and I want to make being here as easy for him as possible, but you have to put the responsibility for all the choices that came before me on him. I get that it's easier to be mad at me because I'm a stranger and I won't be around for very long, but eventually you're going to have to put all that anger where it belongs . . . on Church."

A deep-throated laugh burst out of her and she seemed to transform right in front of my eyes and the woman that belonged in that ridiculous owl shirt appeared. Her frail and severe features morphed into a smile that was as sunny as the one I usually had plastered on my face. I was so dumbstruck by the change that my jaw dropped and I couldn't stop my eyes from blinking rapidly.

"You *do* have a backbone somewhere underneath all the pretty hair. I was starting to wonder if you were ever going to get your knickers in a knot. My boy needs a woman that can step in and save him from himself. He's got a good heart like his mama and he's brave like his daddy, but somewhere along the way he forgot both those things. I want a good woman to remind him of who he was, but that's gonna be a fight you can't win with only a smile, even if it is a pretty one."

"It's a fight worth fighting no matter what I have to use to win." It wasn't a battle I'd realized I was engaged in until she pointed out what was at stake, but I'd been in the trenches since I blindly agreed to jump feetfirst into the middle of his homecoming.

I knew he couldn't see past the scared kid that had made some bad choices to protect himself from further hurt and heartache. He couldn't see the man that I saw, the man I loved before I even knew how much he really had to both love and loathe. He wouldn't recognize the man that Rome saw and trusted with his life and his livelihood if he was staring at his own reflection in the mirror. He couldn't see the man his little brother worshipped and the man his father was proud of. He couldn't see the man Elma Mae loved like a son, the one that had dropped everything and come running the minute he knew she needed him. All he could see was that kid that packed a bag and turned his back on everyone that needed him. I wanted to be there when he finally opened his eyes and saw the light, the brightness that was waiting to shine out of him.

"What keeps you from being happy on the days you don't smile, Miss Dixie?" She sounded genuinely curious and now that I was making headway I couldn't seem to keep the truth in that painful place where I always kept it.

"I love my job and I enjoy my life, but I wanted something different. I wanted someone to love me in a way that I'd know they could never not love me. I wanted a family, a big one, and a pretty house with flowers outside. I wanted the kind of happy that only happens when your dreams come true." My voice trailed off when I realized she was staring intently at me, like she was trying to see inside of my head and my heart at the same time. "My folks had that, so I grew up with something beautiful and special all around me. My sister found it, too, so I always assumed it would find me." It had but the person behind all those hopes and dreams had no idea he was the one.

"Honey, you are far too young to throw in the towel on those daydreams. If all you want is some pretty flowers and a nice house, you go out and get those yourself. You don't need a man to provide that for you. And you have to know after spending time with Dashel that even a love that feels like it will last forever can be cruelly taken away. Doesn't matter how tightly you hold on to it."

I gave a lopsided grin because I liked this spark of feminist outrage so quickly after she had been throwing around how a woman should look and sound. I was glad she wasn't stuck in old ideals and traditions after all. Now that she wasn't purposely pushing at me I could see how easy it was to really like her. She was a character and had no trouble speaking her mind.

I was saved from having to make my brain work by several nurses entering the room with a wheelchair. They were all smiling, and it was clear *this* was the real Elma Mae. This was the kindhearted older woman that held so much of Church's heart, the woman that all these people enjoyed taking care of and were sad to see go. The harpy that greeted me, the shrew that raked me over the coals, was all an act. She put me through the gauntlet to see if I was worthy of her boy and by some miracle I passed.

"You ready to go home, Elma?" It was a male nurse that lowered the rails of her bed and helped her move her long legs over the edge. The brace that held her leg straight and secure went all the way up to her hip and seemed very cumbersome and awkward to move.

"More than ready. I've been missing all the new episodes of *The Blacklist*. I can't wait to get back in front of my DVR."

He chuckled as I still stood there openmouthed and unable to move. "You're the coolest, Elma. I'll have Jenna bring the kids by with cookies once you're up to having visitors. If you need anything don't hesitate to call."

It took some maneuvering and a very delicate touch to get her settled in the chair. Once she was comfortable with her leg extended out in front of her she patted the male nurse's arm and offered him a warm smile. "You do that but now that all my boys are home I have everything I need." She lifted an eyebrow at me and tilted her head in my direction as she fake whispered, "And Dashel even brought me a pretty girl to help with all the things he won't want to do. My boy has good taste, doesn't he?"

All the nurses turned to look at me and I noticed the looks again, only this time they didn't feel judgmental but more considering.

"Dash always got all the best-looking girls. Looks like time hasn't changed much. We were all wondering if your new friend raided your closet when she walked in." The male nurse chuckled and I looked down at my cow shirt and then over to Elma's owl shirt. I couldn't stop the almost hysterical laugh that burst out of me. No wonder they had been watching me like a hawk. I reminded them all of their favorite eccentric. Quirky was cute even when you were in your eighties. That was good to know.

I shoved my hands through my hair and gave a tug at the roots to kick myself back into gear. "I'm going to go move the truck around to the front of the building. It's lifted to the sky, so I hope you're prepared to pick her up and put her into it."

The male nurse nodded at me and told me like it was obvious, "We know all about that monster Jules drives. That's why I made sure I was on shift when it was time for Elma to go home. We look out for our own around these parts."

It was like something out of a movie. All that was missing was Tom Hanks eating chocolate, or Brad Pitt reverse aging, or Julia Roberts dying a tragic death. It made me all kinds of warm and fuzzy on the inside to think of them collectively looking out for each other and worrying about the well-being of the community as a whole. This little southern town had every single thing I ever wanted in my life, including the difficult man I couldn't get my stubborn heart to let go of.

"Of course you look out for one another, because that's perfect and this place is made of magic and dreams. I'll meet you outside." When I made my way back to the front doors I realized all the people that I thought had been sneering at me were actually smirking and trying not to laugh at the fact that the girl Church went halfway around the world to find had the same unusual sense of style and the same kind of effortless charm as the woman that had been the only constant in his youth. I had none of the long, lean elegance that Elma Mae possessed, even confined to a wheelchair, but it was clear despite our physical and generational differences that we both wanted to love and care for those that needed it most.

I was lost in thought as I made my way across the parking lot. I was thinking that I was foolishly glad I had passed Elma's test, not that it mattered. She might actually like me after all was said and done, but that didn't change the fact that all Church thought we could have was a complicated friendship and some seriously mind-blowing sex. Granted I was really enjoying exploring both of those things with him but I couldn't deny that the closer we got, both physically and emotionally, the more I wanted to build every fantasy I had right on top of him and surround him in promises. He told me I deserved to put myself first, to have everything I wanted, but he was the one keeping the thing that I desired most annoyingly out of reach.

I had the keys to the truck in my hand and my head in the clouds, so I barely managed to jump out of the way when a big, black SUV roared by me disturbingly close. Close enough that I could feel the heat coming off the motor. Close enough that I could see my own startled face in the glossy paint as it flew by. Close enough that if I'd been paying attention I would have locked eyes with the driver. My swift reaction made me drop the keys as I jumped back, my backside hitting the side of the borrowed truck with a thump as I stared after the SUV like an idiot. I hadn't heard a honk. I hadn't heard the engine rev or even the brakes howl when they got too close. It was almost like the person behind the wheel had deliberately aimed for where I was walking. It seemed like they wanted to watch me jump and purposely caused me to freak out. It seemed like they wanted to scare me, because if they had wanted to plow me over they'd had ample opportunity while I was fantasizing about a future I couldn't have with the only guy I'd ever wanted one with.

It was alarmingly similar to what had happened on the highway with the car trying to run the Harley off the road. Close enough to scare, but not close enough to kill. I looked down at my shaking hands and swore long and loud at the fact I hadn't had my wits about me enough to look at either the driver or license plate. I knew Church was going to be even angrier than he already was when I told him what happened. He might not want to play house with me, but I had no question about how protective and fierce he was over me. It was one of the things that had made me fall for him from the start.

Elma Mae was right, something wasn't right here and it was becoming more and more obvious that it was directly related to Church bringing me home with him.

Chapter 14

Church

Locating Dalen was easy enough when I got to the convenience store. He was crouched down on the curb in front of the ice cooler out front, the hood of a gray sweatshirt pulled up over the top of his head and both of his hands wrapped up in white bandages that I assumed came from inside the store. He looked like a prize fighter that had gone a few rounds with a worthy competitor and I knew from firsthand experience that both his eyes were going to be dark purple before the day was done. His bottom lip was already swollen to twice its normal size and there was a line of dried blood down the center of it where it was split in half. He was going to be hurting even though it looked like he had put up one hell of a fight. As pissed off as I was, I also had a good dose of masculine pride working that he had been able to hold his own when things got rough.

He rose gingerly to his feet as I swung off the bike and made my way over to him. "Got in touch with Jules. Turns out the call out to the Holler was bogus, so he was already on his way back when I called. He should be here any minute." It didn't escape either of our notices that the call that took him way out of town coincided perfectly with Dalen getting attacked. Someone was pulling on the strings of my return, making us all dance around like puppets and playthings. What started out as annoying and problematic was quickly turning dangerous.

"I told you they weren't from around here. I didn't recognize the truck or any of the guys. They were a bunch of backwoods types, the kind that don't come into any town very often. Think *Deliverance*." He took his hood off and licked at the slice in the center of his lip. "There was something weird when they rolled up on us though."

"Weird how?" The side of his head had a nasty scrape on the side of it and there was a furious red line along the side of his neck like someone had tried to strangle him. The marks made my vision go red and I couldn't stop the scowl or the furious flood of dirty words that rolled off my tongue.

Dalen looked at me with wide eyes and shifted his weight on his sneaker-clad feet. He tucked his bandaged hands in the center pocket of his shirt and looked down at the ground as his brow furrowed while he tried to concentrate. "Well, I was supposed to be in class. I don't usually ditch, today was a fluke, but when they stopped, the guy that was riding in the back pointed at me and yelled 'There he is!'" He shrugged his shoulders and let them fall. "It was like they were looking for me, but that's impossible because I wasn't supposed to be here. It didn't seem like they were out looking for just anyone that didn't look like them to mess with. I mean there aren't a lot of us in Lowry but there are enough that I couldn't have been the first dark-skinned guy they came across today. It seemed like they were looking for a very specific person of color." He pointed to his face. "This color."

I exhaled a long breath and felt fear, frigid and chilling, curl around my spine and slither out of the darkness where it always lurked. That voice that reminded me what happened when I was around those I loved whispered ugly insinuations and taunts in my ear. That poison that infected the people I cared about was starting to seep out, and it had only been a handful of hours that I'd been home.

I looked at the young man who bore a striking resemblance to the image I looked at every day in the mirror. He was obviously years younger and favored Julian in ways I couldn't, but there was no mistaking we were related. There wasn't a single doubt in my mind that the guys that had put a beating on Dalen were looking for me and found him instead. The convenience store was one of the first stops in Lowry when you were coming into town. I bet they saw him standing outside of the building and thought they got a lucky break.

My little brother had taken a beating that was meant for me.

Ten years of peace and quiet.

Ten years of a fairly normal childhood minus the fact he'd lost more than one mother.

Ten years of security and serenity, things the poor kid deserved more than most, and it only took one day for the bad that always seemed to work its way into my life to blow it all to hell.

"They were more than likely looking for me, kid. It's your bad luck that we happen to look so much alike." I shook my head and lowered my gaze to the ground. "You took a beating that was meant for me. I'm sorry." Sorry for the fact he was hurting. Sorry that it was my fault. Sorry that I brought ruthless things with me wherever I went.

He snorted, which had me lifting my head so that we were staring at each other. It was like looking at a better version of myself. Dalen had been through all the same horrors of love and loss that I had, but even though he was just a little boy at the time he'd handled everything that'd happened better than I had.

"I'm not sorry I look like you." His bloody lip twitched as he tried to smile. The motion made it bleed and had him wincing in pain. He used the bandage on his hand to stem the flow of red and lifted his eyebrows at me. "When you weren't around, sometimes looking at myself was the only reminder I had of you, Dash." Right in the fucking heart. This kid was going to be the end of me with his truth bombs and unvarnished honesty. "Plus I can't even handle all the girls that are up on me all the time. Looking like you has its advantages."

I couldn't hold back a chuckle, but the seriousness of the situation and of his words didn't allow the levity to last very long. "When I left I didn't plan on staying away. At first I couldn't leave because of boot camp, and then I got shipped overseas and there was a whole learning curve there that kicked my ass. Eventually it was easier to keep some distance because I had a job to do and I couldn't think about both staying alive and all the what-ifs happening back here."

He narrowed his battered eyes at me and gave me a dirty look. "It was better for you, Dash. It was never better for us. Your country might have needed you, but so did your family." He scoffed at me and pointed one of his wrapped fingers in my direction. "Do you have any idea how long I thought it was my fault you took off?"

That made me take a step back like he'd hit me in the face. "What? Why would you think that? You were five when I left, Dalen."

"Yeah, you left because Caroline got sick. You loved her, but so did I, and losing her hurt me just as bad as losing Mom hurt you. Caroline was the only mom I ever knew, and I know she never would have met Dad if I hadn't been born. I'm also smart enough to know neither one of you would have lost Mom if it hadn't been for me. She wanted me so badly it cost her her life. I was the reason you lost Mom and the reason Caroline was around in the first place. That all leads to you leaving because of me. I used to cry about it to Dad. I missed you. Dad missed you. Elma Mae missed you but you were nowhere to be found and I blamed myself for that. It took years and years for him to convince me your choices had nothing to do with me and everything to do with you. He still tells me all the time that even though he lost Mom, he got me, and he got to have Caroline even if it wasn't for very long. He always tells me that he gained as much as he lost."

Thank God he'd had Jules to set him straight and to battle the blame and guilt that I'd allowed to suck me under. Dalen hadn't been allowed to become a victim of all that grief and sorrow that tore apart my insides. "I left because I was a coward, Dalen. I can't lie about that. I didn't have it in me to hold Jules up under the weight of losing another woman he loved, even though I owed it to him to at least try. I was pathetic and I was pitiful . . . honestly, I still am because I *should* have been here. The army took me in, gave me purpose and regimentation. I was lost and they put me on a path that was easy to navigate after I felt like every move I made here pushed me closer to the edge of catastrophe. The army told me where to be, what to do, how to act, how to look. I didn't have to think, all I had to do was follow orders and it worked for me. I knew if I came home all of that would go away, it already has." I waved a hand at his face. "Look what happened to you not even a day after I got home, kid. Shit gets fucked up and I don't even have to try . . ."

His swollen eyes widened and he took a step closer to me, which brought him off the curb and had us almost chest to chest and eye to eye. He was tall for his age, but I still had a solid three or four inches on him. That didn't stop his anger from making him seem much larger and far older than he was. He poked me in the center of the chest and his voice raised as he spit furious words at me. "The people we've lost, the heartache we've suffered . . . none of that makes us unique or special. People lose loved ones all the time because bad stuff happens to good people every single day."

I thought about Dixie's dad and all the families I'd had to contact while I was overseas when one of their sons, husbands, or fathers had come to their end at the hands of our enemies. Good men dying while doing what they were trained to do. I thought about the bullet Rome took in the center of the chest when he was home because he made the wrong man mad during a bar fight. He could have easily died and left Cora and their daughter behind when he was supposed to be living a safe, quiet, civilian life. I couldn't ignore the fact that my brother, young, innocent, and blameless, had simply been in the wrong place at the wrong time today and paid for it heavily. Bad things did happen to good people every single day because fate was a bitch and there was no controlling her, even if you desperately wanted to.

"You know what does make us special, what does make us unique?" He put both of his hands on the center of my chest and pushed. "That we had not one, but two moms that loved us unconditionally for as long as they could." He pushed me back again and I caught his wrists so that he didn't hurt himself more than he already was. "We have a dad that has never given up on us, never walked away. He lost just as much as we did, even more because he lost you, too, but he's always been there and he always will be. He could take a bullet tomorrow while he's on the job, Dash. He could be taken away just as easily as Mom and Caroline were, but I don't think about that because he won't let me. He wants me to appreciate the time we have together and not get lost in what could happen because if either of us did that we would stop living, stop caring about each other . . . just like you did. Do you know how lucky we are, Dash? You ran away from everything that you lost and totally turned your back on everything you still had. Maybe you had an excuse at first, because everything that happened with Caroline did suck, and it was scary and you never really got over losing Mom, but every time you chose not to come home after that, you chose wrong because we were still here." He shook me loose and turned his back on me as he pulled his hood back up over his head. "You're right. You are pathetic."

I'd faced off with armed terrorists and insurgents wearing explosives. I'd gone toe to toe with extremists and militants. I'd brawled in bars and in close-quarters combat. I'd taken bullets and been sliced open by tactical knives. I'd been put through the ringer by drill sergeants and the opposition but none of it had leveled me out and taken me down like my little brother just did. He'd just inflicted wounds that wouldn't heal, but they were ones that were necessary in order for the poison inside to start to leak out. He'd lanced the infection that had lived inside of me so long by showing me what a man that had been through hell and back looked like when he just kept going. My brother and Jules kept walking no matter how high the flames got and no matter how hot the fire burned. I had stopped and let the heat consume me. I quit walking and gave up while everyone else marched on. It was time to get my ass in gear and catch up to the rest of my family.

I reached out and clasped his stiff shoulder. It took some work to get him turned towards me, but when he did I pulled him to me and wrapped him up in a hug he struggled to get out of. I wasn't a hugger by nature, though I was getting used to the ones Dixie kept pulling me into, so it was awkward and uncomfortable, but I held on to Dalen until he realized I wasn't going to let go.

"Everything you said is the truth. I did choose wrong many times over, but I swear on all that I love that I will work on it now that I'm home."

I squeezed him until I felt some of the tension exit his tall frame. Hesitantly his arms lifted to return the hug. Because he was a teenager and because he had a reputation in the town, I got a very stiff pounding on the back like we were bros instead of brothers. It made me chuckle but I would take it. I let him go and gave him a serious look. "I'm serious. I owe you and Jules the world that I worked my ass off to make a better place. I will show up, Dalen, and I'll keep showing up. I will be here."

I could see he didn't believe me fully, and I didn't blame him. I'd been lying to everyone for so long about so many things it was hard for him to know if I was actually being truthful.

"We'll see. That girl you brought home with you is hot. When she goes I bet you run after her." We both turned our heads as a patrol car pulled into the lot and stopped next to my Harley. Even from this distance it was easy to see Jules was not a happy parent or police officer.

"She is hot, but she's not mine to keep." Even if the idea of a guy showing up to give her everything she wanted, that fuzzy future with all the trappings, made me feel murderous and alarmingly possessive. Jules got out of the car and slammed the door with enough force that the entire vehicle shook.

"You okay, son?" He walked right up to Dalen and grabbed him on either side of the face and turned his head this way and that while assessing the damage. "They got some good shots in didn't they? Gonna take you to see the doc. I don't like the look of that ding on the side of your head."

Embarrassed, Dalen swatted Jules's hands away. "I'm fine."

Jules snorted and put his hands on his hips. "You might be fine but if you want to finish out your season we're gonna make sure you don't have a concussion. You think you learned your lesson about skipping school?"

My brother nodded and looked sheepish. "Yeah, Dad. It was dumb."

"Need the names of the kids that were with you. I also need you to give me a description of the guys that attacked you and what they were driving. Don't gimme no lip about keeping your buddies out of trouble. This is bigger than your next game, Dalen."

I could see my little brother gearing up to argue, so I interrupted before things got too heated. "I'm going to stick my head inside and see if the cashier noticed anything. Maybe we'll luck out and they'll have video of the fight and the license plate of the truck."

Jules nodded at me and waved me off with a hand. "Good thinking. I'll be in right after you."

I pushed through the glass doors and frowned when the girl behind the counter didn't so much as look up as the electronic ding overhead rang to alert her to the fact she had someone in the store. She was propped on the counter, chin in hands as something played on her phone. She didn't bother to look up as I approached either. The closer I got the more obvious it became she was oblivious to everything but what was happening on the tiny screen in front of her. I bet shoplifters had a field day on her shifts and if the owner didn't have some kind of video surveillance in place then they were an idiot.

"Excuse me." I tapped the counter in front of her until she rolled her heavily made-up eyes in my direction. At first she looked irritated but once she got a good look at me she perked up. I decided to use that to my advantage and gave her a flirtatious look and a half grin that was totally fake. "I was wondering if you noticed the commotion that just went down outside. Did you see anything?"

She grinned back at me and rose to her full height. She was probably about the same age as Dixie, but all that makeup and the unflattering red uniform shirt made her look older. She stuck her chest out as she tapped a manicured finger to her chin and I gave her the obligatory once-over. She was fine to look at, but I had zero interest in anything she was offering up. I wasn't the right guy for Dixie, but that didn't stop her from being the perfect girl for me.

"Naw. It's quiet around here until noon when the school lets out for lunch. We get an occasional trucker and a couple of tourists passing through but nothing exciting usually happens in the morning. At least not until you walked in." She batted spidery eyelashes at me and pursed her glossy lips. "Are you new in town? I definitely would remember seeing you around before."

"I grew up here. My family is from around here. In fact, it was my little brother that was the one attacked outside your store." My friendly tone got a whole lot less friendly when I started talking about Dalen getting attacked. "You weren't paying attention. You didn't call the cops when a teenager was being attacked by three racist adults. A teenager who happens to be the sheriff's son. I'm sure you can see how this can end really badly for you." I looked at her name tag through narrowed eyes. "Allison."

"Shit. Dalen got beat up? That's not good. My boyfriend likes to bet on the games and Dalen is the backbone of that team." She put a nervous hand to her throat and looked at me out of wide eyes as she must've heard how callous her statement sounded. "Uh . . . I mean . . . is he okay?"

I didn't respond to her fake concern for my brother's well-being. "Tell me that you got cameras pointed at the parking lot."

She rapidly nodded. "We do. Teenagers like to gas and dash, so the boss put them in a couple years ago. I'll have to call him and ask permission to show them to you."

"I already called since this is an official criminal investigation. Take us to the back and show us what we need." I turned my head as Jules walked in and up to the counter next to me. He was in his no-nonsense police mode but I could tell that underneath he was one furious father that wanted payback for what had happened to his son.

We followed the cashier into the back and both of us stopped breathing as she enlarged the view from the camera we pointed out and started to roll back the feed until the scuffle appeared. It was hard to watch. The images had my hands curling into fists and Jules swearing every five seconds. The guys that attacked Dalen were no scrawny weaklings. They were burly backwoods boys that looked used to hard labor and hard living. I was glad there was no sound because not only would the noises of fists hitting flesh make it harder to take, I knew the things that they were saying to him, the names they were calling him, would push me over the edge. I already wanted to hurt them, but that kind of unjustified hate unleashed on a kid, well, that made me want to kill.

The footage was clear enough to get a plate number and Jules wasted no time in calling it in but it was the oblivious cashier who actually turned out to be the best source of information. After we watched the entire attack, twice, she nervously informed us that her boyfriend with the gambling problem went to a bar called Sassy's a town over to place his bets with his bookie. Apparently the place was a dive that catered to yokels and hillbillies. She gave me a look when she said it that indicated it was a place where I would most definitely not be welcome.

"I've heard of it, but it's out of my jurisdiction, so I've only ever driven by it." Jules gave me a look that spoke volumes. We both knew where this was going and he didn't want me to run off half-cocked. Well, he was in luck because I was fully cocked and more than willing to let the bastards that beat my brother find the person they were actually looking for.

"I've seen that truck in the parking lot. And the big guy who was driving, I think I've seen him at the door a time or two. I don't ever go inside because it looks filthy and my boyfriend says it's not safe, but yeah, I bet you can find those guys there." She shifted her gaze between the two of us and tilted her head to the side. "So, do you think Dalen will be playing this weekend?"

I growled at her and went to take a step forward but was brought up short by Jules's arm shooting out like a metal bar across the center of my chest. "Young lady, if you had been doing your job my son wouldn't be in the shape he is in now. If you had called the police when those men pulled in with obvious ill intent, Dalen wouldn't have had to fight three grown men while he was outnumbered. I'll be speaking with your boss at length and you should mention to your boyfriend that he'll need to find a new bookie because business at Sassy's is about to get shut down."

I continued to glare at her even as he grabbed the back of my shirt and started to haul me towards the door like he had when I was a kid. "Come on, Dash."

Once we were back in the parking lot I wasted no time in swinging a leg over the Harley and pulling weight up off the kickstand. Jules put his hand over mine on the throttle and gave it a little squeeze.

"I know you think you should go after those men, that you want to defend your brother. I know you aren't afraid of a fight, afraid of their close mindedness and bigotry, but if you start something, if you are the instigator that puts me in a tough spot, son . . ."

I shouldn't be surprised that my intention to go knocking at every dive bar in the county until I found the guys that injured Dalen was clear on my face. I was still choking on rage and a desire for retribution for what had happened to Dalen. "They were looking for me and found Dalen instead. He got hurt because of me and I can't let that slide."

"Son, I know exactly what you are capable of and that could lead to trouble. You need to be smart and you need to think through whatever you do next. You may think just because you didn't tell me where you were or what you were doing that I didn't keep tabs on you. You're my son, Dash. I've always known exactly where you were and what kind of hot spots you were in. I'm not too proud to use my badge and my position to get information that my son isn't willing to share. I never wanted you to enlist because I didn't think you were in a place where you could handle losing brothers in arms and seeing what the ravages of war can do to people. You'd already had so much death in your life I couldn't believe you were actively chasing after more of it. I should have known back then that you were looking for a reason. Your mom and Caroline died senselessly, but when you went to the desert, well, that was death and destruction that made sense." I stared at him like I was seeing him for the first time, which maybe I was. I hadn't been trying to see through my darkness, I'd simply become comfortable in it, feeling my way around with my eyes squeezed shut. I was seeing a whole lot of things for what they were now that Dalen had prodded me hard enough to get them open. "I didn't want you to be a solider, but dammit if you weren't the best soldier you could be."

I gritted my teeth and one by one uncurled my fingers from around the throttle. "We both know someone found those guys and sent them on a mission to give me a beat down. Someone called in that bogus call to you so that you were out of town and set this in motion. This is all tied to the stuff that's been happening since Dixie and I left Denver."

"I agree, but I still don't think it tracks with a vendetta drug dealer might have with towards you."

"Then what? I didn't piss anyone else off in Denver except for a few drunks that got handsy with some of the ladies. I put the fear of God into an abusive boyfriend of one of the cocktail servers but he's locked up now as well. So who could it be?"

Jules chuckled and reached out a hand so that he could grab my shoulder. He gave me a little shake and looked at me with lifted eyebrows. "You're smart, Dash, so think it through. If you didn't piss someone off in Denver and the trouble followed you from there then it must be the other person with the unseen adversary. Dixie is a sweetheart, but that doesn't mean the whole world is in love with her. We all have skeletons, even if hers are pink and fluffy."

I couldn't imagine Dixie having any kind of enemy. She was everyone's best friend. She was the constant cheerleader and sun that never stopped shining. "I'll ask her. I doubt she's got skeletons, pink or otherwise, but something's gotta give before someone ends up dead."

"I agree. I'm taking your brother to get him checked out and then dropping him off at the house." He looked at me over his shoulder with a smirk. "That was a good call with the tape. Those are instincts not everyone has. You know that if you stick around we could always use another deputy on the force. You have more training than most of my guys and since you started off as an MP in the service all you would have to do is take the state's test and do the physical."

I stared at him for a long minute and then shook my head. "You didn't want me to be a soldier but you're okay with me being a cop?"

He gave a shrug as he stopped at the door of his patrol car. "What father doesn't want his son to follow in his footsteps? I'm gonna send a cruiser out to Sassy's. I'll let you know when we round up the suspects, though something tells me you're going to find them first. Make good choices, son."

I stared after the car for a long minute until it was gone from sight. Every instinct I had was screaming at me to fire the Harley to life and go exact justice for my brother. My muscles were tense, my jaw was clenched, and my heart was beating so fast that it was all I could hear. I was used to letting my family down. I was comfortable doing the wrong thing for the right reasons. I promised Dalen I would show the fuck up and that was exactly what I was going to do.

Chapter 15

Dixie

I got Elma home without further incident. Getting the wheelchair inside took a little finessing and some muscle but I managed it. I made a mental note to ask Church if he was handy with a hammer and a saw because she was going to need a ramp to help her navigate coming in and out of the house until she was healed enough to use the walker. Once I had her comfortable on the surprisingly chic leather couch (no giant cabbage flowers or pastel prints for Elma Mae) with all her recorded shows fired up on a flat screen I knew most men would be envious of, I went to work finishing the laundry that had caused her tumble in the first place.

After I had that easy chore handled, I discovered that the hand rail leading up the stairs was loose, another thing I was putting on Church's list of things to look at, and I asked for a rundown of other things I could help her with while we waited on Church to get back. He'd sent a message that Dalen was with Jules and that the cop had gone all kinds of protective parent and insisted the younger Churchill get his head checked out. My brooding biker was on his way back home now, and I could tell that Elma was excited to finally get some time with him.

She asked me to organize all the food that people from the community had brought by and stocked her fridge with. There was no way she was going to get to it all before it went bad, so she asked me to find something that would feed all of us, plus the nurse that was coming in and staying with her for dinner, and divvy up the rest and freeze it. She also asked me to water her flowers in the yard and to bring all the stuff she would need that was upstairs in her master bedroom downstairs since there was no way she was making that trip until the brace came off. Her kitchen was something that would leave even the Barefoot Contessa impressed, so it was no chore to bop around the fancy marble countertops and stainless steel appliances.

I left something that looked like a giant dish of lasagna in the fridge for dinner and then made my way outside to tackle the flowers as the sun was going down. Being from the city and living in an apartment most of my adult life I'd never had a garden. We were lucky to have a small square of grass in our front yard to play on when we were kids, so Elma Mae's sprawling, lush landscape was like something out of a fairy tale. I had no problem picturing Alice and the Mad Hatter at tea amongst the flowers and fauna. I spent more time touching the velvety soft petals and smelling the fragrant blooms while daydreaming about the perfect intimate garden wedding than I did actually watering the plants. It was so very easy to get lost in all the wonderful things Church's home had to offer that I couldn't imagine how hurt and how scared he must have been to leave it all behind without a backwards glance. I knew he would hate it, but it made me feel sorry for him. He was absolutely right that there was a lot of goodness here to turn your back on.

Lost in my own little world I didn't hear his bike or the heavy fall of his boots as he walked up behind me. I also must have tuned out him calling my name because when his hand landed on my shoulder it freaked me out. I jumped. I screamed. I flailed around like a lunatic and when I whipped around to confront my unseen assailant I sprayed him right in the face with the hose that was still dangling out of my hand.

Stunned that it was friend and not foe, I stood there with the hose trained on him as he swore at me, yelled my name, and tried to evade the water. It didn't work. He was drenched. Head to toe, sopping wet as I gave him an unwanted shower. He snatched my wet weapon out of my hand and bent the green rubber until there was a kink in it big enough to stop the flow of water. He shook his sandy head, water droplets flinging every direction as those better than hazel eyes narrowed threateningly at me.

"Seriously?" He ran a hand over his face as I struggled to contain a laugh. The humor died when he shrugged out of his soggy leather jacket with a grimace, leaving him in nothing more than a soaking wet T-shirt that clung to every defined muscle he had. The boy looked good without even trying, get him wet and make him a little angry and everything that made me a girl sat up and took notice. Jeans that clung to all the parts of him that I didn't want to share made my mouth water and my cheeks pink. I wanted to snap a picture of him so I had it when real Church was gone and battery operated Church was all I had left. Hell, I might not even need the vibrator. The picture would be enough to get off on.

He shook his head again and swiped a hand down the back of

his neck, where water was rolling down the collar of his shirt. "Didn't you hear me calling your name?"

I threw up my hands in exasperation. "Obviously not. You scared me."

He looked down at his dripping front side and then back up at me with a smirk. "Are you sure you didn't just want to get me wet?"

I laughed and let my eyes roll over him in an obvious way. "I mean, I'm sorry-not-sorry that I got you all wet."

One of his eyebrows quirked upwards and I felt like an idiot for not knowing exactly what was coming next. Before I could let out a sound or put my hands up in a defense he let go of the hose and I was hit in the face with an onslaught of water. It was cold, so I squealed and he was too fast for me to evade when I darted to the side to escape the spray. The chilly wetness stuck my shirt to my chest and had my curls falling heavily into my face.

"Stop!" I held my hands up in surrender and barked out the order over a laugh. I had to shake my hair out of my eyes to look up at him and when I did my knees almost buckled. It wasn't a full smile; the light didn't reach his eyes or shine out of him and it didn't make his perpetual scowl lighten up, but man oh man, did it transform his face from something beautiful to something that was better than beautiful. The barest hint of his teeth, the tiniest indent in his cheek that hinted at the fact he was probably hiding a dimple or two, the lift of his brow from frowning to not . . . it all made my heart turn inside out and solidified that I might want him for myself but I wanted that smile for the rest of the world. No one should be kept from something so stunningly special.

While I was enraptured and unable to move he made his way

over to the spigot to turn the water off. When he came back his shirt was in his hand and the late afternoon sun was kissing his bronze shoulders, making him look like an ancient bronze statue come to life. "What were you daydreaming about so hard that you didn't hear the Harley or your name?" It was an innocent enough question but one I wasn't going to answer truthfully because he didn't need to know that I had him standing at a flower-covered arch in Elma's yard waiting for me to walk down the aisle towards him. I was afraid that would kill that glorious smile when it was so newly resurrected.

"Uh . . . I had a little run-in at the hospital." I pulled the front of my sticking T-shirt away from my stomach and wrung it out in my hands. It would serve him right if I pulled the thing off in front of God and everyone but I didn't want to give Elma Mae a reason to go back to being nasty to me. I was sure a half-naked redhead running around her yard would have the neighbors talking, that was if they could get past all the golden glory that was Church.

"What kind of run-in?" His rumbling voice dropped lower and all the humor fell away from his handsome face. Leaving the grumpy, glowering one I was so familiar with back in place. "Elma Mae still giving you the business?"

I shook my head, which sent water flying in all directions. He had to step back to avoid getting wet. "No. We came to a truce. She was testing me and I finally stood my ground and passed. We're pretty much best friends now." I wiggled my eyebrows at him but his stern expression didn't waver.

"What happened at the hospital, Dixie?" There was no room for argument or further beating around the bush.

"I was in the parking lot moving the truck and I had my head in the clouds as usual." I was daydreaming about him then as well. It was like an addiction; one I was going to have to quit cold turkey pretty soon. "This black SUV came roaring out of a parking spot a few yards away. They almost hit me. It was close enough I could see my reflection in the door. There were no other cars around because I parked that big-ass truck like shit, so it was obviously deliberate." I held up a hand before he could speak. "And no, I didn't get a look at the driver or a license plate because I was too busy thanking my lucky stars I didn't get run over."

"Dixie." My name was coated in concern and exasperation. He dropped his soggy T-shirt to the grass and reached out and pulled me to his bare chest. I was so stunned I didn't immediately react because I couldn't believe he was hugging me of his own volition. "Are you okay?"

I let out a shaky sigh and leaned into him. His skin was like warm silk stretched over iron and stone as I rested my cheek on his naked pec. I wrapped my arms around his narrow waist and let my fingers trace lazily over the twin little indentations that rested right above his backside. It was the best hug I'd ever had in my life, partly because I hadn't had to ask for it, it'd just been given, but mostly because it came from him and I knew a few days ago there was no way that he would have willingly pulled me into his arms. He cared. He might not care the way I wanted him to, but he cared nonetheless.

"I'm okay. It shook me up a little and it made me nervous to have Elma in the truck with me on the way back here but nothing else happened." At least nothing else happened that I was aware of.

"You know all of this is connected somehow, right? You almost getting run down, someone setting the good ole boys on me and getting Dalen instead. Someone is mad we left Denver and the more incidents that occur the more it seems like someone is downright pissed we left together. My drug dealer seems unlikely but Jules is going to check into him and I spent all afternoon looking for the boys that put a beating on my brother but they must have gone to ground, so there won't be answers from them until I find them. This all feels like it might point to someone you rubbed the wrong way, pretty girl."

I jerked back and looked up at him with wide eyes. "I don't rub people the wrong way, Church." In fact, I went out of my way to make sure I didn't.

He grunted and lifted his hands so that he could tunnel his fingers through the damp spirals that were a kinky mess all over my head. He used his palms to tilt my head back even farther so that we were staring into each other's eyes. "I know you don't think you do but I need you to think back, is there anyone that gave you any kind of bad vibes lately? Anyone from the bar seem unusually irritated or annoyed at you? I know you've been online dating and there can be some real oddballs on the internet. Did any of your dates strike you as strange or off?" I wanted to squirm after he asked the question. I wanted to forget the disaster online dating had been and I wanted to forget the reason I had been so desperate in the first place was because of his irrational fear of getting close to anyone.

"There were only a handful and they were all pretty weird." I let my hands fall from around his waist and went to take a step back but he wouldn't let me go. His multicolored gaze kept me rooted to the spot as he told me to explain what I meant by weird. I groaned and raised my hands to hold on to his wrists while I talked.

"The first guy seemed nice enough but halfway through dinner I went to the bathroom and when I came back he was gone and so was my wallet. He took it right out of my purse and disappeared."

"The fuck?" His outraged growl actually made me smile.

"Yeah well, I preferred him to the next guy, who never bothered to disclose that he was married and that he and his wife were swingers looking for a third to play with while the kids were out of town. He also used a picture that was wayyy out of date, because when I went to meet him I hardly recognized him. He was like . . . the same age as my dad." I wrinkled my nose at the memory as Church swore again and tightened his hands on the sides of my head.

"The last guy was actually very nice. He was quiet. He was shy. I don't think he'd ever been on a date before." His eyes narrowed to slits and his mouth pulled down into a frown that I was sure had scared men that were far bigger and fiercer than I would ever be. "I might have given him a chance, or at the very least a second date if—" I paused as an animalistic sound rumbled loud and possessive out of his chest. "If he hadn't brought his mother along with him. Our entire date was chaperoned and monitored, and while he was nice enough she was a shrew and a bully." I felt my brows draw together as memories of that evening played through my mind. "In fact she was angry when I wouldn't let them into my apartment for a drink. Way angrier than the situation called for. It was obvious that she was the one that set the date up and was the driving force behind it, so she was far more upset than he was when I pulled the plug."

"You got a name on the mother and son duo? It may be a long shot but it's as good a place to start as any."

"But that's crazy. It wasn't even a real date. She couldn't really have been so angry that she followed us down here and tried to run us off the road. Who does that?"

He leaned forward and kissed my forehead before stepping back and rolling his heavy shoulders. "You'd be surprised how little it takes to set someone off, especially if they've only got one oar in the water."

I snorted at his very southern turn of phrase and pointed at him. "Better watch out, Church, your southern is starting to show." It'd always been around in the sensual, sexy drawl but now that he was back where everyone sounded like him his accent was getting stronger and his speech was slipping into familiar phrases and patterns that I'd never heard him use back in Denver. "I'll look at my phone and give you momma's boy's number and name. I meant to delete all those dating apps I downloaded but I never got around to it because you showed up and made everything go crazy."

That unpracticed and rusty grin flashed back across his face. "That's what I do." It sure was. My heart had been crazy for him since day one. "No more online dating, Dixie. You don't need it. The right guy is going to come along and he will be everything you ever wanted him to be." He bent to pick up his shirt and tossed the soggy mess over his shoulder. "I'm going to go in and check on Elma. I'm sure she has a list of chores she's been waiting ten years to hand down to me."

I waved him off and told him I needed to finish the flowers as well as dry off a little before heading inside. I also told him I would handle dinner if he called his dad and brother and told them we were all eating with Elma that night, and more than likely every night for the rest of the week so we could help her with all that food the neighbors had brought over. What I didn't tell him was the right guy for me was standing right in front of me and he did have everything I wanted, but he also had a lot of things I didn't want because that was how the world worked. No one was guaranteed anything, so you made do with the few blessings you did have and tried your best not to squander them. It was a lesson I think he was slowly starting to learn but my time to get it to sink in and make him realize what we could have if he believed, in him, in me, in us just a little bit, was running out.

DINNER WAS GREAT. The nurse that was staying with Elma didn't look a day over nineteen and had her hands full cooing over both Elma and a battered Dalen. Watching Elma and the Churchill men reunite filled my happy heart with all the things that it longed for. Church was relaxed, well, as relaxed as he ever was, and the change was huge as he joked around with his brother and traded lighthearted jabs with his father. Elma couldn't stop smiling and at one point she asked me to help her use the restroom, not so she could actually use the restroom but so she could sit on the closed toilet seat and cry. This was a moment too long denied and it was obviously overwhelming for her.

All I could do was pat her on the back and wait until the emotional storm passed. I helped her erase all the evidence of her sob-fest and served everyone a slice of the coconut cream pie I found in the fridge like nothing out of the ordinary had happened. After pie and a few episodes of *The Blacklist*, Julian ordered Dalen home to finish homework and reminded him that they had an early meeting with the principal and the kids he had ditched school with. In typical teenaged fashion Dalen played up his injuries, though his face did look like it had been smashed into a very unforgiving wall, and pleaded with his father for a sick day.

Church called him out, saying the only reason he didn't want to go to school was because his coach was going to hand him his ass for missing class and getting hurt in the process. He softened the verbal blow by assuring his little brother that teenaged girls couldn't resist flocking around an injured sports star. He urged him to take the punishment because the rewards on the other end would be pretty sweet.

When father and son left I quietly excused myself as well so that Church and Elma could have some alone time. When I was walking out the door he was sitting next to her on the couch, his arm around her shoulder, her head on his chest as he told her about all the places he had been and all the memories he had made in the last year. I couldn't help but be a little touched that his voice lightened and his tone softened when he talked about Denver and all the people that had welcomed him there. I was glad to know that all the efforts put into including him, into letting him know he was one of our own even if he wasn't ready to embrace us back, hadn't gone unnoticed.

I walked up the block and across the street to where the Churchills called home and tapped lightly on the door before letting myself in when there was no response. No one was in the living room, so I helped myself to a quick shower and decided I needed to check on both my dog and my neighbor. I pulled Poppy up on FaceTime and waited for what felt like forever for her to answer. Her pretty face had a tad bit more color in it than it normally did as it filled the screen.

"Hey, Dixie. How's Mississippi?" I heard Dolly bark somewhere in the background and was hit with a pang of longing. I missed my pretty blue girl and her constant companionship. She was my ray of sunshine when I was worn-out from spreading light all over everyone else.

"It's actually pretty amazing. It's like something from a Nicholas Sparks movie." Ugh. Bad reference. No one in those movies ever got a happy ending without something terrible happening first. "It's very pretty and everyone has that slow southern drawl. I kind of love it. How is my girl doing?"

Poppy whistled and suddenly the screen was filled with a happy drooling face that I missed so much. I cooed at Dolly, told her she was a good girl, and promised her I would be home soon. She danced around and barked like she understood what I was saying but then took off when Poppy tossed a ball.

"She's good. I've had her with me at the clinic most days, but Wheeler asked to watch her yesterday. He took her to work with him. I think he's lonely over there all by himself. All he does is work and sleep . . . oh, and order pizza. You might need to air out your place when you get back. It's definitely getting a distinctive dude funk to it."

I chuckled and looked up as Church opened the door. He noticed I was on the phone and half mouthed half mimed that he was going to hit the gym set up in the garage before taking a shower. I guess when you had a future hall of famer and a police officer in the family, fitness wasn't taken lightly and I was glad he dipped out without subjecting another friend to a round of phone sex they didn't sign up for. Especially this friend.

"You've been over at my apartment with just Wheeler there?" I couldn't keep the surprise out of my voice. She avoided strangers and strange men in particular like they all had the plague.

"Just for a minute here and there. I wanted to get Dolly's rawhide and her dog bed that I knew were in your room. She doesn't like my bed. I was there when your sister showed up. It didn't go well."

She bit down on her lower lip and ducked her head so that her face was partially obscured.

"Don't worry about Kallie. She can be a bitch, but she's not all bad. Things are really complicated with her and Wheeler right now and you just happened to be in the wrong place at the wrong time. He's pretty worried about you after the confrontation." I didn't tell her that I thought his priorities were kind of screwed up in that because it wasn't my place or my problem.

"He's very nice." He was. He was also freshly heartbroken and cut loose. He'd been set adrift after a long time spent with the same person and a little too raw to be thinking about the quiet, damaged girl next door. But again not my zoo and not my monkeys.

"He is a great guy. I'm glad things are going okay with him there while I'm gone." I was going to ask how her very pregnant sister was doing when my phone dinged with an alert I didn't recognize. I told Poppy how much I appreciated her looking after my girl and assured her things were going well on my end as well. A slight exaggeration but I figured she didn't know that.

When I pulled my phone away from my ear I froze in shock when the dating app where all my disastrous dates had sprung from pinged with a match. This particular app was set up to narrow down possible prospects within a twenty-mile radius of wherever your phone was. The service was letting me know there were men using the app in Lowry that met all the requirements I'd filled out when I initially set up the app. It also meant that anyone using the app would be able to find me and my profile if my phone was in that same area.

Staring at it in shock as realization dawned I got up and practically ran through the house towards the door that led from the utility room to the garage. The space had been converted into a home gym that rivaled the setup at the twenty-four-hour fitness center I kept a membership to but never used. It was full of serious machines and heavy weights that indicated the men in this family were dedicated to taking care of themselves. The door slammed shut behind me, which had Church looking at me through arms that were bulging and straining as he hefted a bench-press bar loaded down with what looked like more weight than I had on my body straight up.

"I think I know how whoever has been tailing us has known where we've been since we left Denver." I watched in awe as he pushed the bar back up and lowered it a few more times before setting it on the cradle with a loud *clink*. I knew he was strong but watching all those muscles move and work was mouthwatering and mesmerizing.

I held my phone out to him as he leaned his head back on the bench to look up at me. "The dating app where I met all those guys has a location finder. I think it's used for people looking for a quick hookup more than anything, but it notifies you when someone you're interested in or that matches your preferences is within twenty miles of your phone. You can open the alert and it gives you a real-time map that shows you exactly where your match is at. If it's one of the guys that I went on a date with then all they would have to do is be within twenty miles of my phone at all times to know where I am."

He reached for a towel that was lying on the ground next to a half-empty bottle of water and motioned me over with a crooked finger. He was sweaty and shiny, his veins standing out under the glossy sheen of his skin.

"So if you look at the guys you answered the alert on will the map show you where they are currently?"

I stopped by the bar and put a shaking hand on the smooth metal. "If they have the location service enabled." I tapped the screen of my phone and opened the app. He watched me as I poked through the different saved profiles and conversations I'd saved to find the guys I'd agreed to go out with. First up was the thief. He was still in Denver and I wanted to kick myself for not thinking to use the app to locate him after he took off with my wallet. Next was the swinger. He appeared to be somewhere south of Denver towards Colorado Springs but still nowhere near Lowry. Lastly was momma's boy. I scrolled and scrolled but couldn't find any traces of him in the app. His profile was gone and with it any record of the interactions we'd had while he was signed up.

"The first two are still in Colorado, well, their phones are at least. The last guy, the one who brought his mom on the date, is gone. I can't tell where his phone is at and I can't retrieve any of our conversations. It's like he disappeared, which is no big surprise considering it was his mom using the app all along."

"What was his name?" Church took the phone from me and pressed a bunch of stuff on the screen as he messed with the apps and settings.

"His first name was Joseph and his last name was something common." I furrowed my brows together as I tried to remember how he'd introduced himself, or rather how his mother had introduced them. "The last name was Erikson. Joseph and Marie Erikson."

Church handed me the phone and I slid it into my back pocket as he looked at me out of soulful and serious eyes. "Either of them could have made a new profile, clicked on you, and tracked you here. It would make sense. All the things that have been happening seem geared towards scaring you, probably so you'll leave and go back to Denver. The beat down that Dalen caught was meant for me. They want me out of the way so you are on your own and scared."

I put a wobbly hand to my throat and shifted my weight nervously. "So what do we do now? I need to get rid of that app."

He shook his head and laid back down on the bench, which put his head right at thigh level. All I had to do was take a step forward and that unsmiling but oh so sinful mouth would be right where the seam of my jeans was already a little damp from watching him throw those weights around like he was Hercules.

"Don't delete it just yet. I turned off the location locater but left your profile up. We might need it to see where those other guys you went out with are and it won't hurt anything to see who else pings the app while you're here. One of the new hits will probably be the fake profile of whoever it was that followed you from Denver. We can see them, but they can't see you."

He put his hands on the bar over mine and curled them around so he was holding me in place. I bent my head so that I was looking down at him and felt my blood start to heat at the smoldering intent making the brown in his eyes turn darker with desire.

"I'm not going to let anything bad happen to you." It was a promise he couldn't keep but I appreciated that he made it anyways. "Want to work up a sweat with me? I picked up a little something while I was at the gas station with Dalen earlier."

My hair fell forward around my face as I continued to stare

down at where he was lying with his face really close to the part of me that was particularly fond of those full lips and that clever tongue.

"Girls don't sweat. We glisten." He let go of my hands and slid his palms around my waist so that his hands had ahold of either side of my ass.

"I will gladly make you glisten all over."

I sighed. It would take a woman with far stronger willpower and who was far less in love with him to turn down an offer like that.

Chapter 16

Church

I watched upside down and with heavy-lidded eyes as she moved deliberate and unhurried, popping the button open on her jeans and slowly lowering the zipper down. I would have given my left nut, or maybe my right since that seemed to be the preferred one, for her to have had a frilly little sundress on or better yet those leather chaps and nothing else. It was nothing but denim and some flimsy lace that kept my mouth from being where we both wanted it to be. I needed her naked and hovering over my tongue like yesterday. Especially now that I knew how close the danger was. Waiting, insidious and deceptive while hiding out in the open. I didn't like a sneak attack when it was my stronghold that was vulnerable.

It took her a few minutes to scramble out of her clothes and another second to dart across the gym naked as a jaybird so that she could flip the lock on the door. I had no worry that my dad or my brother would be naïve enough to walk into any room I was in with her unannounced, but if it made her feel better and got her to sit on my face faster then I wasn't going to tell her she didn't need to bother.

When she came back I could see the way her pretty, pale skin quivered as she got closer. She wrapped her hands back around the bar that was sitting a few inches above my chest and took the last few steps required that would have my mouth lined up with her glossy center perfectly. I let out a breath that made her whole body shudder and had me flashing a wolfish grin that was all teeth and wicked intent. I grabbed the back of one of her knees and pulled it up next to my head on the weight machine and swallowed back a groan as she leaned over the bar slightly, rusty curls falling in front of her face and the tips tickling my stomach. The heavy weight of her breasts hung in front of my hungry eyes as I coasted a caress up the back of her thighs and pulled her closer.

She was already shiny and wet. Her hidden flesh my favorite color of pink and so obviously aroused and ready for me. I kissed the inside of one of her thighs and heard her let out a quiet gasp. She was so responsive, so easy to set off and please. I liked to think I had a special touch where her pleasure was involved. Something magical and mystical that only occurred when it was my hands on her, when it was my mouth eating her up and licking her clean.

My chin bumped into her cleft, where that single center of pleasure lived. The contact made her eyes flutter closed and had her thigh muscles tightening where they were next to either side of my head. It made me chuckle in satisfaction, which vibrated low through all of her tender folds. I let my tongue swipe all along the damp slit and stopped at her velvety opening so I could flick it in and out of her sweet heat. Her hips bucked in my hold and her breasts swayed enticingly above me. The thin track pants I'd snagged from Jules were doing little to keep my growing erection in check as I continued to work my tongue in and out of her as she made little panting sounds and rubbed herself against my face. She was always so uninhibited and ready to take hers when we were together like this. It was the only time I ever saw her get greedy and when she didn't seem hesitant to take exactly what she wanted.

I needed to get my hands on those perky nipples. I needed to get my tongue on her hungry little clit. I needed to get my cock back inside that silken channel that was fluttering around each lick and swipe in a delicate caress. She didn't feel like she was going to last very long, which made me feel like a savage, sexual superstar. There was something to be said for making your girl so quick on the trigger as long as she knew I was far from done with her.

I gave one of her ass cheeks a little tap, which made her yelp. Her eyes popped open and narrowed down at me where she was hovering over me as I continued to devour her. I was relentless as I licked and sucked at her. Brutal as I worked her over and helped her ride my face like she would win a big shiny belt buckle and be crowned rodeo queen after she came all over my face. These were the times I relished not having to be gentle in how I handled her. In our day-to-day I knew I was going to crush her, that all those feelings that were catching up to me were going to bury me, but here, with her mewling and rocking back and forth like her life depended on it, there was no place for a soft touch and a hesitant heart.

I tried to pull her down as she suddenly moved, dragging my tongue along more secret skin and hidden places that I didn't think she was ready to let me have access to yet. She let go of the bar with one of her hands and placed it on the rigid lines of my stomach. The already tight muscles pulled even tighter and she maneuvered herself farther over the bar between us so that she was almost kneeling over me. Once she found her balance in the new position she let go of the bar with her other hand and used it to push the lightweight fabric of my pants down until the towering length of my cock sprang free of the confines. I had to lift my hips a little, which was tricky since I was practically holding her up. It was a good thing I hadn't slacked off in the gym since getting out of the service or else this fucking explosive 69 wouldn't be possible.

She wrapped a hand around the base of my dick, looked back at me with a sexy little smirk that had my erection swelling even more in her hold, and then she bent her head and I forgot how to breathe. She sucked the head into her mouth, wrapped her lips around it, and rolled her tongue over the tip like she was licking around the outside of an ice cream cone. I wasn't going to melt in her mouth but there was a good chance I was going to explode all over that quick and clever tongue. She started to move her fist with a little twist up and down the straining shaft and it took me a solid minute to remember I was supposed to be holding up my end of the deal.

I had to lift my head to get back at all her luscious and juicy places, so I was sitting in a perpetual crunch. My abs burned and my shoulders screamed but there was no way I was tapping out. Not when she was sucking more of my cock back as she moved her fingers lower, between my legs to gently run them across sensitive globes that were aching for some kind of release. I got my mouth on her, got my tongue back inside of her, and managed to hold her up with one hand so I could use the other to tease and taunt the puckered tips of her breasts where they swayed seductively over me. She hummed around the thick flesh in her mouth as I tugged on the rosy peak and the vibration made my eyes cross and had my balls pulling up tight as she continued to manipulate them.

I threw my head back and blew out a heated breath that had her hips undulating and swiveling in my hands as she chased the phantom kiss.

"Dixie, I need to be inside you. As good as your mouth feels and as good as you taste I need to feel you come on my cock." She let go of my dick with one last lick and looked at me from where she was practically lying flat across my body.

"Okay." Her whispery acquiescence had me fighting down urges to toss her on the floor and rut into her like an animal. She shouldn't give me free rein. I would take everything because I was a selfish, needy bastard.

Once she was on her feet back by my head I maneuvered myself out from under the bar and leaned over to where I had tossed my jeans when I changed out of them to start my workout. I fished out one of the condoms that I'd stashed in there earlier and handed it to her as I stripped out of the rest of my workout gear. I grabbed her hand and pulled her around to the end of the bench, urged her to sit on the end of it where my cock was eye level and insistent that she do something with it.

I wrapped my own fist around the rigid length and gave it a few swift pumps, sliding it along the moisture left over from her mouth. She licked her bottom lip and looked up at me from under her lashes as she tore open the foil packet and pulled the circle of latex out. I was going to hate being inside her with the barrier between us after having a taste of her dangerous and raw this morning, but as much as I wanted to leave everything I had inside of her, I knew that wasn't fair to her.

She batted my hands away and replaced them with her own. She had me covered in seconds and before she laid back she leaned forward and placed the softest, sweetest kiss right below my belly button. My stomach clenched and my thighs bunched up like I was preparing for an attack, and really, I kind of was.

I put a hand in the center of her chest, spread my fingers wide, and urged her to lay back. I followed her backwards and pulled her hips down to the very edge of the bench so that only her spine was making contact with the surface as I supported the rest of her body in my hands. She wrapped her legs around my waist and leaned up to meet my lips as I let gravity and the moisture we'd already stirred up pull me into the waiting warmth of her body. I kissed her. Lips seeking, tongue swirling as she took me into her body fully. I had to release her mouth so I could stand up and move.

I held her hips to mine as I started a steady, powerful rhythm. She lifted her arms up over her head and stretched them out so her breasts bounced and swayed with every thrust. I couldn't look away and I was happy to say she didn't seem like there was anything that was going to pull her eyes off of me either.

We rolled into one another, her stuck with the pace I set even as she used her heels in my ass to go faster, to pound harder. I liked watching the way the slow and deliberate thrusts made her eyes darken to almost black and I liked that the slower I went and the longer I took to drag myself out of her the more she flushed and the more her pale skin did indeed glisten. She strained towards me, hips grinding, legs squeezing, but she was my captive and this was my magic trick.

I moved her legs so that her knees were resting over the bend of my elbows, giving me the perfect view of the spot where we were joined. It made me groan every time her body fluttered and trembled around mine as she took me in. She was so welcoming, so willing to take me as I was.

"Need a hand here, pretty girl. Mine are occupied."

She made a noise of satisfaction low in her throat and slowly started to trail her hands over her skin. She stopped to play with her breasts, which she knew would make me lose the steady rhythm I was using to torture us both. My hips kicked into her and she gasped. She smiled up at me and continued to let her fingers dance over that freckled skin. She circled her cute little belly button and then, after what felt like hours, finally touched that place where I had her spread open and shimmering with sex and saliva. Her touch was butterfly light as I watched her fondle herself. She circled and circled with the pad of her finger until her breathing got choppy and her gaze got hazy.

When I felt her start to tighten around me, when I saw her legs quiver and felt her stroking rhythm get erratic and wild, I finally let loose. I plowed into her, dick hammering and balls swinging against her ass. She moaned my name and scrambled to find something to hold on to as I pounded into her so hard it started to move her farther up the bench. Her slick skin squeaked on the vinyl but neither one of us stopped to readjust.

I took her harder and more viciously than I had ever taken another woman and I knew I was driven by the fact that I didn't want her to be able to forget me when it was time for us to go our separate ways. I wanted to fuck her better than any man that may come after me could.

I felt my orgasm start to coil and wind into a spring that was beyond ready to snap at the base of my spine. "Dixie." It was a warning but it was also a plea. I never wanted her to get shortchanged when we were together like this, not after all the big promises I'd made to her about giving her the time of her life in the sack, but her demanding and serious way of fucking me back was unraveling me and blowing all my restraint to hell. I wanted to give her what she deserved, but she was just as determined to give me all the things I didn't deserve.

She gave a wobbly smile and I saw her toes point and stiffen as her body broke under mine. The rush of pleasure from her orgasm pushed me ruthlessly into my own.

I'd had more than my fair share of sexual experiences since I lost my virginity when I was fifteen. But none of them compared to this one. None of them would be remembered because this one was the only one that felt like it mattered.

Sex with Dixie had proven to be different, deeper than any other sex I'd ever had, but I hadn't realized until this minute that that was because she made it as much about me as I tried to make it about her. I wanted her to come first, figuratively and literally, but she wanted us to come together. She wanted to make sure that it was as good for me as I tried to make it for her.

I let her legs drop and watched as gravity pulled her body away from mine. Sex looked good on her. Sex with me looked perfect on her.

I let my gaze drift over every satiated, satisfied inch of her and couldn't stop one of those grins she'd forced me to find from pulling at my lips.

"You glisten good, pretty girl." And I wasn't so sure anymore that I was going to be able to hand her off to someone else that might take better care of her if that meant I didn't get to see her shine anymore.

THE REST OF my workout was put on hold since all my muscles felt like they were made of taffy and my bones had the rigidity of water after Dixie was done with me. She was yawning and barely able to keep her eyes open, so I walked her back to my childhood bedroom, but there was no way I was going to sleep. Not with my brain swirling around the information she had given me about the dating app and not with the realization that letting her go and handing her off to someone else might not be as easy as I'd once had myself convinced it would be. I was used to guarding my heart but somehow she had slipped under those ironclad defenses and imbedded some of her optimism and unshakable belief in the territory inside of me I thought was toxic and contaminated. Everything needed sunlight and care to flourish and grow. Dixie had both in spades and was relentless in her quest to turn my insides from something barren and lifeless into something that flourished and thrived with light and color.

After her breathing turned steady and even, I maneuvered my way out from under her freckled limbs, pulled on the black track pants I'd snagged from Jules, and quietly made my way through the house towards where the master bedroom was located. The silent journey was one down memory lane as well as down the hallway. It felt like yesterday that I'd been creeping down these same floors searching for comfort during angry storms or when I'd had a bad dream. Even after mom had passed, Jules was always there, always with an open door, ready to offer comfort and soft words that made everything in the world seem better. I'd always thought he could keep all the monsters at bay until we lost another amazing woman. It was then I realized there were some things even the bravest men couldn't battle, so instead of staying to fight I chose to flee.

I didn't make it to the bedroom because the sliding back door was open and the rich scent of a lit cigar wafted in from the outside. There was a big deck on the back of the house, where the barbecue to end all barbecues lived, and ever since I was little Jules had liked to sit out there with his feet propped up on the rail, smoking a stogie after a particularly long day at work. The smell was one of comfort and fond memories. It was one that made me feel like no matter how much had changed, more things, the important things, had stayed the same. The smell held regret and remorse for all the nights I'd missed it, missed the simple, quiet times with the man who raised me.

I pushed the door open wide enough to accommodate my shoulders and made my way over to the chair that was next to the one Jules was lounging in. The only light was coming from the half-moon overhead and the cherry glowing at the end of the cigar clamped between Jules's teeth.

I propped my feet up and crossed them at the ankles, copying his pose without even thinking about it. I'd been emulating the man my entire life, tried to live up to all the big examples he set, but when it came down to it, I'd failed at being the man he raised me to be.

"I need you to dig up whatever you can on some people named Erikson. Joseph and Marie. I have a friend," I used the term loosely, "in Denver who is dating a cop and I'm going to see if she'll look into them as well. Dixie met the son online and went on a date that went sideways. It sounds like they might be our culprits."

A puff of smoke billowed out in front of him and his chin dipped down in a nod as he pulled the cigar out of his mouth. "I can do that. I have a car parked outside Sassy's looking for our yokels as well. No sign of them yet. They're probably lying low or they may have figured out they got the wrong guy and are keeping their heads down so the person that hired them doesn't come looking for a refund." He stuck the cigar back in between his lips and when he talked the red end bounced up and down. "Keep that pretty little thing close, son. She's a keeper and you don't want anything happening to her."

I laced my fingers behind my head and rocked back on the chair so that it was balanced precariously on the back legs. "I'm more the catch and release type." I wasn't actually a fisherman at all because the catch of the day tended to land in the boat without me reeling them in. "And I promised her I wouldn't let anything happen to her while she's with me. It's a promise I intend to keep."

The cigar twitched as he turned his head to look at me and then he sighed long and loud, which sent fragrant smoke drifting up around his head. "That's not a promise you can make good on, son. Sometimes the things that happen to those that we love are out of our control. The only thing you can make sure of is that *you're* not the person or the reason she gets hurt. That you can control completely. If you hurt her, that pain falls squarely on you, Dash, and you don't get the luxury of blaming God or piss-poor luck."

His words dug themselves deep inside my skin. It was a fatherly warning, but it was more than that. It was hard truth that

I couldn't bury my head in the sand and ignore. I was always waiting for the bad to work its way into my good thing. I rarely stopped to wonder if I was the bad working myself into someone else's good thing because of my long-held hang-ups and refusal to let anyone close.

"I owe you an apology. I know the words don't make up for my actions, but I am sorry." I kicked the chair back even farther so that I was looking up at the night sky. "I'm sorry I didn't tell you what I was really risking when I was overseas. I'm sorry I never made it back home. I'm sorry I left the way I did and I'm more than sorry I wasn't here when you needed me the most. You have always been the best example of a father any kid could ask for and I'm sorry you got stuck with me instead of a kid that deserved you."

There was absolute silence from the man next to me, so I turned my head just as he was shifting in his seat so that he was looking directly at me. He pulled the cigar out of his mouth and gingerly placed it in the glass ashtray that was resting near the leg of his chair.

"Did I ever tell you I loved your mom long before she ever agreed to go out on a date with me?" At the abrupt change of subject I gave him a quizzical look and shook my head. "Well, I did. I thought she was the most beautiful girl I'd ever seen when we were in high school together. I used to watch her in the hallways, and I had a picture that the paper ran of her from her pageant days stuck on my mirror in my room. I would have given anything for her to look at me, for her to see me the way I saw her, but she never did."

I snorted. "Probably because her parents would have lost their shit if she tried to bring home a black boyfriend while she was still living under their roof. It probably never occurred to her that you were a viable dating choice back then."

He nodded and lifted a shoulder and let it fall. "Maybe, but I didn't know that. I didn't know she was raised by racists and had been taught that different skin color was something unacceptable. What I did know was that she came from money, and I did not. I came from the Holler. My home had wheels and aluminum walls. I shared that space with a mom who had a drug habit and a dad who liked to knock her and me around when he was home. I didn't have a lot, and what I did have wasn't anything to brag about, so I never asked your mom out. I never took a chance." His eyes were intent on mine as he kept talking. "When I saw her again when she came back to town the rumor had spread that she left school and had a baby. This is a small town, so it was no secret she was on the outs with her folks because the baby wasn't enough like them. By that time, I'd been on the force for a few years, I'd gone to college, I'd bought a home, and had a life any man could be proud of, but I saw your mom and all those old fears came back. I wasn't good enough for her and there was no way I had anything impressive to offer her. I didn't deserve a woman like that because I didn't know what I would do with her even if she gave me a shot. My life was violent and ugly, that was the reality of things. I didn't know if I had it in me to be a different kind of man than the one I was raised to be and that terrified me."

"That's shitty." We'd never talked much about his childhood since so much if his focus had been on making sure I had a great one, before and after my mom.

"It is shitty, but it turned out I wanted your mom more than I wanted to keep her safe from all the things I was scared of. I asked her out without meaning to and almost had a heart attack when she said yes. I was already in love with her, so I was surprised how easy it was to be the kind of man she needed me to be. When things got serious and she told me it was time to meet you—" he stopped talking and had to clear his throat "—I remembered every single time my dad hit me. All I could think about was how short-tempered and angry he was with me all the time. I'd always had a thing for your mom but you were this tiny, innocent stranger that I was going to have to fool into thinking I was worthy of love and affection. I didn't think I could do it. All I could imagine was doing the wrong thing with you, screwing up and having your mom leave me, and worse than that, having her leave me because I'd been right all along and I wasn't good enough for her." He gave me a pointed look that I could see clearly even in the dark. It was like he was looking right into my soul. "I broke up with her before she could bring you around me. I left her with some lame excuse about things moving too fast, lied through my teeth that I wasn't ready to be a daddy, told her it wasn't her, it was me . . . all the stupid stuff idiotic men say when they know they are breaking a good woman's heart."

I felt a frown pull at my face as the sides of my mouth turned down. "I don't really remember that." I had vague recollections of my mom being sad after we were back in Lowry, but I always figured it had to do with my grandparents' ignorance and the mean things people would say about me when they thought she couldn't hear. Maybe there was a time before I remembered Jules being a part of my life when she had cried more than normal but I was too young to have any clear memory of it.

"That's because it didn't last long. I realized pretty quickly that I was an idiot. Fear can make a smart man do very hurtful things, but eventually the heart wins out because fear is fleeting and love lasts forever. It took me six months to win her back and another six plus an engagement ring before she would let me meet you. She said she could handle me breaking her heart again but there was no way in hell that she was going to let me mess with her little boy's. She didn't need to worry. It was love at first sight with you, son. I took one look at you and knew I would do everything in my power to be the best dad I could be for you. I knew that what my dad had taught me didn't matter, that being a parent was something you could choose to be good at, and could make the effort to get better at every single day. He didn't want to do the work, I did . . . and still do."

It was my turn to clear my throat. "You were the best back then, and if Dalen is anything to go by you're the best now. You didn't have to keep showing up when things got hard. In fact, I don't think anyone would have blamed you if you'd bailed." Well, he probably would have blamed himself like I'd been doing the last ten years and that was a heavy burden to haul around.

He chuckled but there was no humor in it. "You don't think I wanted to, Dash? I was a county cop in a small town with two kids that had just lost their mom. I lost the love of my life and didn't have anyone to turn to. There were times I would be on patrol and think about driving and driving until Lowry and everything that was here was behind me. There are nights I don't remember getting you kids to bed and there are entire days I can't recall. I started doing stuff at work that had my bosses threatening to put me on a desk. I wasn't living for me, and I was hardly showing up for you kids. Thank the Lord Elma was there because there's a good chance I would have screwed everything up and lost you both."

Again I couldn't remember any of that. After Mom died I was in my own youthful fog of grief and misery. I'd also had my hands full with a little brother that needed constant care and supervision. Plus, I was a new teenager and dealing with puberty that hit like a Mack Truck. Sure, Jules had maybe been a little more distant, a little less affectionate than he typically was, but I figured that was how real men, how men like him, dealt with the loss of a loved one.

"It was Caroline who pointed out how much I had to lose. I brought Dalen in for a checkup and he was underweight, he needed his nails trimmed, and he had cradle cap. She yelled at me, told me that it was awful I'd lost my wife but my son was still here. I still had the opportunity to hold him in my arms, and if I didn't get my head out of my ass I was going to lose that." A soft grin touched his mouth as he spoke about his second wife. "It was a wake-up call I desperately needed because I had checked out, son. I was physically here, but mentally . . ." He blew out a breath and pointed to the stars. "I was long gone."

He cut another look at me. "I didn't want to fall for Caroline. I didn't want to love anyone else. I had my boys and my work and I was happy with that. When she started to pursue me I resisted." He gave me a look with a lifted eyebrow that told me without words he clearly remembered my resistance when he entered my life. "I remember when Caroline was pulled out of school when she was initially diagnosed. She was a few grades younger than me and I remembered thinking it was impossible for someone so young to be so sick. But like I said, love will always outlast fear."

He didn't talk about being afraid like it was something to be ashamed of. He didn't talk about the fear like it was something that made him, or me, weak. He talked about it like it was a fact of life and we had to learn how to live with it, and the hurtful things it made us do, just like we had to live with the fact we couldn't pick the person our hearts settled on.

"I loved her when I didn't want to and I don't regret a minute of it. What I do regret, son, is the same thing you now regret. I regret the time that I allowed fear to steal from me. I regret every second, every minute, every hour I let fear keep me from your mom all the way to when I was younger up until she let me back into her life. I regret every moment of time I lost with Caroline because I was terrified of something I had no control over. She would have been sick with or without us and I thank God every day that she got to spend the last years of her life with our family because we were the only thing she wanted and she gave us back everything we lost and then some."

I felt a ball of emotion lodge in my throat. I had to blink my eyes because they stung. My hands curled around the arms of the chair so tightly the plastic groaned in protest.

"I hated when you left, son. I hated it for you and I hated it for us. You should have been here so I could watch you become the man you are today, Dash, but you let fear take that away from you, and you let fear keep that from the rest of us. It's up to you if you're going to let fear take even more from you." He reached out a hand and put it on my shoulder. "Make good choices, son." That seemed to be his favorite bit of advice now that I was back home.

I ground my teeth together and when my voice made it past the lump in my throat it sounded like sandpaper scraping over razors. "I was scared. I was scared something was going to happen to you, to Dalen . . . to Elma. Everyone I ever cared about went away and it really fucking hurt. I thought it would be easier if I was the one that went away. I took myself somewhere where things are always bad so when shit went south it wasn't a surprise. It didn't feel like my heart was getting ripped out of my chest because over there . . ." I shook my head. "Bad is all you know."

I sighed and lifted up a hand so that the moonlight made my skin glow. There was always a light in the darkness if you opened your eyes and looked for it.

"It took longer than I would have liked but you're finding your way to where you need to be, son."

I was but that was only because one perky redhead had burst into my life and lit the way. I threw my head back, not thinking about the fact I was still on two legs of the chair, and gave a surprised shout as the entire thing started to topple backwards. The sky swirled starry and black before my eyes as I braced for the impact of my head hitting the hard wooden surface of the deck.

But my fall was halted mid-crash by a strong hand on the back of the chair. Like it and I weighed nothing Jules latched on to the back slats of the chair and hauled me back to a seated position.

I looked at him out of the corner of my eye and watched as he bent down to pick up his cigar.

"Thanks . . . Dad." The man had never let me down, never let me fall, and he refused to let me be less than the man he'd raised me to be. It'd taken almost thirty years, two moms, a little brother, and realizing that even though I didn't want to and was terrified of it, I was falling in love with a girl that I didn't want to hurt more than I wanted to protect myself to get the words out of me. With him, I'd never had to earn the title of son. I was a real asshole for ever making him feel like he needed to earn the title Dad. It was who he had been the minute he entered my life.

The cigar quirked between his lips, and in true Jules fashion, even though what had just happened was monumental and life changing, he acted like it was no big deal.

"Anytime. Sometimes you gotta let your kids fall and remind them that you'll be there to pick them up. And sometimes you gotta step in and keep them from hitting the ground in the first place."

There was one fall he couldn't prevent or help me up from. That was the fall that had started when I walked into the bar and felt the warmth of the sun after what felt like a lifetime spent in the frigid cold. Slipping, sliding, skidding, tripping, tumbling, flailing . . . falling into love with Dixie Carmichael.

Chapter 17

Dixie

I was surprised that I was up and ready to go before Church the next morning. I'd felt him leave the bed sometime last night but hadn't awoken when he returned. It was the best feeling in the world to wake up sheltered in his arms, wrapped up in his strength like he didn't have any intention of letting me go. The feeling was quickly chased away by the disappointment that all too soon he wasn't going to simply let me go, he was going to push me away.

Not wanting to wake him I took my time sliding out of his grasp and almost couldn't make a clean escape because the more I moved the more his hand tangled in my hair where it was caught. He mumbled something in his sleep and eventually rolled to his side, his normally fierce expression softened in sleep and making him look almost approachable . . . almost.

I snagged a pair of jeans and a tank top from my meager wardrobe and tiptoed into the bathroom to get dressed and tame my hair for the day. I could hear the other Churchill men up and about when I was done brushing my teeth, so I wandered into the kitchen, where the sounds of masculine chatter and early morning preparations for the day were coming from. Jules was at the stove flipping pancakes and telling a sullen-looking Dalen that there was no time like the present for him to learn that actions, no matter how insignificant they may seem, all had consequences. Dalen was grumbling under his breath about how the game this weekend was vital to the team, and Jules flatly informed him that next time he decided to skip school he might want to consider who else he would be letting down if he got caught breaking the rules.

I took a seat at the counter on one of the high-backed stools next to Church's younger brother and gave him a sympathetic look. His eyes were a startling shade of purple with a halo of yellow and green on the outside. The cut in his lip had scabbed over but the skin around it was still red and angry-looking. The scrape on the side of his head looked sore and the bandage he had slapped over it was doing little to camouflage the damage. I bumped his shoulder with my own and gave him an "Ouch."

He returned with a lopsided grin that made him wince. "Yeah. Getting out of bed this morning wasn't any fun, but Dad is still insisting we meet with the coach and the principal." He narrowed his eyes at his dad's back and pouted with pure teenaged ire.

It made me laugh and had Jules turning to look at me over his shoulder with a knowing grin. "Dash said you aren't typically an early riser, so I only made enough for the human garbage disposal sitting next to you, but I can whip up a couple more if you're hungry."

I shook my head but gladly took the mug of coffee Dalen poured for me and pushed my way. "I think I'll go and see if Elma needs help with breakfast. She has her first physical therapy session today, and I want to be around for moral support."

Dalen lifted an eyebrow at me and then groaned when the action pulled at his bruised face. "You're like a cheerleader for things that happen in real life."

My lips twitched as I lifted the mug up and took a sip. "Sometimes the day-to-day things are the hardest. We take being able to do them without struggle for granted. I'm happy to offer a little bit of encouragement when it's needed."

Jules turned around and placed a stack of pancakes in front of Dalen that had my jaw dropping open. It looked like something that would be on one of those outrageous eating competition shows but Dalen dug in like this was an everyday occurrence and not a meal fit to feed the entire offensive line of the Denver Broncos.

"I'm sure Elma will appreciate the company, but you should wait until Dash is awake to take you over there. He gave me a heads-up that your recent troubles might be an overly amorous suitor. I put calls in to see what we have on them in the system, but until we hear back, you should probably avoid being out in the wild alone."

I stiffened and looked at him over the top of the coffee. "Okay."

Jules nodded and lifted his hands so that he could smooth his fingers over either side of his goatee. "Elma's had a pretty rough go of it here the last few weeks and she is looking at a long road to recovery. I hate to ask, but if you can avoid mentioning that things are a little bit unpredictable right now I would appreciate it. She spent the last ten years worrying herself sick over my stubborn son, I'd like her to be able to focus on getting better and not the fact trouble followed the boy home."

I set the coffee mug down on the counter and rested my chin in the hand of the arm that had my elbow propped up on the surface. "I won't go into details but she's sharp as a tack. She told me yesterday that she knew something wasn't right and she saw Dalen's face last night. It's pretty obvious things haven't been smooth sailing since Church and I got to town."

"She'd be fit to be tied if she knew someone was after you and that they were willing to hurt my boys to get at you. She's wanted Dash home since the minute he left. She's also wanted that boy to find his happy since we lost his mom and let's be honest, Curly Sue, you're probably the best shot he's got at it."

I blinked at the older man and had to take a second to find my breath. I wanted to be Church's happy forever, not just his happy for now, but he hadn't given me a single sign he was on the same page as I was. "Well, he deserves some happiness, you all do, after everything you've been through. I'm glad I can give him a little bit of it while we're together."

Jules braced himself on the counter across from me with his arms crossed against his uniformed chest. His dark eyebrows quirked upwards and his mouth tugged into that grin that had to break hearts from miles away. "I think it's easy for folks to forget that sometimes it's far harder to have a smile ready than it is to find a frown. You should find your happy, too, Dixie girl."

The man was far too perceptive for my own good. "I am happy." And I was most days. It was the days when I got swallowed up by everyone else's wants and needs and forgot to focus on my own that I felt like I was missing out on a little something. I was a caretaker by nature, but the care I allowed for myself often paled in comparison to that which I offered others. "I have a lot to be thankful for and I get to have a hand in making sure that the people I care the most about are living their best lives. There isn't much more to happiness for me than that." Sure, I would be elated to finally have the dreams I'd been hoarding for a lifetime come true but just like I couldn't be Church's reason to find his happy, I couldn't hold him accountable for mine. I was going to have to go out and live my best life without him, even if I wasn't sure that was possible. Even before we were romantically involved my heart had beat stronger, my soul had shined brighter, and my life had been more full and interesting simply by having him in it. Once he was gone I knew there were going to be a lot of stormy days in my future but the truth was the rain was never able to stop the sun from shining for very long.

"Enough of this boring grown-up talk. I'm going to have to sit through hours of lectures and real talk once the coach gets his hands on me. Can we go so I can get it over with?"

Dalen's surly tone broke the somber mood between his father and me, so it seemed like a perfect way to end the conversation. I grabbed my phone and some shoes from the bedroom, surprised Church was still out like a light. I was leaning over to give him a kiss on that tempting mouth when his eyes popped open and I found myself lost in a swirling labyrinth of color and confusion. Those eyes weren't dark and haunted first thing in the morning. They blazed with a million emotions I couldn't name and a few that I wanted so desperately to be something he hadn't even hinted at.

"Mornin'." His eyelids fluttered slightly and all the muscles in his chest stretched and flexed as he lifted his arms above his head. The sight made my mouth water and had me pondering putting our visit to Elma Mae on the back burner when Church's phone rang from somewhere off to the side of the bed.

I lowered my lips to his shoulder as he swiped the screen and put the device to his ear. I let my fingers trip and tickle across his smooth skin with a grin as he lifted an eyebrow and gave me a warning look. I had my mind on payback until he stiffened and reached up a hand to push my hair off my face with a shake of his head.

"Is she okay?" I went still at his question and frowned as a serious look pulled tight across his features. "Give us five minutes and we'll be over."

He tossed the phone onto the bed and swung his long legs over the side. "Is everything okay?"

He looked down at me as he snatched up a pair of jeans and shoved his long legs into them. "That was Elma's home care nurse. Apparently she fell this morning in the bathroom. She's refusing to go back to the doctor. The nurse asked me to come over and talk to her."

"Oh no." The words whispered worriedly between us. I was worried about Elma, but in all honesty I was more worried about Church. He wouldn't take something happening to the older woman well. He would see it as more evidence that every time he let someone get close, something bad worked its way in to harm them. "Well, I'm the new guy, so I have no problem going head to head with her if it's for her own good." I could do tough love for the cause because it was still love and that was sort of my specialty.

"The nurse said she's in a mood, so you can stay here if you want. I got this."

I reached out a hand and put it on the center of his back as he sat down on the edge of the bed in order to tug his boots on. "I know you have this, but I'm here and I want to help you with it."

He looked at me over his shoulder and the corners of his lips twitched as he reached around to snag my wrist so that he could pull me flush against his warm skin. "Always trying to fix everything, aren't you, pretty girl?"

I gulped a little and kissed his shoulder again. "I mean, I have to try."

"No, you don't, but you always do. That makes you something pretty special, Dixie." He let me go and bent over so he could snag a shirt off the floor. "You can come with me, but Elma is stubborn, so if she's in a mood I might have to pick her up and put her in the car and force her to go see the doctor if she's hurt."

I cleared my throat and slid off the bed. "You'll take care of her. That's what you do, and that's what makes you special, Church."

We walked up the block and around the corner hand in hand. We didn't say much, but he never did and the fact he had his fingers wrapped around mine felt like it said a whole lot more than words would anyways.

His eyes never stopped shifting over the area around us. There were obvious lines of tension in the set of his shoulders and in the turn of his mouth. It was like he was waiting for the other shoe to drop, or for whoever had been terrorizing us since we left Denver to jump out of one of the perfectly maintained rose bushes that lined the neighbor's yard. His alertness made me anxious and had me craning my neck to make sure danger wasn't lurking as we rounded the corner and started up Elma's driveway.

The nurse's plain economy car was parked in front and the big white door leading into the home was open. The screen door was still shut and the sound of Elma's TV could be heard well before we reached the porch. I went to run up the stairs like I always did, but Church threw out a hand and gently shoved me behind him as he took the steps one at a time. He was always doing that. He put me first in bed. He put me first when it came to the idea and thought of me getting what he thought I justly deserved. He put me first when it came to my comfort and well-being, and he put me first when it came to my safety and security by putting himself between me and whatever line of fire might be in front of us. I could take care of myself, but around him I didn't have to, because he always stepped up to take care of me. Somewhere along the line on this wacky journey he'd convinced me to take with him, his need to protect and defend felt less like an obligation and more like an honor that he was more than happy to have the responsibility for.

He rapped his knuckles on the frame of the screen and called Elma's name. There wasn't a response for a long minute, which made him frown. "Do you think she can't hear me over the TV?"

I shrugged and reached around him to tug open the door. "She might be in a lot of pain if she fell hard. Her nurse probably gave her some medication to help with that. Maybe it finally kicked in and she's down for the count. That will make kidnapping her and hauling her back to the hospital easier if that's the route you decide to go with."

He gave me a narrow-eyed look as he pushed into the house, me close on his heels. "Not funny, pretty girl."

It wasn't. But I hated the idea of Elma hurting as much as I hated the idea of him hurting because someone else he cared about had fallen to that bad that hung around, heavy and dark like a stormy day.

I was opening my mouth to shout for the nurse when suddenly there was a crack that sounded like a thousand firecrackers going off. One second I was standing behind Church in the entrance of Elma's stately and romantic house and the next I was being shoved bodily through the screen door without it being opened. Another crack ripped through the air and I heard him swear as he pushed my head down and continued to shove me through mesh and out of the house.

I heard him grunt in pain and swear as he yelled at me to run, his hands hard on my shoulders as he kept pushing me farther and farther away from the deafening pops and pings that I belatedly realized were gunshots.

I tumbled and landed on my hands and knees at the bottom of the porch steps. The gravel of the driveway slit the skin of my hands open as I screamed at Church when I realized he was still standing on the porch. He had one hand wrapped around the opposite bicep as crimson oozed fast and thick through his fingers.

"What . . ." I didn't even get the rest of the question out before Church fell back a step as the tattered and torn screen door was kicked open and a squirming, swearing Elma Mae was wrenched through it, clasped in the arms of a man that I recognized immediately. He looked different. Insanity and fury did that to a man. It twisted features and erased any traces of humanity that might have been there before.

Elma had a nasty-looking black eye that she hadn't had the day before, and it was clear she'd been fighting for a while but her already damaged and frail body was no match for the irrational strength that came with crazy.

Joseph had a small black pistol in his hand and it was aimed right at the center of Church's chest. Even with the distance separating us I could see his finger twitch on the trigger as he grappled with the white-haired Tasmanian devil in his grasp.

"He hurt Dharma." Elma's voice broke as she spoke to Church. "He made her call you and then he hit her in the head with his gun. She's bleeding, bad." Elma sounded as angry as Joseph looked as his wild-eyed gaze shifted between the two of us.

"She was supposed to tell you to come alone. She didn't. She was supposed to tell you the old bitch didn't want Dixie here. She didn't do that either." His gaze drifted past Church and landed on me. "I need you out of the way. You're standing between me and what's rightfully mine."

"The fuck!" Church growled the words and went to take a step forward but the gun wavered and switched from being pointed right at him to resting threateningly against Elma's temple. That had Church going stone still and the older woman's eyes popping open wide. I sucked in a shaky breath and climbed to my feet. I wiped my bleeding palms on my jeans and cleared my throat so that Joseph's attention would shift to me and off the two people standing between us.

"This is a bad idea, Joe." I hoped keeping my tone calm and using the name I used when I thought I was chatting him up online would lower his guard and make him more susceptible to suggestion. "Someone is going to report those gunshots. Church's dad is a cop. Elma Mae is their family. This is not going to end well for you."

"It's not going to end well for them!" His voice was shrill and the gun pressed harder into Elma's temple. She cried out in pain and Church couldn't stop himself from taking another step forward. The gun jerked away from Elma's head and once again ended up pointed right at Church. "Someone is always standing in the way of what I want. Someone is always getting what should be mine. At work, at home, I'm always coming in second best. Except with you, Dixie. You were the only one that saw how special I could be, how great I could be. You saw the best in me. I just needed a chance." The gun wavered a little and I screamed as I saw his finger move on the trigger.

The gunshot was louder now without the walls of the house to muffle it but nothing was as loud as the scream that ripped out of me as the bullet hit its target and sent Church to his knees in front of me. Elma Mae shrieked just as loudly as I did but her sound was cut off as she was flung to the side, collapsing in the same position I had as I hit the ground. Joseph stalked to where Church was still kneeling, blood now flowing freely down his arm and soaking into his shirt as his big body listed to the side. He lifted a hand to his shoulder and I could see him tilt his head back so that he was looking Joseph in the eyes as the other man loomed over him, the gun now focused right in Church's face.

"You're in the way of what I want. She was nice to me. She was sweet to me. She liked me and then you showed up and took her away."

That wasn't exactly how it all went down, but I didn't think there was going to be a lot of reasoning with him. "If you keep hurting Church and the other people I care about I'm not going to be nice anymore, Joseph. This has to stop."

His gaze shifted from Church, who was growling low in his throat and breathing hard. He was hurt, but he was also pissed off. I could practically see the wheels turning in his handsome head. He was going to take this all on himself. He was going to think that we were just getting good, and bad had wasted no time getting between us. He was going to think this was his bad even though it was clear it was all mine.

"I just want things to go my way one time. I want to be a winner for once." He sounded whiny and pitiful, which was totally at odds with the firearm pointed at the man I loved.

I sucked in a breath so hard that it whistled between my teeth. I put my raw hand to my throat and did what I always did . . . I tried to fix things.

"Leave Elma and Church alone and I'll go with you wherever you want, Joe."

Church's head whipped around so fast I was pretty sure he was going to get whiplash. "You aren't going any, fucking, where, Dixie." The words were bit out and filled with fury.

I refused to look at him because that was a lot of anger and a lot of frustrated man between me and my objective. I knew he would hate it, but I didn't see any other option. He was shot and Elma was hurt. I didn't know if anyone had called the police and I refused to be the reason anyone I loved was hurt.

Joseph tilted his head and considered me. "They're going to come after us."

That was the sanest thing he'd said since the first gunshot was fired. I put my hands up in front of me and prayed my voice didn't shake the way the rest of me was. "I'll tell them I left with you. I'll tell them I picked you."

His wild eyes widened even more and he looked down at Elma, who was growing increasingly pale. "I hurt people. They won't like it." He sounded like a toddler and I assumed the "they" he was referring to was the police.

"I'll tell them it was all Church. I'll tell them he tried to take me from you and I didn't want to go. I'll tell them you hurt people protecting me." I sounded desperate and frantic, because I was. Church's eyes shot daggers of warning at me. I could feel them prick my skin and stab into my soul but I refused to look at him. I didn't want to lose Joseph's attention.

He considered me for a second and cocked his head to the side before stating, "That might work."

I exhaled slowly and told myself to stay steady. I could do this. I could fix it. "It'll work, but you have to trust me and we have to go, right now." The gun wobbled a little and his eyes shifted back to Church and then slid over to Elma.

"They'll be able to tell the truth." Shit! He had far better reasoning skills than I expected for a lunatic.

"But they won't. They just want me to be happy and if you leave with me then I'll be happy."

"Dixie." My name had never held so much meaning as it did when it was ripped out of Church's broad and bleeding chest. He would die before he let me go and it was my job to keep him alive at all costs.

"Joe, Church and I aren't real. This is all just a fantasy. He was never in your way. He told his family that the reason he couldn't go home was because of a girl. It was a lie, and when he had to come home he asked me to pretend to be that girl. He'll let me go because I'm not his to hold on to." I'd told Church I didn't want him to be a liar and here I was spinning falsehood upon falsehood.

Joseph continued to look at Church and at Elma but somewhere in the distance sirens started to wail, indicating that someone had reported the gunshots. We were running out of time and apparently my psycho online date knew it. "You're gonna go with me." He said it instead of asking it and instead of trying to get through Church to get to me he walked over by where Elma was still lying unmoving and crumpled on the ground and vaulted over the railing on the porch, which landed him in Elma's flowers. She was going to be good and pissed when she could do something about that but at the moment all she could do was weakly lift her head and look at me with pleading eyes.

Joseph was at my side in an instant. His hand was clammy and shaking as it wrapped around my elbow. The gun in his hand dug into my side as he shoved me towards the sedan in the driveway. Once I got closer I realized the keys were in the ignition and the driver's door was still slightly ajar. He'd grabbed the nurse when she'd been either coming or going and used her as leverage to get into Elma's home. He was going to shoot Church as soon as he opened the door, but the man was a terrible shot. Something I hoped would work in my soldier's favor.

"You drive." He put a hand on my head and tried to shove me into the car. With his hand on the top of my head and sirens screaming as they got closer and closer I let my eyes meet Church's as he lumbered to his feet and started towards the car.

"Hey, Church." I whispered the words, not sure that he would hear them over the pounding of my heart and across the distance that separated us. "You know I love you, right?" I'd never tried to hide it but I had to tell him if this was the only chance I was going to get.

"You don't get to do that, Dixie. You don't get to give me that when you're risking your neck like a little fool and telling lies." He sounded so angry and so hurt that it hurt worse than the crack of the gun across the top of my head as Joseph freaked out at my words and hit me.

I let out a strangled laugh and closed my eyes briefly. "You've always had it. I gave it to you forever ago. You just didn't know it."

"Get in the car, Dixie." I did as I was told and folded into the seat. The car was a few years old and needed an oil change but it started right up. I pulled out of the driveway, watching Church with wide eyes the entire time.

Alone in the car with the only person I'd ever met who actually wanted to harm me, I told him exactly what was on my mind. I felt like there wasn't much left to lose.

"Your mom was overbearing and has obvious control issues. If you want to meet a girl and have something special, I would suggest you leave her at home next time." I cut him a look from the corner of my eye and noticed that he was turning an alarming shade of red. His cheeks were billowing in and out like he was having trouble catching his breath.

"She yelled at me." The gun swung in an arc and ended up pointed at the side of my head. "She hit me . . . she always hits. Ever since I was little. She told me I would never be a man, that I would never have what it took to satisfy a woman. She burned me with an iron." He pulled up the sleeve of his arm and showed me a nasty burn that looked like it was still healing. "Then she told me I was worthless and that I would never give her grandchildren." He started to laugh. Hysterical, shrill peals of laughter that hurt my ears and made my skin crawl. "Well, I finally had enough. I finally fought back. So you don't have to worry about Mother or her hurting our children anymore. She got what she deserved."

I cringed and swallowed back a scream. He'd tried to hire someone to kill Church, so I shouldn't be surprised that he was capable of taking a life and sounding so cavalier about it. What really had my skin tightening and my brain buzzing was the fact that he was talking about me being the mother of his children. That didn't bode well for me and whatever future plans he had in mind.

I blew out a breath and lifted my eyes to the rearview mirror. I had to trap a shout behind clamped-down lips. Then out of nowhere a white car with twirling red and blue lights was trailing behind us, dropping in and out of sight, but there nonetheless. I'd tried to sacrifice myself for the greater good, but the greater good wasn't going to let me go that easily. I couldn't stem the flow of tears that spilled over my lashes and ran freely down my face.

"I'm a nice person, Joseph. I like everyone I encounter and chances are if you had asked I would have gone on a second date with you because I always give everyone the benefit of the doubt. Don't do something you can't take back." Don't kill me like you killed your mother. Don't hurt me like you hurt Elma and her nurse. Don't shoot me like you shot Church. I couldn't even get my head around the thought and my heart refused to believe that fate would force Church to attend another funeral of a woman that mattered to him. Nothing in this life could be that cruel.

My captor's eyes went flat. There was no emotion. No regret or fear. There was nothing there but chilling intent and cold-blooded resolve. "I don't regret anything. You're the one, Dixie."

A broken laugh burst out of me as I lifted my hand to wipe my face. All I did was smear moisture around and show Joseph how badly I was shaking.

I'd always wanted to be *the one*. It was my one wish. It looked like I should have been more specific when I was tossing my pennies into the well. I wanted to be the one for the person that was the one for me, not for a lunatic with mayhem and murder on his mind.

If I made it out of this alive there was no way I was going to let the man that was my *one* get away or let him send me away.

Chapter 18

Church

"Hey, *Church. You know I love you, right?"*

There was no stopping my fall after that. My knees hit the ground. My head fell forward on my neck and my heart turned itself inside out. I couldn't breathe. I couldn't see past the haze of everything I had to lose suffocating me and pulling me under. I don't know how the words escaped but I managed to tell her, "You don't get to do that, Dixie. You don't get to give me that when you're risking your neck like a little fool."

She laughed but it was sadder than anything I'd ever heard in my life. It was so final, so fatalistic when she whispered the damning truth and gave me a good-bye I was bound and determined to obey: *"You've always had it."*

Then she was gone and there was no getting her back. I let out a roar that was inhuman and dragged my bloodied, battered body down the driveway even though there was no way in hell I could catch up to the car that squealed away with my entire life inside of it. I fell to my knees again. Leveled by emotion and hammered by pain, none of it coming from the graze across my arm or the jagged hole that burned right under my collarbone. I'd taken a bullet before. It never felt good, but I knew enough and had been wounded enough while I was overseas to know that while these injures hurt like a bitch they wouldn't be the end of me. I felt a heavy hand land on my shoulder and looked up at my dad through eyes that wouldn't focus. My lungs were burning and my mouth felt like it was full of acid and bile. He handed me something that looked like a spare T-shirt and ordered, "Put that on your shoulder and get your ass up. Let's go get your girl, son."

I barely heard him. I was too lost in my own spiral of panic and remorse. I wanted to go back and do it all over again. I wanted to leave Dixie at home so that she was never in danger in the first place. I wanted to take her to bed the first time she gave me the opportunity so that I could tell her with my body what I didn't have the words to say. I wanted to make sure she knew that if I could love her I would. I had forgotten how but I was willing to learn for her and because of her. She made me want to face my biggest fear. She was the only woman that made me want to take that risk. I wanted to wake up with her in my arms every single morning and I wanted to spend all day, every day making sure she knew that she came first. She was the sun in my sky and if something happened to her there was absolutely no way that anything would ever get the chance to flourish and grow in the soul she had been cultivating and nurturing from the moment we met. In fact, all that rich and fertile soil that she had been tilling and digging her way through would go back to ash and dust if anything happened to her. I would be barren and desolate, like I had been before her bright light found its way into all my dark places.

"If anything happens to her . . ." I trailed off and allowed Jules to haul me up to my feet.

"We're gonna make sure nothing happens to her, Dash."

I winced in pain that had nothing to do with the bleeding hole in my shoulder. "I wish I could believe that, Dad. Our track record isn't so great in that department." I followed him to his cruiser all while he was shouting orders and rallying the troops, and we hit the doors at a run and peeled out into the street and after the speeding sedan. Jules tossed his radio at me and ordered me to relay every twist and turn we took as we followed. I knew he was trying to make me feel productive and helpful in the pursuit but all I could feel was panic and fear threatening to choke me. She'd sacrificed herself for me, for Elma. She took care of me when it was my job to take care of her. She would give up everything for the little bit of good we'd had together.

"We might not have a winning track record when it comes to keeping them, but we're undefeated when it comes to finding the best women to make a life with. I think the big guy upstairs owes us a solid, son. Keep your head in the game." I was trying to, but I felt like I was getting sucked into a black vortex that was filled with familiar pain and hopelessness.

"She told me she loves me." The words ripped out of my chest. It couldn't be the last thing she ever said to me, not without me being able to give that back to her. I needed to give that to her regardless of what happened between us in the future. "She loves me and I was so fucking worried about Elma falling that I didn't stop and grab my gun when we left the house. I knew trouble was brewin' and I dropped the ball." I felt my head fall forward as pain and blood loss started to zap some of my energy. She loved me and she very well could die because of it.

"I think that love has been pretty clear from the start. I don't think she would have agreed to come here, to hold your hand as you found your way back, if she didn't love you. And just in case you keep wanting to be stubborn it's obvious you love her, too."

I sighed and told him to pick up the pace and turn once we hit the long, flat stretches of rough road that led out of town and towards the more rural parts of the county. It was obvious neither Dixie nor the guy holding the gun on her had any idea where they were going. The poorly marked roads that seemed to go on forever were causing them to double back and speed haphazardly along roads that went nowhere.

"How could you know I love her before I did?" I wanted to kick myself and take back every second I'd spent pushing her away. That was familiar regret and I couldn't believe I wasn't smart enough to learn my lessons from the first time I had done that with a woman that brought nothing but sunshine and light into my life. "Looks like they're making a U-turn and they're headed back towards the main road. They're going too fast. All that gravel and unfamiliar roads . . ." I trailed off worried Dixie was going to lose control and flip the car.

"We're going to block them in. We'll be at the junction at route 9 in a few minutes. He's not going anywhere with her." The sirens wailed overhead as the car flew so fast over the road that it didn't even seem like the wheels were touching the ground. I'd never been so happy that the man that raised me came with a badge and a gun before. He cut me a look and went from cop to parent in the blink of an eye as he told me, "I knew you loved her because you introduced her to your family. I knew you loved her because you stayed in Denver for her even if you had other reasons for lying low. I'm not a fool, as soon as I saw you with her

I knew she was your main reason. I know you love her because instead of running from whatever is waiting for you when we get to her, you're right here running towards it. You might be scared she's going to get hurt, but your love for that girl is stronger than your fear, Dash."

I couldn't think of a response to any of it because he was right. Even though I'd let fear steal time and important moments with my family away, they were still the most important people in my world and as much as I liked Denver, the Delta was always calling me home. I'd stayed longer than I'd planned because of her. I wasn't ready to go back to gray days and frigid nights alone without her in my life. He was also spot-on about the fact I couldn't get to her and the danger she was in fast enough. I understood that she was in the hands of a madman, that her fate was being held in the hands of a lunatic, and there was nothing I could do about it. But instead of losing control and running from the very real possibility that I might lose her, I was racing towards whatever may come so that any time we had left together wasn't wasted. I would fight for Dixie until the bitter end. There was no giving up on her, even if forever wasn't a guarantee.

We watched in silent horror as the older car started to fishtail and lose traction. It screeched from one side of the road to the other, a cloud of dust swallowing it up. When it came back into sight the vehicle was bearing down on the fleet of police cars thundering towards it. "Doesn't look like he's letting her take her foot off the gas or pull over and surrender." They were blurry through both windshields and the smoke screen of road debris that the tires were kicking up but I could see the stark look of terror on Dixie's face and the gun that was pointed at the side of her head.

Jules nodded and his hands tightened on the steering wheel until his knuckles turned white. “He’s not going anywhere.”

My phone rang and I was jerked out of my pensive thoughts. It was such a normal thing in a situation that was not that it took me a minute to juggle the device and get a finger free to swipe across the screen. I winced when I noticed I smeared blood across the glass when I hit the speaker function. It was a blatant reminder of the kind of violence the man who had my girl was capable of. “Not a good time, Royal. Let me call you back.”

I’d asked the gorgeous lady cop to check out all of Dixie’s online dates but I already knew the culprit was Joseph thanks to Dixie calling his name out while he threatened her with the gun.

“Is that a siren?” She sounded alarmed but I didn’t have time to reassure her everything was okay.

“In the middle of something. Like I said, now isn’t a good time.” I barked the words at her far more harshly than I meant to.

“Okay, well, I’ll talk fast because you need to hear what I have to say.” She took a deep breath and then words erupted out of her so fast I could hardly keep up. “All the guys on the list you gave me checked out except for Erikson.” I grunted because she wasn’t telling me anything I didn’t already know. “We can’t locate him but we did get a nasty surprise when we checked his home. There was a dead body inside the house, Church. An older woman that we’ve identified as Marie Erikson. It was bad, gruesome. If the son is the person behind this murder, you need to be careful and you need to tell Dixie to be careful. This guy is unhinged.”

“Fuck.” I bit the word out and looked over at Jules. My dad’s jaw was clenched and a muscle was ticking rapid-fire in his cheek. “Thanks for the heads-up, Royal. I’ll call with an update when I have one." When Joseph had talked about everyone keeping him from what he wanted I had a suspicion he'd been referring to his mother. This news wasn't good but it was far from unexpected at this point.

"Just tell me that you're in the front seat of that cop car and not the back." She sounded like she was kidding, but I could hear genuine concern in her voice, which let me know she wanted some kind of real reassurance that things were under control. They were far from it but there was nothing she could do to help the situation from Colorado.

"I'm sitting shotgun. My dad's a cop and we have a situation but we're handling it. Chances are I'll be able to hand Erikson over to you at the end of the day."

She made a noise. "Hand him over alive, Church."

That wasn't a promise I could make. "I'll be in touch." I knew what was at stake here and there was no way I was going to be making a phone call to Dixie's family telling them she hadn't made it. I wasn't going to let some lonely, crazy person take her from us. This was a war I was determined to win. I'd lost enough battles when it came to love and loss in my life.

I could hear the motor screaming over the noise of the sirens. I felt my heart drop and everything inside of me go still and on high alert.

"There's a convoy of cop cars behind us. Where does he think he's going to go?" I put a hand on the dash as the distance between me and my girl grew smaller and smaller in a dangerous way.

"I don't think he's thinking. Look at Dixie, she's trying to tell him there's nowhere for them to go." Jules sounded tense as he bit the words out.

Her mouth was moving and her hands were curled around the steering wheel in a death grip. I could see the tear streaks on her face and I wanted to reach through space and time so I could wipe them away and tell her everything was going to be okay.

"You need to stop. He's going to make her keep going. He has a finger on the trigger." He was waving the gun around wildly and screaming at Dixie. She flinched but her eyes never left mine as the struggling sedan continued to thunder closer and closer.

"Think he's got every intention of running into us whether we're moving or not." Jules started to slow the cruiser down but he was right. It was clear that he wasn't going to let Dixie take her foot off the pedal. In fact, as the car slowed he jammed the gun so hard into the side of her temple that the action jerked her head to the side. I said her name even though she couldn't hear me, but she must have seen it because her lips twitched.

She turned her head and looked at her captor. I couldn't make out what she said but whatever it was it pissed the guy off. The gun waved around some more and then he held it in two hands as he pointed it right at her face.

I screamed her name again as she turned back to look at me. The sedan picked up speed again as her eyes locked on mine. Her lips moved slowly and deliberately. She mouthed the words *I love you* over and over again as my heart stopped and my soul tried to jump out of my body to stop her from doing whatever it was she was going to do. I couldn't watch her sacrifice herself for me, even if that's what she had been doing from the get-go.

"No!" I put my hands up and shook my head, but she kept repeating *I love you* and I heard it like she was yelling even though there was silence. The cruiser rolled into position horizontally across the road and I was out the door and on my feet running towards the oncoming car before the wheels stopped. I vaguely heard Jules yelling my name but all I could see was Dixie and her unfailing desire to save everyone but herself.

"I love you!" I screamed the words back at her but I had no clue if she heard or understood because the second the last word left my mouth she cranked the wheel as hard as she could to the side, which sent the quickly moving car careening wildly to the side of the road.

Traction was lost.

The overtaxed motor whirred.

Gravel and rocks kicked up and pelted me even though I didn't feel them.

The front wheels hit the dip of the ditch and all it took was momentum and gravity to send the big machine end over end.

It felt like it flipped a thousand times. The sound of metal crunching and glass breaking was deafening. The smell of fuel and rubber burned my nose.

I was frozen to the spot in horror in the middle of the road as my worst nightmare played out before my eyes.

She'd called me a hero, and yet again I'd been unable to live up to the title. I couldn't save her when she was so desperate to save me and everyone else she thought she could help. She was the one who was a hero and I almost hated her for it, but it was the fact I couldn't not love her that finally had my feet moving as my body had no choice but to follow my heart towards the woman that owned every piece of it.

Chapter 19

Dixie

I was flying.

Sure, the car had left the road in a symphony of screaming metal and noisy mechanical parts pushed past their limits, but that wasn't why I was weightless and free, floating above everything bad happening in the front seat of the twisting, turning, flipping sedan. I was flying because Church loved me and he was ready to let me love him. Even if a second was all we got to have of that love, it was enough. The light had pushed back the dark and he was standing in the sun after lurking in the shadows for far too long. It was the only thing I wanted and he had shown up to give it to me, in case it was the last thing I ever laid my eyes on. My last vision would be one of love and courage. It would be one of bravery and acceptance. It would be my dream coming true.

I heard glass breaking all around me as I let go of the steering wheel and covered my face with both my hands. Joseph was still screaming next to me, calling me names, telling me he was going to kill me, yelling that after I was dead he was going to make it his mission to kill everyone I loved, but then there was a sickening crunch as metal made contact with the ground as we rolled over and over again. Joseph quit saying anything and I felt something sharp rip through my clothing and skin at my shoulder. It was my turn to scream as something below the dash broke loose and trapped my foot between the weight of it and the gas pedal.

Joseph wanted me to keep going.

He knew there was nowhere to run, not with the entire Lowry police force stretched out in front of us. He told me it was all my fault. Over and over again he told me I should have given him a chance, that I shouldn't have been leading men on if I was in love with someone else. I tried to stay calm and reason with him. I tried to tell him that wasn't rational. He kept telling me to go faster, to keep my foot on the gas. He jammed the gun into the side of my head so hard I saw stars and I panicked, thinking that he was going to pull the trigger by accident. There was no way in hell I was going to let him murder me in front of Church. I wasn't going to be another slash across Church's barely stitched-together heart. I refused to let him blame himself for the misfortune befalling yet another woman he cared about. It wasn't his fault. None of it had been and now that he could see that, I wouldn't let him drift back into the darkness.

I told Church I loved him. I said it out loud over and over again. I repeated it what felt like a thousand times, each word making Joseph angrier and angrier. His rage didn't matter. All that mattered was that I got to say what needed to be said.

I saw Church run towards me. I could clearly see the fear and worry on his face. I told him I loved him and prayed that he could hear me. I watched with my heart in my eyes and determination coursing through every part of my body as he told me he loved me back. I didn't need him to give that to me, but I was overjoyed that he had. It made what I had to do next far easier than it would have been otherwise. Love was stronger than fear and I felt that strength fill me up as I cranked the wheel of the speeding vehicle as far to the right as it would go. There was no hope for the sedan. It left the road and started to summersault instantly, the farm fence meant to keep in livestock and trespassers out was no match for the tumbling vehicle.

My head was spinning. I could taste blood and dirt all across my tongue. There wasn't a single part of my body that didn't hurt and I couldn't get my eyes to focus. Every breath I took burned and it felt like there wasn't enough air. The world was upside down and sideways but I figured I must still be alive if I could feel all the things that were wrong with me. I tried to turn my head to see if Joseph was still in the seat next to me, or more accurately to see if there was still a weapon that could be pointed at me, but I screamed as white-hot pain scorched down the side of my neck when I tried to move.

"Dixie!" I heard my name, but it didn't sound like it normally did. Church was screaming it and it sounded like both a prayer and a curse. None of that smooth drawl was present. All I could hear was a frantic man worried about the woman he loved. He sounded tortured and stripped bare. It was his soul screaming out in search of mine, but I couldn't answer. I tried to, but I couldn't make my muscles work. I couldn't get my tongue unstuck from the roof of my mouth and I couldn't speak around the tang of blood at the back of my throat. Luckily I didn't need to because within seconds that familiar face with those remarkable eyes, twice their normal size and flooded with fear, were hovering in front of me. He was upside down, but I could make out the lines of worry and concern on his face as he reached into the mangled side of the car and put his fingers on the side of my neck.

I had a pulse. I must have. I could hear my heart pounding between my ears and every thump of it made my chest ache with pain. I tried to blink heavy lashes so I could give him some indication that I was okay, but even that feat proved to be too challenging. I couldn't make anything cooperate.

"She's got a pulse, but it's thready. She's bleeding all over the damn place and there's a piece of the goddamn fence sticking out of her shoulder."

"Don't move her until EMS gets here. They're two minutes out." I heard Jules like he was speaking through heavy fabric. I could see his legs somewhere beyond where Church was kneeling and holding on to my face with his hands.

"I've got you, pretty girl." He did have me, and now it seemed like he wanted to keep me. "Where's Erikson? He isn't next to her. He must have been thrown clear when they rolled."

Joseph hadn't had a seat belt on. That and one too many Jason Statham movies had given me the idea to drive the car off the road. I figured if either of us was going to survive I was the one with a better shot since I'd buckled up. It sounded like my instinct had proven to be correct. Not that surviving felt all that awesome at the moment.

"Hurts." The word wheezed out as I lifted the hand that wasn't pinned to the crushed seat behind me towards my shoulder.

Church caught the unnaturally pale and weak appendage in his own hand and gently pulled it away from the razor-sharp glass that was imbedded in my flesh. "I know it does but you can't touch it." He curled his fingers around mine and gave them a little squeeze. "You stole about a hundred years off my life, you know that?" He shook his head and leaned forward so that he could touch his lips to mine. It was upside down and too brief but I swore the touch of his lips against mine stole away some of the pain that was making it hard to think. "I already lost ten years, I don't want to lose any more."

That was good, but I was having a really difficult time keeping my eyes open. I was seeing three of him and all of those versions were fuzzy around the edges.

I heard voices, all talking fast and loud. I heard Church grumbling when I tried to protest when his face was replaced by one I didn't recognize. But I was too tired to argue and the pain was getting to be too much to fight. I could feel oblivion trying to suck me under and its embrace was warm and welcoming.

"Her foot is caught under the dash. It's probably got some significant damage. We need a machine in here to cut her loose."

I heard Church order them to be careful with me. But one of the paramedics jostled my side as he tried to make room for himself next to me so that he could get to my captured foot. It wasn't a big bump but it was enough to make me scream like I'd never screamed before. I felt like lightning was ripping through every limb. I saw stars but they were blinking rapidly in a field of black and that darkness was calling to me, promising me relief from the searing agony that was pulling my body apart. I heard other voices yell. I heard a loud *pop* and smelled gunpowder as well as the blood and gasoline that I was choking on . . . then everything went black and I finally stopped hurting.

Chapter 20

Church

I was going to pull the paramedic that made Dixie scream out of the crumpled wreckage of the SUV by the back of his neck and shake the ever-living shit out of him for causing her more pain. She looked like she was barely holding on. Her face was as white as chalk and there was blood covering most of her skin. The crimson droplets were dripping from her curls at an alarming rate, and I could barely stomach looking at the way her shoulder was cleaved open by that piece of glass. I'd seen battlefield triage up close and personal, but none of that prepared me for seeing the woman I dared to love clinging to life as everything vital and necessary drained out of her.

The little fool had risked everything to save everyone but herself.

"Step back, son. Let them do their job. The quicker they get her out the quicker we can get her the help she needs."

I let my dad pull me away but I couldn't take my eyes off the smashed vehicle where her small body was trapped. The sense of helplessness, of not being able to do anything to help her, had all those old feelings of inferiority and unfairness rearing their ugly little heads. I wanted to help her, but I couldn't and if she died . . . I didn't want to think about what that would do to me, but it was almost impossible to keep the stark and dreary thoughts at bay. I'd just found my way home, but I knew if Dixie didn't make it there was a really good chance that I would end up lost and adrift once again, no matter how sturdy and strong my roots were.

"This is all your fault!" I heard the accusation screamed at me, but I was so lost in thought and tied up in my concern for the woman stuck in the wreckage that it took a minute for me to realize that the words were being hurled wildly at me from a hundred yards away.

I turned to look at Joseph Erikson, bloodied, listing to one side, but still able to stand under his own power with that gun he'd used to terrorize Dixie clutched in his shaking hand. He had police on either side of him, moving slowly towards him with their weapons drawn. Once again he was surrounded with nowhere to go but he refused to give up.

"How did he manage to keep hold of the gun when he was thrown?" I asked the question under my breath and saw Jules shake his head in response.

"No clue, but his luck ends right here." He unsnapped the holster that held his service weapon and smoothly pulled the gun out. "Joseph Erikson, you are under arrest for the murder of Marie Erikson and the kidnapping and false imprisonment of Dixie Carmichael. Put the weapon down."

The man laughed hysterically and wavered on his feet. One half of his face was covered in blood and I couldn't be certain but it looked like he was missing a couple of his teeth. He hadn't escaped unscathed but I wanted him in as much pain and suffering as Dixie was fighting her way through.

"She could have loved me. She should have loved me. I did everything right." His words were garbled and he started to cough, which made the gun wobble in his hands. The deputies that were closest to him started to move in closer but stopped when he snapped the weapon back up and pointed right at me. I heard Jules swear under his breath but my attention was stolen as Dixie's pale and fragile form was finally freed from the twisted metal that had kept it captive. They maneuvered her onto a stretcher but she wasn't moving and I couldn't tell if she was still breathing or not. It was every fear I'd spent a lifetime running from chasing me down and forcing me to face it head-on. I'd done everything in my power to avoid this very situation, a woman I loved hovering on the brink of death with my heart in her hands, but there was no denying this was where I was meant to be.

"She was never going to love you because she loved me. I didn't want her to, but she never does what's best for her, because she's always doing what's best for everyone else." I turned to walk towards the ambulance not caring what happened behind me because I was only moving towards what waited in front of me . . . the best thing that ever happened to me. I wasn't going to let the bad that was threatening take any more of it away. I trusted Jules to watch not only my back, but to keep Dixie safe as well.

There was screaming, some obligatory ugly words, and then the sound of gunfire. I didn't know who pulled the trigger but the crazy talk stopped, so I figured it was one of the good guys and I selfishly hoped it was my dad because that was almost as good as me getting to pull the trigger.

"How is she?" I asked the paramedic that was closest to me as they loaded Dixie into the back of the ambulance.

"Better than she looks. That slice in her shoulder is ugly and deep. I won't be shocked if she needs surgery. She's lost a lot of blood, which is why she blacked out, but she's coming around. Her ankle was stuck pretty good, but by some miracle I think it's only a bad sprain. She's incredibly lucky. I've seen crashes less severe than this one where I still had to use the Jaws of Life to get bodies out instead of patients. The debris from the fence they went through did a number on her clavicle and I would place good money on her having a couple busted ribs. She's having some trouble breathing, so we're watching for a collapsed lung, but right now there's no need for a tube. We're taking her to Tupelo but they might need to airlift her to somewhere more well equipped to handle her injuries."

I nodded and stepped around him to climb into the back of the ambulance. None of the first responders tried to argue with me as I took a seat on one of the narrow benches and picked up the limp hand that was closest to me. Her doe eyes flicked open and locked on mine as the guys rushed around her and tried to get an IV line in her arm.

Her droopy gaze drifted over me and landed on the point where her hand was trapped in mine. Scarlet red coated our fingers and stained the backs of our hands. Her eyebrows pinched together and her mouth pulled into a little pout that I wanted to kiss.

"You're bleeding." Her voice was ragged and I could tell every word was a struggle to get out.

I looked down at our joined hands and couldn't stop the dry bark of laughter that escaped my chest. The wound from my shoulder and the gash across my arm were indeed leaking drops of blood onto the back of her hand where I was holding it. The minute I knew she was okay I forgot all about my own injuries. "You were just pulled from one of the worst accidents these guys have seen and you're worried about me?" I sighed and lifted her hand to my lips so that I could put a kiss on the back of it. "It's my turn to take care of you, pretty girl. You've done all you can do for me, now it's up to me to show you that I was worth every sacrifice you made to make me see that love wasn't something to run from. I don't want to be a coward. I want to be the man that's brave enough to love a woman like you."

Her eyes blinked rapidly and I could see moisture gather behind her lashes. They put an oxygen mask over her mouth, so she couldn't respond, but I didn't need her to tell me what she was feeling, she'd been giving it to me from the start without a single word spoken. She never had to tell me she loved me because everything she'd done since agreeing to get on the back of my bike showed me she did. She loved because her heart was strong and she was the bravest person I had ever met. They said that love was war and if that was the case Dixie was winning and well on her way to being undefeated.

Chapter 21

Dixie

I was in the hospital for a little over a week. My shoulder and the damaged muscle and tendons underneath were in bad shape and needed surgery, but all the doctors and surgeons I saw were cautiously optimistic that I would regain full range of motion once it healed and I did some physical therapy to regain strength. Surprisingly it was my sprained ankle that proved to be the biggest hindrance. It was swollen and bruised a grotesque shade of blackish green. I couldn't put any weight on it and there was no balancing myself with one of my arms out of commission and strapped across my chest in a sling. The stupid thing screamed at me whenever I tried to move it, so I spent a week immobile and antsy as Church barely left my side complete with a matching sling that he promptly discarded as soon as his own wound started to feel better. He acted like catching a bullet was no big deal, which I found totally aggravating. He kept saying that the gun was a small-caliber weapon, so the shot to his shoulder was far less involved compared with the way mine was mangled.

Like that was supposed to make the situation better. Begrudgingly I told him I thought it was cute that we were going to have matching scars.

I wasn't used to being the one that was fussed over, so it took some getting used to. I didn't want to be a bother but eventually it was obvious I was limited in what I could do for myself, so I settled in and let everyone around me fret and fuss. Church and I didn't talk about the future, the fact that he admitted that we were going to have one was enough for me. He wasn't running away from me and the way I loved him anymore, in fact he was sprinting towards it and chasing me with his own chaotic, wild kind of affection. Frankly I thought our story was going to kick my parents' story's ass!

Currently his booted feet were propped up on the edge of the hospital bed and he was scrolling through something on my phone. He's been tasked with explaining to my family why I was a leading story on the national news and with convincing half of Denver to stay put until I was up to seeing visitors, so he'd had my cell in hand pretty much twenty-four/seven since I got out of surgery. I was getting my walking papers in an hour and I couldn't wait to get out of the hospital and back to some semblance of reality.

My parents had arrived the day after the crash and were currently staying with Elma Mae. They hovered but quickly realized Church wasn't leaving my side and had spent most of their time in Mississippi falling in love with Lowry and Church's family the same way I had. I was going back to Denver with them at the end of the week.

I still had an entire life in Colorado I needed to situate before Church and I could make some decisions about what was next for us. I missed my dog, and I didn't want to push Church when I finally had him where I so desperately wanted him to be. He loved me. He wanted me. He needed me but I didn't know if he was planning on doing all of that here or if he was going to come back to the Mile High. I couldn't imagine him leaving his family when he'd spent so long hiding from them, but he hadn't said anything one way or the other.

I nudged his boot with my good foot until he looked up at me. "What are you doing on my phone?" There was nothing incriminating on the thing unless he'd managed to get onto Pinterest and found my wedding boards, that might be embarrassing but he had to know that's where all of this was heading for me regardless of what state we called home.

"I'm looking through that dating app." He looked up from my phone and lifted his eyebrows at me. "I'm reading all the things you filled in to find your perfect guy."

I groaned and held out my good hand. "Stop that. I still need to delete the dumb thing. Hand it over." I wiggled my fingers and was promptly ignored.

A grin tugged at his mouth and his eyes danced with a million colors as humor lit them up from the inside out. "Over six feet." He held up a finger. "Check." I groaned and demanded the device again. "Though why that's a must when you're barely five-foot is beyond me."

"I'm five-five, jackass. Can you stop?"

"Open to all ethnicities." He wiggled his eyebrows up and down and I felt myself blush. "That's good to know." I slapped a hand over my eyes and sighed in defeat. He wasn't going to stop until he got all the way through my list of must-haves.

"Fit, some formal education, gainfully employed, kids okay.

Man, you weren't being very picky here, Dixie." He was laughing at me, so I closed my eyes and tried to block him out. "Where's the box for no murdering psychopaths with mommy issues?"

I groaned again and turned to look at him through narrowed eyes. "I must have missed that one."

He chuckled again but then his expression turned serious and his eyebrows dipped in a V over his colorful eyes as he dropped his feet off the edge of the bed and leaned over the phone, reading intently. "Prefers the strong, silent type because when he has something to say it's always worth listening to. Looking for a man that is chivalrous, adventurous, and has a sense of pride and duty." His eyes flicked up to mine and I would have shrugged if I was able. Instead I bit down on my lip as he continued to read. "Loyalty is a must. You can tell a lot about a man by the company he keeps. Searching for someone that knows the importance of family and home, that is willing to go above and beyond for the people he cares about. Looking for love and forever."

I gulped a little as he tapped the screen, shutting the app down and turning the phone off before setting it on the bed next to me. He rose to his feet and made his way over to the side of the bed. The mattress sank under his weight as he propped his hip next to mine.

"You described me."

I looked up at him from under my lashes. "Well yeah. You're supposed to describe your perfect man, and even when you were driving me crazy and making me chase my heart around in circles you were still my perfect guy. You're the only one."

He reached out a hand and moved some of my hair away from my face so I couldn't use it to hide behind. "How can you be so sure?"

I blew out a breath and reached up to catch his hand in mine. "I just knew. There was no explaining it. There was no denying it. My heart picked you."

His lips twitched and it happened.

He smiled.

I knew it was going to be my undoing.

That mouth was made to be happy. That face was created to have joy and delight stamped across it. He was so much more than beautiful with that smile. He was stunning. He stole my breath and made it hard for me to think.

"You're smiling." I reached out and touched the indent in his cheek that wasn't quite a dimple but was close.

"I guess I am." He caught my hand in his and kissed the backs of my fingers. "I have a lot to be happy about lately."

I smiled back at him. "I'm glad."

"I've got an errand I need to run real quick and then I'll come pick you up when it's time to take you home. I've only got you for a little bit before your folks whisk you back home." He hadn't left my side in days, so I was surprised that he was doing so now when I was so close to freedom.

"Uh . . . okay." I frowned at him but he bent over and placed a hard kiss on my lips.

"I'll be back, pretty girl, and I know we need to talk about what's next. I'm not running. I'm right here in front of you even when you can't see me. Trust me." It was hard not to give him everything he asked for when he was smiling at me.

"All right, soldier." He nodded and slipped quietly out of the room.

I had no clue where he was going, but I knew with everything inside of me that he would be back.

Chapter 22

Church

I knew I had to take the good with the bad from here on out, but there was some bad that needed a reminder that I could and would fight back. There was some bad that needed to know there was no place for it in my life or the lives of the people I loved. There was some bad that needed to learn I was bigger and badder than it could ever be.

Plus I'd made a promise to my little brother that I would show the fuck up and I wasn't going to renege on it. In fact it was a promise I was more than looking forward to keeping.

I heard the rusted door to the trailer rattle and leaned forward on the ugly couch that was cream and brown with pheasants all over it. It was straight out of the '80s and smelled like it. I rested my hands on my knees and didn't take my eyes off the doorway as the door swung open and a burly man in dirty jeans and a torn white T-shirt stumbled in. It was the middle of the day but he smelled like cheap booze and there was no missing his blurry-eyed surprise when his gaze landed on me.

A sneer pulled at his mouth as he wiped the back of his hand across his mouth and he stumbled a little until his eyes hit the broken coffee table that was in front of me and the lethal black firearm that was sitting just inches away from my fingers. It was a clear warning so I didn't have to waste time or words. After he'd shot and killed the crazy man that abducted and terrorized Dixie, Jules had located the ringleader of the crew that attacked Dalen at the bar. It took no time at all for the man to rat his cohorts out, including this guy. And while I was disappointed I didn't get to have a chat with the man who'd taken the money to hurt a stranger just because he didn't like the way they looked, I was grateful that Jules had given me enough of a head start that I could make my point with the muscle that had no qualms about beating on a kid.

"Whaddr you doin' here?" The words were slurred together and he stumbled again, one beefy hand slapping onto the thin wall of the trailer to keep him upright.

I sighed heavily as I stared at him through narrowed eyes. He was too drunk for anything I was going to have to say to get through. The guy before him had taken one look at the gun and the look on my face and pissed himself in terror. I hardly had to utter a word for him to understand he had picked the wrong kid to mess with. He was curled in a ball on the floor of his pitiful one-room apartment in tears when Jules and his boys arrived right behind me with a warrant for his arrest. He was actually the one that gave up the location of this hidden trailer, deep in the valley and almost impossible to find. Luckily I had more time to make a point with him, since words would be wasted.

I sighed again and reached for the weapon. I made it disappear into the back of my pants and rose to my feet. The other man's eyes went up . . . and up some more as he took in my height and the set of my shoulders as I crossed my arms across my chest. I had to ignore the pull in my still healing shoulder. It was going to have to suffer through far greater strain by the time I was done with this guy.

"My little brother isn't going to be little for very long." I watched his Adam's apple bob up and down as he tried to straighten. I had several inches on him, but he was stocky and there was no telling how fear and alcohol would make him react.

A sneer worked across his face. Hatred was ugly. Hatred for no reason was silly. I felt my lips twitch and took a step to the side as he suddenly lunged at me.

"Get outta my house!" The words were furious and loud but they lost some of their power when he hit the edge of the already trashed coffee table and was thrown off balance. I shot a hand out so I could latch on to the collar of his T-shirt and used his momentum to drag him towards me.

He struggled in my grasp, hands lifting to pry at my wrists, but I was bigger, angrier, and sober.

"You were looking for me, you found my brother instead. You put a beating on a kid for a few bucks and because you're a racist fuck. You wanna lay all that shit on someone, you lay it on someone that's the same size as you so they can fight back. You lay it on a grown-up who has the experience to know the world is full of assholes like you."

The hands continued to claw at mine as his eyes went wide and his stank breath started to wheeze in and out of lips that were making sounds but not words. I gave him a shake that snapped his teeth together and hefted him up so that just the toes of his boots were touching the filthy floor of the trailer.

"If I was a different kind of man, if I was a man like you, you'd have a bullet between your eyes. You understand the point I'm making?"

The man's watery eyes blinked at me slowly as he tried to jerk himself free. "It weren't like that." His words were garbled because of my hold, so I gave him a shove backwards that sent him flying across the narrow living space. His arms pinwheeled and faltered but nothing could stop him as his big body hit the wall opposite me. He landed with a thud and then slowly slid to the floor with his legs extended in front of him.

"I didn't want to get dragged into that mess with those boys from Sassy's but I didn't have a choice." He rubbed his elbow and scowled up at me. "I knew that kid wasn't the right target, but those idiots wouldn't listen to me. They were so fired up to get some cash and to make some kind of fucked up point." He shook his head and rubbed his eyes as I continued to loom over him, hands on my hips. "The sheriff's son . . . the fucking sheriff. Doesn't matter what color he happens to be, you don't go messing with a lawman's kin. Idiots, all of them."

I cocked my head a little bit and narrowed my eyes. "Why did you go along with it if you knew you had the wrong guy?"

He threw his head back and let out a dry and bitter laugh. "Drink too much. Gamble too much. Don't got any family or any money. Got myself in deep with Sassy and her crew. It was go along with the lynching or get myself a new asshole torn. Do I look like a man that makes good choices?" He threw his hands up in the air and let them fall. "I ain't got nothing good in this life, so I let all the bad stuff take over."

I stared at him in silence for a long minute realizing I'd been really close to being in the same boat. It got way too easy to ignore the scrapes of good when they came because the bad felt so consuming and encompassing. I knew moving forward I had to make the effort to focus on what mattered and not what may or may not be lurking on the horizon. My stance shifted as my phone vibrated in my pocket letting me know that it was time to cut out before Jules's boys showed up to issue the arrest warrant.

I stepped over his legs and gave him one last look as he stared up at the stained, dented ceiling of the trailer. "Goes without saying that you end up in a situation where you have to come after a member of my family again it isn't going to end well for you."

His eyes rolled to mine. "Don't think it's gonna end well this time either."

He wasn't wrong, but I didn't have even an ounce of sympathy to waste on him.

I made my way down the back embankment behind the trailer and down to a little creek that ran behind it. Jules's truck was parked behind a moss-covered outcropping of rocks and well out of the sight of the incoming cavalry. He was going to chew my ass when he saw the mud caked on the tires but I figured when I told him I was giving serious consideration to taking his suggestion and walking in his footsteps it would smooth things over.

I wanted to take care of people. I wanted to be the man he raised me to be. I wanted to put the years of training and sacrifice I'd survived through to good use. I wanted everything I'd learned to matter. It seemed like strapping on a badge and signing up to protect and serve was a good way to accomplish all of that.

When I drove out of the Holler and made my way back to town so I could get my girl, I drove past the cemetery where both my mom and Caroline had been laid to rest. I made a mental note to take Dixie by so we could both pay our respects before she went back to Denver. If those two women hadn't loved me as fiercely and ferociously as they had I never would have figured out how to love the woman that felt like she was my everything. I owed them the world and I wanted to make them proud. I knew they would both be proud of the woman my heart picked.

I would hold Dixie while she cried, because I knew she would.

And I would let her hold me while I cried, because it was long past time I let myself really and truly grieve for all that I'd lost. Then I'd kiss her until neither one of us could breathe because it was long past time that I celebrated and reveled in all that I had gained.

Dixie was waiting when I got back to the hospital. I wanted to kick myself for not thinking ahead and grabbing her some of the unpronounceable flowers as well. I needed to up my romance game, needed to put some oomph in my wooing skills. Not that you would think I'd dropped the ball by the smile on her face. She glowed. She shined. She shimmered. She was so bright and vivid it was easy to overlook the bandages holding her together and the thick brace on her foot. Any day that I got to see her smile was my best day and I was looking forward to having a whole hell of a lot of them in the future.

She pulled me to her for a hug as soon as she saw me and I didn't hesitate to return it. I was getting pretty good at being a hugger. It was nice to have my arms around someone I never wanted to let go of and it was nice to be held like she had no intention of ever letting go of me.

"How are you? Did you get that door closed?" She curled her

good hand around mine as a woman dressed in scrubs rolled her and the wheelchair she was seated in out of the room and towards the elevator. It didn't surprise me one bit that every staff member we passed knew her name and wanted to wish her well and a speedy recovery. That was simply the effect she had on people.

When it was time to put her in the truck I didn't give her the chance to try to lift herself up while she balanced on one leg. I picked her up and hefted her into the cab as she laughed in my ear and curled her arm around my neck so that she could strangle-hug me. I kissed her hard on the mouth and lingered a little longer than I'd intended. She didn't seem to mind as she slid her tongue between my teeth and gave it a little flick.

I pulled back and smoothed a hand over her cheek. "I should have brought you flowers or a balloon."

She grinned at me and leaned forward so her lips could touch mine. "I liked the kiss better."

God, how could you not smile at that?

I climbed into the driver's side of the truck and headed home . . . well, home for now. That was a conversation we were going to have to have sooner rather than later.

We were on the outskirts of town and settled into what I thought was a comfortable silence when I felt her staring at the side of my face. I looked at her out of the corner of my eye and watched her watch me.

"What?" She jumped when I asked the question and lifted her hand to her throat.

"Nothing." She tilted her face back around so that she was looking out the windshield but her lips were pressed tightly together and she was tapping her fingers nervously on her knee.

It was all very un-Dixie-like, so much so that I kept an eye out for a place to pull over and when I found one I drove the truck off the road, found a little spot that was secluded and out-of-the-way, and parked behind an outcropping of cypress trees that had branches that touched the ground. She gave me a curious look but didn't say anything as I twisted around to look at her.

"What's working in that pretty little head of yours, Dixie?" I stretched an arm along the back of the seat and touched the tips of my fingers to her hair.

"I was just thinking. It's nothing important and it can definitely wait until we're back at your dad's place."

"It's not nothing. It has you fidgety and quiet. Lay it on me, pretty girl. I told you there is nothing you can say that is going to scare me off." I watched as she bit her lip and then stuck it out in a pout. The plump little curve was slick from her tongue and I wanted to put my teeth into it.

She took a deep breath and then started talking so fast that it made my head spin. "Well, I love you and you love me, but I have to go back to Denver. Because I have a job that I might not be able to do because of my shoulder, an apartment which is nothing special, my dog who I really do miss, and my sister who is still in a mess and who still hasn't told Wheeler she likes girls. You haven't mentioned if you want me to stay there or come back here, and you haven't said anything about where you're planning on living long-term or what you think you want to do for a job, because it's clear you don't want to be a bouncer forever. And your family is here, so I'm sure you don't want to leave, but I don't want to overstay my welcome at your dad's place, and I want to get married and have babies, but I don't know if that's what you want because you didn't even know you could love me back until like yesterday and it's all just a lot. I don't want to scare you away but some of it I've been thinking about for a long time, the rest just recently when you told me you loved me back."

I watched her as she looked everywhere but at me. "Is that all?"

Her head whipped around and she narrowed her eyes at me. "Do you need more?"

I chuckled and slipped out of the truck and walked around the front end so I could pull her door open. She gave me a questioning look but didn't pull away when I picked her up and carried her to the back end of the big 4x4. It was a little tricky getting the tailgate down one-handed but I managed and got her propped up on the surface so that I could put myself between her legs. She had an arm wrapped around my shoulders and her eyes locked on mine and I leaned forward and kissed the end of her nose.

"I told you that you deserved to come first, so I'll be wherever you want to be. You want to stay here then we'll stay. You want to go back to Denver then we'll go. You want to move to Austin and be Jet and Ayden's neighbors then we'll go there. I want you to be happy, Dixie."

Her eyes got wide and it was like drowning in chocolate. "Oh."

I brushed some of her hair to the side and nuzzled along the curve of her neck. She tilted her head back to give me better access and rubbed her fingers through the short hairs on the back of my head. "Nothing needs to be decided right now. We will figure it out."

She muttered something into the air above my head then yanked on my ear to get to me look up at her. "I'm serious about getting married and having kids, Church. I want you, but I want it all with you. You keep telling me to put my own wants and needs first, well, that's what I want."

I chuckled into her ear and pulled back so I could see her face. She was deadly serious and had every hope and dream she'd ever had shining out of her eyes. "I don't have a ring, so I'm not going to drop on a knee and propose right this minute, Dixie."

Her gaze shifted away, but I nudged her under her chin with my fingers to get her to bring it back to mine. "But that doesn't mean it won't happen. It needs to be right. I've screwed a lot up over the last few years, pretty girl, so this is something I'm determined to get right. The right time, the right place, the right everything. But you have to know that you will always be the right girl for this completely wrong guy."

Her lips twitched a little and some of the seriousness fled. "I can wait for the right time and the right place because you are the right guy for me, Church. There is no wrong anywhere in that."

I lifted my eyebrow up and leaned into the cradle of her hips, careful not to put any pressure on the brace around her ankle. I slid a hand up her back on the side where her good arm was wrapped around my shoulders. Her injuries were on opposite sides of her body, so I had to handle her with the utmost care. Her skin was warm and soft. So were her eyes as they melted and went liquid with lazy desire and languid passion. "So your sister digs chicks now? That's an unexpected turn of events."

She laughed, her teeth flashing and that glow that was so much a part of her bursting out. I knew as long as I lived I would never tire of her constant cheer. I'd been sad for so long that I don't think I ever would have remembered how good happy felt if it wasn't for her.

"Yeah, I don't know if she told Wheeler yet, but she was having an affair with a woman. I mean, it's still cheating and she still should have been honest about what she was feeling and her doubts, but I'm hoping that overall the fact that it was another girl will lessen the blow." She let out a little sigh as I curled a hand around the side of her neck and used the side of my thumb under her jaw to tilt her head back so that I could touch my lips to hers. When I pulled back she slicked her tongue over the moisture left behind and smirked at me. "Out of all of that I just threw at you, that was the part that stuck out?"

I put my forehead against hers and moved a hand to her hip so I could pull her even closer to the edge of the tailgate. We were pelvis to pelvis, hard to soft, and my dick was achingly aware of the fact that the only thing separating it from her velvety center was my zipper and the flimsy cotton of the sundress she was wearing. Elma had procured emergency provisions for Dixie so that she wouldn't have to struggle into her normal uniform of silly T-shirts and jeans. The gauzy material clung to all of her curves and had adjustable ties at either shoulder so she didn't have to maneuver her damaged shoulder in and out of an armhole.

"Everything else we'll handle as it comes. We'll cross all those bridges together so that we're both always standing on the same side or walking towards each other to meet in the middle. The info about your sister isn't a problem you are required to handle or worry about. She'll do the right thing and come clean to the grease monkey, or she won't. That's not your situation to set right. They gotta get there on their own. Plus, if your sister looks anything like you then the idea of girl on girl is pretty hot." I fake grunted as she lightly head butted me with her forehead against my chin.

"Not funny." I disagreed. I thought it was plenty funny but I wasn't laughing when she gave her hips a little wiggle that pressed her even closer to the erection that wasn't even trying to be discreet behind my zipper. Her breasts pressed into the center of my chest as her arm tightened around my neck where she was holding on to me. She rubbed her forehead against my chin where it was already resting and let out a whispery breath that tickled the front of my throat.

"I could have died." Her body shuddered and I smoothed a hand down her spine to soothe her.

"Not your time to go, pretty girl." And when it was I would make sure I was by her side. I would be there and I would be everything she needed me to be, because the love I had for her was far more powerful than the fear I had of losing her.

"In the moment I wasn't afraid at all. I knew I was doing the right thing, knew it was the best option but after—" she shook her head and her entire body quaked against mine "—all I could think about was how risky it was and everyone that I would have left behind." She pulled back and looked at me, tears making her eyes shiny and bright. "The idea that I would never get to be with you, to touch you, to tell you I love you while we were making love, that hurt almost as bad as the sprained ankle and the sliced-open shoulder. I want you to know I love you always, not just when I'm worried I won't get the chance to love you anymore."

Her words wound their way into the parts of my heart that were held together by frayed strings and pulled the mangled thing back into some semblance of order. She made it beat the way it was supposed to. She made it hum with life and anticipation. She shaped it into something that was far stronger than it had ever been before her gentle touch.

"I know you love me, Dixie." I took her precious and adorable face between my hands and kissed her until neither of us could breathe. I tasted every misstep and every triumph on the tip of her tongue as it flicked against my own.

"You wouldn't have gotten on the back of my bike even though it made you nervous enough to shake if you didn't love me." I slipped a finger under the tie at her shoulder and lightly traced her collarbone. She sighed and lowered her hand so that it was resting on my heart and tapping along to the rhythm that was beating a love song she orchestrated.

"You wouldn't have left your family, your friends, your dog and come on this crazy trip with me if you didn't love me." I pulled the dainty little bow loose at her shoulder and watched as the thin fabric uncoiled and released. She didn't have a bra on and the rosy tip of her breast was immediately bared to my hungry gaze. The little peak pulled into a tight little pebble and goosebumps dotted the soft, pale globe as I visually traced a pattern across her freckles with my eyes.

"You wouldn't have put my dick in your mouth without caring where we were or who might come across us if you didn't love me." I used a knuckle to brush that pink tip and bent so I could kiss her again.

"You wouldn't have put up with Elma's initiation and the hostility between me and Dalen while we figured out how to be brothers again if you didn't love me." I lowered my head so I could flick my tongue over the sensitive flesh I uncovered and feathered soft kisses all across her chest. I loved on each bruise, each mark that marred her perfect skin, as she tossed her head back and looked up at the trees that shrouded us.

"You wouldn't have risked your life to save the people you

know matter most to me if you didn't love me. Everything you've done, every move you make tells me how much you love me, Dixie. I never doubted it, I just didn't want to see it because I knew there was no way I was going to be able to not love you back. I loved you long before I almost lost you, pretty girl."

I slipped a hand under the hem of her dress and slid it up the silky skin of her thigh. She shivered into my touch and her eyes encouraged me to keep on going with my words and with the deliberate caress. I couldn't manhandle her in her current condition, couldn't be rough and forceful. She needed a tender touch. She needed soft hands and an open heart. She needed to be loved, not fucked.

My lips quirked up into a grin that made her smile back at me as she tugged on the material of my T-shirt. I leaned back so I could pull the thing off over my head and bunched it up and put it behind her in order to keep the metal of the truck from rubbing against her bare ass as I hooked a finger in the side of her panties and started to work them carefully down her legs.

"I didn't do it right because I was out of practice and it scared the ever-living shit out of me, but I loved you from the get-go." Once I had the nothing scrap of fabric free of her feet I tucked it into my back pocket and put both my hands on her hips as I shifted my cock so that it pressed insistently against her center. Her good leg wound its way around my hip as she leaned back in my hold so that her good hand was free to trace over the muscles on my chest. She used the tip of a fingernail and roughly ran it over my nipple. The motion made me suck in a breath and had desire unspooling throughout my limbs. "And now I'm going to *love* on you because we are both here, together, and that's something I won't ever take for granted." That was the main lesson

I learned in all my mistakes and fuckups. Make the most of the time you had with the people that mattered because tomorrow wasn't a guarantee and the memories you made with them could keep you warm or leave you out in the cold.

Everything with Dixie was warm. Her smile. The expression in her eyes. The skin on her hip and belly as it quivered under my hands and the touch of my tongue. The brush of her fingers as they wrapped around my dick when she finally wrestled my jeans out of the way. Her lips were hot as they landed on the side of my neck and she practically burned between her legs as my thumb slipped along the bend of her thigh and arrowed in on her damp opening. Her muscles clenched, her pussy fluttered, and pleasure soaked my fingers. I used my thumb to slip through silky folds and found her distended clit. I brushed the little nub lightly as she continued to nibble her way along my neck. I didn't want to jostle her or move her any more than necessary. I was careful of her bad shoulder as I brushed the tip of my nose along the ridge of her good one. I whispered promises I was going to keep into her sweet skin. I growled all the dirty things I was going to do to her once she was better into her ear. I planned a future out between kisses as she panted in time to my stroking fingers and worked her hips slowly and carefully against my hand.

I touched her with every ounce of care I could muster. I fondled her with every bit of reserve and restraint I possessed. I played with her like she was something rare and treasured, because she was. I watched her desire build, slowly and steadily. I watched as pleasure started to work its way across her pale skin and found its way into her dark eyes. Her chest rose and fell with quick breaths and the light hold she had on my dick tightened as her body shifted and turned more towards mine. A grimace of discomfort crossed her features and some of that pleasure turned to pain. I kissed the furrow that found its way to her brow and trapped her slippery little clit between two fingers and gave it a little tug. "Easy, pretty girl. This is supposed to help, not hurt."

She grinned up at me and used the heel she had resting against my backside to pull me closer. Her wetness coated the head of my cock and the sensation made me groan. "It is helping. It feels so good it made my toes curl and right now that hurts. You're too good at what you do, soldier."

"You will always get my best." I pressed into her and we both groaned as flesh parted and heat speared through both of us. "But now I plan on giving it to you in all ways, not just when we fuck."

She rolled her eyes at me as I started to move in and out of her gripping channel. Her body pulled at mine, squeezed it and flexed around it. My cock jumped at the attention and thumped with the need to let loose. My balls ached. Pleasure pulsed hard in my blood. A tingle started at the base of my spine and spread upwards along my back, making my shoulders bunch and bulge with the effort to stay slow and careful.

"You're loving on me, not fucking me, remember?" The words were broken and breathy. She was moving against me as much as her injuries allowed. Our pelvises bumped into one another and it made her moan. I kept one hand open wide on the center of her back to keep her upright and braced, and moved the other back between her legs so I could give her the friction and pressure she was wildly searching for.

"Gonna give you my best when I love you *and* when I fuck you, Dixie. Don't ever doubt it." Her mouth dropped open a little at the declaration and I took advantage of that to kiss her wetly and messily. Our bodies were hardly moving, grinding against each other seductively and sensually, but I took her mouth with the way my body was screaming at me to have her. I bit at her, I licked her, and I probably bruised her in my voracity. I made love to her body but our mouths fucked furiously and frantically.

I felt her inner walls start to flutter. I felt her get wetter and wetter. I felt her hand clutch at the rigid arm that held her and I felt her thighs tense and lock stiffly around my gliding hips. She muttered my name against my lips and I swallowed her strangled scream as she burst all around me.

I was riveted by her beauty.

I was stunned that I could make her feel that way.

I was honored that she wanted me and planned to keep me.

I was captivated by the life and love that shined out of her.

She told me she loved me and I lost it. Raw and unrestrained I let loose inside of her, flooded her with every ounce of desire and passion she inspired in me. I held her close as my heart raced and rested my cheek on the top of her head as reality started to swirl and settle around us.

Her hand was on my ribs and she was tracing one of my many scars. "We might be walking across one of those bridges sooner than you planned, Church."

We hadn't used protection and when I finally stepped back and separated myself from her the evidence of the fact was there, glossy and slick on her skin. I rubbed a thumb across her cheek and smiled. "We'll make our way across it. Don't worry."

She nodded but she didn't look convinced, so I decided it was well past time I give her something she always gave to everyone else . . . I needed to give her happy.

"Hey, Dixie." I helped tie her dress back up around her shoulder and sacrificed my shirt so she could clean herself up.

She looked up at me, her strawberry brows arched. "What?"

"You good?"

Her lips twitched and she leaned forward so her cheek was resting against the part of my chest where my heart beat with a renewed rhythm. "Yeah, Church, I'm good."

She was better than good. She was the best, and nothing bad that could or would happen was ever going to change the truth of that.

Epilogue

I knew two things for sure as I listened to Church talk dirty to me through the phone that was pressed tightly against my ear.

One was that his voice in all its raspy southern sexiness was enough to get me off. I barely felt the low hum and vibration coming from the battery-operated device that was a sad substitution for the real thing and was currently circling my clit and driving me crazy.

The second thing I knew without a doubt was that long-distance relationships sucked and I wasn't cut out for distance making my heart grow fonder. The space between us was making me cranky and had my typically sunny disposition all kinds of gloomy and gray. I missed him and as close to the edge of orgasm as I was barely a couple of minutes into his filthy words and husky encouragement, it was obvious my body missed him just as much as my heart did.

"Be sure you pack your little friend when you start throwing things in boxes." He chuckled as I gasped my way through a full-body shudder. The vibrator was good, but he was better and I was starting to resent that every quiver of pleasure, every quake of desire hinged on his words and the brush of his rough words against my ear. "Next time we're together I'll put it to good use. I've been thinking up lots of new ways to get you off. Think you can handle real me and plastic me at the same time? I bet you can. I bet you're drenched with the thought of giving me that cute, freckled ass while that toy fills you up and buzzes against your clit." His voice dropped and it was obvious the words meant to entice me had a pretty powerful effect on him as well.

I choked on a laugh and tossed my head back on the pillows as my toes curled and my legs tensed as pleasure unfurled slow and steady throughout my blood. It wasn't the same kind of mind-melting, body-bending orgasm I had with him buried deep inside of me, but it would hold me over until I got the real thing.

"Promises, promises. You have a lot of them stored up to make good on the next time I see you, soldier." It had been two months and we had one more to go before I was throwing everything I owned into a U-Haul and heading back to Lowry. I flew in to see him one weekend each month, but that hadn't been enough. One thing the distance had shown us was that we were far happier when we were together than we were when we were apart no matter where we decided to call home.

"I should have made you FaceTime me." There was a grunt on the other end of the phone and my breath quickened as I imagined the look on his face as his fist pumped up and down the strong, thick column of his cock. I could see the heavy muscles of his chest rising and falling. I could see his massive thighs tensing, one leg bent so that I would have the perfect view of all his impressive masculinity. I could almost feel the delineation between each carved ab muscle and the flex in the defined V that arrowed down on either of his sides.

"Your voice works wonders. It gives good sex," I purred into the phone and heard him pant as he got closer to his own completion.

"Yeah, but I like your face. I like to see that soft smile you get when you come. I like the way your eyes go out of focus and the way your cheeks get pink. It makes your freckles stand out and that gets me off, every, single, time."

I sighed and reached up to twist a sweaty curl around my finger. "You know what else gets you off?" He grunted and I could hear the sound of flesh against flesh. It had my already sensitized sex doing a lazy little clench and release of appreciation. "When the tip of your cock hits the back of my throat. When I suck you back as far as you can go and look up at you in awe because there is still so much of you that doesn't fit. When I trace the tip with my tongue and hold your balls in my hand. When I hum because I like the way you taste and feel in my mouth. That always gets you off."

"Fuck me." I was more than ready to. Stupid miles and miles between us.

He panted his way through his own orgasm, threw in some dirty words for good measure, and once he caught his breath he grumbled, "I would give up my bike right now to finish inside you, hell, I'd even take coming *on* you at this point. I've been wanting my cock between those pretty tits for a long time. Anything would be better than my hand and making a mess on my stomach." I heard sheets rustling as he moved around to clean up. I didn't tell him that I had no problem watching him finish all over himself, it was hot. But I had to agree finishing together was a thousand times more satisfying.

"It won't be much longer. Speaking of which, how is the training going?" He'd decided to take Jules's suggestion and go through Mississippi State testing so that he could join the sheriff's office and work with his dad. The three months we were spending apart was not only so I could get things settled and squared away in Denver but so he could focus on the training and his future in law enforcement with the minimum of distractions. The job opportunity was only one of the reasons that I ultimately decided it made more sense for us to look at building a life in Lowry instead of Denver. As feisty and fierce as she was, Elma Mae wasn't getting any younger and I didn't want to take Church away from whatever time he had left with her considering the years he had squandered. He might be willing to drop everything and be where I wanted to be, but what I really wanted was to be there for him as he made things right with the people that he loved.

Plus I liked Lowry. I liked the slower pace of things and the laid-back vibe, especially since Kallie had finally come clean and told my parents the wedding was off. She refused to tell them why and as a result Wheeler was persona non grata in the Carmichael home due to my parents' belief that it had been something he'd done, that he was the one at fault for everything falling apart. I begged Kallie to come clean, to tell my parents and Wheeler the truth about why she was willing to lose everything but she refused. So everything was a mess that I felt caught in the middle of and I'd made the decision that Church was right, none of it was mine to worry about, not my circus and not my clowns. What was mine needed to be back home making amends.

Frankly I couldn't wait to watch Dalen play football and to help Elma make cookies. Church had already found an adorable home similar to Jules's in a neighborhood close by to rent. He told me I was in charge of making it a home because he didn't have a clue what that meant. His only requirements were a garage for the Harley, a big TV and a comfortable couch in front of it, and of course a big-ass bed with me in it. I could give him all those things and I was dying to do so.

"Training is fine. I guess it's like riding a bike, you never forget the basics no matter what they apply to."

"I think it's more likely that some men were born to protect and serve others and you happen to be one of them. It doesn't seem hard because it was what you were meant to do."

He snorted. "You always think the best of everyone, me included." There was a long pause and then he sighed. "Don't ever stop doing that. It's one of the things I love most about you."

I laughed a little and got up when I heard Dolly making noise in the living room. She had no use for me when I was a puddle of goo after Church talked me into a bone-melting climax.

"I've always seen your best and now everyone else can, too. You aren't trying so hard to hide it anymore." Dolly started barking and prancing around the door as someone used a heavy hand to pound on the wooden surface. "Hey, I have to go, someone is at the door." I pulled on a long T-shirt that had a fox on it and the words "No Fox Given" scrawled around it and a pair of yoga shorts and willed my still-rubbery legs to find some strength.

"What? It's after midnight there, why is someone at your door this late?" I smiled as all his alpha protective instincts fired up. He wasn't around to keep an eye on me and he hated it. Something I knew for a fact since Rome had been hovering like a mother hen. I finally asked him to back off and he sheepishly shrugged and told me when a brother in arms asked you to keep an eye on his girl when he couldn't that's what you did. Then he hugged me until I thought my ribs were going to crack and told me that there was no one that was ever going to be able to replace me. I knew he meant I would leave a void in more than just the bar and it made me want to cry.

"I don't know, but if you quit barking at me I'll go find out." I had a pretty good idea who it was as lately both my sister and Wheeler had the annoying habit of popping by when they weren't expected, each to bitch about the other and the tension their split had caused in the family and between their friends. Canceling the wedding should have been the end of it but it turned out when you broke up with someone you had been with for so long untangling the ties that bound your lives together was quite a tricky feat.

"Don't open the door until you know who it is." He snapped the order at me over my sigh.

I petted Dolly on the head and shushed her and drily replied, "I can adult, Church." I looked through the peephole and wasn't all that surprised to see a familiar tattooed form on the other side. "It's Wheeler. I love you and I'll call you tomorrow."

He grunted. "I love you, too, and tomorrow we FaceTime."

"Goodie." I made a smacking kiss noise and hung up the call as I pulled open the door. Dolly did her typical overenthusiastic greeting but Wheeler walked in and immediately launched into a tirade without even acknowledging the poor pooch.

"Did you know? Did Kallie tell you? And if you did know how could you not tell me? This is getting insane, Dixie."

He ripped off the red ball cap he had on his head and ran his hands through his hair. His blue eyes were alight with fire and there was an angry flush staining his neck beneath the ink that lived there. I'd never seen him this keyed up before and I couldn't believe this was his reaction to finding out that Kallie was a lesbian or at least curious enough about the same sex to be bisexual.

I closed the door and leaned my back against it. I held up a hand in front of me and gave him a pointed look. "First of all it's not my place to share news like that with anyone. It's Kallie's life and she's the one that has to be held accountable for her choices. This isn't the end of the world, Wheeler."

He threw his hands up in the air and let them fall. "How can you say that? This changes everything, and it's not just her choices at play here."

I scowled at him and crossed my arms over my chest, starting to get a little defensive on my sister's behalf. "Sometimes things happen. They hurt the people we care about, but we can't control them. You can't be mad at her for being who she is."

"I'm furious with her for keeping this from me."

I sighed and walked over and put a hand on his shoulder. "She hasn't told anyone. I think she's scared. Realizing that you've been wrong about your sexual identity your entire life has to be terrifying. I'm sure she never intended to hurt you."

His pale eyes widened at the same time his eyebrows snapped down. His mouth opened and then shut like he was a fish out of water. "What are you talking about?"

His voice was sharp and it startled me, so I took a step back. "Uh . . . the fact that Kallie was cheating on you with a woman, didn't she finally tell you the truth?" I couldn't imagine what else would have him so riled up.

He let out a whoosh of air and put his hands on his knees as he started to laugh almost hysterically. This went on for a solid five minutes before I put a hand on his back and said his name questioningly.

"That's not what you were so worked up about?" I frowned at him in confusion.

He slapped the ball cap back on his head and his jaw clenched as his back teeth clicked together. "No, that's not what I was upset about, but at least now I know that I won't have to question whether or not the baby is mine."

"Baby?" The word whispered out and I put a shaking hand to my lips. "You've got to be kidding."

He shook his head and lifted both his hands to drag them over his face. "Nope. She showed up at the house tonight to get the rest of her stuff with a positive pregnancy test. It wasn't a conversation that went well."

"I can't believe this." I really couldn't.

"You and me both." He eyed me speculatively. "Are you really going to leave me here to wade through this mess on my own? Your parents aren't talking to me and apparently Kallie has more than one secret she's holding on to."

I gave him a lopsided smile and nodded. "I'm really going. I've finally got my own happy and I'm gonna hold on to it."

He sighed and turned towards the door. "I'm gonna miss you."

"I'll miss you, too, and I'm here in spirit if you need me." He gave a sharp nod and then showed himself out of the apartment. It didn't escape my notice that when he hit the hallway he turned his head and looked longingly at the doorway where my pretty neighbor lived.

This was a mess that had just gotten even messier. But for once I knew it wasn't all on me to clean it up. I wanted everyone I loved to have their own happy and to live their best lives possible, but I knew now that it wasn't up to me to take them by the hand and lead them there. They had to find their own way, just like I had found mine and Church had found his. That didn't mean I was going to stop lighting the way to all the good things I knew were waiting out there. That was intrinsically part of who I was. I was simply done being the one holding the torch.

The sun was a trillion, billion, million miles away from the Earth and every day we managed to feel its warmth. That would have to be true for those that I loved while I went and lived my own version of the fairy tale I'd always wanted. My story wasn't perfect but the ending was and that was all that mattered.

Good things did come to those who were willing to wait.

AUTHOR'S NOTE

I already know I'm going to get all the e-mails asking how this can be a Saints of Denver book when it takes place in Mississippi. The truth is I always knew I was going to give Church a story (from the second he hit the page in Rome's book) and I always knew it was going to be a homecoming story. I knew his past and his upbringing were going to have a major impact on his present and if I'm being really real I wanted another character with that thick southern drawl because goddamn is that sexy ;)

It was fun to take a little bit of Denver on the road and the reality is that you follow your heart when it's right. You sacrifice your own comfort and your familiarity if that's what's best for the other person. Leaving Denver was Dixie following her heart instead of sticking around to fix Wheeler and Kallie's problems for them. Dixie and Church had to go and it was a lot of fun for me to go with them. Who knows . . . I might end back up in Lowry down the road . . . I'm pretty fond of Jules and something tells me Dalen has a story to tell . . . not that I have time for any of that at the moment . . . lol.

I also want to take a minute and say that if you have a Dixie or if you know a Dixie give them a hug. Take a second to tell them how much you appreciate them. Give them a smile back and tell them thank you for bringing the light in a world that is often so dark. Every second of every single day we're flooded with hate, shame, blame, degradation, complaints, arguments . . . it takes a person so much bigger and brighter than me to tune that out and focus on the good. It takes a special kind of person to know the clouds eventually have to part. Having a smile and kind words when people don't deserve them takes a strong soul and a warrior's heart. People LOVE to scream and shout about all the things they hate, and the whispers about the good, about the joy and the things that make us happy, get lost in all the noise. That makes me so sad. It should be a thousand times easier to share our excitement over what we love than it is to commiserate about what we loathe.

To all the Dixies out there . . . we need more of you, so don't ever let the world steal your sunshine. If you smile at me I promise I will always do my best to smile back. ☺

RIVETED PLAYLIST

Heartless Bastards: Out at Sea
The Cactus Blossoms: You're Dreaming
The Wild Reeds: Let No Grief
Smooth Hound Smith: Forever Cold
The Lowest Pair: The River Will
Bob Dylan: Mississippi
Mountain: Mississippi Queen
Johnny Cash: Jackson
Kings of Leon: Back Down South
Tom Petty: Down South
Calexico: Bullets & Rocks
Dave Rawlings Machine: The Weekend
Rhiannon Giddens: Black Is the Color
The White Buffalo: I Got You
The Stray Birds: Shining in the Distance
Shakey Graves: Dearly Departed
Band of Horses: No One's Gonna Love You
Punch Brothers: This Girl
The Sea The Sea: In the Dark
Lewis & Leigh: There is a Light

ACKNOWLEDGMENTS

To all my friends ("readers" seems so formal at this point), thank you for going on another journey with me. Thank you for trusting me with your time. Thank you for supporting me and for loving these characters as much as I do. You've encouraged me to do better, to reach further, and to invest more with each book. Your words have influenced my words, which means these books tie us together forever. Letting my books into your life when we're all so busy and so hectic with other things is a big deal and I'm ALWAYS honored that you choose to spend some of that time with me and my guys. Thank you for reading, and thank you for continuing to read. I promise it's always going to be a good time!

To every blogger that has ever shared a post, participated in a tour, asked for an interview, put up a review, or asked me to be involved in any way with your followers . . . THANK YOU! Thank you for sharing. Thank you for caring. Thank you for loving books and sharing that love with others. Thank you for doing what you do, often with little thanks. Thank you for your time and for the space, I know those are both a valuable commodity!

I have to thank my fellow author and fellow dog lover (shout-out to Gus) Andie J. Christopher. I asked her to read through *Riv-*

eted at the zero hour to make sure I gave Church and his heritage the respect it deserves. Her feedback was brilliant, thoughtful, moving, and insightful, which reinforces that the characters we love should represent people from all walks of life. Love is love is love and there really should be no formula or standards for how that looks.

I gotta thank my people: Cora, JLA, Heather, Stacey, Ali, Debbie, Kristen, Karina, Jen Mac, Tucker, Dee. Find your tribe, they really do make it all better. We all need people that force us to be better but also accept us when we're at our worst.

To all the people that go above and beyond to make sure these books are the best they can be . . . you have my eternal thanks. They say you aren't working when you're doing what you love . . . that's a lie! Lol . . . so much work goes into getting a good book to the reader but you guys make it a treat rather than a chore. Amanda, you wrangle words in a way that I am both in awe of and intimidated by. You've set the bar high and frankly I thought by now I would be tired of reaching for it . . . somehow you always have me jumping up to catch on. Stacey, you talk me both down and up without getting dizzy. KP, you are a wizard and a visionary and without a doubt the hardest-working woman I know. Mel, thank you for being an adult when I just can't do it. Thank you for being my partner in crime and for being reasonable when I just can't be. You are the oil that keeps the machine running and I'm well aware I would be broken down on the side of the road without you. To the rest of the team at HarperCollins . . . thank you for continuing to believe in me and encourage me. Thank you for giving my books a home and treating them like they are family.

To my folks . . . thanks for being rad. Thanks for not being afraid of adventure and whatever is waiting around the next corner. Thank you for the endless support and both the hand-holding and the real talk. Mom, thanks for giving up an entire month of your life because I wanted to see the world and didn't want to do that with anyone besides you. Thanks for not murdering me when I couldn't get my giant suitcase under seventy pounds no matter how hard I tried!!

Mike, thanks for being the guy who gets shit done. Thank you for your creativity and for your willingness to be there when I need you the most. You are the best right-hand man a gal could ask for . . . don't forget to get my Opie Funko signed at Comic-Con!

To my pack . . . thank you for inspiring a love that is special. Thank you for inspiring this book in a roundabout way. Thank you for being fuzzy and warm no matter how cold it is outside.

I WILL LOVE you forever if you made it this far and you take the time to leave a review on whichever retail site you purchased *Riveted* on!

GUYS!!! I FINALLY have a newsletter, so if you want to sign up for exclusive content and monthly giveaways you can do that right here:

http://www.jaycrownover.com/#!subscribe/b7mto

You can also contact me at all these other places on the interwebs:

You can email me at: JayCrownover@gmail.com

My website: www.jaycrownover.com

https://www.facebook.com/jay.crownover

https://www.facebook.com/AuthorJayCrownover

Follow me @jaycrownover on Twitter
Follow me @jay.crownover on Instagram
https://www.goodreads.com/Crownover
http://www.donaghyliterary.com/jay-crownover.html
http://www.avonromance.com/book-author/jay-crownover

Can't wait for Hudson and Poppy's story? Keep reading for an exclusive excerpt to the next Saints of Denver Novel from *New York Times* bestselling author Jay Crownover,

SALVAGED

Hudson Wheeler is a nice guy. Everyone knows it, including his fiancée who left him with a canceled wedding and a baby on the way. He's tired of finishing last and is ready to start living in the moment with nights soaked in whiskey, fast cars, and even faster girls. He's set to start living on the edge, but when he meets Poppy Cruz, her sad eyes in the most gorgeous face he's ever seen hook him in right away. Wheeler can see Poppy's pain and all he wants to do is take care of her and make her smile, whatever it takes.

Poppy can't remember a time when she didn't see strangers as the enemy. After a lifetime of being hurt from the men who swore to protect her, Poppy's determined to keep herself safe by keeping everyone else at arm's length. Wheeler's sexy grin and rough hands from hours restoring classic cars shouldn't captivate her, but every time she's with him, she can't help being pulled closer to him. Though she's terrified to trust again, Poppy soon realizes it might hurt even more to shut Wheeler out—and the intense feelings pulsing through her are making it near impossible to resist him.

The only thing Poppy is sure of is that her heart is in need of some serious repair, and the more time she spends with Wheeler, the more she's convinced he's the only man with the tools to fix it.

Coming June 2017

Prologue

I was the kind of guy that thought I had it all figured out. That mostly came from my entire childhood being spent in chaos and upheaval. When I was old enough to call my own shots and make my own way, I did with a single-minded determination and unwavering dedication. I knew what I wanted and every move I made, every step I took moved me towards that perfectly planned future I had been dreaming of from the minute I realized I was all on my own. A realization that came far too early and was brutally reinforced every single time I was forced to switch from one temporary home to the next.

I clung to the idea that I would do everything differently which would lead to a life that was easy, smooth, and as steady as a car with a new alignment and high end shocks. I found the girl that was meant to be mine and held onto her in a death grip. I went out of my way to be whoever she needed me to be, to never give her any kind of reason to go. I made her the center of my entire world, not realizing she might feel trapped there over time. I started a business, bought a house and made plans . . . so many plans. Plans that would be considered simple and boring to some, but they covered everything I wanted since the time I was four years old.

I had my eyes on the prize, the promise of what could be if I worked hard, took care of my woman, and did everything the person that was supposed to love me and care for me didn't do. I would have held on to the bitter, burning end but there was nothing I could do when the rope was cut. All I could do was fall.

I felt my grip on everything slipping the day she walked into my shop with one of my friends. Rowdy St James worked at the tattoo shop where I got most of my ink done. He had called and asked me to clear out my shop one weekend afternoon so that he could bring his girlfriend's sister in to look at a car. He didn't need to explain why the shop needed to be cleared out. The girl had been all over the news months before. You couldn't get away from her terrified face and shaking body as her horrifying ordeal was splashed all over the media. Her husband had taken her at gunpoint, Salem, her sister and Rowdy's lady, had been there as well. The girl only went with the lunatic to keep her sibling safe but it had resulted in a nightmare that I couldn't imagine anyone coming back from. So, I cleared out the shop so she wouldn't have to worry about being surrounded by a bunch of dirty, boisterous men that wouldn't know how to behave around someone as fragile and delicate as she appeared to be.

Things at home had been rocky, rougher than class five rapids in winter but I was paddling for my life and prepared to ride it out. I couldn't let go, I wouldn't let go, but I saw her the day she walked through my shop and I started to feel how sore my hands and my heart were from holding on.

Her head was down, focused on the tips of her shoes. Her shoulders were hunched over and her long hair hid her face. She was skinny, so skinny, nothing but skin and bones. She was nothing that I should have noticed, not because she was clearly doing everything in her power to be invisible but because I was supposed to have my eyes locked on my future and doing whatever I could to salvage it. But I did notice her and I couldn't look away once I did.

She was obviously terrified, clearly out of her element and uncomfortable but it wasn't her unease that called to me . . . it was her loneliness. I could feel it filling up the space that separated us. Stretching, growing, expanding until it was all I was breathing in and exhaling back out. It was bitter on my tongue and heavy across my skin because I knew the feeling well. The reason I was so set on the way things had to be, the reason I was single mindedly set on settling down and building a life with the girl that was slipping through my fingers was because I never wanted to be as alone as this girl was again. I didn't want to be left and forgotten. I'd barely survived it the first time.

I did my best to sell her a car that was as beautiful as she was . . . a classic with clean lines and a flawless finish. She picked something practical and boring but that was ultimately safe and reliable. I understood her choice but it grated and annoyed me long after she left the shop. When she wasn't standing in front of me, she should have been easy to forget after all, everything in front of me, everything I had been working for and towards was falling down in front of my eyes. My world was collapsing in on itself and everything I thought I was so goddamn sure about turned out to be nothing more than lies and illusions. In the middle of all of it, I couldn't forget her sad eyes and shivering, shaking form. Her loneliness clung to me, unshakeable and unforgettable. I didn't think I would see her again but I often found myself wondering how she was doing and if she had gotten a handle on all the things that seemed to be crushing her under their weight.

I was wrong about seeing her again, just like I was wrong about doing everything differently from my mother would ensure my happiness and a future build on an unshakeable foundation. I was wrong about hard work and sacrifice being enough. I was wrong about holding on when what I was holding onto desperately wanted me to let go. All I was left with was bleeding palms and rope burn around my heart.

The next time I saw her it was my loneliness that was filling up the space, suffocating me, choking me, making me forget to handle her with care. I was nothing more than a vast, open wound. One that was raw, aching, throbbing, and leaking my heart out everywhere. I felt like I lost everything, like my entire life had been nothing but a waste of time, nothing more than building blocks knocked over with the swipe of a careless hand. The girl I loved didn't love me back, my future was now nothing more than a fuzzy, fractured blur in front of me and I couldn't see anything but what would no longer be.

I scared her.

It was the last thing I wanted to do but my loneliness was just as big and just and consuming as hers was. It spread out, hungry and angry, looking to consume anyone that might try and challenge its reign.

I tried to pull myself together, apologized because I knew our paths would cross again and I didn't want to be just another man that she was terrified of. I locked the loneliness down, wrestled it into submission and tried to quiet the wild inside of me that was howling, screaming at the loss of its mate down. I wanted to be nothing more than gnashing teeth and tearing claws but I swallowed that down and became the kicked puppy that just wanted to whimper and cry.

This girl that had been through more than I could imagine, the one I couldn't look away from slipped past me and disappeared. She looked like honey but she moved like a ghost. I had memorized everything about her even though she hardly let me see her face.

I wasn't supposed to be looking at anything other than how to best fix the mess my life was in, but she was all I could see.